THE LOS

MW00987096

DARKNESS AND STONE

PETER NEALEN

THE LAND of
ICE & MONSTERS

THE TEETH
of WINTER

GRICHENCOS'
CITADEL

POHLOJA

S'UMNOTH

MENNINKAI

VAHAVA
PAYKHAH

N
W E
S

WARGATE

An imprint of Galaxy's Edge Press
PO BOX 534
Puyallup, Washington 98371
Copyright © 2021 by Galaxy's Edge, LLC
All rights reserved.

ISBN: 978-1-949731-73-6

www.forgottenruin.com
www.wargatebooks.com

CHAPTER 1

THE coast had just come into sight, a faint, dark line to the north beneath the lowering gray clouds, when the sea serpent hit us.

I looked up at Eoghain's cry and saw him standing in the high, swan-carved prow, pointing off to the starboard side. I hadn't caught the words over the wind, but the tone of alarm was unmistakable. I snatched up my M110 from the sea chest at my feet and started working my way across the deck to join him.

If it had been the marksman rifle that I'd left behind on the USS *Makin Island*, I probably would have had it in a waterproof bag, slathered with silicone spray. But King Caedmon's *Coira Ansec*, the mystical cauldron that could produce ammo, weapons—whatever you asked for, really—produced some fine firearms. That thing was practically impervious to salt water.

The deck of Nachdainn's ship was neat, every line, chest, and tool in its place, but that didn't make it clear. It took me a minute to cross to the prow, where I joined Eoghain, Bearrac, and Gunny Taylor at the gunwale.

Gunny was already up on his rifle, peering through the scope. The whole platoon had switched from our M4s and M27s to M110s and Mk 48s from the *Coira*

Ansec after we'd seen how little 5.56 did against some of the monsters in this world.

Eoghain and Bearrac simply peered out across the water. The Tuacha da Riamog didn't use optics. Their eyes were far better than ours.

I squinted through the gloom. The overcast had thickened as we'd sailed north, and though it was about midday, the ship was wrapped in a gloomy twilight as it heaved over the gray chop of the sea.

There. A V-shaped wake cut across the waves, undulating slightly as it bore down on us. Whatever was making that wake, it was big, and it was fast.

"Brace yourselves." Bearrac, barrel-chested and black-bearded, was holding onto the gunwale with one hand.

I was about to open fire on whatever it was, but it was apparently bigger and faster than it looked, because a moment later, something hit the ship with a bone-jarring impact.

The ship heeled over, and every timber groaned after the *boom* of the initial blow. I grabbed ahold of the gunwale in time to keep from going over on my back and sliding across the deck, hearing the awful scrape of something big dragging across the keel beneath us.

The deck swayed and shuddered alarmingly under our feet for a moment. The terrible scraping noise subsided, and Gunny and I moved quickly to the port side, scanning the water over our rifles. Only dark gray water topped with whitecaps where the wind whipped the spray off the tops of the waves met our eyes.

Movement stirred in the depths, as if something huge and pale was turning over. Then it struck again.

I felt the planks of the hull bend torturously beneath the deck as something massive slammed into the ship's flank. Despite being braced for it this time, we all staggered, and I almost slipped backward. I still got a glimpse of a massive, pale gray back just beneath the waves, arcing as it dove underneath, once again battering at the keel as if the thing was trying to tip us over.

Tipping over a Tuacha ship is far more easily said than done. While she groaned and rocked under the impact, I heard no cracks of broken planks, and she righted herself, rocking slightly from side to side, the sail flapping overhead, as the monster passed to the starboard side again. There is a virtue in everything the Tuacha build that is difficult to overcome.

"Hold." Mathghaman stood at the mast, tall, auburn-haired, and bearded, his feet planted wide, one hand on the mast itself. "It cannot sink us thus. Let it give us a better opening." Grim as his voice was, there was still that lilting Tuacha music to his words. I had lived and fought among the Tuacha long enough that I no longer needed the "mind speech" to understand him.

Mathghaman was King Caedmon's champion and our brother through fire. Thrown together in Taramas's dungeons, we had fought our way out of the Land of Ice and Monsters together. At the King's own request, we had then fought our way through haunted forests and cursed deserts to rescue the mystic, Sister Sebeal, from an ancient vampire in its own lair. As vastly different as our origins might have been, we were closer now than any kin we might have left behind in The World.

He stood firm while the ship rocked and shuddered under the continuous onslaught, as the monster dove and returned, battering our hull with increasing fury. But while the planks creaked and flexed, they held.

Finally, the monster seemed to realize that it wasn't doing much by simply bashing its skull against our keel over and over again. The battering stopped. But none of us relaxed. Weapons stayed at the ready as we scanned the waters around us. The impacts had driven us aside from our course, and the darkness of the coastline now lay off to starboard, drifting farther away.

I was looking off that direction as the chop picked up, when the serpent came up out of the water on the port side with a noise like the roar of a waterfall.

We all spun, guns coming up, both our more modern weapons and the more elegant, engraved rifles the Tuacha had adopted after joining us.

Almost twenty feet of scaled monstrosity, topped by a blunt, stony-looking head with jaws that split it clear back to its gills, lined with forked, dripping teeth, towered above the ship's hull. Those jaws gaped above us as the serpent struck at the forward gunwale.

None of us just stood there gaping, though. We were Recon Marines and Tuacha warriors. Every man on deck shouldered his weapon and opened fire as that huge, dripping maw descended like a falling mountain.

Suppressed 7.62mm gunfire roared as that massive head dropped toward us, bullets punching through scales and into rubbery flesh. One fang was blasted off. The monster shuddered and twisted aside, then dove back into the water to avoid the stinging blows, hitting with a splash that sent a massive wave crashing against our hull.

"Hell." Gunny was still watching the chop and foam left behind where the sea monster had disappeared over his rifle. "It's going to take more than bullets to kill that thing."

He'd barely finished speaking when the deck heaved under our feet as the sea serpent struck the keel again, only this time it wasn't just beating against the hull as if it could wreck us with its skull. Instead, a moment later that massive head came slithering up the starboard side, snapping at the lines and at Synar, even as he reared back from the rail and reflexively pumped another pair into the massive, blunt-faced head, with no apparent effect.

The monster's tail came writhing out of the water behind us, slithering over the gunwales and wrapping itself around the ship's stern. It kept moving, too, twisting its slime-dripping body around once, twice, the coils tightening as its huge head loomed over the bow, jaws gaping as it hissed at us. I was right there next to Bearrac and Santos, dumping rounds into that mountainous skull, forcing it back as it hissed and shook, trying to protect its eyes from the stinging impacts.

Gunny was right. We weren't going to kill that thing with bullets. It was just too big, and it seemed like its skull was as thick as a grizzly's. But we couldn't exactly regroup and come up with a better plan while it was trying to crush the ship like an egg.

The hull groaned as a third coil wrapped around it, and the big serpent started to squeeze. It snapped at Mathghaman, who was now closest to it. It darted in despite the gunfire, its maw suddenly gaping wide to close like a steel trap where Mathghaman's head—his entire upper body, in fact—had just been.

Mathghaman, however, was faster than the monster. He danced out of the way, leaving those huge jaws to snap shut on empty air, pivoting as he ducked beneath and away, bringing the muzzle of that elegant rifle of his almost in contact with the thing's beady, unblinking eye just before he squeezed the trigger and obliterated the orb. The monster reared back again with what might have been a deep, angry moan of pain, blood and slime running from the ruined socket. Then Mathghaman was moving again, ducking back beneath the huge head as the thing shook itself, then firing another shot into the soft tissue under its jaw.

I half expected the round to do nothing. Half expected the jaw to be as armored as the rest of that thing seemed to be. But Mathghaman's rifle blew a hole through it with ease, punching through scales and cartilage and into the roof of its fang-laden mouth.

That still didn't kill it. It hissed and roared, lashing its tail and its head alike and smashing its skull into the prow, then the deck just in front of the mast. It snapped at us, even as Fennean and Gurke went to town on its coils with axes and swords. But while their blades were biting into the slimy flesh, the creature's body was a good four feet thick, all muscle and scale and cartilaginous bone. It was going to take a long time, even with Tuacha weapons, to hack through that.

Which was why Bailey suddenly muttered, "Fuck this," and shouldered past me, his rifle slung and a short, stubby black tube with a pistol grip and collapsible stock in his hands.

He fired before I could say anything, snapping the 40mm grenade launcher to his shoulder and barely aiming. The *thunk* was followed immediately by a hollow *clock* sound. The grenade had just bounced off the top of the sea serpent's head as it recovered from the wound Mathghaman had given it and reared back for another strike. The 40mm "egg" went sailing off into the water.

"It's too close to arm, and if it wasn't, then you'd kill us all with that damned thing!" Gunny didn't usually lose his cool in a firefight, but Sean Bailey had just forgotten a couple of things in his eagerness to get his kill on. One being the fourteen-meter arming distance, the other being the fact that we were right in that creature's face, and an explosion would have fragged us at the very least.

With a snarl, Bailey let the thumper fall and looked around for some other way to do enough damage to kill the sea serpent. Several of us were still shooting, but that was only burning through ammo and sort of keeping it at bay. Meanwhile, the hull groaned even more as it continued to tighten its coils around us. That ship was strong, but there was only so much even Tuacha handiwork could take.

Mathghaman had ducked back beneath the thing's head, and now, as it poised to strike again, he leaned over the gunwale and shot out its other eye.

The monster shuddered and spasmed, making several of the hull planks scream in protest, but then it was uncoiling and slipping back into the water, blind and in agony, before retreating quickly back beneath the waves.

For a few moments, we just stood there, panting, sweating despite the chill of the northern wind and salt spray, hardly believing it was over. We weren't just staring in shock, though. Every man had moved to the sides, watching the water with guns up.

All that met our eyes was the white-tipped, gray waves as rain swept in from the east, dropping visibility to a few hundred yards. The only sounds, beyond the beating of our own hearts and the rasp of breath in our ears, were the creaks of lines and timbers, the faint snaps of canvas in the wind, and the whispers and wails of the wind itself.

Until the serpent came out of the water like a breaching whale, just off the starboard stern, sailing toward the mast with its jaws gaping wide.

CHAPTER 2

IT hit the mast like a freight train, its jaws clamping shut on the towering oak pole, fangs sinking into the wood with an awful *crunch.* The ship heeled hard to port, nearly capsizing under the sheer force of the monster's full weight hitting it that hard. We all went tumbling toward the gunwale and the sea, as gear and lines broke loose and clattered across the deck.

I caught myself on a sea chest, almost getting the wind knocked out of me, even as the ship heeled back to the starboard under the monster's mass. The virtue of Tuacha construction meant that the mast hadn't given way yet, though it was only a matter of time as the serpent chomped spasmodically on the mast, splintering the white-painted oak even further.

More gunfire hammered at the thing as Recon Marines and Tuacha alike got their feet under them, but the bullets may as well have been gnats for all the damage they were doing.

As I regained my feet, though, I saw an opening. The monster was still trying to bite the mast off, which meant it was stationary for a moment. And while Fennean's and Gurke's axe and sword might not have been enough to cut through its body, their weapons weren't quite like mine.

I let my rifle hang on its sling and drew my own sword. Nearly three feet long, the blade a shimmering gray, the hilts accented in gold that never seemed to wear or tarnish, inlaid with runes that reminded me of an ancient Greek Chi-Rho, that sword had come through fire and storm with me, though it was immeasurably older than I. I still don't know its full history. I might never know it. I knew that the blessed blade was far more potent than bullets against certain enemies, though. So, ducking beneath whipping lines that had been severed by those awful jaws, I waded in and brought the blade down with terrific force on the sea serpent's neck, just behind what might have been its gills.

The smoky blade bit deep, shearing through scales and even cartilaginous bone with greater ease than even I'd expected. Rubbery flesh parted as my sword cut deeply into its spine. The creature shuddered, its jaws tightening on the mast as the oak creaked and cracked alarmingly. I brought the sword through its circle to keep the momentum going, then hacked deeper into the wound I'd already inflicted, as Mathghaman came around on the other side with his own leaf-bladed sword in hand. His blade bit as deeply as mine, and watery, reddish black blood flowed out onto the deck beneath our feet.

With only a few more strokes, the great coils of the serpent relaxed and slithered over the side and into the sea, floating and bobbing on the waves for a moment before slowly drifting down into the depths, leaving clouds of dark blood that obscured the paleness of the carcass for a moment before the darkness of the abyss swallowed it up.

The head was still clamped to the mast, rigid in death, but it almost seemed as if there was still some awareness there. I can't explain how that sense came to me. The creature's eyes were destroyed, and it had just been beheaded. It didn't move but stayed in place, its jaws locked onto the mast with those weird, multi-pronged fangs.

For a few moments, we just stood there, gasping for breath, as the ship rocked on the waves, seeming to wallow in the trough of the swell, no closer to the shore on the northern horizon than we had been before the serpent had attacked. It was as if the sea serpent had arrested our progress, leaving us stilled on the sea, despite the wind that still flapped our sails atop the cracked and splintered mast.

"Let's get this thing off." Gunny, as was his wont, was the first one to get us all moving again. He stepped forward, drawing his own axe, a gleaming, bearded affair with a wicked curve to the blade and a dark, carved and studded haft. He'd been given an old Tuacha sword from the abandoned armory in Teac Mor Farragah, but after we'd arrived at the Isle of Riamog, he'd decided that an axe fit him better. He sized up the severed head, as if trying to decide whether to just hack it off in pieces or try to pry the fangs out of the wood.

Mathghaman and Bearrac were ahead of him, though. They had grabbed boat hooks from the equipment in the bow, and were already prying at the jaws, and Gunny seemed to nod to himself, as if realizing that prying was probably better than chopping. The mast was already damaged enough. Cutting through the sea serpent's head might only bite deeper into the oak, further weakening it.

We'd all seen just how incredibly durable the Tuacha's work could be, but none of us figured it was limitless.

The fangs were deeply embedded in the wood, and it took a lot of effort to wrench them out, prying against not only the bite of those weird teeth, but also the stiffness of the dead jaws themselves. The bones and fangs groaned and cracked, several of the thing's teeth shrieking like rusty nails as they were slowly drawn out of the wood, every inch won with terrific effort against the tension of the clamped jaws.

Finally, the hinge of the jaws gave with a snap, and the head fell to the deck with a heavy, wet *thud*.

We had just picked it up, and were about to heave it over the side, when its eye moved to stare at us.

Baldinus dropped his part of the head, taking a step back with a loud, "What the fuck!" I can't say I blamed him. We'd all seen Mathghaman obliterate both of the monster's eyes. Yet there was an intact orb shifting in that bloodied socket, its pupil as big as my hand, moving from one to another of us.

As the weight shifted, we all let go, allowing the head fall to the deck once more, and our hands reached for weapons as we put some distance between us and this new threat.

"*Better for you had you surrendered to fate.*" The voice was low, sepulchral, and while it seemed to be coming from the severed head's gaping jaws, it could just as well have been in our heads. That we all could hear it, though, I was sure, as every man on deck glanced around and then stared back at the head.

The eye continued to swivel from one to another of us. "*My master knows you. He has seen. I sent one of my servants out of mercy. Now there shall be no hope for you.*" The eye turned to Mathghaman, then to me. "*You shall be dashed to pieces against his might. Devoured for all eternity, shriveling beneath his thousand eyes.*"

I glanced at Mathghaman. A faint frown creased his brow. He didn't have any more of an idea of what this thing was ranting about than I did. But it was equally clear that it was addressing the two of us, him and me. And I had no idea why.

After all, we weren't out to topple any of the Fohoriman Warlock Kings, at least not as a primary objective. We had left Recon Marines behind when we'd escaped the Land of Ice and Monsters, that low, dark line of land now on the northern horizon, months before. Mathghaman had been up there in pursuit of a Tuacha traitor. He was still hunting that one. We were after our own.

If we happened to overthrow or kill a Warlock King, so much the better, but that wasn't why we were sailing north.

Even if we had been, though, there was something exceedingly weird about this. The Warlock Kings were powerful, there was no doubt about that, but they were still killable, and from what I'd seen, they held no sway over the Deep Ones, the ancient evils that lurk in the depths off the coasts of this haunted world. They even had sorcerous watchers along the coast to keep the Deep Ones' minions at bay. And I couldn't think of anything that might call a sea serpent its "servant" that wasn't a Deep One.

Granted, I still had a lot to learn about this world. But from the look on Mathghaman's face, he was reaching many of the same conclusions I was.

Gunny acted first. He brought his axe whistling down to split the new eye. It bit deep into the socket, but the eye seemed undamaged and unfazed.

"Close your ears. Cover them if you must." Mathghaman bent and lifted the head on his own, his broad shoulders and arms rippling as he heaved it to the side. I stepped forward as that baleful eye turned toward me again. "Quickly. Before its words do more damage than its puppet's teeth ever could."

We shoved at it as the head with its gaping mouth, the hinge of its jaw broken, began to laugh. At least, I think that was what it was doing. The sound was a maddening rumble of inhuman, insane mirth, a gurgling thunder that battered at the mind more than the ears.

Then we had it over the rail, and it turned over once before it hit the icy waters with a splash. Like the body, it floated there for a moment, that awful, not-quite-there eye still staring at us, before it sank out of sight.

Mathghaman and I stood there at the side, watching that terrible head dwindle into the darkness of the ocean deeps as Nachdainn and the rest of the crew set about repairing the damage as best they could to get us underway again. Gunny was already getting the rest of the platoon to work, helping out, but left us be for the moment.

"What was that all about?" I might have been able to understand the Tuacha's tongue, but I still wasn't all that fluent, so I relied on the fact that Mathghaman would understand me whether I was speaking English or Swahili.

"I do not know." While Mathghaman was perhaps the most composed man I'd ever met—he made Gunny Taylor look overly emotional at times, and that's saying something—he was clearly troubled. He turned his gaze toward the dark line of the coast ahead. "We do not know what all has happened in the north since we left. I fear that greater powers may be moving than we had expected." He looked at me then, meeting my eyes with an unfathomable expression in his own. Was it worry? I could hardly imagine this man, preternaturally gifted by the standards I'd grown up with, ever worrying, but there was an echo of something like that in his gaze now. "The vampire wanted to draw *you*, specifically, to his lair. He wanted to know why you had been drawn here, through time and space." He leaned on the rail and turned back toward the north. "I confess that I have wondered that myself. I do not think that your coming to our world was an accident. Apparently, neither do our enemies."

When he turned back to me once more, I saw what was definitely concern in his eyes. "Whatever greater purpose brought you here, let us pray that we discover it soon. Because terrible things have now taken notice." He sighed and turned around. I found most of the platoon, including Mathghaman's companions, who had joined us before we had gone to the Land of Shadows and Crows after the vampire, watching, listening to the King's Champion voice his concerns.

"Steel yourselves. We believed that we sailed north for our own purposes, to pursue the one who betrayed and wronged us, or those who were separated in battle and left behind. We believed that we sailed on our own terms, known only to our friends and allies." He glanced over the side, where the sea serpent's carcass had disappeared. "It would seem we come against enemies prepared and waiting, and perhaps more dangerous than we realized."

He turned back toward the prow, which Nachdainn was even then turning back toward the north. "Fear not, though. Trust in Tigharn, your weapons, and your strong right hands. And whatever the cold and dark of the north holds for us…

"Let it come."

CHAPTER 3

IT took most of another night and day to finally reach that coast. Leviathans rose out of the depths, and more than one scraped against our hull, but none surfaced, and none sought to attack us. I thought I might have seen sea trolls just beneath the surface once or twice glaring up at us with their too-large eyes, but every time I thought I saw one, it quickly ducked beneath the keel and disappeared.

Finally, near sunset—though it was hard to tell; the overcast had never quite gone away over the last week—of that second day, we neared our destination.

We had escaped the Land of Ice and Monsters through the ruins of the ancient Tuacha outpost of Teac Mor Farragah. Mathghaman and his companions had entered that cursed land through those same ruins, but their quest—which Mathghaman was still awfully tight-lipped about—had ultimately failed, as they'd been detected, ambushed, and captured. Mathghaman had said little about the details, but I gathered that several of his Tuacha companions had been killed in the process. I didn't see any of them giving up without a fight. They must have been up against truly staggering odds to have allowed themselves to be taken prisoner.

We had only barely escaped through Teac Mor Farragah, however. Two of the Fohoriman Warlock

Kings—well, Queen in one case—Uergal and Taramas, had put their differences aside to pursue us when we'd escaped from the catacombs beneath Taramas's citadel. It had been a hell of a fight, with what remained of the platoon going black on ammo, our backs to the sea, before Nachdainn had arrived at the quay to take us off. It had been a near thing.

Near enough that when we set sail for the north again, King Caedmon had admonished Mathghaman not to try to go it alone in enemy territory this time. Mathghaman had reluctantly agreed, though it would put us far to the east of where we wanted to go.

So it was that we sailed into the shallow bay at the base of a towering stone hill, surrounded by thick walls of stone and blackened timber, studded every few hundred feet by massive, square guard towers. Gates faced the strand where several dozen longships were drawn up. Above the walls, the rocky promontory the city was built on rose several hundred feet above the water, studded by timber-built, sod-roofed houses. Above it all, atop the stony prominence at the peak of the hill, stood a massive stone great hall with a peaked and gabled roof, that looked far more ancient than any of the rest of the place.

Cairbre ran the Tuacha's standard high, silver-white with a rune upon it in gold that looked very much like the rune in my sword's pommel. It flapped in the wind coming off the mountains in the distance, mostly obscured by the low-hanging clouds.

We had hoped that our arrival at Vahava Paykhah would be a quiet one. But the signs of battle, the smoke rising and hanging over the fortress city in a thick pall, the barred gates and the distant glints of wan light on spearpoints on the battlements, dashed those hopes.

"This isn't good, is it?" I was in the prow with Bearrac. Both of us were armed and geared up, even though, like I said, we'd hoped to simply make landfall, meet with the Menninkai, the short, stubborn people who clung tenaciously to this strip of wooded land on the coast of the Land of Ice and Monsters, and prepare to move inland on our mission. I was still wearing my woodland digital camouflage trousers and infantry combat boots, though instead of my cammie blouse, I was wearing a green, woolen, padded gambeson under a supple mail shirt of green-enameled steel rings. My chest rig went over all that, my sword hanging from the belt just beneath it. The helmet under my arm was also steel, light and peaked for close-in combat, though with an NVG mount riveted to the front.

Bearrac was dressed much the same way, though his trews were of fine, blue-dyed wool rather than my cammies from another world. "No, it is not." He squinted through the mist and the smoke. There was no snow on the ground, at least that I could see. Even this far north, this close to the Teeth of Winter, the enormous ice sheet that locked the far north in its frigid grasp, it was getting into late spring. We shouldn't face the brutal cold that we had the last time we'd been up there. "It would seem that the Lasknut of Sumnoth have seen fit to try once more to drive the Menninkai into the sea."

"Who are the Lasknut?" Mathghaman had told us something about the Menninkai. They were men, though generally short enough to be thought to be dwarves among some of the men of the south. Known for being stocky, somewhat close-mouthed, and quick to take offense, they were nevertheless old allies of the Tuacha, dating back to before the fall of Teac Mor Farragah. But there had been only so much time to talk, and sometimes the Tuacha left things out. I'd never thought it was out of any malice—that seemed outside their character—but rather from their own tendency to be sparing with their words, plus the fact that most of them were far older than we were, and there was a disconnect there as to what was common knowledge and what wasn't.

Gurke had muttered some discontent about that reticence to talk. "We're obviously the newcomers here. How come we have to ask for every bit of information like we're pulling teeth?"

"Maybe they don't want to just give us everything." Bailey hadn't looked up from the knife he'd been sharpening as he spoke. I wasn't sure if it was one he'd gotten from the Tuacha, one he'd taken off an enemy, or one he'd brought with him. Bailey was one of those guys who always had at least two or three knives on him, even before we got to this place and found that swords were actually pretty useful at times, especially when you're a *long* way from resupply with limited ammo. "I mean, they haven't exactly been reticent about telling us what we want to know. We've just got to ask."

Gurke hadn't liked that answer, but Gurke had apparently decided that he needed to be the platoon devil's advocate since Zimmerman had gone missing beneath Taramas's citadel.

True to what Bailey had said, though, Bearrac was happy to answer when I asked the question. "They were once kin to the Menninkai. Men who dwelt in these lands and held the line against the Fohorimans and their servants."

He sighed. "Yet as has happened so many other places, one by one, many of the Menninkai's outer strongholds fell. Not to external siege, not all of them. Many fell to treachery and deceit from within. Rotted from the core as their rulers and their great men fell to dallying with the Outsiders they call the 'elder gods.' One by one, the lesser holds fell under the sway of the clan that called itself Sumnoth, to the point that all those under their domination are now sometimes called that, though the Menninkai call them 'Lasknut,' which means 'Betrayer' in the Menninkai tongue."

"So, we're walking into the middle of a civil war?" I'd been there before, and I wasn't looking forward to going there again. Syria had been no joke.

"Not anymore. Sumnoth and Menninkai have been separate kingdoms for long enough that there is little kinship there, despite their history." Bearrac glowered at the smoke on the horizon as we continued to drift into the bay, an answering flag in red and white waving from above the gate, signaling that they saw our standard and recognized it. At least, I hoped that was what it signaled.

At any rate, we moved in toward the beach without any of those longships coming out to challenge us. I could hear horns and drums in the distance. We were still too far out to sea to be able to tell what was happening on the far side of that massive rock that was Vahava Paykhah. But the sense of desperation was as palpable as the smoke was thick, even on the seaward side.

Nachdainn was shouting commands, fine-tuning the approach to the beach, as Subne, his first mate, beat a drum to keep time for the oarsmen. The ship could be beached, like any longship, but she looked far larger and more imposing than the low-slung ships already drawn up on the beach ahead.

The sails were furled, and only about half the ship's oars were pulling. Part of that was because that close into shore, we didn't need the speed. Part of it was because we would have been on the other oars, and we needed to be alert and ready to fight, instead.

Mathghaman was very much of the "trust, but be ready" sort of mindset, even when it came to people he'd been friends with in the recent past. I could appreciate that.

Still, Bearrac and I had our own part to play as we glided in toward the beach. We both leaned out on either side of the prow, arms raised as we looked down at the rocks and sand beneath the keel. When it looked shallow enough, we both swept our arms down, and with a heavy double note on the drum, Subne signaled the oarsmen, who brought their oars up and dragged them inboard. It was an awful lot like beaching a Zodiac, only with a Zode we had to pull the engine up to keep the propulsor from getting driven into the bottom, whereas the oarsmen were trying to keep from snapping an oar.

For a brief moment, I wondered what had happened to the Zodiacs we'd abandoned on the shore of the Land of Ice and Monsters all those months ago. Probably still rotting on the shore, if they hadn't just floated off into the ocean. That shore was no man's land between the sea trolls to seaward and the Fohorimans and their followers to landward. We hadn't exactly beached them that thoroughly, either.

The keel scraped on the strand, and then Bearrac and I were jumping off into ankle-deep water, the cold seeping through my boots despite the GoreTex insulation. Grabbing hold of the lines, we leaned into them and slogged up the beach, hauling the ship higher and most of the way out of the water. Her momentum helped, and more of the platoon jumped off to join us on the lines as she mounted higher on the strand. Finally, her keel scraped more loudly, and she seemed to get heavier. Nachdainn shouted from the prow after it had come about six feet out of the water, and we let the lines drop. He didn't want her so high on the beach that we couldn't cast off quickly.

Especially not with the smoke on the air, redolent of burning timber, pitch, tar, and less wholesome things.

Mathghaman leapt down to join us, followed by Gunny and the rest of the platoon. Funny, I wasn't thinking in terms of "the platoon plus Mathghaman and his companions" anymore. We were all just "the platoon."

Granted, of the original twenty-nine of us, there were only eleven Recon Marines left. Maybe we'd find some of our missing and shore those numbers up a bit.

But a part of me could only hear the echo of Mathghaman's words as I thought that. "*If they are prisoners, then you must prepare yourself to find that they are no longer the men you knew. It may have been a mercy if they were killed.*"

I shook the thoughts off. There would be a time for such questions. Right then, as the massive seaward gate in Vahava Paykhah's walls creaked open, was not the time.

A full company of warriors came out to meet us, armed and armored. Their breastplates were lamellar, formed of dozens of overlapping plates. So were their pauldrons, which ran from a high, lamellar collar guard down to their elbows. Even their helmets were made of overlapping plates sewed to high, peaked caps. Each man carried a spear and a small, round shield. Most also wore swords or short-bladed axes.

The man in front was one of the tallest, and as they closed the distance toward us, I saw that he was about five foot two, if I was being generous and granting him a bit more of that peaked helmet than his skull might actually fill. The rest were roughly five foot nothing. The Tuacha hadn't been exaggerating when they'd spoken of the Menninkai's short stature. I just hoped they didn't all have Short Man Syndrome to go with it, but from some of what Bearrac had said under his breath, I wasn't all that optimistic on that front.

We waited on the beach, hands on weapons but otherwise keeping our cool and looking as non-threatening as we could. Mathghaman didn't even have his rifle in his hands but had it slung across his back, his arms folded over his armored chest.

The company of Menninkai warriors halted about ten yards from us as the leader lifted a hand. He sized us up, then stepped forward and continued to advance down the beach toward Mathghaman.

He halted about an arm's length away, thrust the butt spike of his spear into the sand, and held out his hand.

Mathghaman clasped it. They spoke briefly, then the Menninkai warrior turned back toward his own people, spread his hands, and raised his voice. I couldn't make out the words, though there were some common-alities with the Tuacha's tongue. But from the look on Mathghaman's face, we had little to worry about.

At least, we had little to worry about from the Menninkai. Mathghaman turned to face the rest of the platoon, raising his voice. "We are among friends, and we are welcome here. I confess that I had wondered. It has been many years since I have sojourned among the Menninkai." His voice turned grim. "I fear that the welcome and help that we had hoped for will be slow in coming, however.

"It seems that we have landed in the midst of a siege."

CHAPTER 4

THE Menninkai warriors led us through the gatehouse, past the second set of thick, timber doors, and then out and along the winding lane that led from the gate up the hill toward the hall at the peak. I was somewhat surprised to see that as soon as we crossed under the massive gateway, instead of the turf-roofed houses we'd seen from below, we faced a barren, rocky hillside without any mark of man on it except the road.

It made sense, I realized. The outer wall was not the only line of defense, and the city had been built with defense in depth in mind. If the outer wall fell, then there was a secondary killing ground between the outer wall and the secondary.

I looked up as we hiked along the narrow road from the gate, circling around toward the east. There were fighters stationed on the outer wall, though few of them seemed to be facing the sea, most of them armed with bows. Above, more could be seen moving within the timber-roofed watchtowers on the secondary wall as well, doubtless there to cover for the outer wall's defenders as they retreated.

Which meant that the Menninkai were prepared for such a retreat. I didn't know if it was just preparedness—

these guys seemed pretty stolid—or if things were really getting that desperate.

I couldn't see any more of the siege as we climbed higher, since we were moving along the south slope of the hill, but I could still hear. Distant echoes of shouts and more horns and drums could still be heard even on the far side of that mammoth rock that formed the foundation of Vahava Paykhah.

I wondered, as we reached the second gate, a third of the way around the city—doubtless by design, so that if an enemy forced an outer gate, they wouldn't have a straight shot at an inner one—how long this siege had been going on. What I knew about ancient and medieval warfare pointed to sieges mostly turning into long contests of patience, the attacking force staying outside the range of whatever weapons the defenders could bring to bear, relying on starvation and dwindling water supplies to force a surrender. Trying to storm a prepared fortress was often a meat-grinder that most such forces couldn't afford.

But then, that applied to a sane world, not this nightmare land of berserkers in service to inhuman sorcerers. And even as we started up toward the third wall, I realized that the enemy had no blockade out at sea, otherwise we never would have been able to land. That meant that storming the walls was their *only* real option to take the fortress.

The inner gate was almost as tall as the outer, a double door of hewn timber, bound in iron, set in a stone arch that stood nearly thirty feet in the air. It creaked open for us, and the warriors led the way through, after the man in the lead shouted up to the watchers on the battlements above.

Passing under the arch, we found ourselves in a short tunnel, with yet another double door on the far side. It was almost a clone of the gatehouse below and led into the first level of the city proper.

Even on that circle, which formed the outer districts of the city, the timber and stone houses with thatched or turf roofs closely clumped together, there was still a wide space between the walls and the buildings. The lower houses were all small, mostly stone, partially dug into the hillside itself, and roofed with turf. It was obvious that this was one of the poorer quarters of the city. The people still went about their business, but there was a furtiveness to their movements, though most of them gave the warriors respectful nods.

In general, the Menninkai were small but stocky, with faint epicanthic folds at the corners of their eyes, their skin almost as ruddy as their hair. And as we climbed higher, turning to weave in and out of the blocks of rude houses, I saw that even the poor had spears, bows, and axes kept close at hand.

They were under every bit the threat that the wealthier warriors were, and it seemed that the Menninkai lived accordingly. I had to approve.

The route to the third gate was somewhat less meandering, but it still wasn't straight. We wove through the clumps of houses, none of them all that regular, getting stares from the huddled people in the shadows of the turf roofs. We Recon Marines weren't that big compared to the Tuacha, but most of us were still practically giants compared to these people. And our green enameled mail and digital camouflage would be strange enough without the chest rigs, the NVG mounts on our helmets, and the rifles, machineguns, and grenade launchers we carried in addition to our blades and axes.

The third gate was every bit as strong as the first two. Square towers of stone and charred, oiled timber loomed above it, with red and white banners hanging limply from poles above their peaked roofs. The great doors creaked open—I noticed then that all the gates opened *outward*, making them more difficult to break in—and the warriors led the way up into the next circle.

On we went, through three more circles of the city, the houses getting larger and more well-built the higher we climbed. We still kept getting looks, but they were more curious than hostile. These people clearly knew the Tuacha when they saw them. It was us Recon Marines and our weapons who were getting stares. But we were with the Tuacha, so we must be all right. We were just strange.

Finally, after well over an hour of hiking, we reached the hall.

It was huge, far bigger than I'd thought when I'd been looking at it from below. Standing nearly five stories tall, it was nearly sixty yards wide at the base. The only wood in its construction appeared to be the eaves, the roof, and the doors themselves. Everything else was stone.

That place looked like it could stand forever. Only I knew better.

Looking over my shoulder, I saw the coast spread out beneath us. And now I could see the siege more clearly.

The land around Vahava Paykhah had been cleared for farms for several miles, though the dark, coniferous woods closed in quickly after that, cloaking the foothills of the mountains that loomed in the distance. Many of the farmhouses appeared to have been burnt down, those that had been built of timber, anyway. The fields, still fallow from the winter, were now churned and muddied by the passage of feet and hooves.

A great semicircle of tents and barricades stretched across the farmland, not quite surrounding the landward side of Vahava Paykhah. Fires guttered behind the barricades, none of which looked particularly well-built. But there were clearly enough archers out there to make an attack in either direction, across the open ground below the fortress, a risky proposition.

Bodies, bones, broken weapons, and the other detritus of battle littered that open ground. What might have been hide shields for rams or something similar smoldered on the bare, trampled ground. That must have been the source of most of the smoke.

The doors to the hall opened with an echoing creak, and while most of the company of warriors that had accompanied us up from the gates stepped aside, the leader beckoned to us just before he turned and walked through the doorway and into the gloom beneath the roof.

I looked around as we entered, trying not to be too much of a gawking tourist. It was dark and honestly a little crude, compared to King Caedmon's palace in Aith an Rih, the Tuacha's capitol. It was still far homier than any of the other places we'd been in the north.

A massive stone fireplace stood in the center of the main hall, which was vaulted two stories above us, putting only three floors above. The fireplace's chimney looked to be about six feet wide as it arrowed straight up toward the roof high above. A fire roared in the fireplace, spilling golden light out in four directions around the stout stone pillars that held up the chimney.

Benches and tables were set around the outside, and tapestries woven in stylized scenes of hunting and mythic battles hung on the stone walls between alcoves where tapers burned on iron sconces.

There weren't many people in the hall. A handful of obviously senior warriors stood or sat around the upper tables, and some women and younger boys came and went, carrying food, drink, fuel for the fire, or messages to the warriors at the tables. The city was under siege, and it appeared that the Menninkai were not given to an aristocracy that huddled in the deepest of fortifications, trying to ignore the threat while the common people and the warrior class bled to protect them.

I liked these people more every minute.

Our guide led us around the fireplace, toward the dais at the head of the hall, where the high table and the tall throne at its center were lit by the fire and the wan sunlight that streamed through several slit windows high in the building's second story.

The man in the high seat was ancient, bent and gray, the Menninkai burliness seemingly wasted away to a large extent. As we got closer, I saw that he was wounded, too. Bandages were wrapped around his arm, shoulder, and chest, barely peeking out from under the mantle he wore. That a man that old had been out on the field said even more about the Menninkai than what I'd seen already, not to mention the gold band around his white hair, studded with agates and amber.

This was King Karhu who sat there, huddled over wounds that might have felled a younger man.

He looked up as we approached, and even at a distance, I saw his eyes light up as he spied us. "Mathghaman!" He started to stand, winced, and sank back into the throne as the younger woman next to him fretted over him, glowering at us for prompting him to make such an attempt in the first place.

The king recovered, his ragged breathing eased as the pain subsided, while we closed to the foot of the dais. Gunny, Bailey, Gurke, and I held back, letting Mathghaman take the lead.

"Mathghaman." The king's voice was almost a sigh. There was relief in his voice, almost painfully so. "How many men have you brought?" He spoke the Tuacha's tongue, which meant I could understand him, though his accent was thick and his pronunciation halting. He knew the language, but it had been a while, and he was rusty. Still, he took pride in being able to speak it to the Tuacha themselves, that much was obvious.

Mathghaman inclined his head, though he neither knelt nor bowed. This man might be a king, but he wasn't *his* king. "Forgive me, old friend. I brought no army." He spread his hands to indicate the handful of us who stood behind him. "We came on a mission of our own. We had no word that you were under attack."

The king's shoulders might have slumped slightly, but he otherwise maintained his composure, though I saw the sadness in his eyes. "I feared as much. We sent word, but none of the ships we sent have ever returned."

Bearrac, standing at Mathghaman's shoulder, frowned, a thunderous darkening of his already beetling black brows. "Corsairs?"

The king shook his head. "We do not know, but I doubt it. The corsairs of the east have all but vanished from the Narrow Sea in recent months."

Bailey and I shared a wry glance at that. *I wonder why that is?* Having allied with a vampire, followed by that creature's sudden but inevitable betrayal, the northern corsair tribes had been ravaged not long ago. We knew. We'd gone through the burned and blood-soaked settlements. That had to have a dampening effect on piracy.

Who would have thought that a vampire feeding on people—or just gruesomely murdering them for fun—would actually have some *good* come out of it?

Gunny's eyes had narrowed, and when he glanced over at the two of us, I suddenly had an idea what he was thinking about.

The sea serpent.

Someone—or some*thing*—had set that thing on us. Was the same creature responsible for the disappearance of the Menninkai's messengers?

"How long has this siege endured?" Mathghaman asked, stepping closer to the throne. "And who has come against you? Has Sumnoth grown so powerful as to sweep past your outposts, your other villages?"

King Karhu's face grew haunted. "Would that it were only Sumnoth." He took a drink from the horn cup the younger woman held for him. His hand shook slightly, though that might have been from pain. These people didn't have the drugs we'd had, or even the herbs the

Tuacha possessed, which made water, Motrin, and a change of socks look like a witch doctor's dancing.

"Sumnoth began it. It started the usual way, with raids along the western frontier. But they did not cease with the descent of winter. Settlements began to vanish, burned to the ground and all the people gone. Then the enemy's numbers began to swell, and the few survivors who reached us spoke of terrible sorceries and unnatural monsters. Things of shadow and smoke that could hardly be touched but could tear a man open in a single blow." He took another shaky swig of whatever was in that cup. "They reached our walls within days of the thaw. They nearly hammered down the front gates the first night. Since then, every assault has been a near thing. The northern clans cannot reach us. There are savages from the west and north among the Lasknut. We have seen symbols of those tribes serving the Fohorimans from Grichencos to Morc to Colgrun. Yet the Lasknut of Sumnoth seem to have all become sorcerers now. Or at least enough of them have. That is what beleaguers us."

He looked up at Mathghaman with a squint. "If you heard nothing of our plight, what *does* bring you here? It has been many years."

"It has." Mathghaman fell silent for a long moment as he thought over what he would say. Finally, he sighed. "Some months ago, my companions and I came to these shores in pursuit of one of our own, one who had committed a terrible crime." He never had told us what exactly this man had done, and it didn't seem like he was going to say now. He indicated us with a wave of his hand. "These men from afar rescued us from Taramas's catacombs, and now they have come to seek out some of their own who went missing here in the north."

King Karhu's eyes flicked to us, taking in our strange weapons and equipment. There was no recognition there, only curiosity and some fear. Fear tempered by the trust he apparently held in the Tuacha. He didn't believe that Mathghaman would side with monsters.

I felt some relief that I hadn't expected, seeing that lack of recognition. The mention of *things of shadow and smoke* had put icy claws around my throat. It wasn't an exact description of the horrors Dragon Mask had conjured, either in the hills above Taramas's citadel, or deep beneath, in the chamber where she had kept the Athame of Urkartikar, the evil artifact that Dragon Mask had dragged us down there to steal, all with Captain Sorenson's eager assent. But it was close enough that I wondered.

It didn't mean that Dragon Mask, Captain Sorenson, Zimmerman, or any of the rest were still alive. After all, if Dragon Mask could figure out how to summon those horrors, anyone else with a sufficiently deadened conscience could, too. But it still put a cold, hollow feeling in my gut, hearing that description. That was why I was relieved when the king didn't seem to recognize our weapons or chest rigs. It told me that he hadn't seen or heard reported any other strangers like us among the enemy.

There was still hope.

"Well, I cannot fault you." King Karhu leaned back in his throne, visibly pained. "But you may have come to the wrong place. I cannot aid you." He spread his one good arm, encompassing the entire walled city. "If the northern clans are not simply cut off, but have been over-run, then we here in Vahava Paykhah are all that remain of the Menninkai. And we lack the strength to break out, except by sea." He looked up at Mathghaman again, his eyes hooded, as if fearing what the response would be to his next words. "You could, perhaps, slip past the enemy in the confusion, if your errand is that pressing. But we cannot help. It is all we can do to hold."

Mathghaman glanced at Gunny, who had stepped up at his right hand. I could see the wheels turning. He was bound by his mission, the same as we were. Yet just leaving these people to their fate stuck in his craw.

"Our task is urgent, but all the same, it will take time. And if there is such sorcery afoot here as you have de-scribed, it would be folly to leave it at our backs." He sighed. "And there would be no honor in pursuing our mis-sion only to leave you to the mercies of the Fohorimans." King Karhu hadn't said that the Fohorimans were there yet, but if their followers were... He glanced down at his rifle with a faintly amused expression, then looked over at Gunny. Probably thinking about the thumpers and the machine guns, too. "Perhaps we can even the odds a little for you."

CHAPTER 5

THE sun was setting when Mathghaman joined my team in one of the towers.

The inside of the enclosed turret was dark, since the only openings to the north, east, and west were arrow slits, just barely wide enough to fire our rifles through. Right at the moment, Farrar and Santos were sitting against the wall, while Rodeffer and I watched what we could see of the enemy camp through the northern slits.

We all turned, straightening unconsciously as Mathghaman entered. Technically, he had placed himself and his companions under Gunny Taylor, but there wasn't really a chain of command there. We weren't so much a unit with a rank structure anymore. We were a band of brothers, Marines and Tuacha both. Mathghaman and his companions came along with us for the same reason we'd gone with him into the Land of Shadows and Crows.

That sort of brotherhood, however, didn't quite ever take away the man's sheer *presence*. If I hadn't met King Caedmon, I would have assumed that Mathghaman was a king, himself. And I'm not exactly what you might term a monarchist.

So, we all sort of reflexively stood whenever he entered the room. It wasn't something we'd ever talked about and definitely wasn't anything we'd ever mandated. It just kind of happened.

As was his wont, Mathghaman ignored it. I didn't think he was comfortable with being treated like, well, an officer, but he was equally uncomfortable drawing attention to it. So, he ignored it. It was almost oddly human for a man who seemed otherwise more than just a man.

He stepped up next to me and peered out the arrow slit. "They still wait?"

"Still." I leaned against the wall and ducked my head to look past his shoulder through the narrow opening. There was movement out there on the barricades, but so far, none of the Dovos or the Lasknut had ventured out into that no man's land between the barricades and the outer wall. "Not that we're in a position to do too much if they decide to push the walls tonight."

Mathghaman glanced at me with a glint of what might have been amusement in his eye. "You are still frustrated at being back here on the second wall?"

"Yeah." I waved toward the first wall. "We offered to help them out, and we get stuck in reserve."

Mathghaman chuckled faintly as he turned back to watch the enemy out there in the dying light. "You must understand, Karhu is a man torn between responsibilities and obligations. He cannot afford *not* to ask our help, yet he feels that he owes me, and thus is burdened by asking for help once again without having discharged what he feels is his debt from years past." He turned and leaned against the wall, his arms crossed over his chest. "I met Karhu years ago, when he was much younger. We fought the Lasknut together, and then we ventured high into the mountains to hunt the giant Cormu." His gaze got far away. "The giant was cleverer than we had suspected. It ambushed us near its cave and nearly crushed Karhu. I was able to kill it before it could end him, and he has held himself in my debt ever since."

"So, he needs our help, but at the same time he's afraid that you're going to get killed before he can repay his debt." Santos had relaxed since Mathghaman had entered, and now had gone back to sitting against the wall. "Or else, he's worried that he's going to end up *deeper* in debt, so he wants to keep Mathghaman back until there's no other option."

"You take his honor too lightly." Mathghaman turned stern. "It is true that he is torn between his duty to defend his city, and therefore accept any help that we might offer, and his debt to me. But there is no duplicity in the man. You may trust in that."

Under any other circumstances, I might have let years' worth of cynicism color my response, but I knew Mathghaman well enough from the last few months not to doubt him. If there was anyone in this world who really *didn't* have a duplicitous bone in his body, it was Mathghaman. But he was also keenly observant and wiser than most of us. It was unlikely—at best—that King Karhu could have pulled the wool over *his* eyes.

"So, because he's conflicted, what?" Rodeffer turned from his own arrow slit. "We just sit here until the first wall falls while our own mission gets postponed indefinitely? Again?"

Mathghaman looked over at him calmly, and then the lightbulb came on in my head.

"We didn't stay out of sentiment, did we?" When Mathghaman turned back to me, he'd raised one eyebrow, but he said nothing, at first. He was going to let me figure it out. "There's something else going on here, something that you think we ought to stick around for."

He nodded solemnly. "Indeed." He turned and looked out the arrow slit again for a moment. "Karhu spoke of the *followers* of Fohorimans from Grichencos, to Morc, to Colgrun. Yet he named none of the Fohoriman Warlock Kings themselves." He pointed out toward the barricades. "They are close enough to see with your optics. Have you seen any Fohorimans among them?"

I frowned, stepping to the slit and bracing my rifle against the wall, finding the besieging forces with my scope. I'd studied their general dispositions, but that had been about the limit of it so far.

Working my way from east to west, I scanned those figures I could see between gaps in the barricades. None of the incomplete circumvallation was particularly well constructed.

I saw a man with a familiar mask above the hides he wore. Beaten bronze, engraved in the semblance of a snarling beast, it marked one of the leaders of the "Dovos," the followers of one of the so-called "younger gods" of the Fohorimans. As near as I'd been able to figure out, the "younger gods" were mostly sorcerers who'd reached a level of power that convinced their followers to worship them. It had also warped them physically, turning them into fearsome monsters.

As for the "elder gods," I didn't know enough about them to say exactly what they were, except that the Tuacha referred to them as "Outsiders." What exactly that meant, I couldn't be sure, but it sure *sounded* ominous.

I'd find out more than I'd ever wanted to know. But that came later.

Continuing my scan, I spotted the Lasknut, somewhat more civilized looking than the Fohorimans' Dovos, dressed in mail and colorful capes. The emblems on their banners and shields, however, were all of death and destruction—crows and vultures, wolves and ravening bears, skulls and flayed skeletons.

But nowhere did I see the telltale deformities of the Fohorimans. No gray-skinned, red-eyed monstrosities, built like men but taller and out of proportion. Whatever was happening, the Fohorimans seemed to have nothing to do with it.

And yet…

"If it isn't the Fohorimans throwing this sorcery around…" I glanced at Mathghaman as he nodded.

"The Fohorimans were the first of the 'younger gods,' as they style themselves." Mathghaman leaned back against the wall again. "They were the first to trick the Outsiders, the so-called 'elder gods,' stealing their power and imprisoning them in the deep places. They did not declare themselves gods at first, and not all at once, either. But they have held their sorceries close ever since, lest their slaves turn on them just as they turned on their masters."

"So, you're saying it's not normal for ordinary men to be able to throw supernatural powers around?" Santos didn't seem to want to *quite* make the leap to say, "spells," even after everything we'd seen on this side of that mysterious fog bank, but sometimes you've got to hold onto your sanity by any means necessary, even if it means not quite looking at the whole picture all at once. Guys like Bailey and me, we seemed to be more at home in this place than we had been in the "modern world" we'd left.

Some guys, though, like Santos, were still making the transition, months after we'd found ourselves fighting sea trolls off the coast of what was definitely not Norway.

"No." Mathghaman shook his head. "Oh, they are given trinkets, charms, cursed things that have been touched by the power that the Fohorimans stole from far worse creatures. But true power is always withheld from them, kept secret by their lords." He nodded toward the barricade. "So, when there are true sorceries in use, and not a Fohoriman, or any other such sorcerer lord, in evidence, it means that something else is happening."

"Like what?" I was curious. Especially if Mathghaman considered it serious enough to have put our mission on hold.

"I do not know." He was still watching the barricades, his brow furrowed. "The magic unleashed beneath Taramas's catacombs was not like that which the Fohorimans have managed to control. It was more like that wielded by the Outsiders during the height of their power. The Fohorimans and their like have never dared to delve so deep."

"Didn't you say that the Fohorimans stole their powers from the Outsiders, though?" Santos glared at Farrar and Rodeffer, as if daring them to question his apparent acceptance of the idea of magic powers.

"They did," Mathghaman answered. "But there are some things no man can control. The Outsiders are not of this world. They are *other*, in a way that the Fohorimans are not. Their true power can unmake the world, or at least a portion of it." I suddenly imagined that if he was more given to emotional displays, Mathghaman might have shuddered. "They are the stuff of nightmares and madness. Beings given great power and gifts who refused to serve Tigharn with them, but rejected all that he is instead." Even in the dying light, it seemed his eyes were haunted. This man had seen things, things beyond even the weirdness that we'd already witnessed here. This conversation made my earlier, reflexive cynicism seem downright childish. "And the Outsiders the Summoner brought here, all those ages ago, are but the least of the *Cinn Tith*."

That was one of those terms that I hadn't heard before, but I understood it through the Tuacha's strange sort of background telepathy, the "mind speech." It literally meant "Fallen Ones." There was a metaphysical aspect to it, though. A sense, if you will, of something so turned aside from its very nature that it was an affront to Being itself.

We'd probably call them demons, in the original sense of the word.

There was a long silence, even as drums started to beat a new, frenetic rhythm in the enemy camp below. I turned back to the arrow slit and put my eye to my scope. Whatever was happening down there, it was behind the barricades, invisible to us.

"So, if even Uergal and Taramas don't dare mess with this stuff, how did Dragon Mask ever find out about it?" Rodeffer was thinking things through.

"That is the question, is it not? The Fohorimans sought to destroy all the artifacts of their masters when they sealed them in the depths of the earth—appealing even to Tigharn in many cases, as hypocritical as that may be—and it is unlikely that they would have told their followers much about the beasts they 'freed' them from."

Mathghaman was thoughtful. "But if the Outsiders—or even one of them—are stirring again, perhaps that explains things. They have abilities far beyond even the Fohorimans' comprehension."

Silence fell again, broken only by the weird thumping of the drums outside the walls. "That…doesn't sound good."

"It is not." His voice turned grim as a strange droning rose above the drumbeats in the distance, and even from where we stood or sat, a strange, electric tension began to fill the air. Santos scrambled to his feet, and in a moment, we were all at the arrow slits, weapons up and ready, looking for targets.

"This is why I chose to stay." Mathghaman himself had his rifle to his shoulder, though the Tuacha didn't really need optics. "If the Outsiders are stirring again, then the fates of those we seek pales in comparison." He didn't move or take his eyes away from the enemy as he paused.

The droning got louder. I could have sworn I smelled sulfur on the wind. The Lasknut began to come out from behind their barricades in tight formation, huddled behind their oval shields. The first questing arrows arced from behind them but fell short, only getting the range to the outer wall.

"Unless Dragon Mask is behind all of this." Santos's speculation hit like a bolt of lightning. "If it's the same weirdness, and he's still got our guys with him, maybe the Outsiders are more closely linked to our search than we thought."

Before anyone could comment on that, the attack began.

CHAPTER 6

FOR a while, we could only watch, and even then, we could only see bits and pieces of the larger fight. We could see the tight formations, roughly rectangular and protected by overlapping shields in front and overhead, moving across no man's land, as archers launched arrows high overhead to plummet down onto the battlements of the outer wall. There were three main forces moving across the open, muddy ground outside the outer wall, and unless I missed my guess, the center was bringing a ram or something similar against the north gate. There was enough movement near the middle to suggest that they were struggling to move the ram while maintaining the roof of shields overhead.

The other two groups out on the flanks were tighter, but they still might have been carrying something big beneath those shields. Through my scope, even in the dying light, I could see that the overhead cover seemed looser in several places, suggesting that the men couldn't get close enough to completely overlap their shields, though they were still holding more tightly than the center.

On the battlements, the Menninkai weren't just sitting there waiting. Arrows arced down toward the advancing formations, and though it looked like very few were getting through the overlapping hide shields, some were, and even at a distance I could see some of those shields falter and disappear, though the gaps were closed quickly. The Lasknut were surprisingly disciplined, though when I thought about it, no Hollywood barbarian rabble would last long against any disciplined, cohesive fighting force.

Step by step, the close formations closed in on the walls, as the Menninkai added sling stones to the rain of arrows. "They're just shooting normal arrows." Roddefer frowned as he watched through his arrow slit. "Why no fire arrows?"

"Probably because the flight would put the fire out." Santos snorted. "You shouldn't believe everything you see in movies."

I frowned as I watched. The Lasknut and their Dovo allies were certainly numerous, but this still seemed a little off. Why would they simply throw bodies at hardened fortifications like this? I didn't consider myself any expert on ancient siege warfare, but it seemed like there were better ways to reduce a fortification.

Of course, their options were limited. Without the ability to blockade Vahava Paykhah from the sea, they couldn't starve the Menninkai out. Undermining the walls was probably out of the question, given the rock the city was built on. That pretty much left storming the walls and the gates, as much of a meat-grinder as that promised to be.

Soon we couldn't see much beyond the defenders raining arrows and sling stones down on the attackers as the shield formations closed on the outer wall passing under our view over the top. Then for a while, we could only hear the rising clash and the first *boom* as the ram hit the gate.

All the while, the drums kept thundering, and that weird droning continued, only seeming to get louder as the night began to descend.

I didn't think the assault was starting after sunset because the Lasknut wanted to avoid being spotted, either. This was a world without NVGs, for the most part, and there were other things involved that didn't seem to like the sun.

Boom. I could just see the gate from our position, but the inner gate was closed, so I couldn't see the outer doors anyway, where the ram was hitting them. Still, from the looks of the inner gate, barred by a timber that looked like it had been hewn from most of an entire tree trunk, it was going to take some serious time and energy to get through that gatehouse. And that was without the head-sized stones that the Menninkai defenders were hurling over the top of the wall, or the steaming—or smoking, it was hard to tell—buckets that were being carried from the fires at the lower level to be poured over the battlements.

The Lasknut weren't just focused on the gates, though. Ladders rose to the battlements, and armored warriors clambered up, shields held up to fend off the worst of the defenders' projectiles. Say what you will about them, the Lasknut were tenacious. No one would have gained the top of the wall while being shot, crushed, burned, or boiled alive, otherwise.

The defenders were trying to throw the siege ladders off, but there were more of them than I'd suspected from first looking at their formations as they'd advanced. The enemy archers had moved closer to the walls, too, as the rain of arrows from above dwindled, focused more on the advancing assaulters. Even as I watched, one of the Menninkai warriors on the wall took an arrow through the throat and dropped, clutching at the shaft through his windpipe, already dying before he struck the walkway.

At almost the same moment, the first of the Lasknut came over the wall.

His shield came first, held over his head to fend off the rocks, arrows, and boiling water or searing hot sand raining down from the defenders. He hooked the shield over the top of the battlements, swung a leg over, and then he was on the platform, his back to the no man's land below, crouched behind his shield as Menninkai warriors closed quickly on him from either side, intent on either slaughtering him or simply throwing him back over the wall.

He was good, I'll give him that. He shifted from one attacker to the next with lightning quickness, driving first one back with a flurry of blows, then turning before the other could stab him from behind. He never stayed still, never got sucked in by one or the other, and the narrowness of that walkway worked to his advantage, as the Menninkai defenders could only come at him one at a time in either direction. He *would* miscalculate, sooner or later, but the whole time he was up there, the next man was climbing the ladder behind him.

That didn't take long, either. In moments, half a dozen Lasknut warriors were up on the battlements, forcing the Menninkai back as the ram continued to *boom* against the gates. One of the Menninkai warriors, several ranks back from those engaging the men who'd gotten to the top, lifted a horn to his lips and blew frantically, the blasts of the horn sounding even over the rumble of the drums.

I had my sights on the big bruiser who'd just come up the ladder. Two arrows were stuck in his armor, apparently having failed to penetrate all the way. He stood taller than any of the others and wore a bearskin over his shoulders and helmet. Unless I missed my guess, he was a leader of some sort. The others seemed to have stepped up the ferocity with which they battered at the defenders, now that he was up on the wall.

The light was bad, but I knew the range to that first wall down to almost the inch. We'd had just enough time to build our range cards before the attack had come. So it was an easy enough matter to put the ghostly glowing lines of my reticle on his chest, my rifle braced against the side of the arrow slit, clamped in position by my off hand as I leaned into it, let my breath out, and squeeze the trigger.

The *crack* of the shot echoed across the open killing ground between the first and second walls, and my bullet took him high in the chest.

He staggered back as the 7.62 round punched through whatever armor he was wearing. He stared down at the hole in his chest for a moment before he toppled over backward and went over the top of the wall, presumably wiping out several of the warriors that were following him up the ladder.

That shot threw the entire battle into doubt. At least, on the Lasknut's side.

The assault faltered, and the Menninkai rallied as the archers in the guard towers rained yet more arrows down on the ladders. Several Lasknut warriors were cut down, stabbed, or simply shoved off the wall, crashing down to break their bones on the rocky ground beneath, on either side of the wall itself.

Rodeffer shot another one, and he fell against one of the lead Lasknut who was trying to fall back from an axe-wielding Menninkai fighter. That gave our ally the opening he needed, and the axe crashed down where neck met shoulder. Blood splashed dark against the wood, glistening in the faint light of the lanterns in the nearby guard tower.

A couple of the Lasknut managed to retreat to the ladder, but were probably killed or maimed a few moments later as Menninkai spears levered the ladder itself away from the wall and cast it down onto the rocks below. More screams joined the clash of arms, the drums, the *boom* of the ram, and the cries and grunts of the fighting.

For a moment, then, we could no longer see the fight, as the Lasknut were forced back below the level of the wall. The Menninkai continued to pelt the attackers with arrows and stones, even as several of them dragged their own wounded back toward the towers. That presented some difficulty, given how narrow the platform at the top of the wall was, but I'd just seen the reasoning for that, as it didn't allow an attacker to get more than one man abreast pushing the defenders if they did get to the top and over the battlements. But they managed it, hauling men cradling gashed or broken limbs or trying to staunch terrible bleeds with their bare hands past the defenders and toward shelter.

We had to go back to watching and waiting. We had no targets, and the wall had held.

Then things got weird.

The droning reached a new pitch, and the drums went insane, no longer holding any real rhythm but just turning to hammering noise. The thunderstorm tension in the air got suddenly worse, and I could have sworn I smelled something metallic on the air. There was something familiar about all of it, and not in a good way.

Something drew my eyes back toward the barricades, where the archers had suddenly made themselves scarce. I frowned, peering through my scope, though the fires had all been shielded by the barricades enough that it was extremely difficult to see. But I almost didn't need to see it. I could *feel* what was coming, and my stomach twisted as I realized it. To make matters worse, there was nothing I could do about it.

Reality itself seemed to heave, as if the very ground and air rebelled at what was happening. In the same moment, dark, amorphous, winged shapes shot into the sky from behind the barricades and stooped on the walls with high-pitched, earsplitting shrieks. None of them had a form you could focus on for long, and it made my head hurt just to look at them for more than a second or two.

Just like those oily black horrors in the catacombs beneath Taramas's citadel.

I'd hardly noticed the fact that the ram had stopped. Those winged abominations, so black that they seemed to *glow* with darkness, if that makes any sense, fell on the defenders right where the Lasknut had gained the top of the wall, and proceeded to tear them apart. The screams were beyond inhuman. Blood and torn body parts rained down into the killing ground. One man was seized by the throat and dragged screaming into the air as great wings of smoke and deeper darkness flapped, hauling him higher and higher into the darkened clouds above, winging over the city until it dropped him, screaming, atop the hall itself.

But even those nightmares were only a diversion.

The world seemed to shudder again, and then the wall just a few yards to the east of the main gate blew up.

There was no flash, no fire, no light at all. The ground seemed to heave under the stones and timber, many of those stones blasted to inky ash. The very air seemed to get blurry and dark, and then a section of the wall about twenty feet wide just seemed to drop into nothingness.

That unnatural stink only intensified. Rodeffer actually puked, doubling over beneath the arrow slit. I felt pretty queasy myself. This was far worse than what Dragon Mask had unleashed in the hills above Taramas's fortress. And that had been bad enough that I'd threatened to kill him in an eyeblink if he ever tried something like it again.

Mathghaman had stepped up to Rodeffer's arrow slit, ignoring the vomit on the floorboards, and fired. I got my head up to try to see what he'd shot at, but nothing had fallen. And I knew better than to think that Mathghaman, of all people, had missed.

He snarled, the angriest I'd ever seen him. "Bullets will not harm those things. As I feared." He turned toward the steps leading down toward the ground below. "Prepare to cover the defenders as they retreat." He paused for a moment. "I have to find a way to banish those things back to whence they came."

Then he was gone, as the Lasknut and the Dovos surged into the blackened breach, and the Menninkai ran for shelter.

CHAPTER 7

I'D dropped my NVGs. The sun was down, and the over-cast was still unbroken, but it was already far darker than it should have been. And even my PVS-15s weren't lighting the world up as much as they should have. I had no doubt that the summoned horrors were sucking up the light by their very presence.

They were still tearing at the Menninkai on the walls. One of them had alighted on the tower immediately to the west of the spot where the Lasknut had mounted the battlements, and it was tearing at the doorframe, reaching through the gap for the men who were even then screaming in abject terror, doubtless as they discovered that they couldn't hurt the creature of smoke and darkness with axe, sword, spear, or arrow.

As much as it stuck in my craw, there wasn't anything I could do about that thing. So, I turned my attention to the breach, canting my rifle to bring the red dot into my NVGs' field of view. It made it harder to aim, but even at two hundred fifty yards, I could still pick out man-sized targets. And that was all I had to do at that point, because the breach was teeming with enemies.

They weren't rushing through like screaming idiots, not like the Dovos nal Uergal had tried to rush our position in the tor, far to the west, only a few months before.

Granted, the Dovos I could see, dressed in skins and masks, seemed somewhat inclined to break ranks and run at the gate, but they were still smart enough to realize that they couldn't do much against that much timber with just axes, and that the more disciplined Lasknut, formed up tightly behind their shields, had a much better chance.

Let's see how your shields stand up to 7.62 NATO.

My first shot blew through the hide and wood, though I didn't hit the man carrying that particular shield. The one next to him fell, but the gap was quickly filled. These guys didn't stampede easily, despite how they'd faltered when we'd opened fire before. They hadn't been prepared, then. In the face of the sorcery unleashed in their support, though, I supposed gunfire from the walls wasn't all *that* impressive.

At least, until Chambers opened up with his Mk 48.

That stuttering roar was unmistakable, and the stream of four ball, one tracer tore through the shields, armor, and flesh of the front rank like a buzz saw. Dead and wounded Lasknut fell on their faces and the shattered remnants of their shields, bleeding out where the bullets hadn't torn the life out of them immediately.

The ranks behind them faltered, then a harsh voice rose above the din, echoed by blaring horns, and they fell back, though they were still huddled behind their shields uselessly as we raked them with gunfire. At least a couple dozen more fell before everything really went to hell.

With a soul-searing shriek, two of the flying nightmares descended on the tower where Gurke's team had set up, battering it so hard that we could feel the entire wall shudder under their blows. Entire timbers and bits of the roofing were torn off to fly into the air over the open killing ground below. Chambers' fire on the advancing Lasknut ceased, but he was still shooting, wasting bullets uselessly on the flying nightmares.

Another one stooped on our tower, shaking the entire structure as it hit. A clawed limb bashed its way through my arrow slit as I scrambled backward. Splinters flew as it clawed at the floor after me, and I realized with a growing, sick sense of horror that there was an eye in the thing's wrist. It couldn't see me through the arrow slit, but it didn't have to.

Santos started shooting at it. Rodeffer was occupied, trying to fend off the second limb that was coming through his slit. Farrar was freaking out, especially as I ended up with my back to the wall, and that limb kept coming for me, its claws skittering across the floor almost as fast as I could move. The limb was growing as it stretched across the inside of the tower.

Bullets wouldn't hurt it. But just maybe…

Transition drills were something we'd trained a lot back in The World. But those were always from the rifle when it went down—empty or jammed—to the pistol. It had taken a lot of practice to get smooth at transitioning from rifle to sword. But I'd drilled it countless times on the Isle, and so I quickly and smoothly swept my rifle to my back with one hand while I drew my sword with the other.

The creature grabbed me by the ankle and yanked my leg out from under me even as the sword cleared its scabbard. It was horribly strong, and that was leaving aside the fact that it felt like I'd just been grabbed by a rope made of white-hot barbed wire. The pain knocked the wind out of me, and I couldn't even scream.

The pain was so bad that I might very well have passed out and gotten eaten right then and there. Even if I hadn't, a lot of people would have simply shut down at that searing torment. If I hadn't had the no-quit attitude beaten into me through BRC and after, I might not have been able to swing that sword at my own ankle. I could barely see through the agony to know for sure where I was aiming.

But God looks after fools and little children, and, apparently, guys swinging a sword half-blind at their own appendages. The blade missed my foot by a hair, and bit deeply into that terrible, black limb.

It *caught fire.* I kid you not. Blue-white flames enveloped the claws and that awful, inhuman eye, and the shriek as it let go and hauled the limb back through the arrow slit ventured into the ultrasonic. A spike of pain rammed through my skull at the noise, even as the pain in my ankle subsided.

Then it was gone, flapping away even as it burned, slowly disintegrating as the blue-white flames ate it alive. It didn't make it back to the outer wall before it had collapsed into a shower of ashes and sparks.

I rolled over and shoved myself up to my knees with a groan. The pain was starting to ease in my skull, slightly faster than my ankle. Looking down, I saw tears in my trouser leg, but none of the burns I'd more than half expected, given how badly that thing's touch had hurt.

The unholy screams and bursts of gunfire from the next tower over were still going on. Gurke and his boys weren't going to be able to scratch those things, and it was only a matter of time before one of them got dragged out through an arrow slit. I had no doubt that those things would shatter every bone in a man's body to do that.

Limping on my aching ankle, I staggered out of the tower and along the top of the second wall, keeping low just in case there was an archer down there who was feeling lucky, my rifle on my back and my sword still in my hand. I could hear Santos yelling after me, but I had a weapon that could hurt those abominations, so I had to get in there and drive them back. Every one of us had taken to carrying a sword or axe—it just made sense in a world where close combat was the norm, and we had limited ammo and resupply was rare and far away—but I was the only one carrying a blessed artifact for a backup weapon.

The story of how that weapon had come to me had to be pretty damned complicated, but I had no way of knowing it. It had been taken by a Dovo warrior at some point, who had been bothered enough by the runes inlaid in the grip to wrap the entire hilt and pommel in rawhide, so he wouldn't have to look at them. Then one of us had killed him, and I'd picked up the sword. Beyond that, I had no idea.

The two eldritch winged things were tearing at the tower in a shrieking frenzy. It didn't look like they'd reached inside yet; they were still ripping timber off in splintery chunks. As I got closer, though, one of them turned its faceless head toward me, and with another juddering, unearthly howl, it leapt off the tower and stooped on me.

If it had a mind, it figured out a moment too late that I held a bitter thorn that could pierce even its unnatural hide.

I ducked beneath the battlements as it dove on top of me, jabbing the point of the sword up at it as it descended. It tried to arrest its rush at the last moment, as the far too many eyes sprouting out of its oily, tar-like black flesh spotted the gleam of that sword—which never seemed to take a stain no matter how evil the crud it was plunged into—but fortunately, despite the unnatural nature of these things, they were at least still *somewhat* subject to the laws of physics when they manifested. They still had mass, and that meant momentum that couldn't *quite* stop on a dime.

It didn't take much, when blessed steel met unholy abomination, either. The point might have sunk an inch into its awful flesh, but the blue flames erupted from the wound as it flapped back toward the sky. They spread rapidly, the creature, or manifestation, or whatever the hell it was letting out that same mind-shredding howl as it burned. It made it about halfway toward the outer wall before it disintegrated.

I reached up, grabbed the sharpened top of the nearest timber, and hauled myself to my feet. My head was swimming, the unholy stench of those things making my stomach churn. Actually, that's oversimplifying things. I could *feel* the madness of their very presence clawing at my mind. Their twisted affront to reality was what was making me nauseous.

Gritting my teeth, I staggered toward the tower, bouncing off the door frame as I swayed.

The scene inside was pandemonium. Chambers was still shooting at the horrific form outside the arrow slits, while Franks was down, shuddering violently, his eyes rolled back in his head, foaming at the mouth. Gurke was on top of him, pinning his arms to the floor, trying to get something between his teeth to keep him from biting his own tongue off.

The creature outside was still howling and tearing at the walls. It hadn't reached inside yet. It seemed to be intent on tearing the tower itself apart, instead. The entire structure shook under the onslaught as I moved toward the nearest arrow slit, looking for an opening.

That thing must have realized that something that could hurt it had just entered the game. It had clambered higher on the tower's roof and was tearing at the slate shingles, sending them flying down into the gap between the walls, heedless of the advancing forces that had resumed coming through the gap as the fire from the second wall had ceased. I could see them moving in, now that Chambers was occupied with trying to fend that horror off. With the arrow slits clear, he was crouched in the corner, his Mk 48 pointed up at the ceiling, where the timbers and the clapboards beneath the shingles shuddered and creaked with every blow.

Then, suddenly, a light shone in the darkness.

It lasted only a moment. But at the same time, it wasn't really a "flash." It was as if the sun came up, briefly. The source of the light was near the top of the hall, at the peak of the rock upon which Vahava Paykhah stood, shining down on the walls and the land beyond, forcing me to flip up my NVGs as they were whited out.

Something made me glance up through the rear slits in the tower, toward the hall and the source of that light. It was bright but not painful, somehow.

For a moment—just a moment—I thought I could see a brilliant, glowing figure in the sky above the roof of the hall.

It took a second to realize that the battering and shaking had stopped. A thin, quavering wail might have drifted by on the wind. Then the light faded, and it was night again.

CHAPTER 8

IT was dark, but it was a natural dark, the darkness of night, rather than the eldritch blackness that clung to the sorcerous abominations the Lasknut had summoned to support their assault. We hauled ourselves back to the arrow slits, dropping NVGs again and getting back on guns. For the moment, I stayed in that tower with Chambers, since Gurke was still looking after Franks, though his seizures seemed to have stopped as soon as the creatures had vanished.

The Lasknut and their allies were flowing through the breach and across the gap between the walls, spreading out to cut off the Menninkai defenders who hadn't made it to the gates yet. The open ground below us was teeming with armed men, though they were still in formation, shields up to protect them from arrows from above.

"Thumpers!" I didn't have one, but Gurke did. He turned and unslung it, tossing it to me as I turned back from the arrow slit, Lasknut arrows hammering into the battered, splintered timbers around it. One actually sailed through the rather widened slit itself with a whistle and smacked into the beams overhead with a *thunk*.

I caught the standalone 40mm grenade launcher, a pretty faithful replica of the LMT M203 standalone, opened the action just far enough to make sure there was an "egg" in there, clapped it closed, and moved back into the slit.

Aiming wasn't even all that necessary. They were so thick down there that all I really had to do was point and shoot.

The stubby grenade launcher kicked about like a twelve-gauge shotgun, sending its explosive surprise spinning downrange with a loud *thunk*. I was already yanking the action open as I brought the tube down from recoil, then I had to reach back for the belt of 40mm HE grenades that Gurke was just then holding out.

With a heavy *thud* the grenade went off on impact, having just slipped between a narrow gap between shields. A knot of Lasknut disappeared in a flash and an ugly black cloud, the shockwave surging through the rest of the formation, as men crumpled from the impact or the frag. When the cloud dissipated, almost a dozen Lasknut warriors lay broken and bleeding on the ground.

They were quickly joined by more as Chambers opened fire. Santos soon joined in from the tower I'd left, and soon the two of them were raking the oncoming warriors with alternating bursts, the guns talking smoothly to keep the rate of fire up without melting the barrels.

I honestly had no idea if barrels produced by the *Coira Ansec could* melt down, but we could only react according to our training. If we pushed it, and *did* manage to melt a barrel, we could be in a world of hurt.

Shaking the spent casing out of the 203, I slid another grenade in, smacked the action closed, and dumped another ogive into the midst of the falling windrows of slain Lasknut warriors. They weren't quite as densely packed where I fired, but several still fell to the shrapnel whickering away from the detonation. Two lay still, savaged by the shockwave and the frag, but one kept crawling away, dragging a leg turned to hamburger.

Then the Lasknut were fleeing through the breach, still getting cut down by savage bursts of gunfire as I dropped the 203 and got back on my rifle, knocking another one off his feet with a shot between his shoulder blades. As the last of them ran through the hole in the wall and into the dark beyond, we finally ceased fire.

The open ground between the first and second walls was littered with the dead. Unfortunately, not all of them were Lasknut or Dovos.

The northern defenses had been ravaged, and now there was a breach in the wall. We might have thrown them back, but the outer wall was already effectively lost.

It would be a long night.

* * *

It was indeed a long night. The Lasknut didn't attack again, but we had to stay alert the entire time. Despite the fact that they were men, not monsters—at least, not by the definition we'd been using since we'd come to this haunted world—the Menninkai had told us that the Lasknut usually attacked after dark. Mathghaman and Gunny had agreed that it had more to do with their sorcery than with their skill as night fighters.

A little before dawn—at least, I figured it was getting close to dawn; the days and nights were slightly longer here, so using my watch to judge the time was still more a matter of guesswork than anything else—

the Menninkai reinforced the second wall. Gunny came along the battlements, accompanied by Bearrac and one of the Menninkai's leading warriors, a wiry man with his hair shading toward blond where it wasn't white, his armor and weapons slightly higher quality than most of the rest. He also wore a red mantle over his armor, and he quickly started setting a band of archers in on the wall and in the tower.

"We're being relieved, gents." Gunny looked down at Franks. He was still sick and lethargic, and could barely stand, but he was better.

I saw the faint cleft deepen between Gunny's brows as he watched Franks. But when Franks looked up and shook his head, indicating he was all right, Gunny just kind of shrugged. It would be addressed. Once Gunny Taylor had taken note of something wrong, you could bet it was going to be dealt with. But right then and there wasn't the time or the place, so long as Franks was okay for the moment.

The Menninkai looked around at the devastation, his face blank. I could tell he was trying not to show how shaken he was by the extent of the damage the sorcerous monsters had done to the tower. The arrow slits were more than twice their original size, and the night sky could be seen through gaps torn in the roof. The tower was still defensible, but if the Lasknut sent more of those things, it might not be for long.

As he looked around at us, I saw a new respect in his eyes, coupled with a certain degree of wariness as he looked at our weapons. He'd seen the carnage below already. He wasn't sure whether to welcome the havoc we could wreak, or fear it.

Gunny had also taken in the destruction. "What are you doing over here, Conor?" Meaning, *Why aren't you with your team?*

I tapped the sword in its scabbard at my side. "Turns out that those things their sorcerer conjured up don't like blessed weapons very much. They only sent one at our tower. Once it got smacked down, there were still two of 'em tearing at this one." And while I wouldn't have said it in so many words, after Mathghaman had told me to continue to bear the sword—I'd offered it to him here in the northlands, shortly after we figured out that the Tuacha were the good guys—I wasn't inclined to loan it out.

Gunny nodded his understanding while the Menninkai warrior looked from one to the other of us, clearly uncertain about the outlanders speaking a strange tongue who could slaughter Lasknut in job lots from a distance. And with a lot of thunder, too. There was no way anyone in the city hadn't heard the gunfire, even though all of us were running suppressed.

Bearrac spoke quietly to him. He was speaking the Tuacha's tongue; he didn't need to speak Menninkai—or whatever their language was called—thanks to the "mind speech." He explained that I bore an ancient, blessed sword from the Time of Martyrs and Heroes, and that our other weapons were much more mundane than it was.

The Menninkai leader didn't look that convinced, and given the bloody mess we'd made of the Lasknut assaulters, I can't say I blamed him that much.

"Go check on your team, then move back to the great hall, Conor." Gunny kept his voice low as the Menninkai filtered into the tower and took our places at the arrow slits. There were still more behind them, some of them looking as tired and worn down as I felt. I was sure that some of them had been down there on the outer wall.

So, I understood why Gunny was keeping his voice down. The Menninkai probably couldn't understand us, but there was still a bit of discomfort in facing the guys who'd faced the enemy much more up close than we had, and were now taking our place while we retreated to a place of safety. I could see from the look on Gurke's face as he watched our allies move into the tower that he was thinking much the same thing.

But we had our orders, just like they had theirs. So, I nodded, turned, and headed back toward my team's tower.

As I did, I wondered. Orders. Discipline. We'd maintained our cohesion as a platoon mainly for survival's sake, but also because we were the only ones we knew in this strange world. Would that last, as time went on? Unless we found some way back—and that didn't seem all that likely, from what we'd gathered just talking to the Tuacha, who were as mystified about how we'd come there as we were—as we got more comfortable with the world? Would we find other paths, other lives to live, apart from the platoon? After all, there wasn't much of the original platoon left, and not all of us had particularly liked each other even before this mission had gone haywire.

We'd act on orders without much question for now, but how long would that last? And could we keep it together long enough to find ourselves secure enough to go our separate ways? After all, aside from the Isle of Riamog, we hadn't seen much in the way of idyllic, pastoral places to live in this world. The entire north and what we'd seen of the east were infested with monsters, haunted by evil spirits and eldritch abominations, and those men who dwelt there were savage tribes who would probably kill you as soon as look at you. And then probably eat you. *After* you died, if you were lucky.

I don't know why I was thinking about this as I headed for our tower ahead of our relief. Probably because I was exhausted and trying really hard not to think about those things we'd been fighting, or what it meant that the Lasknut could wield the same mind-shredding, unholy magics that Dragon Mask had pulled out.

The team was good, Santos still at the arrow slit with our team's Mk 48. I passed the word as more of the Menninkai came in after us, and we headed down the steps into the city, hauling our gear with us, trying not to think about how glad we were not to have to face those nightmares again that night. At least, not right away.

* * *

Mathghaman was waiting for us at the great hall, standing next to a bent, white-haired ancient. The man was clearly Menninkai—he hadn't come in with us, for one thing—but unlike most of the rest, he was dressed in gray robes, belted at the waist with a simple cord. His attire reminded me of Brother Melchorius, in Lost Colcand, though the cut was still somewhat different.

"I believe we will have some respite, at least for another night." Mathghaman sounded fairly sure. The old man just looked tired, leaning on a stick even though he was already sitting on a bench. "It will not last, but it will be difficult for the Lasknut sorcerers to summon such powers near here for some time."

"Why? What happened?" Gurke looked at the old man. "I was sure we were cooked."

The old man smiled faintly, almost as if he understood what Gurke had just said, even though Gurke had been speaking English. Mathghaman echoed the expression as King Karhu came around the great fireplace and put a hand on the old man's shoulder. Karhu was old, but he seemed much younger then, standing next to the man in the gray robes.

The king looked curiously at Mathghaman, who quietly explained what Gurke had said. Then he nodded. "Brother Saukko's prayers were answered." He said it as if that was all that needed saying.

I suppose, in retrospect, that it really *was* all that needed saying. Any other explanation probably would have fallen short. The fact was, something had happened, and that light had driven away the sorcerous summonings before they'd managed to tear through our defenses.

"Well, then, thank you, Brother Saukko," Gunny said in the Tuacha's tongue. It was halting and accented, but he was learning the language, better than I was.

"Thank Tigharn." Brother Saukko also spoke the Tuacha's tongue fluently. "He sent deliverance. I but asked."

Gunny inclined his head to accept it, though he probably didn't understand exactly what had happened any better than the rest of us did. He looked at Mathghaman. "What do we do now?"

"We rest today. The Lasknut might attack again tonight, or they might wait until they can conduct the foul sacrifices that they must offer if they seek to draw the Outsiders' power back to this place." Mathghaman's voice dripped with contempt as he said that. I could imagine what he was talking about. We'd seen the Dovos' hands red with blood just to satisfy their "younger god," Uergal. If the Outsiders were as bad as Mathghaman had said...

I didn't know that we were going to be able to sleep much with that in mind. But with another fight on the horizon, we had to. Always try to sleep when you have the chance. You never know when you might get another.

It was still a fitful rest.

CHAPTER 9

IT was still mid-afternoon when we slipped out the south gate and started to work our way around the base of the outer wall toward the north. The clouds still loomed overhead, spitting rain from time to time, but it was still bright enough that it felt wrong to be moving through what was essentially enemy territory.

Of course, the enemy hadn't tried to force the breach again since the night before, meaning that the open ground between the walls, about two hundred yards of it, was empty and abandoned, no man's land in actual fact. We'd exited friendly lines from a direction the enemy couldn't see from their positions and quickly moved down to the base of the outer wall, so we had all that cover to work with, while the archers—and Gurke's and Bailey's teams—provided overwatch from the second wall.

In a Ranger file, we moved along the uneven, rocky ground at the base of the wall, Rodeffer on point, Bearrac and I just behind, Farrar and Santos bringing up the rear. We could move fast, since we didn't really have to keep checking six.

It still took the better part of half an hour to reach our planned position, a tower just to the west of that one closest to where the Lasknut had gained the top of the wall the night before. We'd considered just going to that tower, or even the gatehouse, but that had kind of gone against the grain. The enemy might be watching those.

Now, they didn't have rifles or machineguns, it's true. But we'd been hearing the drums and awful screams all day, rising from beyond the barricades. There was bad stuff going on out there, as the sorcerers tried to regain their standing with whatever evil thing granted them their power. The screams had only paused for just about long enough for a dead man to get dragged off an altar and a new victim to get stretched out.

At least, that was what it seemed like to me. It had been nearly continuous since just before dawn. That thunderstorm tension was building with every bout of screaming, nearly drowned out by the frenetic drumming.

I didn't think that we had a full day, like Mathghaman had hoped. And just before we'd left, he'd agreed. That was why we were heading out to the outer wall.

When we reached the base of the tower, we paused to watch and listen for a moment. We hadn't *seen* anything climb the wall or slip through the breach, but in a world full of weird things that shouldn't exist, it was still possible that while the Lasknut's leader out there hadn't managed the really freaky Outsider stuff again yet, they might still have slipped something a little more "mundane" through. After all, even corsair shamans had been able to summon flying spy creatures. If the Lasknut were ostensibly vassals to a Fohoriman Warlock King, they might still have access to that level of sorcery, even if the Outsider stuff had been banished by the Menninkai's holy man.

We didn't know enough to be certain about any of this stuff, but it paid to be cautious.

Our halt didn't last that long. Ordinarily, a SLLS halt—Stop, Look, Listen, and Smell—lasts about ten minutes. But the screaming out there was putting my nerves on edge, and it had only been about five before I reached out and squeezed Rodeffer's shoulder. He stood, put his hand on the wooden door handle, his rifle tucked back under his arm in the retracted gun, muzzle pointed at the gap in the door, and swung it open.

It was dark and still inside. Bringing his rifle back up, Rodeffer stepped through the doorway with me right behind him. We moved in as one, weapon lights flashing into the corners. It was standard tactics for dealing with physical enemies. I didn't know if it would work if there was some creepy shadow *thing* in there, like some of the other monsters we'd encountered in the Land of Ice and Monsters, but short of bringing in a firehose of holy water or burning the tower down, I wasn't sure what else to do.

The base of the tower was dark, quiet, and empty. I wasn't getting any more of the heebie-jeebies than the sounds of constant human sacrifice outside had been giving me for the last several hours. Rodeffer was on the steps, his muzzle pointed up above, toward the fighting platform two stories above. I moved up next to him and we mounted the steps.

They creaked under our boots, the timber old and well-seasoned. , but. We worked our way slowly and carefully up to the top of the tower, our muzzles up and ready, watching for any movement, any threat. Nothing came out of the dark to attack us, nothing appeared at the top of the steps. Finally, we flowed quickly into the turret atop the tower, muzzle first.

Empty and quiet. Gray light filtered in through the arrow slits, softened by the light, misting rain that dripped down the charred and oiled timbers. I pointed Rodeffer toward the door that opened onto the walls to the east, then Farrar to the west. Santos, Bearrac, and I moved to the arrow slits looking out on no man's land.

There were even more bodies out there than we'd left in the space between the walls the night before, and many of them in far more advanced states of decay. The damp and the chill seemed to be keeping the stench down, but the open ground both inside and outside the walls was thick with carrion birds, picking at the dead.

I was glad that the enemy's sorcery hadn't included bringing the dead back as murderous meat puppets. So far, at least.

Looking past the arrow-studded bodies being picked over by the dark, squawking scavengers, I tracked over the barricades and the tents to where the real horror show was going on.

Stakes had been erected around a wooden platform, and men and women hung from them, bloodied and mutilated. Most of them were red-haired or blond, and I suspected they were prisoners taken during the fall of the Menninkai's northern settlements. They *could* have been Lasknut—they seemed to be essentially the same people, divided by their beliefs more than tribal bloodlines—but I didn't think so.

I tried not to study those bodies too closely. They'd been horribly disfigured, most of them. Fortunately, they were all facing the platform, not the city.

The platform was where the sacrifices were happening.

Somewhat to my relief, the group of a couple dozen black-robed fiends was facing away from the city and blocking my view of most of the carnage. That didn't hide the pile of bodies off to either side of the dais, but at least I didn't have to watch what they were doing to the poor soul they had stretched out over a log just then, screaming his lungs out.

Those men in black robes were gathered in a semicircle around the platform, their hands in the air, droning their weird chants while most of the rest of the army of Dovos and Lasknut stood well away to either side, beating their drums. As I watched, I wondered if they were beating the drums to invoke the Outsiders, or simply to drown out the creepy droning and the high-pitched shrieks of terror and agony.

Glancing at my companions, I saw both Santos and Bearrac watching, stony expressions on their faces. If anything, Santos seemed even more disturbed by what we were witnessing than Bearrac. Both also had their weapons already aimed in.

We couldn't let this continue.

I got on my scope, judging the range to the black robe in the center. Just over four hundred yards. An easy enough shot.

Unless that writhing, curling blackness around him was more than an optical illusion.

It almost looked like smoke, but thicker, almost viscous. Like suspended oil, it curled and wove around his arms and shoulders, like it was alive. It almost looked like it was lapping at the blood that soaked his hands and arms.

He lifted his arms toward the mountains, a knife dripping red in his left hand. As the robe slipped back, I saw that he was armored beneath it. His splint vambraces, clotted with gore, shone dully in the gray light.

Armored or not, lamellar wasn't going to stop a 7.62 NATO round. I came off glass to make sure Santos and Bearrac could hear. "On me. Let's end this." Then I was back down on my scope, my rifle braced against the wall, placing my reticle right where it needed to be to put my bullet right between that murderer's shoulder blades, my finger slipping inside the trigger guard as I flipped the selector to "Fire" and let out a breath.

The trigger broke as my lungs bottomed out. It was almost a perfect shot. The reticle was perfectly still as the shot broke, and the wind was nonexistent. It should have blown right through his spine and torn out his heart, just as he'd done to dozens of people already that day.

Instead, that swirling blackness that clung to him seemed to swallow the bullet without it even touching him.

He looked over his shoulder then, and even at four hundred yards, from where I stood in a darkened hide, through the arrow slit, I locked eyes with him.

Those eyes were completely dark, the whites themselves subsumed in a combination of oily blackness and darkening blood. There was something feral in them, something deeper and more threatening than even his bloodstained hands might have suggested. It was as if there was something else in there with him now, something even darker and more evil than a man who would willingly cut the throats of the defenseless for the sake of power.

Bearrac shot him, then, and he actually staggered slightly at the impact, but it didn't look like the bullet had penetrated. I was already taking up the slack on the trigger again, though I was starting to wonder if we weren't far too late, when Santos opened up with the Mk 48.

The muzzle blast muffled by the suppressor, the machinegun still sent a ripping roar echoing out across the open fields as he walked his burst into and across the semi-circle of black robes. They weren't protected by the same swirling blackness that was wrapped around the murderous sorcerer up on the platform, and the stream of fire tore through them, bullets punching through flesh, bone, hearts, lungs, and guts, and dumping their bodies across the platform and the corpses they'd already celebrated over.

That bastard on the dais turned and faced us, lifting his hands and glaring at us with those blackened, blood-filled eyes, then started to chant again.

I shifted my aim. I had no idea if this was going to work, but it had worked against Fohorimans before.

Letting out my breath, I took the shot.

Headshots are tricky at four hundred yards, even on magnified optics and with a 7.62. That's a pretty small target at that distance. It's why we always trained to shoot center mass, rather than try to get fancy. But when the enemy's wearing body armor, or in this case some unholy aura of protection gained by slaughtering defenseless prisoners, you've got to aim for what might work.

My first shot missed. It distracted him, because no matter how absorbed in incantations you might be, the *snap* of a bullet going past your ear has a way of diverting your attention. Unfortunately for him, he didn't think he could be hurt, or he just didn't *quite* understand what that *snap* really meant. He just turned toward it, frowning slightly, which gave me a good idea of which way I had to correct.

My second shot hit just behind Bearrac's. It looked like our two bullets might have crossed midway through his skull, blowing his brains all over his own altar.

He didn't fall right away, which was weird, but said something about the powers he'd invoked. We'd just gotten what should have been a "circuitry kill." We'd blown his central nervous system to hell. But he was still on his feet, swaying, glaring at us with the one eye that hadn't been blown out of its socket by the overpressure, as blood and brains dripped from the cavernous hole in the back of his skull.

Finally, as the blackness seemed to explode off him, he crumpled.

A faint shadow seemed to slither along the ground toward the north with a thin, keening cry, that might have just been in my head.

The drums had fallen silent. For a long moment, it was as if shock had rendered the entire enemy encampment still and stiff, staring at the carnage we'd just wreaked.

I was looking for the next target. From what King Karhu had told us, I didn't think that that black-robed monster was the only sorcerer, or the only leader. I was looking for the next one to step up.

But the camp stayed still. Somewhere, a thin wail of despair went up into the gray sky as the rain started to fall.

We might have just won our respite for the night.

CHAPTER 10

WE stayed in place, waiting and watching. I was curious to see what was going to happen next, and I was pretty sure Bearrac was, too. Santos stepped back from the arrow slit, turning on his radio. We hadn't used them much since coming to this place, simply because there hadn't been much need. We'd been operating as a platoon, only rarely separating into teams, and then it had largely been in places where we didn't want to risk making noise by talking on the radio.

Sure, as Recon teams we had other options on comms. We'd been communicating via text over HF and Satcom since before I'd gone to BRC. That took time to set up, though, time we rarely had in this place, and we frankly didn't know if sorcerous monsters could detect radio waves. When we could stay low-tech, it had seemed like a good idea.

Some of that was probably a holdover to the way we'd had to start operating with the Russians as our presumed adversaries. They'd moved on recon teams by direction finding radio transmissions before, so we'd stuck with very brief comms windows in training.

But we were in a hide with friendly overwatch, and from what we'd just done, it didn't seem likely that the enemy could come after us quickly, even if they magically picked up our transmissions.

"Magically." That had been a sneer where we'd come from. Here, it was deadly serious.

"Gunny, this is Santos." We might have still been somewhat concerned about radio discipline, but with only us on the radio, there really wasn't a need for call-signs, to several of the junior Marines' great chagrin. They'd had some pretty wild ones lined up, all with the understanding that in the real world, when you try to give yourself a badass callsign, you are lining yourself up for the most merciless mocking you've ever endured. "Target is down. I say again, target is down."

"Roger. Status?" Gunny's voice over the radio was as calm, bland, and professional as he ever got. There was no celebration, no indication that he felt anything at the announcement.

"We are still secure. Enemy forces appear to be in some shock, and haven't moved toward us at all. We'll advise if that changes." Santos looked up at me with a raised eyebrow, and I nodded. "We are planning on staying in place for now."

"Good copy. Keep me posted." There was a pause, then Gunny came back. "King Karhu is sending a sortie to the north gate of the second wall as we speak. If we've got an opening, we need to exploit it."

I went back to my scope, watching the barricades. There was movement back there now, and I tried to focus on it, tried to see what was happening. Most of view was blocked by those barricades, but after a moment I could tell that someone, at least, was trying to rally some of the

Lasknut. A horn sounded, and I could see some of them gathering near the west end of the encampment.

From what I could see, everyone down there was watching everyone else very carefully, and every man of them had his weapons close at hand.

Soon, as I dialed the magnification back to get a wider view, I thought I could see at least three different factions forming. And that was just among the Lasknut themselves. One seemed to have formed around the big guy who was shouting first, and they appeared to be the most organized. They were pressing a second, which had formed up around an older man, his gray beard coming down below the faceplate of his helm.

"We are witnessing a war of succession on the battlefield." Bearrac sounded almost amused. I couldn't say I blamed him.

But letting them fight it out and get organized again didn't seem like a good idea. Especially not if some of those new leaders had access to the same kind of sorcery the dead black robes did.

I already had my sights on the big bruiser, who was waving his axe in the air and openly threatening the old man. "Should we help it along?"

Bearrac considered. He was generally more of a fighter than Mathghaman, quicker to anger and quicker to the sword. That doesn't make Mathghaman a slouch— far from it. Bearrac was just more eager, more likely to get stuck in first and ask questions later.

Before he could answer, though, the situation changed again.

I noticed the movement a moment before everything went to hell. One of the Dovos, his face hidden behind a bronze mask of some snarling monster I couldn't identify, had been slipping closer to the corpse-piled dais while the Lasknut had been bowing up on each other. Now he darted forward, snatched up the bloody knife that the head black robe had been holding, and held it over his head, letting out a shout.

That yell suddenly got *way* louder than it should have, and the late afternoon started getting darker.

"Drop him." Bearrac was already on his own rifle, and he got the first shot off as I moved to transition to our dark horse target.

The first round hit high, just under the armpit as he held up the athame, or whatever it was. It was clearly something that the Outsiders liked, because the darkness—that I'd hoped had fled when we'd killed the Lasknut's king, or whoever that guy had been—was already gathering around him.

I wondered, as I squeezed the trigger and shot the Dovo through the throat, how much that artifact was a path to power, and how much it was a conduit for its true master to enslave the narcissistic morons who tried to grab it.

Spraying blood, the Dovo dropped, the athame falling from his hand. Then the blackness went berserk.

Black mist seemed to erupt out of the ground, tendrils whipping between tents and barricades. Screams erupted, throat-rending sounds of pain and madness, and while the scene below us blurred, I could see the Dovos and the Lasknut falling upon each other, hacking each other to pieces in a frenzy of bloodshed. All the while, those inky tendrils of smoke or mist threaded through, wrapping themselves around the most berserk.

Blood and body parts flew as they slashed and chopped and stabbed at each other. There was no rhyme or reason to it; tribesmen fought tribesmen, regardless of colors or kinship.

We could only watch. We *could* have further thinned the enemy's numbers if we'd opened fire, but there was something… wrong about it. As if something was telling us that we'd only feed the horror, make it stronger.

So, we watched and waited, while our enemies tore their own guts out.

If only that had been the end…

* * *

Night fell. We'd already seen horrors I'll remember in my nightmares to my dying day—and after having been in an ancient vampire's lair, that's saying something—but we still had to drop our NVGs and keep watch. We were in position, on overwatch, and we couldn't afford to look away. We didn't have to watch the worst of the horrors, but we still had to be alert, in case things took a turn and we came under attack again.

It wasn't much better, seeing the slaughter, mutilation, and cannibalism out there in the green-scale circle of my PVS-15s. It gave me a little more distance, and I'd stopped watching through my scope a long time ago, but I still *knew* what was going on out there.

And there was no blocking out the noise.

Santos had turned aside a while ago. Rodeffer was dutifully watching the wall, just in case. He'd made some noises early on that had sounded like a bit of dry heaving. He wouldn't say anything about it, because that might look like weakness, being bothered by the utter carnage out there. But it nauseated him, possibly even more than it did me.

I wondered if that didn't say something about me.

Farrar, on the other hand, was watching with rapt fascination. I glanced over and saw him outside, on the parapet, peering fixedly over the wall. I nodded at Santos, who looked over, saw Farrar staring, and levered himself away from the wall.

"Come on, Mike. It's no good to watch that too closely."

Farrar seemed to shake himself a little. When he turned and came back inside the tower, however, he was visibly trying to brush it off. As if it was no big deal.

Maybe it wasn't, if your mind was in the right place. I'd seen the aftermath of airstrikes, IEDs, suicide bombers. The carnage was pretty bad, objectively every bit as bad as what was happening in the enemy's camp.

Yet there *was* something worse about this. Something that sparked a visceral, animal revulsion and fear. It's one thing to see people torn apart by the impersonal forces of explosives, however much hate had been behind their emplacement. It's something else to see a man hack into another man's flesh with the frenzy of a wild animal, then lap up the other man's blood while he was still alive.

Farrar, despite all we'd seen and been through, wouldn't accept that difference. Not yet. So, he tried to play it cool.

"Santos, Gunny." The radio crackled before I could have a word with Farrar. We had the handset turned up so we could all hear it. "Status?"

"They're still slaughtering each other out there, Gunny." Santos didn't even look out the arrow slit as he reported in. He didn't really have to. The noises were bad enough. "It's like they all lost their minds all at once."

"We're holding at the inner gate." Gunny still sounded relaxed. It was his talent. Despite the madness going on out there, which he could hear if he couldn't see, he wouldn't get perturbed over the radio. "Be prepared to fall back if they come too close. I don't want you getting cut off out there. You hear me, Conor?"

I took the handset from Santos. "I hear you, Gunny." I thought about protesting that there was no way in hell I was going to stick around if that happened, but Gunny Taylor was just being thorough and making sure that the team leader acknowledged the order.

There wasn't much more to tell. The fighting out there had been going on for hours, ebbing and flowing from one end of the encampment to the other. I handed the handset back to Santos and joined Bearrac where he leaned against the outer wall next to the center arrow slit, keeping an eye on what was happening without becoming preoccupied with the slaughter.

"Why are they doing this? Wouldn't it make more sense to assault the city?" I didn't get it. The whole thing was insane.

"It would, if the city was the goal." Bearrac seemed unperturbed on the surface, but I'd known him long enough to hear the haunted tone in his voice. "The Outsiders are evil, evil in a way that men cannot truly comprehend. They do not have the same priorities that an evil man would. And they are imprisoned, so they are only partially conscious of what occurs in the waking world."

He waved at the bloody nightmare out there in the dark. "They revel in slaughter and corruption, it is true. Hatred between men gives them the closest they can ever know to joy. Perhaps whatever abomination they sought to summon simply decided that tearing them apart would be more satisfying than aiding them in taking the city. Perhaps it has greater plans. Perhaps it was simply a whim. These things do not think like you and I."

A particularly piercing shriek rose above the din outside.

"What kind of 'greater plan' could it have?" I wasn't sure I wanted to know the answer.

Bearrac turned to look at me. His eyes seemed to glow in my NVGs. "What greater plan would you expect from an ancient false god, imprisoned for centuries after being tricked by its greatest servants?" He sighed. "Perhaps it was simply angered that they sought its power to conquer a city instead of awakening it. There is no telling." He glanced out the slit. "They will all be destroyed, one way or another."

He'd barely finished speaking when everything went quiet. Then a voice was raised out there in the dark, speaking some language that I hadn't heard before, but that something told me was ancient beyond speaking. It was a language that had no word for "honor," "friendship," or any other good thing. It was a tongue of hatred and ancient malice.

Then they came, screaming like banshees, heading straight for the breach in the wall at a dead sprint.

CHAPTER 11

THERE was no formation, no cohesion to that assault. The Lasknut seemed to have come out on top of the internecine fight, as there were hardly any Dovos in that shrieking mob. But their discipline and tactical skill had seemingly fled with any last shreds of their sanity. Most of them didn't even have shields in their hands as they ran at the gap in the wall, roaring, howling, and gibbering.

It made for one hell of a target-rich environment, if we could drop enough of them fast enough.

Santos opened fire immediately, raking the oncoming horde with long, roaring bursts, playing tracers back and forth across the leading knots of howlers. Bearrac, Rodeffer, and I were taking them a bit more slowly, engaging single targets as fast as we could drop one and transition to the next.

I shot the man in front, his face all but concealed by his visored helmet and a massive beard that probably went almost up to his eyes. My shot was a little high, punching through his lamellar coat and smashing his collarbone, but he staggered on for only a couple more steps before collapsing, dark blood flowing from the wound as he fell on his face.

Transitioning to the next man behind him, I shot him in the face, punching a hole through the goggle eye shield of his helm and sending him spinning into the man behind him. Rodeffer and I both shot that one a moment later, knocking him to his knees with two rounds almost so close together that they formed a single hole in his upper chest.

Then it was a matter of dragging my muzzle across the mob, firing as fast as the trigger could reset, barely registering a human shape through my red dot between shots . They were moving fast, and they were already almost to the breach in the wall.

Horns sounded behind us, high and clear compared to the evil-sounding brays of the Lasknut's battle horns, a welcome sound even though it was only barely audible at that point, between the *crack* of our own weapons and the screaming and howling below us. The Menninkai on the second wall had seen what was happening, and they were preparing to reinforce.

I just hoped we had the time to fall back, though I was seriously beginning to doubt it.

We were dropping the enemy in job lots, but the rest were so far gone that they didn't even notice. It was worse than the assault on the tor, as berserk as the Dovos had been then. There was no way we were going to break this assault by killing *just enough* of them. "Just enough" would be all of them, at the rate this was going.

More gunfire thundered from behind us as the mob reached the break in the wall and began to stream through. The other two teams' Mk 48s—Mathghaman and his companions hadn't elected to carry a belt-fed—raked the breach with long, roaring bursts, red tracers flickering through the overcast gloom like something out of *Star Wars*, except that the four ball between each tracer were doing every bit as much damage. Bullets chopped through armor, hides, flesh, and bone, cutting the leaders of the screaming mob down to be trampled by the wave behind them before the streams of flying metal tore them apart, as well.

Arrows rained down from the Menninkai archers on the walls, plunging into the swarm of shrieking berserkers from high above. The arcs of the arrows from that higher wall, well up the hill, kept them above the Marines' and Tuacha's lines of fire, so the arrows weren't getting smashed by bullets.

Still, the tidal wave of bodies, hundreds of men gone homicidally insane, was too thick to be stopped dead even by machinegun fire. Some of them got through, spreading out into the open ground, already littered with corpses.

Santos shifted positions, lifting the smoking Mk 48 muzzle from the exterior arrow slit and moving quickly toward the inside of the wall. "Reloading!" He already had the tray cover up, sweeping the last links away as he moved. He knelt by the interior window—slightly wider than an arrow slit, and apparently meant more for communication with the second wall rather than defense in a situation like this—while Farrar stepped up beside him and opened fire, dumping rounds down into the screamers now swarming toward the stairs.

Those steps had suddenly become our primary threat. They weren't wide open—they still needed to be somewhat defensible for just this eventuality—but the screaming maniacs were already tearing at the timber door at the base, hacking away at it with their axes and swords.

Fortunately, we had quite a bit of wall to work with.

"Get reloaded, then we're falling back." They might gain the tower itself, but we'd be long gone, and well away from the machinegun fire that was already chewing into the men at the base of the tower.

Rodeffer was already at the door leading onto the battlements as Santos slapped a new hundred-round "nutsack" into the clip underneath the Mk 48's receiver, pulled the belt over the feed tray, and slammed the feed tray cover shut with a *clack*.

"Go," Santos barked. "I'll take six."

We hustled out onto the top of the wall. The battlements were just wide enough for two men to move abreast. While the lower half of the wall was stone, the upper half had been built of two separate walls of charred timber, filled with earth between. The planks beneath our feet were as solid as the ground itself, as they lay on tons upon tons of packed dirt.

That said something about the spell that had blown a hole in that wall.

The inside timbers still rose a good three feet above the walkway, so you couldn't just fall off, though the timbers had been cut flush instead of sharpened to points like the outer posts. Three feet of tree trunks was enough to keep anyone from falling off, but not enough to conceal the defenders from anyone below in the no-man's land.

Screams of hate echoed from below, though they were almost drowned out by the hammering gunfire from above. Glancing over my shoulder, I saw several of the Lasknut, one of them with an open-faced helm, frothing at the mouth, pointing and screaming as they ran along the base of the wall after us.

I turned and shot the man with the open-faced helm through the throat. Blood sprayed and he started choking, but he still kept trying to run after us, ignoring the wound until he fell on his face.

It had been a hasty shot. I'd been aiming for his chest.

One of the teams up on the second wall had seen what was going on and they were shifting fire. At least, someone was. The machinegun fire was still focused on the breach, but even as I transitioned to another target—a wiry little bastard who looked like he'd probably already been a berserker even before whatever weirdness had set the whole army to foaming at the mouth, since he was wearing no armor, was bare-chested, and covered in tattoos—a bullet took him through the side. It had been a damned near perfect shot, leading him just enough that it tore right through his heart. He made it about two more steps and dropped.

I turned and hustled to catch up with Rodeffer and Farrar, who had almost reached the next tower already. Santos was still behind me, pausing just long enough to lean out over the top of the inner battlement and rake the Lasknut below us with another staccato burst before coming after me. Rodeffer had already gotten inside the tower, and while Santos and I ran toward the entrance, he leaned out the back window and started putting rounds into the leaders of the now-considerably thinned mob.

Santos and I got to the tower, but with Rodeffer, Bearrac, and Farrar already in the windows facing the killing ground between walls, and no point anymore to hoping to hide in the tower, we got down on a knee, resting our weapons on the inner parapet, and started reaping souls.

Despite the droves that had been killed already, hundreds were still pouring into the breach. The entire combined army of the Lasknut and their savage allies had lost their minds and were trying to tear their way into the city with swords, axes, and bare hands. They were dying in job lots, but it was starting to look like they might just have the critical mass of bodies to soak up our entire ammunition supply.

After that, it was going to get down to blades, and that was a considerably dicier proposition.

I shot another one of the skin-clad savages, putting a bullet high center chest as he howled and gnashed his teeth, waving one of those single-edged brushcutter swords we'd seen in the hands of so many of the Dovos nal Uergal. Once again, he kept coming a few steps, blood spraying from his mouth as his lungs filled up, before he collapsed, knocked against the stone wall by another man rushing up behind him, heedless of the corpse he'd just knocked out of the way.

Santos cut that one down with a short burst. The bad guys were getting spread out this far from the breach, where they were still getting piled like cordwood by the defenders up on the second wall, so he could conserve a bit more ammo. Well-placed shots were still killing these madmen, but it was taking a few extra seconds before they dropped, as the adrenaline and whatever insanity was pushing them kept them moving.

They were closing the distance faster than we could kill them.

I glanced up for a moment as Santos mowed down a knot of three or four of them, taking a brief second to get some better situational awareness. The horde was pushing over the mounds of dead in the breach, slowly gaining ground toward the second gate.

We were cut off. Unless we ran like hell for the port and the south gate, and there was no guarantee we wouldn't drag the lot of them along with us if we did that.

My next shot took a hulking Lasknut warrior, his face hidden by a veil of linked rings, right in the guts. He staggered, one knee buckling slightly, but then he caught his breath, roared his defiance, and kept coming, reaching the barred door of the tower and whaling on it with his axe. That had to hurt like the very devil, as blood soaked his breeches, but he was so insensate that he didn't seem to notice.

I leaned out over the parapet and shot him again, this time down through the torso, the bullet blasting out through his groin as he sagged against the door and slid toward the ground.

My bolt locked back on an empty mag after that shot, and I had to duck back behind the parapet as a thrown axe skipped off the parapet, splitting a sizeable chunk of wood off the log right next to my head before flipping away, back into the open ground between the walls. Quickly swapping mags and letting the empty fall to the walkway beneath me, I popped back up just as Santos went cyclic, holding the trigger down as he braced the Mk 48 against the interior parapet, playing the stream of fire across the increasingly strung-out mob of murderous lunatics. His rounds smashed bones and tore through muscle and organs, spilling blood onto the already-muddied ground. Finally, as I popped back up, he went dry and dropped to a knee below the parapet to reload.

It became almost a rhythm. Find a target, shoot, reset, shift targets, repeat. Lasknut and hairy, hide-clad savage alike went down, piling up beneath the tower in a vague echo of the mound of corpses still rising at the base of the second gate. Guns got hot, brass piled at our feet, and the day got darker as evening closed in.

They kept coming.

My bolt locked back on another empty, and I dropped the magazine while reaching for my chest rig. My hand closed on a solitary twenty-rounder. "Last mag!" They hadn't gotten through the door yet, but enough had reached it and hewed at it that some of the timbers were looking a little iffy.

Santos ripped through another long burst, then dropped the smoking Mk 48 to the planks. "I'm out." He drew his sword, a leaf-bladed Tuacha weapon, but right then, we still had standoff.

A moment later, Rodeffer yelled the same report.

I leaned into my rifle, down on a low knee, the forearm braced against the top of the parapet, and dropped two more with as many shots. My suppressor had left scorch marks on the wood already—or would have, if the Menninkai hadn't already charred the timbers to make them fire resistant. It was smoking almost as badly as Santos's barrel.

More blows rained down on the door beneath us, and I stood, firing almost straight down, bullets smashing through helmets, skulls, and collarbones. I stacked over a dozen more in front of that door before my rifle went dry again.

That was it. The gunfire from the second wall had slackened considerably, as well, though the Menninkai were still raining arrows and rocks down on the mob below. The whole platoon, Tuacha included, was almost out of ammo. And still they came.

The tower shook under the rain of blows, and the door below started to crack. Leaving my rifle leaning against the parapet—it wouldn't do anyone any good without ammo, and I could fight hand to hand more easily without it on my back—I started down the steps, drawing my sword as I did so. Santos was already halfway down, his own blade in his hand.

We could have held the landing, but I didn't want to let the Lasknut get even that far in. We only had to worry about the stragglers who'd gotten distracted chasing after us, while the bulk of that army run amok was trying to claw its way through the second gate. But even the stragglers were still in the dozens, and they could still overwhelm us.

Santos and I continued all the way down to the bottom of the tower, where the door shook and shuddered under the assault, the *crack*s coming from the wood starting to get alarming. Bearrac had beaten us there, and he stood at the second to last step, his sword in his hand, waiting. The bar holding the door shut was still untouched, but it rattled in its stone setting as the berserkers hammered at the door.

One of the heavy planks cracked, and a moment later an axe splintered the rest of the way through, ripping a chunk of the board away as it was yanked clear and leaving an opening about three feet tall and as wide as my fist in the door itself. Santos was already there, and he quickly thrust his blade through, eliciting a scream from the other side. More blows rained onto the door, and the wood splintered still more, the opening widening as slivers and chips flew.

I could see a crazed, slavering face through the opening, and stabbed the Dovo—or whoever those savages were—through the mouth, my blade transfixing him as the point slipped right through his spine. His weight dragged my sword down as his knees buckled, and just for a moment, as his soul fled his body, I saw the haze of insensate rage lift from his eyes, leaving nothing but fear. Then I had dragged the point back, scraping him off on the remnant of the door, the sword coming free with little effort.

An axe came crashing through the same gap a moment later, biting deep into the bar, which actually bent and began to splinter under the blow.

With a shriek, the axe wielder brought it crashing down again, and the *crack* as the bar began to break was almost as loud as the blow itself. The door shuddered hard under more wild strikes, and then the third blow actually snapped the bar in half.

The man with the axe was suddenly swept aside by a big, blond gorilla of a man, gnashing his teeth as he smashed through the remains of the door, armed with little more than a club. He swung it wildly, and Santos ducked beneath it, letting the stout branch hit the stone wall with a *thunk* before stepping in and skewering the big man through the groin.

He'd cut deep. Blood gushed and spurted from the wound, and the big bruiser got one more half-hearted swing in before he collapsed, only to be trampled by the axe man.

That one came in with his axe held high over his head, and he got the point of my sword through his chest, just beneath his sternum. He couldn't stop himself and was impaled, his heart beating itself to shreds on the tip of my blade, and his fingers went limp around the axe, dropping it behind him.

Then more of them came crowding in, slavering and bellowing, and it was all Bearrac, Santos, and I could do to hold our ground, fending off the shower of blows and getting in a thrust or a cut where we could.

Blood soaked the ground. Weapons got heavy in our hands as sweat rolled down under our gambesons, mail, and chest rigs, and we gasped for air. Rodeffer and Farrar stood on the stairs above us, their own weapons ready, but there was no room for them to join us, and if we'd tried to fall back, we'd have been torn to pieces.

It got dark, the only light coming from the lanterns atop the second wall. I took a blow to the shoulder, fortunately turned by my mail, but the shock almost drove me to my knees, and for a moment I thought my arm had been broken. Another blow skipped off my helmet, and I riposted blindly, my sword sinking into flesh for a moment before an insane gibbering was cut off with a scream.

Every muscle ached. My breath rasped in a throat long since gone as dry as the Syrian desert. As light and well-balanced as that sword was, it felt like I was lifting a lead weight with every blow, every parry. Despite the spring and give of the blessed steel, it couldn't keep the shock of each blocked attack from traveling up my arm and jarring my hand anymore.

Then Santos staggered, his foot slipping out from under him, and fell back onto the steps behind us.

A long-limbed, scrawny man in stinking furs, with a brushcutter sword in one hand and a spike of a knife in the other, leapt at him, snarling. I ducked under the wild swing of an axe, exposing myself for just a moment as I swung and slashed open the scrawny man's throat. He fell on Santos, who stabbed him through the chest as he fell, rolling to one side to avoid the bulk of his weight, and I turned back toward the axe-wielder, sure I was dead, only to find that Rodeffer had lunged out over my head and split that one's skull, even as Bearrac had beheaded the next one who'd tried to come through behind him.

And then, suddenly, just as I was sure that we couldn't hold for another minute, and we were all going to die in that narrow doorway, it was over.

They hadn't fled. Bearrac had stepped forward, putting himself between Santos and me on one side and the enemy on the other, going to work like only a Tuacha warrior could, given room to swing. He swept a leg off with one stroke, opening the Lasknut's throat with the backswing, then parried a notched sword and stabbed the Dovo warrior through the heart with the riposte.

That was the last one. There were no more. Bearrac stepped out of the doorway and looked toward the inner gates, then motioned for me to follow a moment later.

The gate would not be useable for some time. The mountain of bodies leaking blood and other fluids out onto the ground stood over six feet high, piled directly against the gate itself. That massive portal of timber and iron was scarred and gouged by weapons and fingernails, splashed with more blood where our fellow Recon Marines had used the last of the 40mm we'd brought into the city.

We could only stare and gasp for breath. Night had fallen, but the battle was over.

At least, this phase of it was.

CHAPTER 12

IT was an utterly exhausted platoon of Recon Marines and Tuacha warriors who gathered in the chamber provided for our use above King Karhu's great hall. My team had cleaned the blood off as best we could, but the fatigue remained. It was the middle of the night, but none of us would sleep yet.

Gunny had led the hot wash, the immediate after-action debrief, going over what we might have done better or not done at all. The best we could figure was that we really had needed a second team out on the wall, and we should have brought the thumpers with us instead of leaving them behind for weight's sake when we hustled to the outer towers.

All of this happened while we reloaded magazines and the machinegunners prepped fresh belts of 7.62 in their drums and pouches. Even the Tuacha had gone dry, and were levering 7.62 rounds into their somewhat more elegant magazines. The *Coira Ansec* had given us the equivalent of 25-round Magpul P-Mags, but the much more "Long Rifle" styled Tuacha rifles took sleeker mags that just looked right.

Now the hot wash was over, and the weariness was taking hold.

I stood up to keep from falling asleep while my mags were still half empty and moved to the window. It was too dark to see very far, but a few of the Lasknut's campfires still glowed, dull red embers flickering out in the blackness under the lowering clouds.

It was strange to look at that encampment and imagine that it was completely abandoned. Yet it was. Every single warrior—and camp follower; there had to have been a few of them—had tried to rush the walls. Uncoordinated, without formation or plan, they'd simply tried to swarm the defenses, solid timber and stone, with swords, axes, and bare hands.

And so they'd died. To a man.

It disturbed me on a level that nothing else I'd seen so far had. That was saying something in this haunted world, where I'd already fought monsters, sorcerous horrors from beyond, eldritch abominations, and the walking dead.

Mathghaman joined me at the window. He didn't say anything at first, but just stood there in companionable silence.

"A great evil is stirring." His words were low and grim. "Greater than we expected when we embarked for these shores."

"What could do that? What could make hundreds of them just lose their minds and throw themselves at us like that?" I'd seen some crazy stuff in The World, even before coming here, but nothing that quite matched the horror that we'd just seen. They'd had no chance to prevail, but they'd thrown themselves into the meat grinder with single-minded rage anyway.

All of them.

"Possession." The word hung in the air like the pronouncement of doom. "It is certain that every one of the men in that encampment had, at some point or other, pledged themselves to Vaelor. Perhaps to another Outsider that still lurks in the north, but Vaelor was always the chief, and it seems the most likely. That opened them to its influence."

"What? Just saying, 'I am a follower of Vaelor' is enough? Enough to do… *that*?" Gurke was even more rattled than I was.

"No." Mathghaman turned away from the window, his arms folded. "It takes more than that. To truly pledge oneself to such a creature… They must commit some crime that they cannot truly take back."

"Murder?" Gunny asked.

Mathghaman nodded. "That would be sufficient. Though I doubt that all of them would necessarily have gone so far." He glanced out the darkened window. "There are other things. Deeds that a man might more easily talk himself into. Still, they are best not spoken of."

I could imagine, and I could barely suppress a shudder.

"This isn't the first time I've heard that name. Vaelor." We'd been deep in the catacombs beneath Taramas's citadel when I'd first heard it. Nuala had mentioned that name when we'd told the Tuacha about the oily black *thing*s that Dragon Mask had summoned deep beneath the earth.

"Vaelor is one of the Outsiders, the so-called 'elder gods.'" Mathghaman spoke slowly, as if he was thinking real hard about how much he wanted to say during the dark of night. "He has been imprisoned for centuries far in the north, beneath the Teeth of Winter. It is said that he dreams in his sleep, and that his dreams can reach out like a dark and foul wind in the night, and touch the minds of men."

As he said that, a breath of wind whispered through the open window, and I felt the gooseflesh rise on my arms.

"I think we had best leave the rest of this conversation for the light of day." Bearrac had finished loading his mags and rose and stretched. "Let us not invoke things of darkness in their element."

It said something about what we'd seen and been through that no one objected or even seemed nonplused by the implications as we finished prepping our gear and headed for bed.

* * *

The next morning dawned cold and gray. The overcast that had swathed Vahava Paykhah in gloom since before we'd arrived persisted, only that day it was even lower. Rain and mist swept across the coast, thick enough to shroud the distant woods in gray, the nearest trees visible as little more than vague, dark shapes in the fog and misting, drizzling sheets of rain.

Below the walls, the carrion birds cawed and shrieked as they picked at the mountain of dead before the gates. There were thousands of them, a black and flapping swarm that circled overhead and darkened the sky when not feasting on the slain.

In the distance, half-obscured by the weather, the fires in the abandoned camp had finally gone out, leaving only the barricades and sodden tents sagging in the mud.

"So, how does this change our mission?" Bailey was the first one to ask the question, around a mouthful of fish and what tasted like rye bread. There wasn't much of the bread left, but there was plenty of fish. That's one advantage—or disadvantage, depending on your tastes—of living in a city right on the water. There's no risk of running out of fish to eat when under siege. "We came looking for our people, but it sounds like everybody's more worried about this Vaelor thing, now."

"There may be some connection between Vaelor's stirring and your missing Marines," Bearrac said a moment later. "Did not your captain disappear in the company of a sorcerer who invoked Vaelor's powers?"

"He did." Gunny was sopping up the last of the fish with his bread. "And it makes me wonder."

"You think that the Lasknut might give us a lead?" Gurke asked. "We're a *long* way from Taramas's territory." Which had been part of the point in the first place. It was unlikely that she would expect us to come from Menninkai territory.

"We are, but suppose that they won free through Vaelor's power?" Mathghaman was gazing out the window thoughtfully. "It is said that Vaelor's resting place lies somewhere far in the north beneath the Teeth of Winter, though no one I know of knows exactly where. The Fohorimans might, but that is a secret they will guard jealously, lest Vaelor wake and take his vengeance upon them. Who knows where they might have gone in search of clues? Vaelor can influence them in his slumber, but mainly through nightmares and madness."

"Problem with Gurke's idea is that the Lasknut're all dead." Bailey had always been blunt, and even Mathghaman's sheer presence couldn't dampen that. "Unless we're gonna dabble in necromancy, we're not going to find anything out from this bunch." It also said something about how much we'd adjusted to this place that Bailey could use the word *necromancy* without batting an eye, as if it was the most normal thing in the world.

Mathghaman actually chuckled, though. "I think perhaps we would find more clues going through that encampment. The dead are dead. They face their judgement. Even were we willing to defile ourselves by such rites, anything we 'brought back' would not be the souls of those who died on the rocks outside these walls last night."

A faint shudder went through the room. We'd faced the restless dead, or the things wearing the corpses of the dead like skinsuits, in the Land of Shadows and Crows. No one wanted to go through that again.

"So, we SSE the enemy encampment before everything sinks into the mud." Gunny pushed back from the plank table and stood. "Though we should probably speak with King Karhu first."

"Indeed." Mathghaman stood, as well. "He should be finished breaking his fast by now. Let us go and speak with him."

* * *

King Karhu looked like he'd aged a century in the last few nights. Bent and weary, his hair and beard unkempt and lank, he had deep, dark circles under his eyes.

He slumped on a bench in his bedchambers, having ordered us admitted despite not being ready to receive anyone of his own people in the throne room below. He was dressed, at least, in a padded aketon and trousers, a long knife at his side. I expected that the Menninkai's king was not accustomed to going anywhere unarmed. "You wish to do what?"

"To search the enemy's encampment." Mathghaman stood over Karhu, though he stood far enough back not to loom. "A grave threat has been revealed here, and it may affect our quest as well as the fate of your people."

"And you believe that you might learn more by searching through the Lasknut's wrack?" King Karhu's voice was thin and weary. He sighed. "I suppose I cannot deny you. Meanwhile, we must clear away the bodies." He coughed, then held up a hand. "Forgive me. We likely would not have survived last night, despite our defenses, without your aid." He sighed. "It is so…"

"A great evil was unleashed here." Mathghaman wasn't unsympathetic. There was, after all, some history between him and the king. Though I wondered just how many years ago it had been that Mathghaman had last visited the Menninkai. How old was he?

He motioned to indicate Gunny, Bailey, Gurke, and me where we stood behind him. "These men have seen this evil before, far to the west. There may be a connection with those we seek. We might find more signs that will point the way down below."

King Karhu waved a hand. "You have freedom of the city and all my lands. You know that. I would only suggest you take the west or south gate. The north is rather blocked at the moment."

Mathghaman inclined his head. "You have our gratitude, King Karhu. Let us hope that we do not find the worst that we fear."

* * *

It was a slog to get out to those barricades and the camps beyond. Just working our way down through the city and across the gap between the first and second walls took almost two hours, and then we had to cross no man's land, much of which had been churned to mud by the Lasknut's assaults and the constant damp. It might have been spring in Menninkai lands, but it was still cold and wet.

Our boots felt like they'd accumulated an extra ten pounds of mud by the time we reached the first set of circumvallating barricades. We hadn't brought our rucks, but we'd otherwise gone out ready to fight, weapons in hand and watching the shifting veils of gray around us as we went. To the best of anyone's knowledge, every last one of the Lasknut had thrown themselves to their deaths against the walls and gates the previous night, but we'd all seen enough of the surprises this world could spring on the unwary that we weren't taking chances.

The place was dreary and abandoned, the tents starting to fall down as their stakes loosened in the mud, the fire pits cold and black. For the most part, the camp seemed little more than that. It was a camp, now deserted. In a few places, ravens and things that looked like a cross between a raven and a vulture, with the same bare head but black instead of red, picked at meat hung up for the Lasknut, much of it looking like it had probably come from the Menninkai's livestock.

As we approached the dais where the ceremony we'd disrupted had been happening, just before the black mist had driven the entire encampment out of their minds, though, things got spookier.

The bodies we'd dropped lay where they'd fallen, untouched by the carrion eaters. In fact, none of the birds seemed to want to go anywhere near the dais, even steering clear of the air above it.

I had my weapon up as we got closer, half expecting some winged nightmare to come bursting out of the blackened mud around the log dais. A thin coating of some black, oily substance covered the dais, the ground around it, and the bodies. The stench was stomach-churning, and my head started to ache as soon as we got close. The sense of *wrongness* in that place was palpable.

Rodeffer nudged one of the bodies that had been thrown to the side by Santos's machinegun fire with his muzzle. It had only been a day. But something *popped*, and a noxious wave of corruption belched from beneath the black robes. It smelled like something that had been rotting in the hot sun for a week, and Rodeffer bent over and retched as he staggered away.

Mathghaman seemed unfazed, though his face tightened as he stepped up onto the dais, one hand on his rifle, the other gripping the hilt of the sword at his side. He looked down at the body of the man Bearrac and I had shot, the black robe with the weird, blood-filled eyes. The man's skull was now semi-deformed, bathed in his own blood from the two bullets that had killed him, precipitating the Lasknut's descent into homicidal, and ultimately, suicidal, madness.

Those eyes were still open, still staring, and it might have been a trick of the light, but even though the body was as motionless and rotten as all the rest, they seemed to follow me as I moved.

I hadn't been able to see the altar where Black Robe had been conducting his ceremony clearly from a distance, but it was as gruesome as I'd expected up close. I didn't know if they'd packed it in or built it there, but it was a pile of skulls, tacked together with mud and clay, bound up with rawhide around the outside, daubed with glyphs and symbols that made my eyes sting if I looked at them too long.

We hadn't killed the black robe fast enough to save the man who'd been stretched out on that grisly construct. He'd been disemboweled and his guts arranged in patterns atop the packed skulls. His blood had run down and stained the rawhide black. But those glyphs still showed through the gore.

The Dovo who'd grabbed the black robe's athame lay crumpled on the back side of the dais, curled around the bullet that had killed him. The athame itself, a crooked, dull gray, single-edged knife, lay in the mud next to his hand.

I blinked. For a moment, the blade had *blurred* as I'd looked at it.

"Keep your eyes away from it and do not touch it." Mathghaman had seen my reaction. He looked up at the city. "We may need to ask Brother Saukko to come down here and cleanse it before we can destroy it."

"Is that the same knife that Dragon Mask was after?" Santos asked.

Mathghaman squinted as he studied it, but then he shook his head. "No. There are descriptions of the Athame of Urkartikar. That does not look like it. This is some different artifact." Then he looked back down at the black robe. "It is hard to say for certain, but I think this may have been Zeiczak, king of Sumnoth, himself."

"Is that normal?" Gunny asked. "I mean, there have been plenty of 'hands-on,' 'lead from the front' rulers in history, but..."

"Sumnoth is tributary to the Warlock King Grichencos." Bearrac was watching the woods in the distance, ignoring the carnage and the stench. "If Zeiczak truly did repudiate his 'god' to seek to invoke Vaelor, things have truly changed."

"So, are we bound for Sumnoth, now?" Bailey seemed to be fine with that. If it meant killing more bad guys, I supposed I was, too. After all, we had a lot of country to cover if we were going to find the captain and anyone else who had gotten separated during the chaos in those catacombs.

And if Dragon Mask had been involved in turning this Zeiczak toward Vaelor, that might mean we'd pick up their trail in Sumnoth.

"Maybe, but right now, I think we need to get back inside the walls." Gurke wasn't looking at the gore-spattered dais, or the rotting bodies, or the athame lying in the mud. He was looking off to the northwest, toward the distant trees.

I followed his gaze with a frown, already seeing movement in that direction, obscured as it was by the mists and the drizzling rain. I lifted my rifle to my shoulder and peered through the scope.

Gunny had been looking, too, and I heard him curse even as I made out some of the shapes moving through the curtains of gray. We couldn't see much, but we'd all seen a Fohoriman-led army before.

And this one looked *big*.

We abandoned the broken siegeworks and headed for the walls.

CHAPTER 13

BY the time we made it to the second wall, mounting the battlements to cover the breach and the northern gate, that vast army had already covered half the fields outside. And they were still almost two hundred yards behind the Lasknut's siege works.

Rank upon rank marched to encircle the beleaguered Vahava Paykhah. The vast majority were hide-clad savages, not unlike the Dovos nal Uergal. In fact, I was pretty sure, watching some of the emblems displayed on shields, that a chunk of them *were* Dovos nal Uergal, marching in mobs around masked riders on the barrel-chested mutant horses of these northlands. But they weren't alone.

Somewhat more civilized-looking Lasknut marched in their own bands, keeping some formation, more than the Dovos. They were identifiable by their taller stature, better armor and weapons, and more colorful clothing. Banners that bore many of Sumnoth's emblems of death and domination waved lazily in the damp.

Disciplined squares of eastern corsairs marched as well, with their own emblems and their own commanders astride more normal looking horses. They kept apart from the others, making it look like they might well have been there as mercenaries, rather than true believers or vassals.

More savages appeared, different but similar enough that they could be lumped in with the Dovos, of whichever Fohoriman Warlock King or Witch Queen they served. Then, several hours after Gurke had sighted their vanguard, the Fohorimans appeared.

There were hundreds of them. No two were alike. Hulking, deformed monstrosities knuckle-walked alongside gaunt, spectral riders atop leonine beasts in lieu of horses. Several legit giants strode behind. I hadn't seen them before, when Taramas and Uergal had chased us for miles and miles down the mountains to the coast and Teac Mor Farragah. I wasn't counting the spectral monster we'd fought in the pass between Uergal's and Taramas's territories. These were considerably smaller than that thing had been, though they still probably stood ten feet tall and had to weigh about eight hundred pounds each.

More Dovos trailed behind them, filing in to join the mass of men and monsters facing the outer walls. Another tribe followed them, tall men wearing what looked like bark capes over round copper breastplates and tall, carved headdresses that looked like stylized beasts and monsters. They were different from the Dovos masks, larger and sporting much different lines, crested with hair and furs. Their weapons tended toward spears and copper axes.

"There have to be thousands of them." Farrar was watching through his scope. We were just to the west of the gate, though not far enough away to escape the stench of death rising from the mound of dead Lasknut piled at its base.

"Easily." I was watching, too, cataloging what I could see. One detail really stuck out. There had been no Fohorimans with Zeiczak's army. Only savages and Lasknut. But here were hundreds of the twisted, sorcerous monsters, marching to crush the Menninkai once and for all. "Tens of thousands."

Had that been the plan? Let the Lasknut bear the brunt, wear down the Menninkai, and then come in after they'd bashed themselves to pieces against the walls? But that didn't quite fit, either. Nor did the fact that they were apparently setting up camp out there, despite the gaping hole in the outer wall.

One thing was certain. If we'd hoped that with the siege over, we could head into the wilds and pursue our search, we were sadly mistaken.

* * *

The camp construction continued, overseen by the Fohorimans. The only exception was the corsairs, who built their own fortified camp off to the eastern flank, their ditch and rampart positioned so that they could defend against their allies as well as the Menninkai.

In the center, the Lasknut built their own fortifications, watched by a man with a gold-chased, goggled helmet sitting astride a barrel chested, northern mutant horse, draped in a dark red cloak. He always kept close to a broad-shouldered Fohoriman who rode another white-furred beast with a massive horn on its nose, almost like a cross between a mountain lion and a rhino. I suspected we were looking at Zeiczak's successor, with his Fohoriman overseer.

That messed with the theory that maybe Zeiczak's assault had been the planned first wave. The longer I watched, the more that looked like the Fohorimans were making sure the new King of Sumnoth didn't step out of line.

"That's a hell of a target rich environment." Gunny was suddenly at my elbow. I'd been so focused on the growing nightmare out there that I hadn't noticed him approach.

"I don't think we've got enough bullets for that," I observed, putting my eye back to the scope. "Even with the crates we've still got on the ship."

We'd planned for resupply this time. It was another reason we'd come to Vahava Paykhah instead of striking directly inland. We could pack the ship with munitions and rations, and if need be, we could fall back to recock and rearm.

We hadn't counted on burning through an entire combat load in the first couple of days, though, before we'd even embarked on the mission proper. And this looked even worse. The Lasknut siege force had been a street gang compared to the army arrayed out there now.

"How are we supposed to get past that?" I lifted my head from my scope to take in the sheer size of that force, as blurred by rain and mist as it was. I hardly wanted to say the next thing on my mind.

The fate of the Menninkai was not our mission. I felt for them, as much as I'd felt for any Syrian Kurdish village that we hadn't been able to stand by and defend. But were we committed to standing and dying beside them? The mission was to find the captain, Zimmerman, Gonsalves, and Owens, or find out for sure that they were dead. Additionally, we were helping Mathghaman hunt down his former friend, who had committed a grave crime and fled to the Fohorimans.

Those were debts of honor. Debts we owed more deeply than we owed the Menninkai, no matter their alliance with the Tuacha.

Yet the question was, could we get past that immense force undetected? And would the Menninkai let us go if we tried?

"I don't know." Gunny rarely sounded at a loss, but right then, he had no answers. It was a bit sobering. We'd all looked to Gunny to have an answer, have a plan, have a way to get us out of whatever idiocy Captain Sorenson had dreamed up. He was a Recon Marine's Recon Marine, and he'd been doing this long enough that he knew just about everything there was to know about the profession. At least, it had always felt that way.

But now we were trapped, with no apparent way out except to go back to the ship, head out to sea, and find another way.

I didn't know how Mathghaman was going to take that, given the way his last expedition to the Land of Ice and Monsters had turned out.

"We're not going anywhere tonight." Gunny looked along the wall, where most of the platoon had taken up firing positions between the Menninkai archers, most of whom were paying us little mind, their eyes fixed on the sheer numbers out there, some shaking, some muttering in their liquid tongue. While I couldn't understand the language, I knew that what they were muttering were either prayers, curses, or both. "Set up a team security rotation. I'm heading below to find us a team room closer to the wall."

He turned toward the nearest tower and the steps leading down to the ground. "We're staying here for the moment. It's going to be up to Mathghaman whether we try to break out or not."

* * *

It seemed that the bulk of the army had arrived by the time night fell. Fires were lit as the light failed, glittering in the dark, despite the damp. There are ways of lighting fires in the rain, but I didn't know whether these people had perfected it, or if the Fohorimans had lit them by *other* means.

We stayed at fifty percent, half up on the wall, half down below in the shelter of a stable near the gate. The rain tapered off and then finally stopped, though patches of fog still drifted between the walls and the fires out in the dark.

Two-hour shifts aren't great for getting sleep, especially not after you've fought hard less than a day before and still haven't caught up. I'm still convinced that I only slept due to sheer exhaustion.

After all we'd been through, I was kind of hoping to see the luminous figure that I'd seen in dreams—or visions, if they weren't truly dreams—several times since coming here. I still didn't know who or what it was, but there was a certain peace that went along with its appearances, an assurance that we weren't alone, that *somebody* every bit as powerful as the monsters and specters we faced was watching over us. That had been the message the first time.

Unfortunately, I didn't see my guardian angel, if that was who it was, this time.

I found myself on the peak of the hill, but there was no city there, only bare rock. The forest grew right up to the base of the mountain. A storm raged overhead, lashing the mountain—and me—with hail and rain, while lightning split the dark above and thunderclaps hammered at me. The tops of the trees below thrashed and waved violently as the wind howled.

No, that wasn't just the wind. Another call went up from the dark, down there in that forest, a call full of hunger and malice.

Then there were eyes in the dark beneath the trees. Red, glowing eyes, full of hatred. And they were coming up the hill.

Low, lupine shapes stalked out of the trees, seemingly unfazed by the hail, rain, and wind. Their eyes were fixed on me, slaver dripping from their fangs as they stalked up the mountain toward me.

Get up.

The words were unmistakable. I sat straight up in my Ranger roll, then scrambled out of it, leaving it for the moment, grabbing my rifle, sword, and helmet. I'd slept in my boots and chest rig.

Without hesitation, I bolted out of the stables and headed for the walls. I couldn't say why or how, but I knew that something bad was about to happen.

The attack was coming. And we weren't ready for it.

CHAPTER 14

THE night was pitch black when I reached the top of the wall, even through NVGs. The overcast had thickened, blotting out the stars and the moon, but that wasn't all.

A creeping darkness was moving through the breach in the wall and spilling over the battlements. It looked almost like mist, except that fog tends to look light green in NVGs, and this was blacker than the depths of the catacombs beneath Taramas's citadel.

Worse, it was climbing *uphill*.

"What the hell is that?" Santos was watching the on-coming cloud of darkness, already down behind his Mk 48, braced between two of the sharpened timbers of the battlements.

"I don't know, but I'd sure like some thermals to see what's inside it." Even as I said it, I knew that even that probably wouldn't have worked. That wasn't a smoke-screen—and even thermals had some difficulty with smoke—it was something else, something not natural.

Which meant that whatever was coming up the hill within it was even more dangerous, presuming that the darkness wasn't the attack itself.

If that was the case, we might be screwed. If that was some sorcerous chemical weapon, then there was nothing we could do but abandon the wall and head for higher ground.

That was no guarantee, either, given the way that black cloud was climbing the slope from the outer wall toward our positions. If it could climb that quickly, we'd be overwhelmed fast, no matter how high we went.

We hadn't thought to ask the *Coira Ansec* for MOPP gear.

Even though it was moving faster than I'd expect a mist to move, there was something almost leisurely about the way it drifted through the breach, spreading out while tendrils slithered over the top of the outer wall and slid down the timber and stone to join the larger cloud. Still, despite the fact that it was a cloud, and therefore had no body language or expression, there was something about it that seemed almost gleefully sinister as it wound its way up the hill toward the second wall.

"Everybody stay cool and hold your fire." I didn't know for sure what was coming, but I *was* pretty sure that wasting rounds shooting blindly into the cloud wasn't going to do much.

Strangely, I wasn't getting the same feeling from that crawling blackness, as similar as it appeared, that I had from the oily, smoke-like horrors that were Vaelor's creatures. It was evil, sure, but it was somehow a lesser evil, not quite as insane as the Outsider's constructs. This felt more like the Fohorimans' power.

The first tendril of smoke, or mist, or whatever it was, reached the base of the wall and shot upward, cresting the battlements in just over a second.

And a Fohoriman warrior sprang out of it, landing lightly on the battlements beside one of the Menninkai archers.

Long limbed and barrel-chested, the creature had two eyes, glowing in my NVGs, but one was set directly above the other, in the center of his forehead. Horns curled to either side of his head, and his mouth was full of teeth too long and sharp to close his lips around them. An axe in either hand, he lashed out, hacking right through the archer's collarbone and tearing through his armor, the blade going nearly to the man's sternum as it crushed him to his knees on the battlements.

Quick as a cat, the Fohoriman spun, the axe still embedded in the archer's corpse, and lopped the head off another Menninkai behind him before the man could bring a weapon to bear. The wickedly curved axe blade sheared through leather, flesh, and bone, and the man's head went flying, still in his helmet, over the top of the wall. Blood fountained from the stump of his neck, black in the darkness, and he toppled.

Another Fohoriman, clad in only wide breeks and boots, leapt out of the cloud on the other side of the first. Wielding a short-hafted spear in one hand and a crescent-shaped shield in the other, this one had the body of a Greek statue and the head of a lizard. His tongue flicked from between his teeth as he blocked an axe blow from one of the Menninkai with his shield, then quickly rotated the shield to slam that short spear through the open crescent and into the Menninkai's teeth.

There were too many friendlies between our position and the enemy, even as the Fohorimans tore through the Menninkai defenders. I couldn't get a shot. Santos was looking for one, too, but he couldn't open fire either, not without tearing right through our allies.

They were probably doomed anyway if we held our fire, but that was a distinction without a difference. If they were going to die, we weren't going to be the ones to kill them.

Then we were under attack, too, and couldn't even try to help them.

I wouldn't have expected that corpulent mass of pale flesh to be able to leap that high. The thing was squat and morbidly obese, its folds of fat bulging down over its short legs. It had to weigh four hundred pounds or more, and it shook the whole wall when it came down, crushing one of our Menninkai allies under it as it landed next to Farrar.

Horns sprouted from the top of its doughy head, and fangs glittered in its leering mouth. Its eyes glowed like all the rest as it cackled and lifted the massive cleaver it had clenched in one meaty fist.

Farrar had pivoted as it came down, and while the impact staggered him, he still got a shot off, the bullet punching into that mass of flesh about where its heart should have been. The thing *huffed* at the impact, but it hardly slowed down, bringing that cleaver sweeping down at Farrar with a hiss as it parted the night air.

I grabbed Farrar by the back of his chest rig and hauled him clear as the massive blade slammed down into the planks beneath our feet with a horrific *chunk*. The wall shuddered again under that blow, and chips flew from the shattered planks, the cleaver driving past the wood and into the packed earth beneath.

That was a fearsome weapon, but it had its drawbacks. As strong as that thing clearly was, the sheer mass of the blade slowed it down. As it wrenched the cleaver free of the walkway, I dragged Farrar behind me, glad that he still had the presence of mind to keep his rifle pointed up and over the battlements, then let go of him, slapped my hand back on the forearm of my M110, and blasted three fast shots through the Fohoriman's teeth.

Fohorimans were tough. We'd found that out the hard way in the west, fighting first Taramas's hunters and then her frontline warriors. They could take half a mag of 5.56 to the chest standing up and keep coming. Some of them had even shrugged off headshots. Their weaknesses were few, but they did have them.

Unfortunately, the mouth wasn't one of this Fohoriman's weak spots.

I might have cracked one of those shark teeth, but that thing just grinned wider and *spat out my bullets.*

Oh, hell.

Stumping forward, it snatched that cleaver up and swung it in a diagonal slash that chopped halfway through the outer timbers as I scrambled out of the way. Once again, it worked against itself, as it had to pry the blade out of the wood by main force, but if it was bulletproof—or simply didn't care what got hit—then it had all the time in the world.

We didn't. We were running out of space. The Menninkai fighting that horned, two-eyed Fohoriman were being pressed back toward us as we got forced toward them. We'd be back-to-back in another moment, with nowhere left to retreat.

There's an old principle in warfare. When in doubt, attack. Recon—and most other such units—had distilled it down to *speed*, *surprise*, and *violence of action*. It was why the immediate action drill in response to an ambush is often to turn toward the ambush and assault through with all the ferocity you can manage.

I dashed forward, ducking under the swing of that massive cleaver, and did what I'd seen Bailey do under similar circumstances. I jammed my suppressor into its eye and pulled the trigger, planting one boot on its gut and the other on the parapet as I bore down, pushing against the 7.62 recoil, dumping five rounds into that thing's skull as fast as I could pull the trigger.

That did it. Fluid spurted from the eye socket around my suppressor, sizzling against the hot metal, and the corpulent Fohoriman froze, the cleaver slipping from its fingers with a crash, before it sagged, still half propped up against the outer battlements.

The reports had been muffled, but for a brief moment, the whole battle seemed to stop.

Just for a heartbeat.

Then a voice, loud but hoarse and strident, boomed through the night. The lizard-headed Fohoriman did a backflip over the battlement and disappeared into the darkness. The horned Fohoriman snarled, wading into the press of Menninkai opposing him, hacking and slashing with both axes. Blood and bits of flesh flew as it threshed through the defenders, battering weapons and shields aside like straws before hacking into armor and bodies. Limbs fell, spraying gore against the timbers, while blades glanced off the Fohoriman's arms and shoulders, one striking his horn hard enough that it chipped the blade.

The voice sounded once more, and then, with a roar of hate, the horned one jumped over the battlements and vanished into the receding black cloud.

I staggered down off the quickly decomposing corpse of the fat one, my chest heaving, sweat dripping from under my helmet. "ACE Reports!" I didn't know if Gunny had gotten up there or not before all hell had broken loose. I could only see Santos, Farrar, and myself in this position, though Rodeffer popped out of the tower a moment later, looking around at the carnage in something like shock.

"I'm up. Only fired like one shot." Farrar sounded disgusted.

"More than I did." Santos was staring at the mutilated, broken, and bloodied corpses of the Menninkai that the horned Fohoriman had left behind him, his Mk 48 hanging in faintly slack hands. The handful of Menninkai who had survived the horned one's onslaught sagged against the parapets, weapons leaning against the walkway or the battlements themselves, gasping for breath, the shell-shocked stares in their eyes a mix of exhaustion, horror, and relief.

We might not speak the same language, but there was an unspoken kinship there, anyway.

I turned my attention back to the open ground between the walls. The black cloud was still there, though it was receding. Somehow it still seemed alive and aware, almost as if it were watching us as it slithered back toward the breach in the outer wall.

"Conor!" Gunny appeared on the far side of the pile of slime and bones that had been my bloated adversary. "You guys up?"

"Up and up, Gunny." I was still watching the blackness recede. It was really weird. Like watching video of an explosion in reverse.

Somewhere in there were the Fohorimans who had slaughtered so many of our allies. I wished again for thermals, so I could at least hurt them. I was developing a pretty intense hatred of those monstrous killers. But I may as well wish for a lightning bolt from heaven.

That might even have been more likely in this place.

The black cloud vanished on the far side of the outer wall, and the night was still, except for the groans of the few wounded who had survived the Fohorimans' attack. The corpse of the monster I'd killed had sloughed away enough that the crushed and deformed remains of the man it had killed on landing were partially visible through the rotten gore.

Movement drew my eye toward the distant encirclement. This truly was a circumvallation, at least on the landward side. If the Menninkai in the north managed to win through the Lasknut forces that had cut them off—presumably—they still wouldn't be able to reach Vahava Paykhah to relieve us, even if they'd had the numbers.

Which I doubted.

I scanned the line of earthworks and tents, barely lit by the low, flickering fires. There. Something was flapping above the center, where most of the Fohorimans had been gathered. It hovered for a moment, then shot off toward the northwest, faster than any bird or bat I'd ever seen.

I had the sudden, sinking feeling that whatever had just happened, killing that big bastard hadn't actually helped us much.

In fact, it might have just made things worse.

CHAPTER 15

THE sky was still overcast when the sun came up, but the clouds were high, lending a clear view all the way to the mountains to the north and west. It was still cold, the damp and the breeze blowing in off the sea cutting through whatever warming layers we had on.

We slumped wearily against the battlements, watching the enemy as the sky lightened. It had been hours since the Fohorimans had retreated, but we were all still up there, just waiting for the other shoe to drop.

Mathghaman, Bearrac, and the rest of the Tuacha "team" had arrived shortly after the fighting had ended. They'd gotten a bit of the side-eye from Gurke, on the other side of the crumbling bones of my adversary of the night before, who probably wondered why they hadn't been on the battlements with us when the monsters had come, but some of that was just Gurke. We all knew that there had been other matters to attend to, that King Karhu had asked for the Tuacha's advice that night. It had taken time for even the preternaturally strong and swift Tuacha da Riamog to get from the hall down to the second wall, and that fight had gone a lot faster than it had seemed.

Gunny Taylor looked as drawn and exhausted as the rest of us. "You think they'll come again this morning?" he asked Mathghaman as the King's Champion watched the enemy's lines in the distance. Thin, pale lines of campfire smoke rose above those lines as the savages, the Lasknut, the corsairs, and the copper-wearing warriors cooked their breakfasts.

I wondered, given our experience with the Dovos, how many of those fires were cooking long pig.

"I doubt it." Mathghaman was studying the enemy closely, his eyes narrowed, his brow furrowed. He could probably see more with his naked eyes than I could through my scope. "There is a grave uncertainty there. Almost fear." He shook his head. "They seem to be… waiting for something."

"Waiting for what?" Santos asked.

Mathghaman turned aside from the battlefield pensively. "I do not know. There is a sense of some strange fear, almost desperation, among the Fohorimans. It is in the way they move, the way they look up at our walls. It is strange. I have only rarely seen such fear among them. There is hate, and the will to crush and dominate, of course. Those are as much a part of them as their own flesh, now. But there is something else, some terror that grips them."

"What about the rest of those bloodthirsty bastards out there?" Rodeffer was peering at the camp through the V-shaped gap between two timbers, barely exposing one eye to the enemy.

Mathghaman looked over his shoulder at him. "They are here for the same reason they always are. Fear of their masters, thirst for blood and violence, and most importantly, the promise of plunder. They are a threat, yes, but hardly the greatest."

"What would make those monstrosities afraid?" I wondered.

"Maybe they found out we were here." Farrar's joke seemed to fall flat in the chill silence of the morning.

That silence. I hadn't noticed it before, but the savages were weirdly quiet. We'd gotten used to the enemy beating drums and chanting. This morning was strangely calm and subdued.

"*Something* sure made them pull back after Conor shot that thing." Gunny jerked a thumb at the grease stain that had been a bloated, murderous butcher the night before. "Damned if I can figure out what, though. They never reacted to gunfire like that before. We sure shot a few of them dead back in the mountains above Taramas's base."

Bearrac was frowning thunderously as he watched the siege lines, his massive hands wrapped around the sharpened tips of the wall timbers. "No, I do not think it was simply the gunfire. Though like Gunny, I cannot imagine what it might have been." He looked over at Mathghaman. "There *is* something else going on here."

"Indeed." Mathghaman rubbed his chin.

Fennean had been quiet so far, but he turned from the distant view of our foes with narrowed eyes. "Could Bres have had something to do with it?"

Mathghaman and Bearrac shared a look. I couldn't tell what all passed between them, but there was an understanding there.

Bres was the name of the man Mathghaman had been pursuing when he, Bearrac, Fennean, Diarmodh, and Nuala had fallen afoul of Taramas and been captured. We never had gotten the full story of what, exactly, Bres had done, but whatever it was, it had been dark and heinous enough that he'd fled north to the Fohorimans, rather than face the consequences among the Tuacha.

"Unless he has somehow seized power among the Fohorimans, it seems doubtful." Mathghaman spoke slowly enough that I could tell he was thinking it over. "We do not know enough."

Gunny stood up and started to scan the landscape. After a moment, it became clear that he wasn't so much studying the enemy as he was studying the terrain itself.

I followed his gaze, taking in the low hills coming off the headland and the rolling farmland, much of it churned to uselessness by battle and the passage of armies. The mountain upon which Vahava Paykhah had been built was the tallest bit of terrain until the mountains, far to the west and north, though even the farmlands and the woods beyond weren't exactly flat.

I knew what he was looking for. A good spot for an OP, where we could keep the enemy lines under constant surveillance, and possibly learn some more—if only from watching the Fohorimans' pattern of life, such as it was—by that means. Unfortunately, it didn't look like there was any place with enough standoff, aside from the walls where we stood even then.

There's reconnaissance, and then there's surveillance. We often lump them together as "R&S," but there are differences between the two. Reconnaissance is defined as *operations undertaken to obtain, by visual observation or other detection methods, information about the activities and resources of an enemy or potential enemy, or to secure data concerning the meteorological, hydrographical or geographical characteristics and the indigenous population of a particular area.* Surveillance is simply continual observation of either an individual or a particular point. Reconnaissance isn't limited to just sitting in a hide and watching an objective, though it's usually the best way to gather information without being detected.

Now, most of the on the ground recon that we'd trained for had been for things like beach profiles, ford reports, bridge reports, stuff like that. Measurements of terrain and man-made features, while they were abandoned. There were stories about *real* close-in recon conducted during World War II, Korea, and even Vietnam, of sappers slithering under the wire and sneaking through enemy camps, but none of those things had been considered "modern" tactics, and so we hadn't officially trained on any of them.

I could only imagine how Captain Sorenson would have reacted if we'd even suggested it.

Under different circumstances, I might have welcomed the opportunity to get outside the box, practice some stuff that we'd read about but never been allowed to do, because somehow it was "too risky" for modern Marines. This place, and the enemy we faced, were different, though.

I'd seen the corsairs' sorcery compromise us when we should have been well-hidden in the forest. I'd seen Taramas's hunters run up on our trail, sniffing us out through the trees. This place was rife with spooky stuff that you couldn't rely on cover and concealment to hide from.

And there was nothing but open ground between the outer wall and any high ground, such as it was, that we might have used to set up observation posts.

I met Gunny's eyes, saw the tightness around them. He had seen the same thing I had, and had reached the same conclusion. We were stuck.

"Dig out the heaviest-duty optics we've got." Gunny squinted toward the distant encampment. "We'll have to do what we can from here."

* * *

The Zeiss spotting scope wasn't actually Marine Corps issue, though it had been in our platoon inventory. Most of what we'd been issued had been the somewhat more compact Leupolds. The Zeiss was big and bulky, but it was considerably clearer and could zoom in a lot more.

Unfortunately, a lot of what we were looking at was stuff we probably would have been better off not seeing so clearly.

For the most part, the encampment was quiet. The normal humans, the Dovos, Lasknut, corsairs, and whoever the copper-armored guys were, were keeping busy digging earthworks. The Lasknut and the corsairs seemed to be the most disciplined, their fortifications considerably neater and more formidable than the others.

The Fohorimans stayed aloof. We saw several conferences, all of them tense, one breaking out into several duels. None of deformed monstrosities seemed to be killed in those duels, but their fractious nature was obvious.

Several of them, clustered around a tall, gaunt figure that looked more human than most of the rest of them, aside from his strange proportions and grayish green skin, approached the dais where the Lasknut had been conducting their sacrifice before we'd disrupted it with a high volume of fire. They stalked forward, weapons in hand, and stopped just short of the dais, on the far side.

I was on glass at the time, so I got to see what happened in detail. The Fohorimans stood around the spot where the athame had fallen, and none of them were any more willing to touch it or pick it up than we'd been. They stood around it, one of them making intricate gestures, mouth moving behind the beard of tendrils that hung from his pale, dead-fish face.

They were afraid of it. Given what little I'd learned about the relationship between the Fohorimans, their "younger gods," and the Outsiders like Vaelor, that wasn't surprising, though it was for different reasons than we might have feared to touch that thing.

The green-skinned Fohoriman turned back toward the earthworks and called out, the hooting, imperious cry reaching us a few moments later. Soon a few dozen of the hide-clad savages were hustling, some of them hurrying off toward the north.

Giving the athame a wide berth, the Fohorimans closed in on the dais.

They still didn't get too close. What had happened there was more than they wanted to tangle with. At least, that was what I could figure, watching them. They spread out around it, forming a circle with at least ten yards between any one of the Fohorimans and the dais, where the decomposed remains of the Lasknut we'd gunned down from the outer wall still lay, rotting but undisturbed.

Once they were in position, they all went completely still. I don't mean they just stood there. Most people can't help but move a little, even when they're trying not to. They breathe, they sway a bit, they shift their weight. The Fohorimans didn't do that. They stood utterly motionless, like thirteen statues placed around the dais. After a while, I could hear a buzzing, droning chant, slowly growing in intensity and volume.

Like a mosquito's whine, that sound almost immediately started to get under my skin. I shifted and blinked behind the glass. It wasn't just annoyance. My eyes started to smart, and I could have sworn my whole body had just begun to itch.

It probably wasn't healthy to continue to watch this, but it was intel.

After a moment, the green-skinned leader lifted his arms, the first motion I'd seen since they'd formed their circle. As he did, a flicker of blue flame appeared in the center of the dais.

A moment later, it had spread until the entire dais, including the altar and the rotten effluvia that had once been human bodies, was completely engulfed.

Timber, bone, and other materials crumbled to ash under the assault of those smokeless blue flames. It took only a few minutes for the entire platform and everything on it to be reduced to cinders.

The flames died away shortly thereafter, and the Fohorimans turned away, starting back toward their pavilions, even as the first of their savage subjects started toward the athame, lugging the biggest rocks they could carry.

So, they'd bury it rather than risk touching it. Interesting.

I wondered, if the Fohorimans' "younger gods" had stolen their power from the Outsiders, just where it came from, and what the dividing line was between, say, Vaelor's sorcery and their own.

Probably not a question I should delve too deeply into.

The pale one with the tendril beard stood by the athame as the savages started to pile stones atop it. The rest headed back to their encampment, a wary distance opening up between them as they moved, the concord that had formed so that they could burn the dais now over.

Stone by stone, the cairn rose over the athame.

* * *

I've done two hour shifts on glass, but they're exhausting. You wouldn't think so. All you're doing is staring at an objective. But concentration takes energy and looking through glass puts strain on the eyes. It's not necessarily all bad—my vision actually *improved* during my Recon career—but you have to rest, or you start missing things.

So, after about thirty minutes, shortly after the burning of the dais, I turned observation duties over to Rodeffer and went down to the stables to lie down for a bit.

The team kept rotating through like that, thirty minutes at a time, until it started to get dark. The cairn was still growing, rocks piled ever higher over the tainted dagger. They really wanted that thing buried. Otherwise, business as usual had continued down in the camp. The earthworks continued to grow, and the green-skinned leader hadn't been seen again since he'd retreated into his pavilion after burning the dais.

I was just coming off my latest shift when things started happening again.

"Conor?" I turned back as Rodeffer called my name, his eye still glued to the scope. "Something's got them all stirred up down there."

I moved back to the battlements next to him, laid my rifle in the V-shaped gap between posts, and scanned with my own scope. It didn't have nearly the magnification of the Zeiss, but right then, my eyes were tired enough that I was fine with that.

Sure enough, there was a *lot* of movement down there. In fact, it looked like the kind of commotion we used to see when a general was coming unexpectedly, and everyone had to get in formation *right now*. Bands of men rushed to get into position on the open ground behind the great pavilion, though mostly by tribe, with predictable results. The savages were mostly milling about in mobs, while the Lasknut and the corsairs formed neater squares.

Taking my eye from the glass, I scanned the wider landscape, looking for what might have prompted that reaction.

I saw no column coming from the north or west, where the vast army had originally appeared. I frowned. *Something* had to have triggered that anthill swarming down there.

A high, croaking scream echoed off the distant mountains, drawing my eyes up.

Four gigantic, winged creatures glided toward the encampment. Two were white, two were more gray. When I lifted my rifle to get them in my scope, I realized that they looked an awful lot like pterodactyls, with long, pointed heads on skinny necks and wide, leathery wings that stretched from their back feet to their forelimbs, kind of like a flying squirrel. If the flying squirrel was thirty feet long, reptilian, and evil.

The flying creatures circled the encampment, one of them letting out that croaking call again. All four bore riders, and two of them were all too familiar.

One was an enormous, barrel-chested armored figure, with a head almost half the size of his torso. That black armor with the vaguely green sheen would have identified Uergal even if his build and his enormous skull hadn't been distinctive enough.

The second was considerably smaller, and while I couldn't see her gaunt, pointed features or the horns jutting from her forehead, I could see the black cloak swirling around her with a life of its own, and I knew Taramas had come alongside Uergal.

The other two were every bit as monstrous as their counterparts. One didn't even look humanoid, but appeared almost draconic, its tail laid flat against its mount's back, reins in clawed hands, its crocodilian head jutting out on the end of a long, snakelike neck. The other was humanoid, except for the antlers and horns sprouting from his head. He looked like a cross between a cape buffalo and a moose, at least from the neck up.

They spiraled down out of the sky toward the open ground on the far side of the Fohoriman pavilions. The vast formations of the Fohorimans' army bowed to the muddy ground as one.

The Fohorimans' gods had arrived.

This was a lot more serious than we'd imagined.

CHAPTER 16

FEAR gripped Vahava Paykhah that night. Even in our OP on the walls, we could feel it. The city was hushed, not a light showing, though I was sure that plenty of lanterns and tapers flickered within the houses and halls, desperately keeping the darkness outside.

The Fohorimans' army didn't budge that night, though. The disturbing chanting and drumming continued from dusk until dawn, and faint screams suggested that some of the unlucky low men on the totem pole out there were being sacrificed to their living deities, but they didn't assault the city. They didn't even probe the outer wall.

The platoon stayed on observation, still switching out the Marines on watch about every thirty minutes, though we went down to only having one man at a time up on the wall as night fell. We didn't have good long-range night vision optics, so the OP was more for early warning than actual surveillance.

I, at least, still didn't sleep well.

Gunny came around in the morning, making sure the team leaders were up. "Meeting with the king and Mathghaman, up top." That elicited a few groans. It felt like a long slog up there, first thing in the morning, and we'd probably just have to come back down afterward.

The summons was the summons, though, and if Mathghaman was going to go to the king, then we would, too. At least the rest of the teams would be able to stay in place.

Honestly, I think the fatigue had really started to set in. We were getting hard and wiry in this world, without cars or other vehicles and without modern food. But we'd been up for night after night, and the rest we'd gotten between fights and shifts on the wall hadn't been great.

Don't get me wrong. I'd take the hay in that stable over half the places I've had to sleep since going to BRC, but I was still exhausted.

It took the better part of an hour to get up to the hall. Despite the chill in the air, we were all drenched, since we hadn't exactly taken our time. You generate a *lot* of body heat hiking uphill for that long.

King Karhu didn't seem to be bothered by our dishevelment. In fact, as ancient and obviously still unrecovered from his wounds as he was, he waited for us in armor, though his face was ashen, and his hand still trembled as he looked out at the army below.

Mathghaman stood at the base of the throne's dais, armed and armored, his rifle slung on his back and his hands clasped beneath it. He spoke not a word, but waited on the king.

"Four." King Karhu's voice was barely above a whisper, but the hall was silent except for the crackle of the fire in the fireplace. The Menninkai were hushed and frightened, and the quiet spread as thickly as the fear.

He turned toward us, looking down at Mathghaman. "Four Warlock Kings." His eyes were as haunted as his voice. "How shall we stand against such ancient hate?"

Mathghaman didn't answer at first. We stood behind him, with Gunny and Bearrac, and held our peace. This was a conference for the leadership.

The fact that perhaps the wisest and oldest of us didn't have an answer spoke volumes, none of it good. We were eleven Recon Marines and seven Tuacha warriors. There was only so much we could do.

"They think their Warlock Kings are gods, don't they?" Gunny broke the silence, a thoughtful note in his voice.

Mathghaman turned to look at Gunny over his shoulder, as King Karhu also shifted his gaze, his brow furrowing. "Yes, they do. They consider them the 'younger gods.' You know this."

"Just thinking everything through." Gunny's eyes were narrowed, staring at nothing as he worked the problem in his head. I traded a glance with Bailey. We'd seen Gunny do this before, and it usually meant we got to do something cool.

Something incredibly dangerous, that would very easily get some or all of us killed, but still cool.

"They're not gods, though. They're just really powerful wizards. Sorcerers. Whatever." He was still thinking things through, talking more to buy himself time. "So, they're still human. On some level." He paused, then moved to the window and scanned the ground below us, beyond the wall. He stared at it for a long moment, then turned to face Mathghaman and King Karhu, both of whom were watching him intently.

"What would happen if we killed or captured one of their 'gods?'"

King Karhu's mouth sagged open a little. He caught himself, shutting it with a snap, but the shock was still there in his eyes. He looked at Mathghaman, who had simply raised an eyebrow as he tilted his head, thinking. Finally, without a word, Mathghaman stepped to the window beside Gunny and peered out at the hillside and the ravaged farmland beyond it.

Bailey, Gurke, and I couldn't talk amongst ourselves right then and there, but the looks we exchanged were both eager and more than a little nervous. We'd all been staring at that terrain for the last several days, and while there were low spots that we might be able to crawl through unobserved if we were up against just the savages or the corsairs, the sheer numbers involved, not to mention the presence of monsters with more than human senses, and the Fohorimans' and corsairs' sorcery, made sneaking in close a serious problem. Unless Gunny wanted to pull a repeat of our hit on the ritual. I wasn't sure 7.62 would do the trick.

Granted, we had the *Coira Ansec*'s version of an M107 Special Application Scoped Rifle back aboard the ship. We hadn't pulled it out yet because we only had so many .50 caliber Raufoss rounds, and I wanted to save them for something special.

A Fohoriman Warlock King might qualify as "something special."

Mathghaman had something else in mind, though. "It will take a great deal of preparation and careful timing." He glanced out at the enemy lines once more. "I will have to go, with only one team."

"We'll draw straws, so you three can put the knives away." Gunny glared at the three of us team leaders. We were already eyeing each other competitively.

"It will not be tonight, whether or not the enemy attempts a renewed assault." Mathghaman bowed his head slightly to the king, who returned the gesture, more a matter of respect than reverence, though Karhu looked a little shell-shocked at how quickly this had all developed. Then he turned toward the door. "There is much to prepare."

We all sort of looked around at each other, almost as blindsided as the king. Then Gunny bowed slightly to King Karhu, again more a gesture of respect than reverence—he wasn't *our* king—and steered the three of us to follow Mathghaman. "Let's go. I think that we're going to have even more prep to do than Mathghaman's got in mind."

* * *

Just in case, I grabbed Rodeffer and headed down to the docks to retrieve the .50 cal and a few other nasty little surprises. We'd loaded up for this hunt, more so than we had for even the pursuit of the vampire Unsterbanak. We hadn't had a potential base of operations then, so we'd had to pack light. Expecting to stage out of Menninkai territory, we'd come loaded for bear this time.

The two of us unpacked the M107, all the ammo for same, more 40mm grenades, a couple of 84mm AT-4 anti-tank launchers, and several satchels of explosives. I couldn't tell you whether it was C4, Semtex, or TNT. Yes, I know there's a considerable difference in burn rates between C4 and TNT. I suspected it was closer to C4, but the *Coira Ansec* gave us explosives that seemed to fit the task we set them to, whether it was cutting or pushing. It was weird. Most of the rest of the weapons it had provided acted essentially just like their mundane counterparts back in The World. Not the explosives, though. They were more…*magic* is the wrong word, but I don't have a better one.

It would have been a long, heavy slog back to the wall, if not for the horse cart the Menninkai had provided. Their horses were short, stocky, and shaggy, but they still looked a lot more like horses to me than the barrel-chested, mutant things the Dovos and the Fohorimans rode.

Gunny was waiting in the stable when we got back. Things were moving, with Menninkai carrying fresh bundles of arrows and buckets of hot sand up to the battlements. In the distance, drums and horns sounded, the braying, discordant notes we'd become all too familiar with among the Dovos and the Fohorimans in the west.

The next assault was already coming.

The Fohorimans, like the Lasknut who had assailed the city before them, had to know that with access to the sea, the Menninkai couldn't be starved into submission. They could only be crushed. The only surprise was that they were moving so quickly after having just gotten there.

Maybe the Fohoriman Warlock Kings—and one Witch Queen—had some new, infernal surprise in store. That wasn't a comforting thought.

"Conor." Gunny tilted his head toward the back of the stable, indicating I should come with him. Leaving the unloading to Rodeffer, Synar, and Baldinus, I followed him back into the shadows.

"Mathghaman wants you on the op." Gunny kept his voice low. "Not necessarily your team; just you. I think it's probably because of that holy pigsticker you've been carrying around." He pointed at the sword by my side. "He hasn't picked any of the rest of his team yet, but I don't think he's going to go with any established team within the platoon."

"Any idea when we're stepping off? Or what he's got in mind to keep us from getting compromised and annihilated?"

Gunny shook his head. "He hasn't told me yet. I think he's still feeling things out, himself." He glanced toward the north as the drumming intensified for a moment. "Not gonna lie, this is shaping up to be pretty hairy."

I nodded. "No kidding." I had to swallow the metallic lump in my throat. I trusted Mathghaman. We'd been through hell together. But this plan, as nebulous as it was, had me scared. If we were just going to try to pop Uergal's skull with a Raufoss round, he would have said so. But I thought, from the way he'd talked, that he was more interested in the "capture" element than the "kill," and that meant going right into the middle of that hornet's nest of monsters and savages down there with five or so guys.

Not gonna lie, that scared the hell out of me.

I'd do it, when the time came. What else was I going to do? But that didn't mean I wasn't facing the possibility with more than a little trepidation.

The door creaked open and Mathghaman came in. I hadn't realized he'd come down to the wall.

His face was pensive. "I have watched them for some time, and now I see the way forward." He fixed each of us in turn with a glance, and seemed to sigh. "But first, I must tell you of Bres."

CHAPTER 17

"OUR people have been at war with the Fohorimans of the north, the Clan of Suth to the south, and the Thulrics of the east since the first of us awoke on the Isle of Riamog." Despite the drums and horns, the enemy advance had not materialized, so Gunny had brought everyone down to the stable to hear Mathghaman. Now he stood near the back, while the rest of us were gathered round in a "school circle." It felt weirdly like campfire story time, even though it was more of an intel brief. "The Fohorimans were the first to raid our shores. They came bringing fire and sword, and we stood against them on the shore, armed with what crude weapons we had learned to forge in dreams. Their sorcery was strong, but we were close to Tigharn, and we prevailed.

"Over the next turnings of the years, word of our defiance spread. The so-called 'younger gods' demanded our worship and our tribute, and we spurned them all. They brought ever greater force against our shores, but each time they were thrown back into the sea. All the while, we mined, and built, and grew."

Mathghaman wasn't looking at us while he spoke. He was, instead, staring at some point above our heads, seeing things distant in time and place. "In time, we took to the seas ourselves, if only to take the fight to our enemies. In so doing, not only did we discover and map the shores around the Great Sea, but we found allies, men not totally depraved or fallen into worship of dark powers. Men like the Menninkai, the Galel of Cor Legear, or the Tervini of Aterinas.

"Yet even with allies, we remained few against the darkness. Where the so-called 'younger gods' did not rule, still more savage tribes worship those ancient evils we call the Outsiders, but they call 'elder gods.' Those tribes, those that worship the younger and the elder idols, claim it was always thus. It was not.

"The Galel retain tales of a time before the Outsiders manifested in this world, a time of high civilization, great cities and greater works, when men even flew upon the winds. As any who have seen the thirst for power can understand, no matter how wealthy, how powerful man became, it was never enough.

"Their quest for knowledge and power slowly turned away from Tigharn's laws, and step by step they fell into greater and greater depravity, all in the name of improving their lot. Truth, justice, and mercy vanished from their minds and souls. It was into that time that the Summoner came.

"To this day, none know from whence he came, or even where he first appeared. He promised ever greater wonders, longer life, powers beyond what even the most starry-eyed imagined. He kept those promises, though at terrible cost. And then, even as it appeared that the apotheosis of man was on the horizon, he offered even greater horizons of power. Control over the very elements, the ability to shape the very world to man's whim.

"Thousands flocked to his clarion call, dissatisfied with even the great wealth and ability they had already unlocked, even at the cost of the blood of millions.

"He sacrificed them all, and with their deaths, he summoned the Outsiders."

The stable fell silent. I think we were all imagining just how bad it must have gotten. Frankly, as distant and vague as the description was, there were some uncomfortable echoes in the story with how things had seemingly been changing back in The World before we'd left. Or slipped through a crack leading away from it. Whatever had happened. It had felt like more and more people had been going out of their way to justify more and more twisted stuff, all while things had been getting weirder and weirder.

It made me wonder.

"Chaos and madness spread across the face of the world like wildfire. The Great Devoid, far in the south, is said to have been the place of the first summoning. It is a great pit, which some say is bottomless. Others say its bottom is in Hell." The name he used was *An Dubnos*, but the sense was roughly the same.

"The Outsiders spread quickly across the face of the world, fighting amongst themselves even as they destroyed or dominated all who had survived the cataclysmic formation of the Great Devoid. Those who resisted were driven back into mountains and fortified redoubts, as those who surrendered were twisted and mutated, while the Outsiders raised beasts into abhumans to serve them when there were not enough men turned to monsters.

"Over the centuries the Outsiders cemented their power, but the seeds of their own betrayal had already been sown. Those who would serve such monsters willingly are never content to bend the knee. Consumed by jealousy and ambition, they delved and spied and twisted their own souls beyond recognition in search of power to equal their masters. Thus were born the first of the 'younger gods,' and the wars of betrayal and sorcery that followed were nearly as terrible as the first summoning of the Outsiders."

He finally looked around at us. "This is how we have lived for centuries. We are a people besieged, at constant war in a dying world. We are not alone, though it often seems as if we are.

"Bres was one of the best of us. He was my brother, just as you are my brothers now. We defended the Isle of Riamog against monsters from the deep and raiders from north, south, and east. For years, we fought side by side, until the day that Korgul came to Aith an Rih."

His eyes were far away again. "They came in the night, braving the storms and the Deep Ones to land at the northern tip of the Isle in the dark before dawn. They overwhelmed the northern watch and swept nearly a league down the inner coast of the Great Bay before word reached us of the attack.

"Bres was awake, pacing the beach in one of his darker moods. He had them from time to time, though we never saw, before that night, how much more common they were becoming."

Mathghaman stopped then, his gaze still fixed on that distant time and place, a tightening around his eyes and at the corners of his mouth the only indications of emotion. Then he continued, though his voice might have been slightly hoarser than before.

"I remember waking up to the bells that sounded the alarm. I took up my armor and weapons, and found Bres already mounted, with my horse held by the reins. 'Hurry!' he called. 'They are already nearly to Aisc Argid!' That was only three leagues from Aith an Rih, and the fires were visible across the water, at least from high up the mountain. I threw my mail over my head and mounted, and we thundered out the gates together.

"We rode as hard as we could, the rest of our war-band forming up behind us as the Fohorimans and their servants put the town of Aisc Argid to the torch. I could *feel* Bres's anger as we rode. My own fury nearly matched his. Never in my memory had the Fohorimans come so far. Never before had their foul steps defiled our Isle so far from thc shore.

"By the time we reached Aisc Argid, the damage was done. The whole town was aflame, the stones themselves burning with sorcerous blue flames. Korgul himself stood in the midst of the destruction and taunted us as we formed into lines to halt their advance. They had no way to go around us. They were trapped between the mountains and the sea. The slopes come down nearly to the water at Aisc Argid, leaving only less than half a mile of level ground between the rock and the waves."

In other words, it was a strategic choke point that a determined defender could turn into an utter bloodbath in short order.

"Korgul is no fool. He stood there amidst the wreck-age of Aisc Argid and held his ground. He would not ad-vance. He is a monstrous figure, twenty hands tall, with no head, his face set in the center of his chest. That face leered and laughed at us, as his Fohorimans dragged the people of Aisc Argid out into the town square as their village burned to the ground around them, the villagers protected from the heat by his sorcery."

Mathghaman's eyes turned haunted. I'd seen that look before, after we'd hauled them out of the pit beneath Taramas's fortress. He wasn't just telling us what had happened.

He was reliving every terrible moment of it.

"One by one, they began to tear them to pieces. Korgul laughed and called us cowards, inviting us to stop him.

"Bres started in. I almost followed, almost brought the whole of the warband with me. Only at the last moment did I see what Korgul had done, even as the people's blood stained the stones and ran down toward the sea. The flames were not just devouring the buildings. They choked off every avenue through the ruins but one. He had turned our advantage to his own.

"Bres did not see it. He saw only the atrocities paraded before our eyes behind Korgul and the hateful visage of the Warlock King himself. He threw himself into the trap.

"He stood no chance against Korgul. He thrust at the monster, only to have his sword knocked away like he was a child with a stick. Catching himself, he riposted, attacking Korgul with a flurry of blows that I would have been hard pressed to defend against. Bres had always been a consummate swordsman. One of the best I'd ever known.

"Yet for all his skill and his fury, he could not touch Korgul. The Warlock King leered at him as he stood in place, battering away every stroke as if he were swatting flies. In the meantime, his Fohorimans continued to butcher the people behind him.

"We could not reach them. Not without committing ourselves to the trap. I could see his monsters in the shadows, beyond the sorcerous flames, waiting."

Mathghaman could never be said to falter, but as he fell silent again, I could see the pain and the doubt there. It was a strange thing to see from him.

He gathered himself. "I held the rest back. Held our ground. To charge in, as Bres had done, would be to abandon our position and the only advantage we had. They would have surrounded us, cut us to pieces, and then driven right through any survivors and on to the city.

"I saw Korgul look up at me, and I saw the anger in his eyes. We were at an impasse, and he knew it. If they tried to force his way through, we could hold them. I had not let Bres's rage lure me into his trap."

He let out a heavy sigh. "He took it out on Bres and the rest of the people of Aisc Argid. With a wave of his hand, he pinned Bres against a shattered wall and barked a single word of power. In an instant, all those of Aisc Argid who had not yet been torn to bits were engulfed in blue flame. They writhed and screamed in their final agony, and we had to watch, powerless to stop it.

"Korgul fell back then, as King Caedmon rode up with the rest of the army. We pursued them clear to their ships, and would have given chase even at sea, but the storm that arose shortly after they cast off quickly snatched them from our sight. We returned to the ruins of Aisc Argid to bury what was left of the dead.

"We found Bres where he had fallen once Korgul had released him. He knelt in the charred rubble, his head bowed, and said not a word. Nor did he utter a word or make a sound as we lifted him from the ruins and helped him on his horse.

"Within a week, he had gathered several disaffected younger men around him, took ship, and vanished in the night.

"He was gone for a year and a day. When he returned, he came alone, one man aboard a ship that needed a crew of ten. That alone should have been warning enough that he had sought powers denied us, but we were grateful enough to have him back that we were less wary than we should have been.

"We should have banished him at once. Instead, we welcomed him back, sought to bring him back into the fold. We had fought many battles in his absence, and the Clan of Suth had pressed us hard for weeks just before his return. We turned a blind eye to the warnings, and welcomed the return of one of our greatest warriors.

"He seemed better, despite the eeriness of his return. He was eager to join the fight, the next time the blood red sails of the Clan of Suth appeared on the southern waters. And at first, everything seemed as if the last year had never happened.

"Bres fought with all the grace and skill we had known him for. He cut his way through the twisted minions of the serpent priests of the Clan of Suth, spilling their blood across the southern sands and driving them back to their ships almost single-handedly.

"They fled before his fury, those who survived. There were not enough left to man but a dozen ships, whereas a full thirty had landed on our shores. We began to fire the hulks that remained on the beach, but Bres would not let the others flee.

"He began to chant in a strange tongue that we could not even comprehend with the mind speech, a tongue of darkness and madness. A great storm blew up at his command, dark clouds racing out of the east. Wind and hail sprang out of nowhere and blew the fleeing ships inexorably back toward the shore.

"Once they came closer, he lifted his arms toward the sky and shouted a phrase in that terrible language. We watched the ships consumed by the same blue fire that had burned Aisc Argid.

"None of the Clan of Suth's raiders lived to return to the south. And we had to decide what to do about Bres. He had delved into ancient tombs and sought out forbidden scrolls, studied under priests of the Outsiders and the Fohorimans both, in pursuit of the power he now wielded."

"Maybe I'm just kind of out of it, but I'm a little confused." Gurke stuck his hand in the air as Mathghaman paused. "If it's being used against the enemy, how is this kind of magic, or sorcery, or whatever, really that evil? I mean, they're bad guys, right? How is it different if you stick 'em with a sword or spear versus burning them with sorcery?"

Mathghaman didn't scorn the question. He thought it over for a moment before answering, but he didn't scorn it. "There is an order to the world, an order that the Summoner and the Outsiders sought to overthrow. No man can reach such power by himself. It is not in man's nature." He looked around at us, as if thinking then of the differences between us and the Tuacha. "Even we, of the Tuacha da Riamog, while we have gifts that other men do not, cannot command the elements or perform such feats.

"Sorcery comes from one source. The Summoner introduced it into this world, and it comes from the Outer Dark from whence he came. No good can come of it. Its promises turn bitter in their fulfillment, and a man must sacrifice a part of himself that no good or sane man would agree to for it. The sorcerer, ultimately, ends as little more than a slave, stripped of all but despair, pinned beneath the gaze of whatever ancient hate he has pledged himself to."

Gurke looked a little nonplused. I'm not sure he had quite expected that answer. Mathghaman returned to his story.

"At King Caedmon's command, Bres was imprisoned, held deep beneath the tower at Aith an Rih, bound with chains, blindfolded and gagged, lest he summon dark powers into our very home. I went to see him, but there was nothing to say. He could not answer.

"Yet our precautions turned out to be for naught. That night, he summoned monsters from the depths, which tore through the guards while he freed himself. Then he and the monsters disappeared into tunnels bored into the rock by some vile spit they spewed from their fanged maws. The first men who followed were crushed as the tunnels collapsed behind him.

"We would not have known where he had gone had he not left me a message.

"I can recall every word, but I will not utter them all here. He cursed me for my 'weakness' and 'shortsightedness.' He praised Korgul for showing him the way, and called the dead of Aisc Argid a 'necessary sacrifice.'"

Mathghaman bowed his head, looking down at the hay beneath his boots. "He swore that he would do what we could not. What we lacked the 'courage' to do. He would overthrow the Warlock Kings, and when he ruled all their domains, then he would take the war to the Outsiders themselves."

"Sounds like he went a little nuts during that year he was gone." Bailey's talent for dry, sarcastic understatement was finally on display again. I hadn't heard it much since we'd come to this world, but he was adjusting.

Mathghaman looked up at him from beneath lowering brows. "Indeed. Only a madman would make such claims. Or a man so thoroughly in thrall to the dark powers that he truly believed he could accomplish it, no matter the cost to himself and anyone near him.

"We knew from his message that he had gone north. He spoke of the Fohorimans. He would pursue Korgul first, to even the score. He may have seen Korgul as the one who opened his eyes, but he was still an enemy, and Bres promised to eat his heart."

"That's a little extreme," Farrar blurted, though when Mathghaman turned his gray eyes on him, he subsided a little. "Or maybe not, if what you said about sorcery is true."

"It should be no surprise, coming from a man who has sold his soul to dark powers, no." Mathghaman looked around at us. "He challenged me, and blamed me for his fall. So it was that I embarked on the hunt to kill or capture him, the first Tuacha in living memory to have fallen so far." He grimaced slightly. "You all know how that quest turned out."

Indeed. We'd found Mathghaman and four other survivors buried in a pit deep beneath Taramas's citadel. They'd been starved and tortured for who knows how long.

"While I'm glad you've seen fit to tell us the story, Mathghaman, since we've been a little in the dark despite having agreed to add him to the target deck, there's one thing I'm still not sure about," Gunny said, leaning against a stall at the back of our little school circle. "What's this got to do with our present situation?"

Mathghaman looked up at him, and around at all of us. I saw a determination there that went deeper than any other such look I'd ever seen on the man's face.

"He is here. Now. I intend to draw him out, and with him, one of the Warlock Kings."

CHAPTER 18

IT was nearly dawn when we landed, Nachdainn bringing the ship just close enough to shore that the prow scraped against the rocky shingle. The oarsmen held water as we jumped off into frigid, knee-deep water, sloshing ashore under the weight of weapons, ammo, mail, and little else, then they backed water and pulled off the beach.

We were in a small cove, sheltered by high cliffs, about ten miles west of Vahava Paykhah. There was no guarantee that we were outside of the enemy's patrol routes, but we were well outside the encirclement.

In the end, we'd decided that the whole platoon would go. We were few enough that leaving anyone behind just didn't make tactical sense. Bailey's team took point, while mine stayed on the cold beach, the wind off the sea biting through our soaked camouflage trousers as Baldinus and our Menninkai guide, Orava, looked for the path leading up off the beach and onto the top of the cliffs. Orava was familiar enough with this stretch of coast, but even he'd said that the path was narrow, treacherous, and difficult to find in daylight, never mind predawn darkness.

It took longer than we'd hoped. The eastern sky was a bright gray by the time my team finally got off the beach, taking up the trail position as we started clambering up the only slightly less steep crack in the cliffside, heading up toward the wind-twisted trees at the top.

Once we reached the top, what had looked like a forest from the water soon proved to be only a narrow strip of woods between the clifftop and the farmland beyond. The Menninkai had cultivated the land for miles around Vahava Paykhah. It seemed strange after the untamed, haunted wilderness that we'd seen so far in the northlands, but Menninkai territory seemed to be an island of sanity and civilization amid a land of savagery and monsters.

If the farmland had been fully cleared, we might have had some difficulty making our way toward the objective unobserved. Once above the cliffs, the land was fairly flat and rolling, aside from the massif where Vahava Paykhah stood, visible even from as far away as this windswept clifftop. Fortunately, lines of trees separated the fields like hedgerows in Europe, providing some concealment as we moved inland.

None of it was guaranteed concealment, when the enemy could summon spectral creatures to spy for them. But it was better than just trying to waltz across cleared farmland, in daylight.

We spread out around the edges of the fields. Despite the disadvantages of moving in daylight, when the enemy might have eyes and ears in every shadow, we were still going to be careful, and moving as a platoon was going to give us more of a footprint than any of us were comfortable with.

At least, any of the Recon Marines. Mathghaman had spent the day and night before in vigil, and while I can't say he was in a trance, there was an air of detachment around him that was different from his usual calm. Whatever lay ahead, he'd gone to some extra lengths to make sure he was prepared on a mystical level as well as a physical one.

He had a bow across his back, too, in addition to his sword, shield, and rifle. I hadn't asked about it, but knowing Mathghaman, he had a good reason for the extra weapon. Especially since he wasn't carrying many arrows for it.

As the morning brightened, the teams moved into the shelter lines between fields and followed the trees north and inland.

* * *

It was slow going. Not that the terrain was bad. Tilled, muddy ground could be agony to walk over under some circumstances—some of those fields in the green zones in Syria had been murder, and not just because the jihadis could see you and shoot at you—but we were staying out of the fields, and the ground under the trees made for pretty easy footing, since the Menninkai tended to harvest any fallen branches for firewood.

No, the slowness of our progress was because of what we were currently watching from about three hundred yards away.

A dozen savages were ransacking the low, stone farmhouse at the corner of the nearby fields. From the sounds they were making, they were not happy that the Lasknut had apparently long since ravaged the steading. Presuming that the Menninkai hadn't stripped it bare before they'd fallen back to the fortifications.

Hell, from where I crouched behind a tall pine, I could see the scorch marks around the window. The Lasknut had burned the steading before they'd moved on to Vahava Paykhah. That hadn't stopped this bunch from sifting through the ashes for anything of value.

Greed was apparently still a motivator, even for a people who lived in hide tents in the wilderness, utterly subject to all-powerful Warlock Kings.

Unfortunately, while they were almost completely focused on trying to find some shiny bauble amid the blackened cinders, they were right in our path. Just like the previous group we'd had to try to slip around.

"There's only twelve of 'em, they're all clumped together, and they're not paying much attention to their surroundings." Santos patted his Mk 48. "I could drop that whole knot of 'em by the corner with one burst."

"And alert everything with ears to hear for miles." Just because our weapons were suppressed didn't mean they were *silent*. That's a Hollywood thing, and even the *Coira Ansec* couldn't magically take away the supersonic shockwave of a bullet passing through the air. "They're starting to give up. Give it a few more minutes." The trouble with killing anyone during an infiltration is that sooner or later, that *will* result in a compromise. Either someone finds the bodies, or someone notices that their outriders haven't come back, or their sentries are late reporting in. Or missing altogether.

He glanced at his watch, which was still probably as accurate as mine to the actual time of day. "We don't have much more time to spare. We're already behind schedule."

"I know. But the 'schedule' was only ever a loose set of guidelines." Which was a good thing. Mathghaman was a seasoned warrior and commander, presumably old enough and experienced enough that he made Gunny look like a boot. He knew that ironclad timelines were never all that doable in a combat situation. We would proceed once everyone was in place. If that meant rolling things a few hours to a day to the right, then so be it.

Even as I said it, I hoped and prayed that the Fohorimans didn't launch a renewed assault on the walls before we could get into position and act. Like it or not, the reality of the situation on the ground aside, we were on the clock, and time was not our friend. The distance we had to cover, just to hopefully stay far enough away from the siegeworks to remain undetected, meant this was already going to take longer than any of us had hoped, but this delay wasn't helping things.

I'll admit, I was getting a little anxious to kill this bunch and get moving, myself. They weren't looking for us, but they were in our way.

I had to force myself to be patient. We had a very specific objective, and jumping the gun would put that objective at risk.

So, we waited, still and silent, until, about half an hour later, they got tired of looking for loot that wasn't there anymore and headed back toward the city and the siegeworks, muttering angrily amongst themselves.

Then, like shadows in the trees, we kept moving north.

* * *

Our rally point was less than five hundred yards away. But we couldn't move.

The sun was shining brightly through a rent in the lowering, slate-gray clouds. It couldn't dispel the gloom around the ruined farm that we watched through the trees.

As far as I could tell, we were still a long way from the edge of Menninkai territory, but the woods had closed in around this particular farm. The house was considerably bigger than most of the rest we'd seen, qualifying as a longhouse by itself. It had been built to withstand the harsh winters of the north, with turf packed about halfway up the timber walls. The steep, A-frame roof had been covered with moss-covered cedar shingles and extended out from the walls far enough that any runoff would have gone into the turf.

Its construction had not saved the people who'd lived there, though. The stench of death still lingered on the faint breeze, wafting from the bloated remains of corpses sprawled outside the door at one end.

The dead weren't what had given us pause, however.

It was hard to make out the thing that was prowling around the shadows behind the hall. It looked vaguely canine, the handful of times we could get a look at it, but that was about where our mental references ended. For one thing, it was big enough that it stood nearly even with the edge of the roof. For another, it was so black that it didn't seem to have any shape beyond a silhouette. It was a hole in the world, shaped vaguely like a giant black dog or wolf.

It reminded me of the black dogs that had guarded Unsterbanak's castle. Except that this thing was far larger, and it didn't have the glowing red eyes those creatures had.

So far, it hadn't given any sign that it knew we were there, but then again, how exactly would we be able to tell?

Waiting on the raiders had been one thing. They'd left once they'd decided that there was nothing to slake their avarice in the ruined, burned-out farmhouse. Somehow, I doubted this thing was looking for shiny trinkets.

Rodeffer and I had barely gotten down behind the hoary old tree at the corner of the field as the shadow thing stalked around the end of the longhouse and out into the open. Rodeffer had been about to take another step when I'd seen movement and managed to grab the back of his chest rig and pull him into cover.

Now it padded slowly toward the bodies, its muzzle bent as if sniffing them. It lingered over one after another.

If it had been a dog, I would have thought it was either looking for a meal, or mourning its fallen masters. This thing was doing neither, though right then I couldn't tell just what the hell it was doing.

Frankly, I wasn't all that concerned with what it was doing. I was worried about the mission and how to get past it without having it come after us. We were late, and even from as far out as we were, I could still hear the rolling drums of the Fohorimans' army. I hoped the assault hadn't started yet, but we were running out of time.

I didn't know how to deal with this thing, though. A dog or a wolf we could have killed, even if we'd had to risk bleeding a little to get a blade into it. This thing wasn't any kind of natural predator or scavenger though.

That much we could be sure of, especially after months in this world where half of what we ran into wasn't entirely natural.

The thing moved from corpse to corpse before padding out into the field and pacing along the length of the longhouse. It disappeared around the far end, though I was pretty sure it was still there.

"I think we'd better go around the long way, Conor." Rodeffer was trying really hard not to look right at the longhouse or the apparition pacing around it. Which was probably smart. I tore my eyes away from the macabre tableau. "If that thing is what I think it is, we won't be able to touch it. At least, not without a whole lot of noise."

"What are you thinking it is?" I had some vague memories of old stories from back in The World about Black Dogs, but it had been a long time. I remembered they'd been thought to have something to do with death, but that was about it.

"Remember the phantoms that were following the vampire? The things that kind of feed on death and despair that Bearrac told us about?" Rodeffer nodded toward the longhouse, again without looking directly at it. "I think that's something like them. I don't think it's really *here*, if you know what I mean."

I nodded, now being careful myself not to look directly at the shadow beast as it came out from behind the longhouse again. It was a pretty good theory. And that thing was so impenetrably black that I suspected he was right. A physical being would have shown *some* kind of detail.

Unfortunately, we were still in the local equivalent of a hedgerow, the line of trees between fields. If we were going to go around, we'd have to cross some open ground. But if this thing really was one of the evil spirits like that ghostly figure we'd seen in the dark while we'd followed the vampire along the eastern shore, then it probably couldn't really *see* the way we could. It was *other*, something of darkness and the spirit world, manifest in this place because the veil between the natural and the spirit worlds was awfully thin in this world.

Drifting back into the trees, I quickly passed the word. We'd go around, cutting across the field to our immediate west. In the process, I made sure the whole team understood that we shouldn't look at that thing, or even think about it real loud. I got enthusiastic acknowledgements. Everyone remembered the phantoms we'd seen in the woods, following the vampire's wake of death and destruction. Everyone was equally creeped out by the memory, as well as the possibility that this was a bigger, nastier version of them.

With Rodeffer in the lead, we left the shelter of the trees and headed out across the field.

It was still fallow from the winter, though fortunately it hadn't been tilled yet, so the furrows weren't as deep as they might have been. They were still deep enough, along with the mud, to make footing treacherous, even though we were only carrying weapons, ammo, water, and not much else. If we'd had rucks, it would have been murder.

We were halfway across the field, the woods looming dark ahead of us, when we heard the growl.

It was deep and distant, like it was coming out of the depths of the earth. Yet it was still loud enough to vibrate in my chest as I turned and looked straight at the hulking darkness of that gigantic, sepulchral wolf-thing as it came through the trees toward us.

It didn't charge. It padded forward a step at a time, utterly unhurried, as that eerie growl resounded around us again. Even as it came, I still couldn't see any eyes, teeth, nose, or even a single hair. It was black as the void, swallowing every bit of light that fell on it.

Santos apparently decided that as long as we were made, doing something to fight back was better than running away and dying tired. He lifted the Mk 48, ready to give the thing a taste of full-auto 7.62.

"Wait." I couldn't be sure this would work, but I *was* sure that machinegun fire wouldn't, and even if we didn't survive this thing, then opening fire in the woods would compromise the rest. We needed the Fohorimans to think that we were all still bottled up in Vahava Paykhah. Otherwise, Mathghaman's plan might not work.

Slinging my rifle to my back, I drew my sword, the blessed blade I'd retrieved from the Dovos nal Uergal, without knowing I'd been doing so. Bringing it up into a forward guard, I stepped out of our wedge formation and toward the void hound.

No, I didn't know if that was what it was called, but the name popped into my head just then, and it seemed to fit.

It stopped as I took another step, that sword held point forward in front of me. It didn't retreat, didn't flinch, but it didn't advance any farther, either.

I took another step. It held its ground. Another. It seemed to turn its head aside—though it was *really* hard to tell, since all I could see, even in broad daylight, was a silhouette—like it was squinting against a too-bright glare.

Continuing to advance, I kept the sword up. I had no idea if this was going to work, but at least it had stopped coming after us.

I glanced over my shoulder. The rest of the team stood motionless in the middle of the field, transfixed. "Get moving!" I hissed. This would be for nothing if we just stood there. I kept advancing on the black dog, as Santos chivvied Rodeffer and Farrar toward the woods.

For a moment, as I got closer, and that spectral growl sounded again, deeper and more menacing, I thought I might have overplayed my hand. But even as I got ready to fight, knowing I probably wasn't going to be able to hurt it, it turned and just *faded away.*

I shook my head. "I don't think I'm ever going to figure out how things work here." Sheathing the sword, I turned and hurried to catch up. We had to get the rally point.

CHAPTER 19

ELEVEN Recon Marines, seven Tuacha warriors, and one short, stocky Menninkai fighter waited in the trees around the small clearing, weapons up and watching not only the clearing itself but also the shadows under the trees, the latter perhaps more keenly. Those shadows were getting deeper as the sun dipped toward the west, half-shrouded in broken, gray clouds.

Movement stirred in the woods off to our flank, and then Mathghaman reappeared, moving through the trees like a ghost. His bow was still in his hand, his rifle slung at his back. He whispered to Bearrac and Fennean, then moved to join Gunny and me near the center.

"The message is delivered." He'd brought the bow not for combat, but to loft his challenge into the Fohorimans' camp, close enough to where he'd seen Bres from the walls to make sure the Tuacha renegade would receive it. I wasn't sure how he'd guarantee that, but the Tuacha were spooky in their own way sometimes. "Now we wait."

Gunny glanced at the sky. The sun would set within the next hour. "How quickly do you think he'll respond?"

Mathghaman nodded toward the far side of the clearing. "It was not a message he could ignore."

A figure stepped out of the trees. Tall, spare of frame, and straight-backed, for a moment, he was only an outline in the shadows beneath the firs. Dressed in a long coat of blackened rings, the man wore a high, peaked helm, not unlike the Tuacha's, all covered by a midnight blue cloak. He carried a naked sword in his hand, the blade blackened, though it still gleamed as a beam of sunlight through a rent in the clouds struck it. His shield was an oval, as dark as the rest of his arms and armor.

So, this was Bres, the renegade.

"You play a dangerous game, Mathghaman." He stepped farther out into the clearing, and I got a better look at his face beneath the helm. Gaunt and angular, his cheekbones stood out like a starving man's, and his eyes glimmered from behind the nose guard. It might have been my imagination, but for a moment, I could have sworn that they glinted red.

Turning to sorcery did not appear to have done good things to Bres.

Mathghaman set his bow down, unslung his rifle, and drew his sword as he stepped out to face Bres. "Far more dangerous for you than for me." He stopped about ten paces into the clearing. "Or do you think that you slipped away before your new lords could notice?"

Bres's eyes narrowed, and there was nothing but hate there. "*My* lords?" He spat. "Was it not bad enough that you refused to reach out and take the power we needed to finally overthrow these monsters? Now you must seek to betray me to them, the same way you betrayed our own people at Aisc Argid?"

Mathghaman's face hardened still further, and his eyes flashed. He barked a humorless laugh. "The man who sold his soul and brought the very powers he claims to oppose to our Isle calls *me* 'betrayer.'" He dropped into a guard. "I counted you a brother once, Bres. Now I will spill your blood to the ground. Make your peace with Tigharn before you die."

Bres echoed Mathghaman's laugh, though there was a hollow sound to it that sent a chill up my spine. I put my reticle on Bres's chest, just in case. I sincerely hoped that Mathghaman hadn't bitten off more than he could chew. Bres was clearly well on the way to becoming a Fohoriman, himself.

The two of them began to circle, weapons held ready, though they were still just outside each other's reach. They were sizing each other up, each man taking the measure of his opponent. It had been some time since they'd faced one another, and many things might have changed.

I knew some of what Mathghaman had been through. Who knew what Bres had seen and done during his sojourn among the Tuacha's inveterate enemies in the north?

Bres moved first, darting in to thrust at Mathghaman's throat. Their blades clashed briefly before he withdrew. It hadn't been a serious attack, but a probe, feeling out his opponent's reactions.

Mathghaman struck back, his blade darting for Bres's head, then quickly circling away from his parry and whipping toward his leg. Bres leapt back, their swords meeting again with a brief clash before disengaging.

The sun blazed through a gap in the overcast, turning the clouds gold and bathing Mathghaman in light, though Bres seemed still to stand in shadow, and then they came together in earnest.

Blows rained on shields and blades, so fast that I could barely track their movement. Steel rang on steel and wood as they feinted, clashed, riposted, and parried with blade and shield alike. Neither man so much as faltered as he stepped forward, back, and circled to one side or the other.

It was awe-inspiring. As thoroughly fallen as Bres might have been, we were watching two absolute masters battle it out, masters with all the preternatural grace and speed of the Tuacha. Steel gleamed in the setting sun as they attacked, parried, and riposted, the fight flowing back and forth across the clearing. Every blow was measured, and so far, anyway, every blow was equally countered. Mathghaman hadn't been kidding when he'd said that Bres had been the best of them.

It was making me worry a little for Mathghaman. He was certainly holding his own, but he wasn't making much progress. Every stroke was deflected, every thrust turned aside.

Tearing my eyes away from the clash of blades and wills in the clearing, I scanned the woods. While taking Bres down had been part of Mathghaman's objectives all along, it was only a part of this operation. And the longer the fight went on without one or another coming out on top, the riskier this got.

None of us believed that Bres had gotten out of the Fohorimans' camp cleanly. And if the Fohorimans came after him before this duel was over, we could be in a world of hurt.

Especially if we were still distracted by the duel. It was mesmerizing, in a deadly serious way.

Mathghaman took a step back, and Bres pressed him, unleashing a flurry of blows that chipped away at his shield and battered at his sword. The renegade's teeth glinted as he snarled, intensifying his assault and driving Mathghaman back another step. Sword strokes rained down on the King's Champion, and Mathghaman gritted his teeth as he fended them off, weaving a web of steel and wood around himself, even as he fell back another pace toward the trees and our position.

I looked over my shoulder. Farrar was watching the fight when he should have been watching our flank. I reached over and cuffed him on the shoulder, and he quickly turned to cover his sector.

Just as we both saw movement in the trees.

Worst case scenario, as we'd figured in planning, would have been a full company of Fohorimans with their savage or Lasknut vassals coming after us. We would have had to break contact and run for it if that had been the case. Mathghaman and Bearrac hadn't thought that would happen—they were both banking on their read of the enemy's situation. They'd figured a few Fohorimans, led by one of the Warlock Kings.

They were right, from what I was seeing.

Six Fohorimans paced through the trees, weapons in their hands, ahead of a towering figure draped in a voluminous cloak, horns and spatulate antlers sprouting from his skull, a long spear held in one hand.

Mathghaman seemed to sense something, even though he didn't turn to look, and none of the Tuacha, who were spreading out and moving to the flank, slipping between the trees swiftly and silently, said a word. He suddenly stopped falling back and redoubled his own assault, driving Bres back with a flickering storm of sword strokes.

Stepping in suddenly, he got the rim of his shield inside Bres's, hammering it aside as he slipped his blade to the inside of his enemy's sword, sending the point slithering inside of Bres's guard to draw blood from under his arm.

Bres leapt back, disengaging and huddling behind his shield for a moment. Malice gleamed in his eyes as he glared at Mathghaman, looking down at the blood on his hand behind the shield.

Mathghaman did not give him room to breathe, but pursued him, crossing the gap quickly, his point questing for any gap in his defense. Bres fell back and even staggered a step, as if his sudden burst of energy had abandoned him, now that blood had been drawn and he was no longer dominating the fight.

He began to mutter, and there was suddenly an electric tension in the clearing, even as the Fohorimans began to close in. A metallic smell stung my nostrils.

Then we had to worry about the Fohorimans, and I couldn't watch the fight any longer.

Bearrac led the attack, coming out of the trees on the Fohorimans' right flank. He opened fire first, blowing a hole through a gaunt, long-limbed, long-necked Fohoriman's temple and dropping him to the loam and needles beneath the trees.

The report echoed through the woods, and in the shocked, nearly frozen moment that followed, we all opened fire.

Bullets tore into the Fohorimans, though many that struck torsos, limbs, and even heads didn't penetrate. Being the sorcerous monstrosities that they were, their weaknesses were few. We battered them back with round after round, but once they got their feet under them, they charged.

Santos put a burst into one, a lanky, wolf-headed, hairy thing that was rushing toward Fennean, its jaws agape and an axe in its hand. The first five or so rounds staggered it without stopping it, but the next two or three went through its roaring maw and blew out the back of its skull. Its momentum kept it moving as it crashed onto its face in the dirt.

I shot another one in the throat, and it stopped for a second before it came after me, moving so fast it seemed to flicker along the ground. I dumped half my magazine into it before I got lucky and put a bullet through its eye. The slate-gray, noseless, hairless once-man spun to the ground, spraying blood from his ruined eye socket.

The gunfire fell silent. All six Fohorimans lay dead or dying under the trees. It had taken far too many rounds, but we'd dropped all of them.

All but the Warlock King behind them. The horned and antlered figure stood beneath the trees, its cloak spread out to its sides, its antlers all but lost in the branches overhead. It hadn't moved as we'd shot its entourage to dog treats, but stood there, stock still, watching, its eyes little more than glints in the shadows beneath that spreading crown of horn and antler.

The duel continued behind us, though from the sounds of things, Bres was not doing well. I was hearing more of his grunts as Mathghaman forced him away from the lot of us. We had to focus on the primary target, though.

Despite Mathghaman's mission to kill or capture Bres, he was just the bait on this op.

Mathghaman had suspected that Bres, despite his use of Fohoriman arts, and his presence in the Fohorimans camp, would have maintained his hatred, and would be looking for an opportunity to turn on the Fohorimans and their Warlock Kings, even as he turned into one of them. It made sense; we'd seen the way everyone in the Land of Ice and Monsters seemed to have their knives out for everyone else's backs. The Fohorimans probably suspected what he was up to, as well, so when he slipped out of their camp, we were sure *someone* was going to come after him. And given who and what Bres was, a Warlock King himself seemed likely.

We'd been right. So now, while Mathghaman dealt with Bres, the rest of us faced the Warlock King Octrallach.

He still didn't move as we formed an L-shape around him, guns up and muzzles trained on that vast head. He was bigger than he'd looked from a distance, when he'd been dwarfed by Grichencos, the crocodilian Warlock King who had accompanied him, Uergal, and Taramas to the siegeworks. He stood an easy seven feet tall, without taking his horns and antlers into account. His head, even swathed in shadow as it was, looked like it was the size of a horse's.

While he wasn't moving, wasn't threatening us with that spear, he wasn't idly waiting for us. Even as the last of his Fohorimans had fallen, I'd started to hear the whispering in the air, and that thunderstorm pressure that had begun with Bres's mutterings doubled and redoubled, and the metallic stink on the air became almost strong enough to make me cough. My head began to ache, and a splitting pain started to build behind my left eye.

Bearrac stepped forward, setting his rifle aside. He seemed utterly unfazed by the growing sorcery in the air. "Cease your foul cantrips, you cursed abomination. Face me as a man, or flee to your depraved masters."

For a moment, the whispers got louder, and the pressure intensified. Synar was driven to his knees, blood dripping from his nose.

With a snarl, Bearrac leapt at the towering figure of Octrallach, his sword singing as he swung at the Warlock King's head.

The spear shifted in an eyeblink, deflecting the blow, but Bearrac recovered as fluidly as if the spear hadn't even been there, shifting his blade away and back, never once allowing the sword to stop moving. The spear was ever in his way, but Bearrac never let up, raining cuts and thrusts on the cloaked figure of the Warlock King with dizzying speed.

Still, despite the unrelenting ferocity of Bearrac's assault, and the eerie fact that he seemed untouched by Octrallach's sorcery, it seemed like he was whaling away at an immovable object, unable to slip his sword past that lightning-quick spear. Fennean, Diarmodh, Conall, Cairbre, and Eoghain were circling, looking for an opening, but even without visibly moving, Octrallach always seemed to be able to face any attacker just as they moved. It was spooky, but no less than what we'd come to expect from a Fohoriman Warlock King, a sorcerer so powerful he was worshiped as a god.

Yet, even as he fought, I realized that Bearrac was chanting, in that ancient tongue the Tuacha used when they prayed. And as the fight continued, while it didn't *look* like Octrallach was moving, he was being forced back, and Bearrac's voice was getting louder, steadily drowning out the whispers that were still susurrating around us. As his voice got stronger, Octrallach seemed to get weaker.

Finally, even as the rest of us were maneuvering, trying to get a shot, Bearrac got a stroke past the spear.

Now, I still can't be sure if I really saw Bearrac's sword shining more brightly in the reddening sunset. I *thought* I did, but I couldn't be sure. There was a lot going on.

But when he got the point into that cloaked shape, Octrallach jerked as if he'd been electrocuted, and the spear nearly fell from his grasp. The whispers stuttered, just for a moment.

Then Bearrac was inside the spear, batting it aside as he seized Octrallach by the throat. A moment later, he had the point of his sword pressed under the Warlock King's jaw.

Immediately, the whispers stopped. Everything went still. The spear fell from Octrallach's hand.

Then Bres let out a full-throated scream. I pivoted, my sights already settling on him before I realized that Mathghaman was very much still in the fight.

In fact, Bres appeared to be retreating, favoring his side, as Mathghaman stalked him across the meadow. The last beams of daylight gleamed off the King's Champion's helm as he closed in on the man he had once called "brother."

"Yield." Mathghaman's voice was as cold as the very Teeth of Winter, the massive ice sheet in the north. "You will get no second chance."

Through gritted teeth, Bres sneered. "Yield? And what then? Shall I kneel and grovel before the king and your precious Tigharn?" He cursed. "You'd best kill me now."

"So be it." Mathghaman moved in for the kill.

Bres shouted a word in a language that sent a spike of pain through my skull. A deepening darkness started to gather around his sword as he presented his shield, the point of his blade pointed down at the muddy ground.

Mathghaman ignored the curse and waded in. He feinted for Bres's head, then quickly reversed the blade as Bres lifted his shield to stop the blow. His sword flashed downward before Bres could react, and lopped off his foot.

Bres screamed then, really screamed, a high-pitched wail of pain, shock, and despair. He staggered back and fell on his ass, staring at the stump spurting dark blood out onto the ground. He shimmied backward, his sword still pointed toward Mathghaman, who advanced inexorably. The gathering darkness was gone, and now it was only a sword with a darkened blade.

"Bres Mag Elatha, for the crimes of treason against your people and consorting with diabolic powers, bringing sorcery to the very shores of the Isle of Riamog, I bring the sentence of death, from King Caedmon's own lips." He advanced still farther, batting aside Bres's sword with his shield.

Bres wasn't going to go quietly into that long night. With increasing desperation, even as his life and strength leaked away, he slashed at Mathghaman, but each blow was weaker and weaker.

Finally, Mathghaman stood over him and drove the point of his sword through Bres's throat. The renegade lay transfixed, and for a long moment, Mathghaman stood over him, looking down into his eyes.

He knelt by the body, closing those reddened eyes, and bowed his head for a moment. Then he straightened and turned toward where Bearrac and Diarmodh had Octrallach down on his knees, his spear broken. The Warlock King seemed shrunken, diminished, and there was a look almost like shock in his eyes. He couldn't fathom how this had happened.

I thought I understood. Mathghaman hadn't been the only one to spend the night in vigil before we had embarked on this operation.

"Bring him. Quickly. His minions will be swarming all through these woods soon." With hardly a glance at Octrallach, Mathghaman turned and led the way back toward the coast.

CHAPTER 20

IT was a long movement back to the shore, dragging Octrallach with us, bound and gagged. Gunny had wanted to blindfold him, just in case, but the horns and antlers had precluded that, and if he couldn't see, we would have needed to drag him or carry him the whole way.

He was a *big* dude, anyway, and that would have slowed us down immensely. And in the aftermath of that fight, speed was security, even as the night descended and the darker things of the shadows came out. We didn't go straight across the fields—that would have been a little too careless. We still kept to the tree lines between the fields, though we relied on the shadows to disguise us as we moved alongside the trees instead of through them. We could move faster that way, especially since the fields hadn't been tilled right up to the trees themselves, so there was some flatter, firmer ground at the edges.

Octrallach still seemed to be in shock, which was the other reason we were moving fast. No one gets to be considered a god by being a simpleton, and sooner or later, he was going to snap out of it and turn into a handful again. He was gagged to keep him from uttering spells, and there was a naked sword at his back or against his throat at every step, but he was immensely dangerous, and we all knew it. The faster we could get him some-where secure, the better.

I was wondering just what constituted "secure" when dealing with a Warlock King, but that wasn't my baili-wick. That was on Mathghaman and Bearrac, and they seemed to think they had it figured out.

Eerie howls and cries rose above the trees behind us. *Something* was on our trail.

Bailey's team was on point, the Tuacha right behind with our prisoner, while Gurke and I took up rear se-curity. I fell back to join Santos in the very rear of the formation as the noises got weirder and scarier. "What do you see?"

"Not a damned thing." Santos had paused long enough to take a knee, his Mk 48 held ready, scanning the blackness beneath the trees behind us. "Whatever's back there, it hasn't showed itself yet."

I stood above him, scanning the trees through my PVS-15s. We were still in Early Evening Nautical Twilight, that period where there was still *just* enough light to wash out night vision. Contrast went to crap during that time of day, but sometimes you could still see movement. But the line of trees between this field and the one we'd just left was as still as the grave.

"Let's keep moving." The longer we stayed in place, the worse this was going to get. The howling screech that went up in the distance was chilling, though I'd heard screech owls in the woods back in The World that sound-ed every bit as scary. Still, putting that noise down to a screech owl here, after what we'd just pulled off, was not going to be particularly wise.

The two of us hurried to catch up with the rest of the team, only to find that the platoon had halted. I knelt next to Rodeffer, just a few paces behind Chambers. "What's going on?"

"Don't know. We just stopped." He craned his head to look behind us as that unholy shriek went up again.

"Don't wait for me if we start moving again." I got up and started past him, keeping as close to the trees as I could. "I'll meet you up ahead." Time was flying, and we were getting deeper into the enemy's favorite time. The nighttime is the right time when you're a sorcerously corrupted monstrosity, or a follower of such.

Gurke reached out and stopped me as I hustled past his team. "What's going on?"

I bit back the smartass comment, mainly about the fact that he and his team were closer to the front and should know more than me. "Don't know. Heading up to see."

While Zimmerman had always been the contrarian of the platoon's team leaders before he'd gone missing, Gurke seemed to have decided to take that role for himself. He didn't bother to get up and come with me as I kept going.

Octrallach must have started making trouble, because the Tuacha had him down on his face with Bearrac's knee in his back, blade held to his throat as the stocky Tuacha warrior whispered fiercely to him, one beefy hand wrapped around a horn to keep his face levered just high enough that he wasn't getting his throat cut. Yet.

I worked my way around the Tuacha and found Gunny on a knee next to Bailey, while Baldinus looked around the surrounding woods and fields. "What's going on?"

"We're not sure." Bailey was watching Baldinus. "We both suddenly got the feeling that we were turned around, going the wrong way."

I frowned. I couldn't make out much of Gunny's expression behind his own NVGs, but I could tell he wasn't happy about this situation, and not just because of the deepening darkness and the noises behind us.

It wasn't outside the realm of possibility that we *had* gotten turned in the wrong direction. It happens sometimes, especially when you're trying to move fast through unfamiliar territory. I'd gotten lost as hell during my first patrol exercise as pointman, back when I'd been a Lance Corporal. My team leader, Sergeant Forrest, had calmly and patiently guided me back, making sure I understood what I'd done wrong and that I got oriented again as we got back on route.

He'd had the good grace to wait until we were back in the rear before he thrashed the snot out of me.

But something about this was a little too pat. We weren't in the thick of the wilderness, where it stood to reason that a pointman might get pushed away from the route by vegetation or terrain. That certainly happened often enough even when he was being careful to navigate every step of the way. No, there was something more going on here.

I dragged my compass out, peering beneath my NVGs at the glowing tritium dial. I hadn't been watching the compass the whole way, but we were definitely pointed the right direction, almost due south. "We're still on the right azimuth. What's the issue?"

"I don't know." Bailey sounded simultaneously worried, confused, and angry. The former two were almost certainly the cause for the latter. Sean Bailey didn't like being confused, let alone worried. "We just suddenly got disoriented, and I can't figure out why."

I glanced over my shoulder at where Bearrac was still whispering fiercely in Octrallach's ear. "I've got a good idea I know why."

Bailey followed my gaze and cursed venomously. "I'll kill that son of a bitch."

"I'm sure Mathghaman's called dibs already." I tapped Baldinus on the shoulder. "You're going to have to keep an eye on your compass. It might slow us down a little, but better than staying put while *that* catches up with us." The hooting screech had echoed across the fields again while I'd been speaking.

"Agreed." Gunny got to his feet. "Baldinus? You good?"

Baldinus was swearing under his breath as he dragged his lensatic compass out of the pouch on his chest rig. Back in The World, the compass was one of those things we always kept on-body, usually in a shoulder pocket, dummy corded to one of the buttonholes. With the shift to mail shirts instead of camouflage blouses, we didn't have shoulder pockets anymore, so we had to find a different place to carry some of that "pocket litter."

"Let's go, Thomas." Bailey was already on his feet as well. The shriek came again, louder and noticeably closer. I suspected that whatever it was, despite his shock and the gag, Octrallach was drawing it to himself.

The platoon started moving again, Bearrac and Mathghaman hauling Octrallach to his feet and propelling him quickly along the trees. That horned and ant-lered head turned to look at me as they passed, and while a part of me rebelled at avoiding eye contact, I was smart enough not to meet those glinting eyes. The gag probably helped, but a being as powerful as a Fohoriman Warlock King probably didn't need only his voice to influence people.

I didn't have much of anything to say to Gurke as he passed, though he looked at me curiously. I could almost feel his desire to ask what the holdup was, but he could take that up with Bailey. We were moving again, that was what mattered.

I fell in behind Rodeffer, grabbing him by the arm as he passed. "Keep an eye on your compass. Don't just follow Chambers." I'd be doing the same thing. Several of my old mentors had said it, and I'd passed it on to plenty of my Marines over the years: *If you're not navigating, you're lost.* That counts for the slack man just as much as it does for the guy on point.

We hadn't gotten far, though, when the screamers in the dark caught up with us.

I'd thought, from the sound, that we were being pursued by one, maybe two creatures. But it was a swarm that came at us over the tops of the trees.

They were small, but still roughly humanoid. Except for the tattered bat wings sprouting from their backs, anyway. Their eyes were glowing, greenish lamps, too big for their heads. What I could see of the rest of their faces looked like desiccated, moldering corpses. Their hands were elongated claws as they swooped down on us with high-pitched, sepulchral screams.

Santos pivoted, dropped to a knee, and stitched a long burst across the diving crescent of screaming, cadaverous flying things. He raked the line of them with bullets, the suppressor reducing the reports to a ripping crackle, the can itself already starting to glow in my PVS-15s.

The bullets did nothing. They kept coming as if none of them had even been hit, even though there was no way Santos had missed *all* of them.

"Run!" Cairbre had stepped out of the knot of Tuacha in the middle of the formation, and was now standing a couple yards away, his rifle slung and his sword in his hand, facing the onrushing monsters.

Cairbre had been the most aloof of Mathghaman's companions, rarely uttering so much as a word to any of us. His loyalty was to Mathghaman, which had seemed to be his sole reason for sticking with the platoon. He wasn't a bad guy; he just didn't seem to like us for whatever reason.

Yet now he held his ground, his sword held up rather like I'd held the blessed sword against the ghostly black dog, letting us get past him while he stood against the howling apparitions diving on us.

I took two steps past him before I stopped, turned, and waved at Farrar and Santos to keep going as I slung my rifle behind me and drew my own sword. Cairbre glanced at me, as if to question just what the hell I thought I was doing, but he still stood his ground.

The swarm of shrunken flying corpse-things stooped on us, but Cairbre lifted his sword, holding it up like an exorcist holding up a crucifix, and I did the same. It was, after all, roughly what I'd done to drive off that black dog thing earlier.

The sight of our weapons didn't seem to deter those things any, and they dove at us, claws grasping. Cairbre started to chant, low and deep, the sound not unlike Bearrac's chant before he'd grabbed Octrallach by the throat.

That did seem to slow them, but they still dipped toward us, screaming thinly as one of them grabbed at Cairbre with its long, grasping claws.

He slashed at it, and the blade passed through the thing's wrist as if it wasn't even there. The claw dissolved like smoke, and the creature reared back with hollow wail.

That seemed to make the others reconsider, and they suddenly reversed direction like a flock of starlings, whipping away from us while Cairbre and I slowly back-stepped, before turning and diving toward us again.

They looked humanoid, but they acted like birds or insects. When they came at us again, I took a swipe at one as they came closer to my side. I wasn't quite as fast as Cairbre; I got a single claw instead of the whole hand.

It was enough to make them slip away again, shrieking and flapping in the night, but they were back almost as fast.

This time, though, Cairbre wasn't screwing around.

His leap had to clear six feet as he launched himself right at our tormentors, swinging that sword with an upward slash that I probably couldn't have managed, at least not while trying to jump over my own height.

That slash clove right through one of the closest of the diving monsters. Just like before, it met no resistance, and the thing vanished in a swirl of mist or smoke, with another strange wail.

The swarm dissolved a second later, as Cairbre dropped to the ground, landing as easily as if he'd just stepped off a curb. The spectral monsters scattered like quail, screeching discordantly, and in seconds they had vanished into the night.

Cairbre looked me over for a second, as if making sure that I wasn't hurt, then, without a word, he turned and loped after the rest of the platoon.

Shaking my head and reflecting that for all their differences, the Tuacha still had their share of assholes, I followed. We had to get to the coast with a quickness.

CHAPTER 21

OCTRALLACH didn't give up trying to disrupt or mislead us as we kept going. The confusion got so bad at one point, affecting even the Tuacha, that only a brutal cuff to the head from Bearrac got him to stop. Bearrac hit him hard enough to leave even the unnaturally twisted creature that had once been a man—I wondered how long ago—dazed, and suddenly it seemed that our own perceptions cleared up and we saw we were barely a quarter mile from shore. The sea was dimly visible through the trees just ahead, and we could hear the surf washing against the rocky coast.

We hustled toward the cliffs and the shore below, Bearrac and Mathghaman practically dragging Octrallach behind them. Bailey halted at the top of the cliffs while the rest headed down the narrow path toward the strand, except for my team. We spread out in a semicircle, facing outboard, looking for more monsters in pursuit.

The flying things hadn't reappeared, and nothing else had attacked us, but I'd seen movement back there. Shadows were closing in behind us, moving like people or beasts, it was hard to tell which. So far, nothing had presented a target, but we weren't going to drop security.

The most dangerous point of any operation is extract, and we were getting awfully close.

Bailey knelt by a gnarled, windblown tree, and flashed his IR illuminator out to sea three times. That might have seemed odd, given we were the only ones with NVGs in this world, but the Tuacha can see in a wider spectrum than we can, and they can see in the dark better than cats. They hadn't needed any illumination to make their way through the pitch-black caverns beneath Taramas's citadel, so they had no problem seeing a small, low power IR light on a headland from out at sea.

A moment later, he gripped my shoulder. "Got the signal. They're coming in. Meet you on ship."

I thumped him on the leg with a fist, letting him know I'd heard. We'd stay up on the clifftop until everyone else was aboard. Getting jumped mid-boarding with everyone down at the bottom of the cliff could be disastrous.

Things went quiet after he slipped down the narrow crack in the cliffside that was the only path down to the beach. The team waited and watched, weapons up, as the only sound that met our ears for the longest time was the wind whispering through the trees around us.

A shadow moved on the other side of the field. I tracked in on it, but there was nothing there. I lowered my weapon and went back to scanning.

Beside me, I could feel Farrar starting to fidget. No, fidget's not the right word. He was actually starting to shake, while trying to suppress it.

I moved closer to him, keeping my voice low. "We're almost out." I didn't want to openly address his fear. He was probably biting his tongue until it bled, cursing himself for being scared. After all, we should have gotten used to the spooky stuff after the months we'd spent in this strange world, often confronted by monsters and specters, right?

Don't kid yourself. No sane man ever gets *used* to the sorts of things we'd fought. Combat is one thing. A man can get hardened to that. Even then, every man still has his limits. Those who aren't total psychopaths eventually reach their breaking point. But the unnatural, the *preternatural*, the spooky… There's something about things that are trying to kill you or devour your soul, that you can't always actually shoot or blow up, that gets to a man.

And we'd just captured one of the scariest of those creatures we'd ever encountered. Just because it had gone the way it had didn't mean it wasn't still scary, especially since we'd seen how even a battered and diminished Octrallach had still managed to mess with our heads.

No, I didn't really blame Farrar for being scared. The only reason I *wasn't*, at least not to the degree I could really feel it, was because I'd been too busy, between trying to coordinate with the other teams, watch our sectors, and make sure we didn't lose anyone. Farrar, while he hadn't dropped security, had just had to watch his sector and keep moving. Which meant he'd had too much time to think, and the enormity of what we'd just done— as well as the constant signs of unnatural pursuit—was preying on his mind.

"That's what I'm afraid of." He tried to make it a quip, but I could still hear the faint note of fear in it. I was sure he was hating himself for it, but he'd seen what had come after us already, and there was nothing in his arsenal that could do what a blessed sword could. Not against things that soaked up bullets without flinching, then turned to smoke when hit with something that could actually hurt them. "It's right when you think you're safe that something comes out of nowhere and eats your face."

Unfortunately, I didn't have a flippant remark to throw back in response to that, and the silence that followed wasn't exactly comfortable. Especially since more of the shadows seemed to be moving closer, almost coalescing into something vast and hulking, a monstrous shape on all fours under the trees, about two hundred yards away, just far enough that our NVGs couldn't really make out if there was really something there, or if the dark and forbidding shape was just a figment of my imagination.

I felt my own trepidation building as I watched that thing...or thought that I did. Whenever I dared look straight at it, I couldn't see it. Maybe it was there, or maybe it was just in my head.

As strange and mystical as so much in this world was, that tendency of the human mind to see spooky things in the dark that aren't necessarily there hadn't gone away. Not *everything* really was a spectral monster trying to eat you.

Unfortunately, the existence of such spectral monsters made it harder to tell when it *was* just an overactive imagination.

Whatever it was didn't move from the trees by the time an IR laser blinked on the branches next to my head. The rest were aboard and ready to cover us. I tapped Rodeffer on the shoulder first, and he turned and immediately headed down the narrow path toward the shore.

If he was moving a little faster than a patrolling pace, I couldn't exactly blame him.

Giving Farrar a similar shoulder tap, I turned and followed Rodeffer down to the ship. Farrar was right on my heels, far too close to be tactically sound, but again, speed was security at that point. Santos followed more carefully, his own mass and the heavier Mk 48 slowing him down as he tried to get down the steep path without biting it.

I held my position at the side of the ship, knee-deep in freezing cold saltwater, my rifle trained on the top of the cliffs as Rodeffer and Farrar clambered aboard, hauled up by Gurke and Chambers. Santos hit the beach as I thought I saw movement up above, though when I turned my muzzle toward it, training my red dot on the darkened, twisted trees, there was nothing to shoot at.

Santos splashed into the surf, and I helped boost him aboard before I reached up and grabbed Chambers' proffered hand, clambering aboard the ship.

Octrallach was down on his face on the deck, once again with Bearrac's knee in his back. Mathghaman and Fennean stood to either side, clearly on guard, and I didn't think they were only there just in case Octrallach tried to get up.

The oars heaved, and with a lurch, the ship pulled off the strand with a deep scraping sound. We stayed in the bow, weapons trained up at the tops of the cliffs, still uncertain whether or not we were being watched by hostile eyes even as the heights disappeared into the darkness.

* * *

It was about midnight by the time we reached the tiny, rocky island just outside the harbor, where a simple, square watchtower perched, an early warning station placed to watch for corsairs or any other threats from the sea. Knowing what we were setting out to do, King Karhu had flatly refused to have a Fohoriman, let alone a Warlock King in the flesh, imprisoned within his city. The Menninkai faced a great enough threat from outside. Their king had no desire to bring such a threat within their walls.

"You know, if we'd just offed him, this wouldn't be an issue." It said something about how much we'd been through together that I felt remotely comfortably saying that to the King's Champion. Mathghaman stood next to me, watching as Bearrac and Fennean hauled Octrallach into the tower, his face unreadable, his arms folded.

"There is more going on here than meets the eye." Mathghaman didn't look at me, even as the three disappeared into the torchlit doorway. "What would draw four Warlock Kings from all corners of the Land of Ice and Monsters to besiege Vahava Paykhah? They hate each other, in the way that only those who are equally evil hate one another. Why would they have gathered so, *after* the forces of Sumnoth had nearly crushed the Menninkai?"

I peered after the vanished shapes of the Tuacha and their prisoner, thinking it over. "The Outsider magic?"

"Possibly." Mathghaman's voice was grim. "Vaelor slumbers, but it is no true sleep like you or I might experience. He is bound, rather than truly asleep. In his dreams, he reaches out, seeking release. There is nothing the Warlock Kings fear more, except perhaps Tigharn's justice, which they will face without fail in the next life.

"If Vaelor's followers have grown strong enough to suborn all of Sumnoth, then he may be stirring to a greater degree than ever before." Mathghaman rubbed his chin. "That *might* draw so many of the Warlock Kings together." He looked over at me then. "If Vaelor were to be freed from his prison, it would mean dark times indeed, and not only for those souls who dwell here in the north. As terrible as the Warlock Kings may be, their evil is nearly insignificant compared to the bottomless malice and power of the Outsiders."

I shifted my weight a little. I was conflicted. I understood the threat, at least in part. It was like going into a small Syrian village on a hostage rescue mission, only to find out that the terrorist holding the hostages was about to launch a nuclear strike.

And yet... We'd come north to find our missing Marines. Mathghaman had, unexpectedly, fulfilled his mission. Ours was still unresolved. And I couldn't help but wonder if we were already too late for Zimmerman, Gonsalves, Owens, or even the captain.

Mathghaman sensed my disquiet. He gripped my shoulder. "I know, my friend. But think of this. If your friends still live, they were last seen in company of a sorcerer who invoked Vaelor's powers. Perhaps, what we learn from Octrallach might tell us more of their fate."

From anyone else, I would have thought he was simply trying to make me feel better. That wasn't Mathghaman's way, though. While his tale of Bres's betrayal had shown him to be as fallible as the next man, at least once, experience had shown that Mathghaman was King's Champion for a reason, and not just his peerless skill and agility.

I didn't know what he suspected, what pieces he'd put together that I'd missed. But he was sincere, I knew that much. After fighting our way out of Taramas's territory and Teac Mor Farragah, then all the way across corsair lands, Lost Colcand, the haunted hills of Tethba, and the undead kingdom of the Land of Shadows and Crows itself, I trusted him.

I just hoped that this wasn't one of the rare times he was wrong.

CHAPTER 22

MOST of the platoon stayed aboard with Nachdainn and his crew, but I took my team up to the top of the watchtower, where we had something of a view of the city, and we could hear at least some of what was going on below.

That last part was an immediate source of regret. Octrallach, even gagged, had gotten noisy, and the sounds he was making were not calculated to give a man a sound night's sleep.

Not that we were likely to get much more than snatches of rest for the foreseeable future. A livid, angry glow had sprung up on the north side of the city, and while we couldn't see what was going on, we could hear. The sounds of battle drifted over the sides of the great hill, and the tang of smoke reached us out on the harbor. The Fohorimans and their minions had started their assault.

Santos was watching, his face lit by the dull orange glow. He'd finally started to let his beard grow, much like most of the rest of us, though he still kept his head as closely cropped as he could. "This puts us in an interesting position."

"Bit of an understatement." Another muffled howl of rage and hatred filtered up from below. "For one thing, what do we do with *him* if the city falls while we're out here?"

Santos glanced over his shoulder. "Huh. That wasn't actually the first thing that came to mind, honestly." He turned back toward the fires. "We're out here, while they're getting the full weight of that army thrown at the walls. Not that there's a whole lot we could do at this point. Even with the explosives we've got, it would be a drop in the bucket against those numbers." He squinted, an almost pained expression. "If the Menninkai fall, then we're back to square one with no local support."

"I'll admit, that's farther than I've thought." I'd been a bit more worried about getting through the next few hours, ever since we'd gone ashore to draw Bres out. And his boss.

I leaned against the wall, peering out the arrow slit toward the fires. We couldn't see the flames themselves. The bulk of the hill and the inner walls blocked them out. But they had to be pretty big to be visible from where we stood. "I'll be honest, this whole op has gone pretty far off the plan. First, we end up caught in a defensive action as soon as we hit the ground, because the allies we were counting on to give us a base of operations have got their backs to the wall, and now it sounds like Dragon Mask might have been a part of something a lot bigger and a lot worse than we thought."

Santos shook his head, his eyes still fixed on the walls and the city, silhouetted by the flickering light of the fires. "And we're still no closer to even knowing where to start looking for our missing guys."

"Taramas is here." A vague plan was starting to form in my head, though it was one that I wasn't sure was going to go over very well with the Menninkai, or the Tuacha either, for that matter. "If they were captured, then she's either got them buried in a deep, dark hole under her citadel, or she brought them with her. If Dragon Mask's bag of tricks is as scary to the Fohorimans as Mathghaman says it is, then she might have dragged them along, just so they didn't get up to trouble while she was away."

"Or she killed them to make damned good and sure, and we're months too late," he said darkly.

Rodeffer looked up at that, though he didn't say anything. The possibility wasn't one we'd thought too much about, though it had always been there in the background. We hadn't seen bodies, so nobody was dead. Just missing. We'd planned accordingly.

If they *were* dead, though, we would have to go awfully deep into extremely hostile territory to find out for sure. And now the Fohorimans had to know we were there. Guns were not exactly commonplace in this world, and I didn't think it was a coincidence that the four Warlock Kings had arrived *after* the Fohoriman raid on the walls had gotten several of them shot to death. The word had winged—literally—north after that.

We were hardly the scariest thing in this world, but still, we'd killed a *lot* of Fohorimans and human minions on the way in and out of Taramas's territory. She had to remember that, and I expected that Uergal hadn't forgotten, either.

That didn't bode well for getting out of here. What if they were here not because of the Menninkai, or even the Lasknut's sorcerous insanity, but because of *us*?

I didn't have an answer. Without more information, not to mention Gunny's and Mathghaman's input, I *couldn't* have an answer.

We settled in, fifty percent security set, and tried to shut out the enraged howls from below, while the Menninkai fought for their lives out on the wall.

* * *

The Fohorimans didn't take the city that night. While we were tired and bleary as the sun came up, eyes stinging from fatigue as well as from the smoke drifting out to sea from the fighting on the wall, we could still tell that the city held. King Karhu's banner still flew from the hall, visible through the darker haze, and when we looked through our optics, we could see Menninkai warriors on the second wall.

"I'm surprised. Not sorry, but surprised. With the kind of numbers we saw out there, I fully expected the bad guys to have taken the second wall." Santos was watching the walls through his scope. The Menninkai on the second wall were still there, but they were also clearly taking cover from arrows from the lower wall.

When I shifted my own gaze to the first wall, sure enough, I saw what appeared to be savages, Lasknut, and even a few corsairs on the wall itself. They were cautious when moving between towers, as the Menninkai were showering them with arrows whenever they showed themselves, but they were there. They hadn't fallen back outside the outer wall when they'd failed to take the second that night.

"Maybe losing Octrallach really did throw 'em for a loop." I kept watching, and I couldn't help but notice that I didn't see any Fohorimans up on the wall. Only their regular human minions. "Having one of your 'gods' go missing has to be a bit demoralizing."

"Probably threw their coordination in the crapper, too." While many of us had grumbled for years that we'd do better without our officers, I couldn't imagine that losing a supreme commander had translated into anything but chaos and confusion. And if their assault had been planned as a coordinated strike by all four armies—or however many there were, presuming the corsairs were mercenaries—then losing a quarter of their leadership had to have worked against them.

The tower shook with another tooth-grating howl. Rodeffer muttered darkly under his breath. Farrar just winced. Santos glowered back at the trap door leading to the steps down below. "About ready to go shut that fucker up permanently."

"Mathghaman might have something to say about that." I kept watching the city, which was why I didn't notice when Bearrac came up the stairs and joined us.

"About what?" The big man sounded tired. He looked it, too, haggard and drawn. The Tuacha had never appeared anything but powerful and collected, so seeing Bearrac looking hollow-eyed and drained was shocking.

"We were debating the dubious merits of keeping Octrallach alive." I didn't want to come right out and say that Santos wanted to go down and slit the Warlock King's throat, but there was only so much you could dissimulate with a Tuacha, and I respected Bearrac far too much to try to lie to him, anyway.

If I'd been worried that he might react badly, I was surprised when he just grunted, leaning back against the wall. "Killing him would have been much more easily said than done. We surprised him, in that the purification we underwent before facing him made his sorcery less potent. But he is beholden to dark powers that will not relinquish him easily." He ran a hand over his face. "He believes himself a god, having tricked Vaelor long ago and imprisoned him. Yet without the powers of the Outer Dark, he would be nothing, just another man. It is those powers we contend with now." He let out a heavy sigh. "And while capturing him was one thing, holding him and questioning him have been another matter altogether."

"I'd guess it *would* be hard to get someone like that to talk," Santos observed.

Bearrac shook his head. "It is more than what you think. Even restrained as he is, he is far more dangerous than you realize. Even to speak to him is to place ourselves at hazard. There is less of him left than even he realizes." He met my gaze, and I was struck by the same haunted look I'd seen in his eyes after we'd escaped Taramas's clutches. "The darkness lurks close by him, and any shadow on a man's soul might grant it an opening." He shook his head again. "We may have captured him, but it is for one greater than we to truly confront him."

Farrar frowned as he turned and peered out the arrow slit. "Is that why a boat's heading into the harbor?"

Bearrac nodded. "There is a greater within the city. Mathghaman has gone to beg his aid." He heaved a sigh. "I only hope that we have time."

Almost as if he'd been heard, the horns and drums sounded again, as the Fohorimans' army commenced another assault on the northern walls.

We could only wait and watch, as Octrallach howled his hate from downstairs.

* * *

The boat returned remarkably quickly, Mathghaman rowing with firm, sure strokes. The bent, white-haired ancient in the gray robe we'd met in King Karhu's throne room sat in the stern, looking up at us as Mathghaman neared the island.

"You're going to put that old man in front of that monster?" Rodeffer turned from the arrow slit to face Bearrac, his doubts written plainly all over his face. "Why would you do that?"

Bearrac chuckled as he turned toward the steps leading below. "That 'old man' is far more powerful than you might imagine. He has far less to fear from Octrallach than any of us." He disappeared down the stairs, leaving us to look at each other and wonder just what was going on.

"There's a lot going on here that goes beyond the physical." We'd certainly seen enough in the last months that it should have been obvious that the line between the material world and the spirit world was so thin as to be damn near nonexistent in this place, but it was something I think most of us were still wrapping our heads around. I nodded toward the outside, where the boat had just disappeared below. "I'd say that if Bearrac thinks that little old guy can hold his own, he's probably right."

Santos just kind of shrugged. Rodeffer still looked doubtful. Farrar, for his part, frowned thoughtfully, his gaze far away.

We heard Octrallach started yelling again, bellowing malevolently through the gag. But then the tone changed. Subtly at first, but soon that howl turned to a scream of utter, abject, animal terror, so loud that we had to cover our ears. I could have sworn that the whole tower *vibrated* with the volume of that scream.

The shriek was cut off abruptly, and did not recur again.

Once more, we could only wait, as low voices murmured below us. Whatever Brother Saukko had done or said, it seemed to have worked.

Now we just had to see what came of it. Meanwhile, the assault to the north continued, the clash of weapons and the shouts and screams of men fighting and dying drifting around the hillside toward us, reminding us all just how precarious our position really was.

CHAPTER 23

NONE of us were sure about leaving Octrallach on the island, essentially unguarded, but Brother Saukko had assured us, through the Tuacha, that he was incapable of doing great harm, at least for the moment. He was bound, chained to the floor, his horned head bowed as if under a terrible weight.

I only got a glimpse of him as we'd left for the meeting in King Karhu's hall, but it almost looked like his horns and antlers had shrunk a little.

I had to wonder just what had happened in that little stone room. The Warlock King, so powerful that he was worshiped as a god, was huddled and slumped, beaten down and bent to the very ground. Brother Saukko, the frail little old man, who should have been easy prey, looked calm, composed, and fresh as a daisy.

Most of the platoon would stay below, ready to move to support the Menninkai if the Fohorimans breached the second wall, while Mathghaman, Bearrac, Gunny, and the team leaders accompanied Brother Saukko to the great hall.

That little old man was a lot spryer than he looked. Once we got onto the pier, he took off at a good clip, climbing toward the hall at a pace that would have put a much younger man to shame.

We still kept up pretty easily, if only because we'd been humping over mountains and hills for months, fighting for our lives for much of that time. We were as lean and hard as the Tuacha, just without some of their more otherworldly gifts.

King Karhu looked almost as beat down as Octrallach had when we'd left him. He slumped in his throne, his face gray with exhaustion and pain. There was soot on his face and blood on his armor. He must have gone down to the walls the night before. The young woman was trying to tend to him as we entered the hall. It looked as if his wound had opened again, and she was trying to bandage it, but he waved her away as we approached.

Brother Saukko bowed before the throne before he spoke. It turned out that he spoke the Tuacha's language fluently, so it wasn't hard to understand him. His voice was low and kind of breathy, as I might have expected from a man of his apparent age.

"I have spoken with Octrallach, my king. He remains unrepentant, but he was compelled to speak, nevertheless." Brother Saukko leaned on his staff, but did not seek to sit down, though the king waved insistently for a stool to be brought. "He has confessed to me the reason the Warlock Kings and their army have come here.

"They sensed the invocation of Vaelor from afar, even before Zeiczak's fall and the Lasknut's subsequent madness. The Fohorimans and their Warlock Kings felt the tendrils of Vaelor's awakening power like an earthquake. They have known since last winter that there are forces abroad, seeking to awaken the old idol, and had been on the watch for those forces to reappear." He glanced over his shoulder at the rest of us. "It seems that some of these acolytes of Vaelor escaped from Taramas's grasp some months ago."

Gunny and I shared a glance, eyebrows raised. Unless the Fohorimans thought *we* were Vaelor's disciples, then that meant that Dragon Mask, at least, had lived, and was still at large.

"While he spoke of other stirrings in the months since, Zeiczak's sorcery here was grave enough that the four greatest Warlock Kings, save only Korgul, whose hatred for Uergal surpasses even his fear of Vaelor, joined forces and marched their armies south and east, first to crush whoever might invoke Vaelor, and then to conquer. Even had Zeiczak still been here, they would not have let us be.

"Yet their opening raid, which was to have breached our defenses and left us open to their assault, encountered our friends, and word winged to the north of the presence of the 'thunder warriors.'" The old holy man glanced at us again, appraisingly. "It seems that among the raiders who struck the guardians of the old temple at Sino Akmon Kruwos some weeks ago were several 'thunder warriors.' When word reached them that men with such weapons were here, the Warlock Kings abandoned the sack of Sumnoth and descended on us, intending to end the quest to awaken the old evil themselves."

We all looked at each other at that. Only Mathghaman had heard this already. Brother Saukko had been saving the results of the interrogation so that he only had to tell the story once.

"Well, that tears it." Gunny's voice was low, and I just nodded. This was not the time or the place for that conversation.

King Karhu had certainly noticed, though, and his eyes flicked to us. I wondered if we were now going to be the focus of suspicion, despite the lengths we'd already gone to in defense of Vahava Paykhah.

There was curiosity and thoughtfulness in his gaze, though, not overt suspicion. He waved to Gunny. "Would you know who these 'thunder warriors' are?"

Gunny stepped forward to stand next to Mathghaman, as Brother Saukko stepped aside. "I think we do." He proceeded to tell the story, as completely and honestly as he could. He told the king about our arrival through the mysterious fog bank, the ill-fated alliance with the Dovos nal Uergal, the realization that we'd been conned, and Captain Sorenson's refusal to accept it, right up until Dragon Mask had summoned Vaelor's unholy creatures in the catacombs, at which point we'd lost track of four of our own in the escape.

"If they're alive, it sounds like they might still be moving with Dragon Mask. I don't know if they're hostages, or if the captain is still clinging to his ideas of local force engagement." Gunny sighed. "It's possible that some of Dragon Mask's Dovos took their weapons and learned to use them. I doubt it, but it's possible." He glanced at Mathghaman. "We came north to find them, one way or another. Either to pull them out, or else confirm that they're dead." He straightened a little more, lifting his head higher. "Or, if they really have gone bad, then we planned to deal with our own problems."

I think that was the first time that any of us had openly spoken of that possibility.

King Karhu regarded him with a solemn expression, his eyes moving to each of us in turn. I could just see

Bailey out of the corner of my eye, and his face was as set and grim as mine. The Menninkai king nodded ever so slightly. He knew exactly what Gunny meant.

"We of the Menninkai have had our share of traitors and would-be sorcerers," he said. "We hunted them down and brought them to justice. We know the need to see one's own dealt with when they go astray." His eyes strayed to Mathghaman for a moment. "As do others who stand here in my hall, if I am not mistaken." He looked out toward the wall. "Unfortunately, we can offer you little assistance. And I fear that Vahava Paykhah, and the Menninkai nation as a whole, will no longer be here when you return, if you strike out to find them." He almost seemed to shrink in his throne. He wouldn't look at Mathghaman. "I would beg for your assistance, but I fear that even your weapons, against the numbers and the sorcery we face, would do little."

I could tell why he didn't want to meet Mathghaman's eyes. He had no hold on the Tuacha, or on us. He desperately wanted to ask for aid, but he didn't think that he could. Or should.

Mathghaman's expression was clouded, the weight of the situation settling on his shoulders. Our mission was paramount, even though his was accomplished. But honor made him abhor the idea of turning his back on the Menninkai, especially in their darkest hour. Never mind that King Karhu was probably right, and we really *couldn't* do much to stave off the inevitable.

Something occurred to me then. Ordinarily, I'd keep my mouth shut in high-level briefs or meetings like this. King Karhu wasn't *my* king, but he was still a king. And that counted for a lot more here than it would have back in The World, believe me. I couldn't think of any politician back there who would have been in the rear only because he'd been stabbed in the side and couldn't fight. Let alone one who would have dragged himself back down to the front again, despite the wound. But this idea was worth speaking up about.

"If someone—whether it's Dragon Mask alone, or some cult, cabal, or whatever—is trying to wake this Vaelor up, isn't that pretty serious?" I got nods from King Karhu, Mathghaman, and Brother Saukko. I'd just stated the obvious, but sometimes it pays to go through all the information, even if some of it is already common knowledge. It makes the case for a mission plan clearer. "If four Warlock Kings put aside their differences to come here on the rumor of Outsider sorcery, then they think there's a serious enough threat that it trumps even their squabbling." I'd heard Dragon Mask talk about wars between Uergal and Korgul, and Taramas and Uergal had been at each other's throats until Dragon Mask had summoned those horrors in the underground. "But Vaelor's imprisoned in the north, isn't he?"

"So it is written." Mathghaman responded before Brother Saukko could. My *Tenga Tuacha* was rough and slow, so Mathghaman understood before Brother Saukko, who would have had to translate my stumbling words in his head first.

"So, why would there be such a fuss kicked up down here if they're trying to awaken and free Vaelor up north? Unless it's a diversion?"

"There are artifacts needed to conduct the dark rituals that would loosen Vaelor's fetters." Mathghaman was thinking it through, though, even as he answered my question. "The athame that the enemy buried rather than touch was one. Perhaps they believe that another can be found here." He glanced at King Karhu, who shook his head so violently that he winced as he made a warding gesture to keep away evil.

"Maybe Zeiczak thought there was, or else someone convinced him that there was." I didn't know exactly where I was getting all this, but the idea was making more sense as it came together. "Which would have drawn him here, where he'd throw all kinds of dark and heavy sorcery around and draw all eyes to the one enclave that might *effectively* stand in the way." I didn't doubt that the Fohorimans would try, but from what I'd seen, the followers of Tigharn were not only a *lot* more wholesome, but they could put the Fohorimans to shame when they really put their minds to it.

Or maybe when Tigharn did. He seemed to be that kind of higher power. Maybe THE higher power. I was still figuring that out.

"You think that perhaps this war is a diversion, intended to keep anyone who might oppose Vaelor's release in the south, while Ekersakar and his minions go north?" Mathghaman was catching up fast.

"I think it's worth a thought." I didn't have any answers to the other questions that followed, namely where they were going, exactly, or how we could find them in the vast wilderness of mountains, forests, snow, and ice in the north, not to mention how to get past all the spooks and monsters up there.

The throne room fell silent, as Gunny, Mathghaman, and even the king thought it over. Unfortunately, that only meant we could hear the sounds of battle down below even more clearly.

An explosion drew everyone's attention. Gunny glanced at the king, then moved quickly to the northern window, peering out at the walls below.

It hadn't been an explosion. A hole had been smashed through the gate in the second wall, and lightning still flickered around the splinters, though it was weirdly green or purple, depending on the moment. The spectral figure that had punched through the doors still lingered, outlined in the same greenish, purplish corposant. The most I could see of it was its eyes, glowing purple dots full of hate.

Don't ask me how I could see the hatred in a pair of floating lights. I just could.

Brother Saukko tapped me on the shoulder with his staff, nudging me aside, and then he stood at the window and began to chant. I couldn't understand it, but the soaring melody was the diametric opposite of the sinister droning that was the enemy's sorcery.

The thing made of flickering, electric fire seemed to wince, then it was gone. But the damage had been done.

The Fohorimans' minions and mercenaries poured into the gap, even as the Menninkai put up a ferocious defense. What looked like almost two hundred men had been waiting in reserve behind the gate, and now they moved into the gap, locking shields before the enemy could get very far. In moments, it was pandemonium, as the Dovos, the Lasknut, and some of the corsairs tried to force the breach, while the Menninkai hewed and hacked at them, selling themselves dearly while the rest of the defenders came down off the wall and fell back toward the third line of defense.

"We should get to the third wall." Gunny knew as well as I did that there was only so much we could do, but all the same, our thumpers and machineguns could still put a hell of a dent in the enemy. Maybe enough to make them rethink the wisdom of trying to keep pushing.

The look on King Karhu's face was bordering on despair. He simply nodded as he turned back toward the window and the raging battle down below.

We headed out to see what little we could do to help the Menninkai hold the line.

CHAPTER 24

BY the time we reached the third wall, though, things had settled out, and we really didn't have much to do.

The Menninkai had fallen back to the third wall in good order, while the shield wall in the breach held their ground, aided by arrows and sling stones from above until the very last moment. The enemy had seemed a little nonplused when whatever had smashed through the gate had been unceremoniously banished with hardly a fight, and they'd been more cautious than they might have been otherwise. They had pursued as the Menninkai had fallen back, but the stocky warriors' formation had been tight and disciplined, and the combined forces of the Lasknut and Dovos hadn't been able to break them before they'd fallen back far enough for the defenders on the third wall to start raining arrows and sling stones over their heads and into the enemy.

I got to the battlements above the gate just as the heavy timber doors shut with a *boom*, the massive bars sliding into their sockets in the stone. The Lasknut's horns were calling the retreat, and they were falling back, their shields raised to fend off the arrows and stones that pelted them as they retreated to the second wall, using some of the houses and buildings of the outer districts as cover. Defending the third wall was going to be trickier than the second, because those buildings gave the enemy more cover while they advanced. There was no open killing ground like that between the first and second walls.

Santos laid his Mk 48 on the battlement next to me, and for a moment, he was sighted in, his finger on the trigger. But he let off, straightening up. "Dammit. Why waste the ammo?"

I came off my own rifle. There was something to be said about whittling down the opposition when we had the chance, but all the same, it was entirely likely that we'd need every bullet when they made another big push. After all, we'd already used one entire fighting load, and despite the supplies we'd gotten from the *Coira Ansec*, the ordnance we'd brought with us was still limited.

The Fohorimans' servants fell back to the second wall or some of the houses and stables just inside, places we'd used for shelter not long before. More of the army was moving across the no-man's land outside the first wall, filling in behind the vanguard.

Two walls down. Three to go.

For over an hour, we waited with the Menninkai archers and slingers, watching the enemy's movements. They weren't idle. We could see them moving around the buildings and the battlements of the second wall, but while many of them exposed themselves enough for a rifle shot, we still held our fire. They were hardening their position, strengthening their hold on the second wall, but they weren't moving to assault the third again anytime soon, from the looks of things.

Finally, Gunny called it. Fifty percent security. Half up on the wall, half below, to decompress, eat, sleep, and maintain weapons. We *could* stay on the wall until the next push, but you can get burned out, staying on watch indefinitely. It's why you don't leave a Recon Marine on glass in the OP for more than thirty, forty-five minutes.

Besides, we might be called out to handle a breach elsewhere on the line. The savages were filtering through the breached gate and spreading out through the district. With the first two walls in enemy hands, and a lot more cover for them to work with, we couldn't assume that they'd come at the north gate alone.

So, we settled in to wait, as the wind off the sea picked up and the clouds began to thicken overhead.

* * *

The storm broke with a roar. Lightning flashed over the city, followed almost immediately by thunderclaps that shook the walls, as rain and hail came down in sheets. The walls were abandoned for the shelter of the watchtowers and the buildings below. The defenders in the towers kept their eyes out, but it looked like the enemy was as deterred by the weather as our guys were.

Sleep was elusive that night. The storm didn't seem to want to move on. It raged for hour after hour, lashing the hill with rain until open streams ran in the streets. The thunder was sometimes almost continuous, and the lightning strobed overhead with an almost constant flicker.

When I peered out against the sheets of rain, I saw St. Elmo's fire dancing atop the roof of the hall. "There's something weird about this storm."

"What else is new?" Bailey retorted from across the room. "Everything about this place has been weird from

Day One." But he came up and joined me at the window, peering up at the corposant flickering around the great hall. "Huh. That *is* weird."

Another lightning bolt split the sky from south to north, and the thunder hammered at us with a resounding *boom* that echoed off the distant mountains. "I don't think I've ever seen a storm last this long. Even some of the big mountain thunderstorms that *felt* like they lasted forever."

"Me neither, now that you mention it." Bailey glanced at his watch, then grimaced. "I keep forgetting that the battery died three days ago."

I looked down at my own. "It's been going steadily for three hours, and it sure doesn't look like it's going to let up anytime soon."

Bailey turned away from the window. "You think it means something?"

"Maybe." I shrugged. "Can't say what, though. It does seem to have put a damper on the Fohorimans' offensive, so that's a good thing, at least in the short term."

"But if this Vaelor brewed it up…" Bailey blew a deep breath out past his nose. "Then we *all* might be screwed."

I didn't have an answer. And the tearing roll of thunder that followed the next titanic flash in the sky wasn't particularly comforting, either.

* * *

The sun wasn't yet up, and the storm was still raging un-abated when the messenger pounded on the door, waking me up. I wasn't all that disappointed to be awakened; the dreams had been hair-raising.

Baldinus cracked the door and let the bedraggled, soaked Menninkai kid inside, his red hair plastered to his skull, his cloak held tightly around himself. He looked around at us hesitantly. There were six Recon Marines and three Tuacha in the small inn, all in combat gear, armor, and helmets, the Marines with NVGs mounted but flipped up. We'd been in Vahava Paykhah for over a week, but it was a big city, and not everyone would have gotten a look at the strangers with their odd equipment and weapons that killed at a distance with a crack of thunder.

"I have a message for Mathghaman, or the one called 'Gunny,'" the kid said in halting but passable *Tenga Tuacha*.

Mathghaman chose that moment to come in from the wall, his own cloak dark with rain, his hood pulled far over his face. He drew it back as he shut the door. "I am Mathghaman."

"The King requests your presence. And your companions'." The kid was clearly a little intimidated by the looks he was getting from hardened foreign killers, so he retreated behind formality. "Something has happened, and he must speak with you about it."

Mathghaman inclined his head in assent. "We shall join him shortly."

Gunny had just woken up, too, and was sitting up in his Ranger roll. "What's up?"

"I do not know. I assume this young man knows no more than I." When Mathghaman looked at the messenger, the kid nodded. "I suspect that King Karhu would not call us back to the hall so soon were it not of grave importance."

It was with something of a sense of resignation that I, at least, put my gear back on, slung my rifle, and then pulled my woolen Tuacha cloak over the lot of it. It seemed like we'd jumped into the middle of a no-win situation. Stuck within the siege and unable to honorably disengage, barring some emergency, while our quarry was free to move around and summon more demons and monsters, things didn't look good at that point.

They might look somewhat better than they had when we'd been dragged along with the Dovos, victims of Captain Sorenson's delusions, knowing that we were allies with monsters, with only the fact that the enemies we faced were even worse monsters as justification for it, but that was a pretty low bar to clear.

Our objective still seemed as far away as it ever had.

"Team leaders." Gunny looked around the room. "Where's Gurke?"

"Up top." Chambers was already heading for the door that led to the wall. "I'll get him."

The rest of us were waiting, armed and cloaked, when Gurke came down, his own cloak dark with the rain. The cloaks weren't that different from our old ponchos, though few Marines had worn ponchos instead of Gore-Tex pants and jackets for a while.

It was a harder slog than it should have been. We clutched our cloaks around ourselves as we leaned into the wind, rain, and hail, trudging up the hill toward the hall. We tried to keep close to the buildings, so as to avoid being the tallest thing around when the lightning crashed out of the sky, which it did often. It was a good thing it was raining so hard, too, because just on the way up to the great hall, I saw at least three watchtowers and two of the taller, wealthier houses in the city struck by lightning. If not for all the water pouring down out of the sky, half the city could have been set ablaze. Unfortunately, it also made the climb that much more arduous, as the flagstones were slick with the rain.

When we reached the hall, dripping on the stone floor, Brother Saukko was standing next to the throne, accompanied by a much younger man, his reddish hair an untamed mane around his head and his beard little more than peach fuzz, dressed in the same gray robe, belted at the waist with a simple rope.

The younger man looked nervous. Brother Saukko looked as composed as ever. King Karhu leaned back in his throne, seemingly in somewhat less pain, but his expression was clouded and downcast. When he looked up as Mathghaman strode toward the throne, he quickly looked down again.

My eyes narrowed as I took in the situation. I wasn't sure this was a good sign.

Brother Saukko leaned on his staff and turned to face us as we halted a few paces from the throne. "Brother Toiva has had a dream," he announced.

Bailey, Gurke, and I all glanced at each other, slight frowns on our faces. We all had dreams. I'd just been awakened from some fairly unpleasant ones only about an hour before. But Brother Saukko had said that as if it had some real significance.

The old man's eyes crinkled at the looks on our faces. "Brother Toiva's dreams are not like other men's. They are often prophetic." He turned to the nervous-looking younger man. "This would seem to have been one of them." He nodded encouragingly to the young man.

With a glance at the king, which was answered by a similar nod, Brother Toiva stepped forward. He began to speak, his eyes cast down at the floor, though it was in the Menninkai's language, so Brother Saukko had to translate.

"I dreamed that I stood on the walls, looking out over a sea of foes. Something drew my eyes up, toward the north, and I looked over the mountains to see the Teeth of Winter. A terrible darkness blanketed the far north, deeper and blacker than a clouded night.

"A wind took me up from the walls, and I saw all the Land of Ice and Monsters spread out below me. I saw the Hold of Grichencos, the Citadel of Taramas, the Spire of Octrallach, even so far as the Fortress of Uergal. All were wrapped in shadow, but none so dark as the night gathering in the far north.

"There was a smaller darkness, moving through the mountains, toward the ice. Toward the black shadow in the north. Yet when I looked down, I saw a light. Only a glimmer, clouded and hard to see, but a light. Here, in Vahava Paykhah.

"Then a voice said to me, 'Their quest, and the Menninkai's hope, are one and the same.'"

Silence fell after that. Mathghaman looked thoughtful, studying the nervous young Brother, who was still staring at the floor. Gunny's eyes were narrowed as he considered what we'd heard.

"What do you think that means?" Bailey asked quietly.

"I think, Sean, that it means Conor was right. Our quarry has used this siege to divert the Fohorimans' attention while they move north, toward Vaelor's Throne. And that only by pursuing them might we save the Menninkai." Mathghaman's voice was almost as quiet, though he was watching King Karhu as he spoke. "Remember, Octrallach said that he, Taramas, Uergal, and Grichencos only came here once they had heard that the 'thunder warriors' were here, and they feared that such men were working with the disciples of Vaelor. They did not think that so many of you escaped with us, or if they did, they considered us a lesser threat. They were worried about the quest to reawaken and free the old wickedness in the north."

King Karhu was listening, his eyes hooded, but so far had declined to comment. I thought I saw why he looked so conflicted. If we acted on the prophecy, he lost some of the biggest force multipliers he'd probably ever seen in his life—the Tuacha were legends in their own right, and our weapons were capable of killing the enemy in job lots before they could even get within bowshot.

"If we go north, into the mountains, and let the enemy see us do it, then it is conceivable that the Fohorimans will draw off much of their forces from Vahava Paykhah to pursue us." He looked back at the rest of us. "We will be alone, surrounded by naught but enemies, going from darkness into deeper darkness, but if we wish to find your friends, then there are few other options I can see."

"Especially if they're still in league with Dragon Mask," Gunny said grimly. The implication there wasn't pleasant, but by then I thought we were all expecting things to get dark if any of them were still alive.

"If the king is willing to let us go, then I think I can safely say that we're all in," Gunny said. "There's still the problem of how we find them. If they're as far ahead of us as Brother Toiva's dream suggested, then that's a lot of country to go through. And I doubt that they've been considerate enough to leave a trail behind them the way that vampire did."

Definitely not if they used Zeiczak as a diversion to draw the Fohorimans down here. I was letting Gunny do the talking, but the wheels were turning.

Gunny was right. We'd seen just how much wilderness was up here, and there was a lot of country to get lost in. Without some idea of where they were going, we'd have a hell of a time finding them, even *without* pursuit. We'd known that going in. We'd had plans for zone reconnaissance that we'd started putting together even before we'd gone into the Land of Shadows and Crows. But those had presumed that we'd be able to get in, get established with the Menninkai, and covertly move out, covering the ground we needed to and hopefully getting eyes on or getting some clue as to their whereabouts *before* being detected.

This was going to be different. We'd been chased by the Fohorimans and their servants before, and it had been no picnic.

King Karhu interrupted my train of thought with a deep sigh. "As much as it pains me, both to lose your strength and skill in the defense of Vahava Paykhah, and to see you go into such danger, I can see no other way, except to cling to our position here and fight until the end. That would be doing no justice to you, who hold no fealty to the Menninkai, yet have stood by us to beat back attack after attack." He snatched up the horn cup by his side and took a gulp, almost as if he was looking for a bit of liquid courage to say what came next. Or maybe he just needed something to dull the pain of his wounds, which still were far from healed.

"We will give you horses, that you might stay well ahead of the bulk of the enemy's forces. Few of them are mounted, and while the mountains are wild and steep, there are no finer mountain horses in the world than ours." He looked over at Brother Saukko. "Would that I could go with you." That part was barely audible, but it still got a sharp look from the woman who stood at the edge of the dais, who had been tending him whenever we'd come up there. He cleared his throat. "As for where you are going, I believe that the Brothers might be able to aid you. Their monastery holds records dating back even before the fall of the Old Ones. If the knowledge of where they might have gone exists outside of the Fohorimans' grim archives, it will be there."

Mathghaman bowed ever so slightly to the king. "We would be in your debt, King Karhu." He turned to Gunny. "Come. Let us prepare. I fear we have little time." Thunder rocked the hall again as the wind howled around the peaks of the roof. "A shadow of a threat weighs upon my mind. I fear our adversaries may be farther north, and closer to their goal, than we think."

His words seemed to hang in the air as we hustled out of the hall to pack and plan.

CHAPTER 25

LANDING on the beach with horses was considerably more difficult and time consuming than landing on foot. Nachdainn had to bring the ship all the way up on the strand and put out a long, ungainly gangplank for us to lead the horses down.

The horses had handled the choppy seas better than I'd expected. I had some experience with horses, back in The World, but it had been a long time. I was glad that the Menninkai's animals actually looked like *horses*, not the weird, overly shaggy, vaguely leonine mutants the Fohorimans and their servants rode. It was also apparent that the Menninkai took their horses to sea fairly regularly. They got nervous when the ship heaved and bucked on the swell—fortunately the storm had finally subsided, or we'd never have gotten away from the harbor—but they never panicked and tried to kick their way out of the pen just aft of the mast, never mind throw themselves overboard.

Footing on the gangplank wasn't great, but the animals were almost more surefooted than any of us, except maybe the Tuacha. Cairbre had led his down first, more quickly than any of the rest of us, and was standing near the trees, holding his horse's reins, looking back at us with a combination of impatience and what might have been thinly veiled contempt as we descended much more gingerly than he had.

My horse was big for the Menninkai mounts, his coat a dappled white and gray, almost an Appaloosa. That name had no meaning here, but the silvery animal and I had bonded quickly down in the stables. I'd known enough to approach him carefully, gently, offering a treat, a root vegetable similar enough to a carrot, and speaking softly until he got used to me.

To several people's surprise, Baldinus had turned out to be the natural rider among us. He wasn't even a country boy, but he took to horses with an enthusiasm that almost screamed, "Why am I only discovering how awesome this is now?"

Few of us had a lot of experience riding, though we'd been working on remedying that shortcoming on the Isle of Riamog. With the possible exception of Baldinus, none of us could be considered what you might call expert riders, not yet, but we were good enough that we got all the mounts down to the rocky beach and ready to move without any mishaps.

We had twice as many horses as men, which was going to make the movement more difficult in some ways. With the distance we figured we had to cover, and the difficulty of the terrain, fresh mounts were going to be absolutely vital.

They'd be only so fresh, since they still had to carry gear, ammo, and feed. But that was still better than carrying a two-hundred-pound man with nearly fifty pounds more of armor, gear, and weapons.

I scanned the trees above our landing site as the ship began to back water, Nachdainn and two others using long poles to help the oars as they pushed off the beach. We hadn't landed in the same spot where we had gone ashore on the raid that had netted us Octrallach—who was still locked up on the island in the bay, watched over by a cohort of Menninkai warriors and two of the senior brothers—since that would be far too dangerous if the enemy had tracked us back there, not to mention that the information we'd found in the Brotherhood's library had led us to believe that a somewhat more northeasterly route would work better.

That information was summed up in a carefully packaged roll of handwritten parchment in Mathghaman's pack, notes taken from an ancient, crumbling tome called the Book of Audur Cohm. None of the Menninkai scholars seemed to know the meaning of the name. It wasn't Menninkai, it wasn't Tuacha, and it wasn't corsair. But whoever Audur Cohm had been—presuming that was the name of the author—he or she had chronicled much of the fall of Vaelor. Translation was apparently difficult. It had been written in an archaic language that was still somewhat preserved among the Menninkai scholars, though the list of other languages they could read was shrinking with each generation.

Unfortunately, the notes didn't amount to a ten-digit grid coordinate and detailed imagery that would allow us to plan a precise route. Those days were long behind us. Crude, hand-drawn maps and questionable translations of vague tales from a time of upheaval, heavy on the horror and light on the details, made up the whole of our intel. Well, aside from Brother Toiva's prophetic dream, that is.

If that seems thin, just consider where we are, and how people waged war for thousands of years before GPS, satellite imagery, radios, artillery, radar, helicopters, and anything else that runs on batteries or internal combustion engines. We had certain advantages, given our weapons and optics, but we didn't make the rules here. We had to adapt or die.

Considering what I'd seen of warfare *with* all the high-tech toys, I'd been less than convinced that they were the end-all, be-all in the first place. It's hard to fight goat herders, and lose, for decades, without doubting some of the promises of all-powerful technology.

That said, finding a small force of sorcerers, possibly backed up by our own shooters, *somewhere* in that vast wilderness to the north, based on ancient tales that read like myth and maps that were more illustrations than accurate maps, was a daunting prospect, to say the least.

Still, we had accurate enough maps for the Menninkai lands, thanks to King Karhu. They'd at least get us to the mountains, hopefully with just enough knowledge of the ins and outs of the terrain to keep us at least one step ahead of the Fohorimans.

That was kind of vital, given what we were about to do.

I swung into the saddle and patted Myrsky, my horse, on the neck. He tossed his head a little, as if he was impatient to get going. My backup mount, Kovaves, seemed a little more reluctant, but he followed as I tugged on the lead rope.

In a long, serpentine file, we rode into the trees.

* * *

Part of the reason we'd landed where we had was the stretch of thick pine woods that divided the Upper from the Lower Menninkai. There were mutterings about past feuds between families in the two regions, but most of those seemed to be put aside when the Lasknut came south and east. At least, they were supposed to be. The fact that the Upper Menninkai still hadn't showed, even after the Lasknut and their savage allies had gone nuts, raised some questions.

Those questions weren't our concern at the moment, though. The trees provided good concealment on the move, and the hill named Kontomaak, with its circle of ancient standing stones, carved with what might once have been stylized bear's heads, was the perfect landmark for our ORP. We rode warily, though in part that was necessitated by the thickness of the woods. No one in their right mind, who wanted to keep their eyes, was going to try galloping through those woods.

I wondered why the Menninkai, who seemed pretty settled, hadn't thinned the woods, harvesting the trees for firewood and building materials. Most of their houses seemed to be largely timber-built.

A flicker of movement in the trees drew my eye as I mused on the question. Turning toward it, I saw nothing, though I could have sworn for a second that I'd seen eyes watching me from beneath one of the pines.

Maybe that was why the Menninkai steered clear, except for the few cleared paths that connected Upper and Lower.

We reached Kontomaak about sundown. Since none of us, not even Cairbre, wanted to get into a fight with the Fohorimans in the dark, we tied the horses to trees, set security in a tight perimeter at the base of the hill, and settled in for the night.

I glanced up at the hill, the standing stones stark black against the fading gray of the sky. "Why not put an OP up there? We should be able to see a lot farther."

Fennean looked up at the hill. "The hill is a sacred place to the Menninkai. Not like a monastery or a temple, but it was there that the first stand was taken against the followers of Vaelor, back in the dark times, before the rise of the Warlock Kings. When the Lasknut broke away and swore fealty to Grichencos, it was on Kontomaak that the Upper and the Lower Menninkai put aside their differences and swore before Tigharn to stand together against the darkness, even though the blood between them, after the taking of Mijelikki and the murder of Paivoha, remained unavenged." He shook his head. "Even if no one in the flesh would ever know, it is not a good place to set a lookout. As a landmark, yes, we can use it. To try to fortify it would not be right."

I nodded slowly. Sometimes it was a little odd, coming from the world that we did, to consider things beyond the immediately practical. We'd been raised in an environment where no one was expected to take such things seriously, at least not once they got in the way. That didn't just extend to largely secular Westerners, either. I'd seen too many jihadis use mosques as munitions dumps, FOBs, and sniper nests.

Here, though, things were different. The mystical had every bit the force that the physical did, and if you forgot it, the consequences were far more immediate. I didn't doubt, after a few of the things that I'd seen back in The World, that there had been consequences there, too. They were just subtler and often had to wait until after you were dead.

"We are not alone in this forest, either." Fennean lowered his voice. "Perhaps you have seen them, the eyes beneath the trees."

I nodded. So, I hadn't been imagining things.

"We need not fear them. They are not like the things in the wilds of the Fohorimans' territory. They would not have settled among the Menninkai if they were. They are elusive, and dangerous if cornered, but they bear us no ill will, so long as they remain unmolested."

"Who are they?" I looked around, though I couldn't see any eyes in the dark at that point.

"They are the Otetzi. None know from whence they came. They were in these woods when the Menninkai came to the shore, driven here by the tides of evil that swept across the land. They clashed at first, as all such disparate peoples will, but in time the Menninkai saw that the Otetzi simply wished to be let alone, and faced by a far greater threat from the Fohorimans, who served Vaelor then, they became the Otetzi's protectors." Fennean leaned back against his saddle. "That is why we lit no fire. The Otetzi will not molest us, and they will warn us if the enemy approaches."

I looked around, flipping my NVGs down for a moment, but there was no sign of the watching eyes or any movement aside from the horses grazing beneath the boughs. Whoever the Otetzi were, they were good at hiding. Good enough to make a Recon Marine jealous.

I wasn't used to trusting locals, particularly not locals we'd had zero interaction with. I was equally unused to treating the field as a secure area. But Fennean seemed unconcerned, and so did the other Tuacha, all of whom probably knew about these Otetzi.

So, I prayed briefly and silently, looking up at the single star I could see through a gap in the clouds overhead, that we'd all still be there, with all our parts and pieces attached, when the sun came up. Then I closed my eyes and tried to get some sleep before it was my turn on watch.

CHAPTER 26

LEAVING the horses at the foot of Kontomaak, we slipped through the woods toward the hill of Lohikarmahamas. A great spire of bare rock, it thrust skyward out of a small circle of woods atop a swelling rise in the ground, surrounded by open fields, separated by lines of trees or strips of actual forest, small stone and timber houses stationed at the corners, the barns half-buried in the turf to insulate them against the winter.

The fields were fallow, still unplanted, as the surviving farmers were all huddled within the walls of Vahava Paykhah, trying to hold off the Fohorimans' army. The damage done by the siege had yet to be fully felt. It was going to be a rough winter in these northlands, if the Menninkai survived.

I leaned into the slope as we moved up toward the tower of stone, the weight of the .50 on my back dragging me down. It wouldn't have been *that* bad, except that I had it strapped to my assault pack, which ordinarily clipped to the top of my ruck, and still had my M110 in my hands, with a full combat load in my chest rig in addition to the M107 and its ammo on my back.

Santos wouldn't have been sympathetic if I'd complained, given that he'd been carrying that Mk 48 with a minimum of five hundred rounds of 7.62 since we'd rearmed on the Isle of Riamog. So, I didn't complain. Not out loud, anyway.

I looked back over my shoulder. We'd covered some serious territory since stepping off just before first light. Something about traveling in daylight still bugged me, but we'd all seen enough to know that we *really* didn't own the night here.

Exactly who was going to come on this mission hadn't been decided until we were all ready to step off. There had been some stiff competition for it. Bailey had suggested fighting a duel—"only to first blood"—while Gurke had suggested South Park style Rochambeau. He would, of course, go first.

Gunny had interrupted before I'd managed to stick my oar in, which was a good thing, since it meant I got the mission because I hadn't made a jackass of myself.

Given another thirty seconds, and Gunny might have taken a few of the Tuacha and done it himself, because I probably would have.

Instead, I was sweating even in the damp spring chill as I labored up toward the mountainous upthrust of rock with a .50 cal, hoping to make a target of myself. Just a hard one to catch.

What the hell am I doing this for? The Menninkai could *probably* hold longer. They had fortifications and a lot more numbers than we did. We were about to poke the bear and run, while we had a pressing mission of our own.

Yet I'd seen the devastation the enemy had wrought on those defenses in an awfully short time. I'd seen the Fohorimans get through the second wall in a matter of days. They might be somewhat slowed, but they'd make it through to the great hall in a week at the rate they were going. They might not have rockets, missiles, high explosives, and machineguns, but they had their own unfair advantages.

I understood Brother Toiva's dream. *Their quest and the Menninkai's hope are one and the same.* The Fohorimans weren't there for the Menninkai, not really. I was sure they really didn't give a damn; they were like any other tyrant or terrorist back in the world, perfectly willing to crush people who stood up to them, whether they were their primary adversaries or not. It wouldn't matter to the Fohorimans if the Menninkai just wanted to be left alone.

But they wanted us. Again, it didn't matter that we had nothing to do with Dragon Mask anymore. To them, the "thunder warriors" were a threat that absolutely *had* to be stamped out, fast.

So, we'd let them know that the "thunder warriors" were now in their rear area.

It got steep once we got into the trees, and the going got harder. When we reached the base of the rock itself, it got even sketchier, and soon I had to sling my M110 at my side and climb, one handhold and foothold at a time, toward a narrow shelf on the side of the massif.

I really wasn't looking forward to getting back down that slope, not as fast as we'd probably have to, but that was why we'd brought the .50. We needed the standoff it could afford us.

The shelf was narrower and shorter than it had looked from below. I couldn't get all the way prone, but had sort of wedged myself into the crack in the mountainside. I could just see over the trees, and for a moment, I was afraid that we'd picked the wrong spot when we'd been scanning the hill from back at the abandoned and ransacked farmhouse about a quarter mile behind us. If I didn't have a shot from here…

No. There was Vahava Paykhah, the outer walls about two and a half miles away, a looming, hazy mountain, wreathed in smoke as the fighting went on. And there was the enemy camp, spread out around the walls, smoke rising from their campfires to add to the haze that hung over the city.

My window on the siegeworks wasn't particularly wide, but I had enough. Truth be told, I didn't *have* to kill any of them. I just had to get their attention.

I figured schwacking a Fohoriman warlord would get their attention best, though. A Warlock King would be one hell of a feather in my cap, but right then we didn't know if even a direct hit with a Raufoss round would do it.

Besides, this was going to be one hell of a long shot. Almost a mile and a half. Even with a .50, precision at that range was iffy, at best.

I flipped out the bipods, laid the rifle down, and settled in behind it as best I could. Santos, Rodeffer, and Farrar had stayed below, in the trees, providing security, while Fennean had climbed the rock with me. His eyes were the best of any of the Tuacha, and as weird as it seemed, given that they looked as normal as yours or mine, was that he could see with his naked eyes about as well as I could looking through a spotting scope.

Naturally, he'd be my spotter.

I'd gone over the ballistics of it with him, letting him peer through the scope and get to understand the reticle.

True to form, he soaked it up as if he had been doing long range shooting for decades. I didn't doubt that his corrections would be in milliradians, and as accurate as any I could have managed with a high-powered spotting scope with a full mil-grid reticle.

Flipping up the scope covers, I got my cheek weld and started to search the line of tents, pavilions, animals, and wagons. I wanted a good target. I wanted to make this count.

I halted my scan, then backtracked a little bit. The tall, barrel-chested Fohoriman, his face hidden behind a carved animal skull, one hand gray-skinned and roughly human, the other a massive, bone-white claw, was gesturing at an obviously frightened band of savages who were trying to get what looked like a giant crossbow set up. A scorpion, I think those were called, back in the day. It was a long way from the outer wall, and I didn't know what it was going to do at that distance, but since a Fohoriman was involved, I figured it was a fair bet that some nasty bit of sorcery was probably involved.

I put the reticle on the Fohoriman. "Target. Big guy with a skull helmet and one hand turned into a claw."

"I have him." Fennean squinted, judging things. I'd explained the length of a meter to him, and how important that range estimation was to making the shot. He hadn't needed the latter; he'd been an accomplished archer before he'd ever picked up a rifle, and he understood the forces of gravity, drag, and wind.

His eyeball estimation was probably going to be a lot more accurate than mine. Laser rangefinder accurate.

"One thousand, nine hundred seventy-five meters." He paused, then nodded. "Yes."

"Wind?" I was already cranking the elevation turret to the setting I had written down on my little range card on the inside of the ocular lens cap.

"Four to five miles per hour, right to left."

It said something that not only were his estimates so scary accurate, but he'd deliberately learned the English terms to make sure he was communicating the data to me without needing the mind speech.

While I'd dial the elevation to just shy of two thousand meters, I'd hold for wind. Wind shifts too fast to dial it. It wasn't that much of a hold; four to five miles an hour would hardly faze a six-hundred-seventy-one-grain chunk of metal and high explosive traveling at supersonic speeds.

Finding the right tick mark on the main crosshair, I set it right about mid-chest on the Fohoriman, settled myself behind the gun, shut my eyes, and breathed out, forcing myself to relax. When I opened my eye again, I was ever so slightly off. I shifted my hips, almost bumping into Fennean, who didn't react, then repeated the little ritual. At that range, natural point of aim matters. A lot.

This time, it was right on target. Claw was standing there, his one human-ish hand on his hip, watching the scorpion setup. He wasn't moving. The wind was barely a breath. I slipped my finger inside the trigger guard, flipping the selector to "fire," and let out my breath as I took up the slack on the trigger.

It broke just as my lungs emptied. The round slammed out of the suppressor with an echoing *crack*, and the recoil hammered me backward almost an inch, despite my fairly good shooting position. My jaw ached at that heavy bolt blasting back against the recoil springs right next to my head.

I'd had to practice a mag-dump with an M107 once. I never wanted to do that again. I thought I'd given myself a concussion.

It took a couple of seconds for the round to reach the target. Fennean called it before it even impacted. "Good shot."

The big bullet smacked into the Fohoriman's torso, just to one side of the spine and below the shoulder. The Raufoss round had a small explosive charge just behind the tip, wrapped around the tungsten carbide penetrator, and that charge went off with a flash and an ugly puff of gray smoke as it blew a hole right through the Fohoriman's armor and into his chest cavity.

I'd seen those big bastards stand up to close-range 7.62 fire, only going down when shot through the mouth or the eye. But a .50 is a whole different animal.

The distance to the target meant I was able to reacquire my sight picture just before the bullet hit. I saw the flash and the puff of smoke, saw him stagger and go down to one knee, black blood gushing from the massive hole in his torso. He struggled to stay upright, but I'd done too much damage. He fell on his face.

The savages stared in shock as I shifted my aim and fired again. That one was a little low, I saw as I got back on target. It tore the first savage's guts out and sprayed them across the scorpion, and he fell in pretty close to two separate pieces.

My next shot missed the second man, who was running for his life, presumably screaming bloody murder, but it hit one of the scorpion's arms and shattered it.

Splinters flew as it tumbled through the air. That engine wasn't going to be useful ever again.

I came off the scope, scrambling up to my knees and snapping the scope caps shut. It took a few precious seconds to fold the bipods and get the rifle affixed to my pack, then shoulder into it, all while Fennean stayed on his own rifle, watching the distant encampment. I'd barely gotten ready to move when the Fohoriman's horns began to sound in the distance.

Together, we started to scramble down the rock toward the trees. The horns sounded again, strident and demanding. They were coming.

Right then, our only hope was that they would need time to call enough of their forces back from the city and get them organized. We would use every bit of that time to make tracks. Unless they had a react force waiting for us to raid them again, which might mean we didn't have any time at all.

It was almost more of a controlled slide off the rock rather than a climb down. We linked up with Santos and the rest fast, and then we were moving out through the trees, making the best speed we could back toward the woods and Kontomaak, the horns and drums calling the pursuit behind us.

CHAPTER 27

THEY must have had a react force standing by. They were in full cry behind us when we reached the woods, where the rest of the platoon was waiting, all of them mounted except for Mathghaman, Gunny, Bailey, and Chambers, who were holding our horses.

It still took a few moments to get my pack and the M107 off my back and secured behind my saddle. I worked as fast as I could. We still had a lead on the enemy, but it was closing fast, especially since we'd gotten glimpses of the Fohorimans themselves, atop those shaggy, barrel-chested, mutant horse creatures they rode, coming out of the trees in the distance behind us as we'd hustled back toward the Otetzi's woods.

Swinging into the saddle, I nodded to Gunny, and we headed out.

Mathghaman led the way, since he had a bit better idea of where we were heading than any of the rest of us, given his time up in this territory. It seemed that he, and some of the other Tuacha, had been taking the fight to the Fohorimans off and on for a long time.

Before he set off, he looked over his shoulder, his eyes grave. "Keep your heads down. We must move quickly and stay within the woods." Without another word, he bent over his horse's neck and kicked the beast's flanks, taking off through the trees at a pace I would have probably considered reckless—given my own lack of skill in the saddle—were it not for the enemy forces hot on our trail.

The next hour was a blur of lashing branches and pounding hooves as we clung to our horses' backs and tried not to fall off or get knocked off by the grasping boughs, trying to just keep the man and his mount ahead within sight. Mathghaman wove through the woods with a skill that suggested he knew exactly where he was going and what path to take. He might, if he'd spent enough time in these woods, but I suspected that he was relying instead on his quick perceptions, reflexes, and sense of direction.

We were moving uphill, though the slope was fairly gentle to start with. Several times we skirted bigger hills, Mathghaman almost always darting around the far side before turning back toward the line of march we'd been following since the beginning.

I thought a couple of times I might have gotten glimpses of the Otetzi, though it was hard to say. If I did, it was only because of momentary movement, and I never saw enough to be sure. Maybe a part of a green-dyed arm, or an eye under the branches. Those guys were masters of camouflage, there was no doubt about that.

I wondered, briefly, as I ducked beneath a low-hanging branch that probably would have left me flat on my back behind my horse with one hell of a concussion if I'd hit it, whether they'd fight the Fohorimans or just fade into the woods. Part of me hoped the former; it would slow our pursuers down and give us a chance to open that time-distance gap farther.

But a part of me hoped that they just faded. I knew what the Fohorimans would do to them, just for standing their ground. I didn't wish that on the stealthy forest people who had watched but never messed with us.

I'd seen that movie. Watched it play out in real time in too many villages in Syria.

We reached a clearing and thundered across it at close to a gallop. We had to pace the animals, or we'd kill them before we even got to the really rough country. But we couldn't take it too slow, or the enemy would catch up.

I glanced over my shoulder as we rode. The tall pines and firs rose like walls around the meadow, and we were still too low to see very far. I could hear the enemy behind us, though they had started to sound fainter, as if we were opening our lead, but I couldn't see enough to be sure.

Then we plunged back into the shadows beneath the trees and kept going.

* * *

The day stretched on as we passed through the ever-darkening woods, the slope getting steeper as we went higher. The mountains were still a good distance away, but we hoped to get there within the week. Sooner, if we kept our pace up.

Which we'd have to, with Fohorimans in pursuit. We could have outlasted the Dovos or the Lasknut, but the Fohorimans weren't entirely human anymore. They'd keep going, night or day, until they caught us.

If the plan worked, and the Warlock Kings pulled the bulk of their army to pursue us, lest we awaken Vaelor—as if that would happen, given our experiences—then we could put some serious distance between us and them. But we could be screwed if the react force caught us before then.

Night began to fall, and we paused in another meadow, overshadowed by a line of hills running down from the mountains above, just long enough for Eoghain, one of the oldest of Mathghaman's companions, to pass around a flask. "Only a sip," he cautioned. "It will sustain you for some time, but we must make it last."

I took a sip as it came around to me. It tasted cool and refreshing, but at the same time, a warm glow seemed to rush through my limbs, washing away the soreness and weariness from the last day's running, climbing, and riding. It felt like the way certain fanatics I'd known described coffee.

Then we flipped our NVGs down, switched mounts, and kept riding.

* * *

Night slowed us down, but not by enough to matter. The horses had the hardest part of it; we didn't have NVGs for them. We *had* to slow our pace to keep them from stumbling or plowing into trees or rocks.

From the noises behind us, it didn't sound like the Fohorimans were slowing down much.

Still, we had enough of a lead that they didn't catch us before morning, when we swapped mounts again, took another sip of the strange but vitalizing drink from Eoghain's flask, and kept going. The temperature had steadily dropped during the night, and while we were warm enough from the exertion of riding, as well as the closeness of the horses, which were putting in a lot of work, and therefore generating a lot of heat, there was frost on the ground in the nearby meadow.

It might be spring, but with the Teeth of Winter up there in the north, I suspected that even summer in the Land of Ice and Monsters never got all that hot.

The farms were getting more isolated and farther apart. We were still in the Otetzi's woods, following that band of thick forest toward the mountains that were getting closer and closer as we continued to push north and west. But every once in a while, the terrain pushed us closer to the edge of that band of thick firs, spruces, and pines, and we looked out over fallow fields toward small, stout houses built like fortresses.

They probably *were* fortresses. The locals would have little other option, this far from Vahava Paykhah. And from the looks of things, some of the Menninkai who lived this far out hadn't retreated to the city, either. We didn't see people, or livestock, but occasionally we could see, or smell, woodsmoke from the thick-walled, turf-roofed houses. The locals might not have fled to the city, but they were still keeping their heads down and holding out in case raiders—or worse—came for them.

About halfway through the second day, Mathghaman drew rein at the base of a rocky hill, dotted with wind-twisted pines, and looked back at the rolling hills that we'd ridden through over the last two days. We'd probably covered fifty miles already, at the pace we'd set and given the lack of stops.

I could see the thought in his eyes as he looked us over. Despite the efficacy of Eoghain's draught, my eyes felt gritty and the deep weariness of over two days without sleep was starting to weigh me down. The drink could sustain us for a long time, that and handfuls of the Menninkai's travel rations, firm but tasty bread and a sort of pemmican, but there's no substitute for sleep.

Sure, we'd all trained and operated on short sleep for years. Everyone had stories about hallucinations due to sleep deprivation during Patrol Phase of BRC. But it takes its toll, and one of the old B-52 tips, put together by Recon Teams in Vietnam and Laos, was that fatigue eventually makes even the hardest studs sloppy.

Yet, as I followed Mathghaman's gaze, I saw the first glimpse of the pursuing Fohorimans since we'd broken contact two days before. They were still coming on fast, and they weren't nearly as far behind us as I might have hoped. Right then, they were riding across a clearing we'd gone around only a couple hours before.

"We must halt." Mathghaman took in our weariness, then looked up at the rocks above us. "They will not stop, will not slow, until they have caught us. I say we let them catch us, but on our terms."

Gunny grinned that wolfish grin of his. "Well, that *is* what we brought claymores for."

* * *

Good ambush sites are rarely comfortable. There are a couple reasons for that. For one, you don't want to set up anywhere a normal person would want to go for a stroll. Furthermore, if you get comfortable in an ambush site, then *someone* will fall asleep. It's as inevitable as death.

So, I found myself wedged between a boulder the size of a house and a gnarled juniper, braced with one foot on the ground and the other knee awkwardly crammed into the fork of the tree, the M107 set in another Y between branches. I had the green spider mesh that I'd brought from the *Makin Island* draped over weapon and optic, making sure to kill any glare that might give my position away to the Fohorimans as they came out of the trees, barely three hundred yards from the base of the hill.

I only had three and a half mags left for the big SASR, so I'd have to make every shot count. It was always going to be that way, as long as we were an ocean and miles of terrain away from the *Coira Ansec*. We were at the far end of a *long* supply line, which was why we also carried a variety of swords, axes, hammers, and knives.

The lead Fohorimans were in plain sight now, scanning the trees and the hills, so I had to stay perfectly still. Any extraneous movement might give the game away.

They came on in a rough line, still mounted. They weren't riding the strange mutant horses we'd seen before, but the bigger, nastier-looking beasts, with shaggy gray to white fur, long fangs, horns, and taloned paws. They looked like predators rather than beasts of burden, but we'd seen them carry Fohorimans—and Warlock Kings—just as fast as any horse could. Maybe faster. And they could do more damage than even the most vicious stallion, all by themselves.

One of the problems with setting a trap for Fohorimans is that they're not really human. Their senses aren't limited the same way ours are. They've got some spooky weirdness going on along with heightened senses of smell. I'd heard during conversations with the Tuacha that they'd sacrificed other things for these enhancements, but that didn't make them any less difficult to hide from.

To make matters worse, the Fohorimans were predators, arrogant beyond human ken. They didn't think of us as a threat, not on an individual basis. Which meant that we wouldn't be able to stampede them into a trap with firepower alone. Instead, we would have to bank on that arrogance, and hope they didn't sniff out the surprises we'd set in for them before it was too late.

The lead rider was short, squat, and had a face like a boar hog, complete with the tusks that curled up to almost touch his snout. His bristles sprang out of the neck of his mail coat, which extended to his knees and his wrists. He carried a long spear in one hand, his side covered by a tall, rectangular shield.

Behind him rode a full two dozen. Many of them still looked human, if gray-skinned and red-eyed, though each one had something off, something twisted about him. Most were masked, like those we'd seen in the north, crimson eyes glittering beneath blackened helmets, their faces shrouded with black cloth.

They came on fast, following our tracks. There'd been no way to really disguise them, at least not without running the risk of crippling the horses by taking them on the rocks—which weren't nearly common enough to have done the job, anyway—and right then, those tracks were serving our purpose anyway. In fact, a couple of Bailey's guys, along with Doc, had taken their horses back and forth to make sure the track couldn't be missed, while the rest of us had either held security or set up the ambush.

The horses were tied up on the far side of the rocky hill, where Bailey was probably spitting nails, having drawn the short straw to take rear security with the horses and the packs, while Gurke's team and mine ambushed our pursuers.

Now the Fohorimans came right toward us, following that track, until Boar's Head stopped suddenly, throwing up a hairy, clawed fist, his beady eyes scanning the ground carefully, his snout snuffling as he sniffed the wind. I shifted ever so slightly to put my reticle on his piggy head. Just in case.

The Fohoriman riders spread out, readying weapons. They knew *something* was up. We'd been careful to camouflage the claymore mines as thoroughly as possible, without them looking like green plastic boxes piled with grass. If they smelled something off, though…

Boar's Head scanned the trees, and his eyes met mine through my scope, camouflage and spider mesh notwithstanding.

If he'd had enough human features left, I thought he might have grinned. Instead, he grunted, kicked his mount in the flanks, and turned toward my hiding place, urging the big beast into a run as the rest shifted their formation into a wedge and began to accelerate into a charge.

They moved fast enough that they were almost right on top of the claymores when they went off.

For a moment, the entire front half of the wedge disappeared in a black and gray cloud, and the ground shook with the concussion as twelve M18 Claymore mines, totaling eighteen pounds of C4, went off almost simultaneously, spewing eight thousand four hundred steel balls at the Fohorimans at three thousand nine hundred ninety-five feet per second.

At point blank range.

Fohorimans and their mounts are tough, but not that tough. They went down like bowling pins, their mounts blasted off their paws by the concussion, the flying ball bearings punching through thick hide, armor, and hardened flesh, spraying black blood across the still frost-whitened grass of the clearing. Those that were shielded from the worst of the blast and frag by their compatriots still went down, except for about four on the far wing of the wedge, who managed to break away before they were knocked over by the falling tide of ravaged bodies.

I leaned to the right, bringing the .50 to bear on the one closest to the trees, and blew a chunk out of his shoulder, sending him sprawling off his mount, which just kept going. My follow up shot punched a fist-sized hole through his chest, and he collapsed in a spreading pool of dark blood.

Santos had opened fire on the next one with the Mk 48, hammering a short, tight burst into his back . It didn't seem to hurt the Fohoriman badly enough, so the next burst was longer, and he slumped forward and fell even as I brought the M107 to bear, falling on his face and staying there.

The third one's mount was either panicking or going into a bloodthirsty frenzy. It darted toward the second fallen Fohoriman, its rider struggling to bring it under control. I got a shot at that one, just after one of the Tuacha rifles thundered from above and behind me, knocking the rider sprawling as the mount pounced on the Fohoriman's corpse and began to savage the body.

As the smoke cleared in the kill zone, those beasts that hadn't been killed had gone crazy from the smell of blood and were tearing at each other and the Fohorimans that were struggling to get to their feet. Chambers added to the chaos with savage bursts of 7.62 fire, punching through flesh and bone wherever the M80 ball rounds found a weakness.

One last rider was almost to the trees, whipping his mount viciously, glancing over his shoulder at the carnage behind him before disappearing into the woods. It wasn't that long a shot, particularly not for the .50. I put the crosshairs on him just as he peered back at us, his face still hidden by that long black veil beneath his helmet.

With another jarring shock of recoil and a harsh *crack*, the trigger broke and sent another Raufoss round downrange. I was a little high. I'd been aiming center mass, but the round took him in the head.

The helmet went flying in a spray of black fluids as the upper half of his head was simply blown off. His corpse stayed in the saddle for a surprisingly long time, still swaying and bobbing limply as his mount darted into the woods.

A *thunk* announced that Gunny was finishing things off. The 40mm grenade sailed into the middle of the awful wreck of torn flesh and armor where the Fohorimans still fought each other and their mounts to try to get clear and come at us, and the explosive tore through them with a savage detonation that still seemed like little more than a firecracker after those Claymores going off. A moment

later, Gurke dropped another in, and it detonated right after the second with another flash, black cloud, and heavy
thud.

Four or five more grenades later, and it was all over.
Nothing moved.

I pulled the Barrett out of its notch, gingerly easing
myself back from my shooting position, pins and needles
starting to go through my previously awkwardly bent
leg, and turned toward the back of the hill and the horses.

We'd bought ourselves some time. I had no doubt—
and neither did Gunny; he'd said as much during our *extremely* abbreviated planning session—that as far away
as the main force was, the Fohorimans had heard what
had happened, and they'd be whipping their minions
into a lather to get them to close the distance. But they
weren't going to be nearly as fast as a dedicated force of
Fohoriman riders.

And they'd go even more slowly once we hit the
mountains, which would be in a couple more days.

We had our time distance gap. Now we had to make
the best use of it.

CHAPTER 28

I'D been too optimistic, thinking that we'd make it to the mountains in a few days. It took more like a week.

The terrain was the primary obstacle. While the mountains themselves remained far off, the land got steadily more rugged and forbidding the closer we got. Canyons forced us to one side or another, great upthrusts blocked our path, and more and more we came across hills that were essentially giant piles of boulders with trees clinging to the soil in the cracks between them. Those required often half a day to get around, since the horses couldn't just clamber over the boulders.

Every step of the way, we were painfully aware that the Fohorimans' army was closing in, moving up the easier terrain while we tried to negotiate the hills and ravines. I thought more than once that I'd seen their weird, shadow-bat spies flapping overhead.

Yet we finally reached the mountains themselves, towering, imposing spires of snow-covered rock thrusting up above the tree line, without actually spying the vanguard of the host we were sure was behind us.

Now we just had to worry about finding exactly where our quarry had gone.

The Book of Audur Cohm had spoken of an old temple to Vaelor that held one of the artifacts that Dragon

Mask might well be looking for. The Fohorimans had, according to the text, collapsed a mountain onto the temple to bury it, but there *might* be a way to dig it out.

We weren't worried about digging anything out, but Dragon Mask might be, and it was the southernmost point the book had described, so it was a reasonable place to take up the search.

Finding it, however, was another matter. Again, we didn't exactly have ten-digit grid coordinates.

Mathghaman had halted atop an escarpment that gave us a good view of the main crest of the mountains beyond, as well as some of the broken, rugged hills we'd worked our way through to get that far. Gunny started up to join him, noticeably more comfortable on horseback than he had been a week before. He glanced over his shoulder and tapped his collarbone, where he might have tugged on his collar when we'd just been wearing cammies.

Team Leaders up.

There wasn't a lot of room up on that promontory, so I swung down out of the saddle and walked. In part, I was glad to get down on my own two feet again. I liked Myrsky, and the horse had certainly put in some serious work without tiring or flagging, but sometimes a man needs to stretch his own legs.

Gunny and Mathghaman were bent over the parchment copy of the map from the Book of Audur Cohm, trying to compare the landmarks we could see with the sketches and descriptions etched on the thinned hide.

I joined them, peering down at the drawing, which had been recreated painstakingly from the crumbling pages of the ancient tome. Mathghaman looked up and studied the forbidding peaks ahead of us, then pointed to one of the most imposing, a towering triangle of bare rock, snow, and ice that loomed high above all the rest. It looked like a slightly shorter version of Everest. And I knew that there were peaks in this range that dwarfed even that one. "That should be the mountain called Kivihammas." He looked back down at the map. "The old temple should lie a league to the north of it, beneath the half dome of Murtunut Krunu."

"Except if it's buried, we're still going to have a hell of a hard time finding it." Gurke suppressed a shiver as a breath of icy wind came down off the peaks. The days had gotten cooler and the nights downright frigid as we'd climbed and moved farther north.

"If they've been digging, that should be easy enough to spot," Gunny replied.

"It will still be difficult, and it will require some time and a detailed search." Mathghaman rolled up the map and slid it into the case at his saddlebag before peering keenly at the slopes, ridges, and thick forest ahead of us. The higher trees were still dusted with snow.

He pointed along the ridgeline immediately to our north. "If we go over that ridge, we should find ourselves moving along the shoulder of Kivihammas." He sighed. "There will be no easy way from here on. The mountains will only become steeper and rougher, and we will doubtless face opposition from the creatures that live within them." He looked around at the rest of us. "Steel yourselves. The flight to Teac Mor Farragah will seem easy compared to what we face going forward." Turning back toward the imposing mountains in front of us, his voice dropped to near a whisper. "And that is provided we need not go all the way to the Teeth of Winter."

I don't think I was the only one who didn't want to even think about that. I'd seen that ice sheet from a distance, and I had no particular desire to see it much closer.

There wasn't much more to say. Filtering back to our teams, we mounted up and got moving again.

* * *

As we got higher, it got colder, and the demands we were putting on the horses were getting harsher. We had to stop more often, and finally, after seeing some less than encouraging movement out in the shadows as the darkness fell, we decided we really needed to halt for the night.

Fires were lit for the first time since we'd left Vahava Paykhah, the cold and the threat of the things in the shadows beneath the trees coming together to make it a necessity. We dragged fallen trees and rocks into rough ramparts to keep all but the most aggressive and committed beasties out and away from our horses, set security, and settled in to rest and wait for morning.

Somewhat to my surprise, it was a quiet night. No abominable snowman tried to come after us, no goblins came swarming in from under the trees. We didn't even see any of the faint, glowing specters that Bearrac had warned me not to pay attention to when we'd been following the vampire's swathe of destruction through the corsair lands. It was weird. This was the Land of Ice and Monsters. The night was *supposed* to be a time of terror, where the spooks and monsters came out and tried to eat you.

I glanced over at Mathghaman as we saddled up in the dim gray light before sunrise. I'd noticed him sitting up every time I'd opened my eyes during the night. I knew that the Tuacha didn't require sleep the same way we did. They just kind of went into a sort of light trance, that they could wake from as easily as blinking. But he'd seemed more alert that night, even though he hadn't been watching the perimeter, or even moving around. He'd knelt, motionless, for the entire night, as near as I could tell.

Maybe he'd held vigil, like he'd done before we'd gone after Bres and Octrallach.

Maybe that was why we hadn't gotten hit. It was something to think about.

After all, we'd seen that the mystical factor counted for a lot here. Much more immediately than any of us were used to—even those who acknowledged that it existed. Marines aren't known for being of a mystical frame of mind. Most tend to be practical materialists, given to dismissing anything that they couldn't physically fight, drink, or otherwise touch. We had to get over that mindset here, it seemed.

It gave me more to think about as we swung into the saddle and headed over the next ridge. I just had to be careful not to get to woolgathering too much in my fatigue. I still had the responsibilities of a team leader, keeping track of my team and our position relative to the rest of the platoon, as well as watching our route and holding security.

Oh, and keeping Kovaves from wandering off. He wasn't nearly as reliable as Myrsky was, but it was Myrsky's chance for a rest.

My team wasn't on point at the moment, though, so I still had some time and energy to consider the question. Had Mathghaman's meditation, or vigil, or whatever it was, really kept the monsters at bay that night? Or were they still just sniffing us out, figuring out the best way to come at us?

I couldn't be sure, but one thing was becoming obvious. The standard Marine agnosticism wasn't going to work here. We'd *effectively* taken sides, but I was starting to think of the possibility that if we were going to survive for long, we'd have to take sides a little more emphatically.

It was a somber thought, as we climbed higher into the mountains.

CHAPTER 29

THE monsters didn't leave us entirely unmolested over the next few days, as we clambered over ridgelines and through the woods. Three times we had to fight off big, dark wolves with eyes that gleamed red even in daylight. While they bled like ordinary animals and died when you shot them, there was something eerie about them. Wolves are intelligent creatures; having hunted them back in The World, I can say with some authority that they're some of the smartest animals in the wild. These things were different, though. They seemed to use actual tactics.

To make matters worse, each time, when the smoke had cleared, there weren't as many carcasses on the ground as there should have been.

Finally, after two more days and nights than we'd hoped, we approached the base of Murtunut Krunu.

It was snowing as we came down the defile across the narrow valley that spread out between one of the shoulders of Kivihammas and the sheer side of Murtunut Krunu, where half the mountain had cracked and fallen away in some long-ago cataclysm. It looked a bit like Half Dome in Yosemite, though bigger and somehow more raw. The top of the dome disappeared into the clouds as the fine, grainy flakes came down.

It had to be getting close to the end of spring, but it was still snowing up here, and we'd been riding through fetlock-deep snow for the last couple of days, even under the trees.

Well, it *was* the Land of *Ice* and Monsters, after all.

Gunny called a halt, and we spread out under the trees, the platoon setting security on the knob just above us while the team leaders, Mathghaman, and Gunny got eyes on. The valley was strewn with boulders and scattered trees, most of them tall but bent toward the lowlands, as if the wind off the peaks had permanently blasted their tops downward. There wasn't a lot of concealment down there, at least not at first glance.

Of course, looking at terrain from a distance could be deceiving. And given the number of boulders down there, there was presumably a *lot* more cover than it appeared. You could hide a small army down there without too much difficulty, especially in this weather.

The falling snow made it hard to see much detail past about half a mile. But we didn't need to see much detail to see the scar on the mountainside on the other side of the valley.

My binoculars were still in my ruck, strapped to Myrsky's back, but I could see pretty well through my rifle's scope, at least so far as the weather permitted. It looked as though a massive shoulder of rock, that had escaped the collapse that left Murtunut Krunu half a mountain, had come down at some time in the past, though there were still a couple of stelae carved into the rock above the landslide. That must have been what the book had described as the Fohorimans burying the temple. They'd dropped half a mountain across the entrance.

It said something about the capability of their sorcery. It would have taken a lot of C4 or TNT to cause that collapse.

The hillside, blanketed in snow as it was, was not unbroken, however. There was another scar in that pile of ancient detritus, only thinly covered in white, not deeply enough buried in newly-fallen snow to disguise it. Someone had been digging.

Or, perhaps more accurately, blasting.

The excavation was more of a crater than a pit, and unless I was seeing things, an artifact of the distance and the contrast set up by the dusting of snow over the dig, the ground was scorched black on the inside.

Scorched, or coated in dark ichor. It was hard to tell.

Nothing moved near it. We were too far away and staring through too much falling snow to form an accurate picture of what exactly we were looking at. But something looked off. I couldn't describe it, but when I came off glass and glanced over at Bailey, he was frowning, too. He looked over at me and raised an eyebrow. I only shrugged. We wouldn't be able to tell until we got closer.

We'd have to be *real* careful, just in case it was a trap.

Gunny brought us all together at the base of the knob as we backed off the impromptu OP. "Okay, Gurke's on point, Bailey's rear security. McCall, you've got overwatch when we get above the target site. We'll work around the upper edge of the valley, set up on that shelf up there, above that thick clump of trees, and Gurke will recon the hole before we move in and see what we can find."

It said something about how tired we all were that nobody made the obvious joke about "recon the hole."

Nobody said much of anything, in fact. For one thing, we were smoked, even with stopping each night and lighting fires both for warmth and to keep the wolves at bay. Plus, we had a long way to go, and unknown horrors to face whenever we got all the way there. Nobody was feeling particularly jokey or talkative. Besides, Gunny had been using his, "I don't want any bullshit" voice.

No man in his right mind starts screwing around when Gunny Taylor talks like that. It means he's as tired as anyone else, and he's probably going to bite your head off if you cross him.

So, we filed back to our horses, mounted up, and headed out, Gurke in the lead while I brought my team in behind them. Mathghaman and his companions fell in behind us, while Bailey took up the rear, holding back about fifty yards, just in case.

We started uphill at first, circling around the valley. The going got harder as the snow came down thicker, swirling around us and forcing men deeper into their cloaks. The horses put their heads down and slogged through it, though the deepening powder made footing treacherous among the rocks and along the sides of the mountain slopes. It slowed us down considerably.

I rode cautiously, keeping Myrsky's pace slow, my rifle in my hands as I scanned the slopes and the trees for more wolves, or something akin to the little frosty rock goblins we'd fought in the passes to the west. But the only sound was the whisper of the faint breeze, the only things moving were the falling flakes and our column.

The quiet of the movement so far hadn't been comforting. It had only put my nerves more on edge, given what we'd seen in the wilds of the Land of Ice and Monsters before. I was always waiting for the other shoe to drop.

I think I would have been more relaxed in the middle of a fight. This constant waiting for one that didn't materialize was murder.

It took a couple of hours to get around to that shelf. The snow thickened and then thinned again, and it had all but stopped by the time we got to the shelf. We tied the horses to a couple trees at the base of the formation before we crept up onto the narrow flat rock and got down in the prone, despite the snow, to watch the pit and the valley below it.

The Tuacha joined Gurke's team as they also left their horses in the trees and moved down toward the pit on foot, guns up and watching every direction as they moved from rock to tree to fold in the ground. The snow made it a lot easier to see their gray-green cloaks, even though the flakes that fell on them never quite seemed to melt, allowing us to track their progress even as we watched for any threats, ready to cover them with accurate rifle and machinegun fire.

The wind whispered in the trees just below our perch. A few flakes continued to drift down from the lowering gray clouds. Nothing else moved.

Gurke and the others reached the pit, rifles leveled as they approached the edge cautiously.

Movement caught my eye. I shifted, lifting my rifle and searching the trees on the far side of the pit with my scope. Nothing. But I'd definitely seen something move, and not with the wind.

Carefully scanning the slopes and the trees, I waited for whatever it was to show itself, but I still hadn't seen anything by the time Gurke signaled the all clear.

We headed down to join up at the lip of the crater, security set high and low along with the horses. I headed down to the pit itself with Rodeffer.

The ground under the snow *was* blackened, though it looked more like scorching than the inky ichor that had characterized Vaelor's horrors. The pit itself burrowed deep into the hill of debris, disappearing into the blackness below. I glanced down into the darkness, unsure if we really wanted to go in after whatever had brought Dragon Mask here. *Especially* if this had been a temple to Vaelor. I'd seen enough of Vaelor's horrors. I wanted no part of his temples.

"Conor. Gunny." Gurke was standing next to a boulder just uphill from the crater. "Check this out."

I slogged up to join him, getting there just ahead of Gunny. It didn't take much to see what Gurke was talking about.

About thirty or forty 5.56 shell casings lay in the dirt, scattered under the boulder. Some had been tramped down into the snow and the semi-frozen ground beneath, but they were still hard to miss.

"Well, that answers that question, don't it?" I looked up and scanned the slopes again. There was no trace of whatever they'd been fighting. Bodies had been policed up, and any bloodstains were probably covered by the snow.

I had no doubt that if they'd been fighting, something had died. Sorenson might be a shithead, but he was almost as good a shot as the rest of the platoon. Zimmerman, Owens, and especially Gonsalves were no slouches, either.

Turning my eyes back to the ground, I started scanning for tracks. Gurke's team had contaminated the scene quite a bit with their own, but soon enough I found the depressions in the snow that had to be their trail, heading farther north, into the mountains. There wasn't enough to tell how many there were, but there had to be a decent number. And at least one of them was a Recon Marine who still had his rifle and his combat load. What was left of it, anyway.

"You think they found what they were looking for?" Even without concrete, identifiable traces, aside from the shell casings, there was a lot of information to be had from just the circumstantial evidence.

We knew that at least one of the men we'd lost was alive. Alive, and still working with Dragon Mask. The location and the shell casings told us both of those things. If they'd escaped and been on their own, they shouldn't have known how to find this place. I would have hoped they wouldn't have had a reason to. We knew Dragon Mask was probably trying to wake Vaelor, or at least steal some power from him in order to overthrow Uergal. That much had been obvious long before, even if we hadn't known the specifics when we'd briefly been "allies."

Mathghaman was looking down into the pit. "I fear they did. Otherwise, they would still be here. Or else their bodies would be staked out on the slopes, their ribcages torn open."

All eyes turned toward him. "You know what they were fighting?" Bailey asked.

Mathghaman looked around us, his eyes narrowed. "I suspect. The Book of Audur Cohm spoke of Duergar who joined the fighting when the Fohorimans buried the temple. They would not necessarily have moved on, if they lived beneath these mountains."

"Duergar? What are Duergar?" Bailey asked.

"Kinda like dwarves, only evil." Bailey looked up with a frown at Synar.

"How the hell did you know that, Synar?"

There was a sheepish silence.

"I'm not kidding, how the fuck did you know that?" Bailey was tired, cold, and grumpy, and he was not going to let this go, whether Synar was right or not.

"It was in D&D, Staff Sergeant."

"You fuckin' nerd." Bailey turned back toward the hole as the rest of us chuckled. "What?"

"We're in a world where sorcery and monsters are real, and you're calling Synar a nerd for playing a game about sorcery and monsters." Gunny shook his head.

"Well, yeah, it was a game for nerds back there. Things are different here." He peered down into the darkness. A faint, sarcastic grin might have lifted the corner of his mouth. "Besides, I can't let him start to get a big head."

"So, the Duergar follow Vaelor?" Gunny asked Mathghaman.

"No. They hold no loyalty to any deity, though they still serve the likes of Vaelor through their thirst for bloodshed. They are dark, crooked, greedy beings, who hate all who are not of their sept. Even other Duergar."

Mathghaman was still watching the rocks and the trees around us. I suspected that these Duergar were known for popping out when least expected.

It was kind of weird, the same name being used between two such different worlds, but I'd seen enough weirdness so far that it didn't especially bother me. Maybe it meant there was more of a connection between the world we'd come from and this one than we'd been able to dig up so far.

"Are they territorial then?" Gurke was watching the mountainside, too, though it seemed unlikely that a threat would materialize on that sheer slope above us.

On top of the peak, hidden by the clouds, though… I suddenly wanted to get a long way away from that mountain.

I'd dropped a boulder the size of a minivan on a giant in the mountains to the west. I had no desire to be in the giant's place.

"Oh, yes. You hardly need to get close to one of their dens, though. They are always watching from the high places. If they spy anyone not of their sept from afar, they will cross great distances to slit their throats." Mathghaman's tone suggested he'd fought Duergar before, and that he'd had no great liking for the experience. "We should not linger long."

"How far would we have to go to get out of their territory?" I asked.

Bearrac snorted from where he'd come up to join us, standing with his feet spread wide next to the lip of the hole leading down into the ancient temple of evil. "Far away from these mountains. Duergar will spread wherever they can find a hole in the earth and burrow in like maggots in a corpse."

That was a cheerful thought.

Gunny nodded, looking down into the hole, and changed the subject to our targets. "What were they here for?"

"There was a cauldron kept here, used in the darkest of sacrifices to Vaelor." I could imagine something of what that might entail, and Mathghaman's tone suggested that I was probably right, and that none of us should inquire too closely anyway. "I imagine it would be difficult to carry, so it might slow them down."

"Who went to Combat Tracker last?" Gunny looked up as Chambers, Applegate, Rodeffer, and Farrar raised their hands. I'd been through the course, but it had been a while.

"Find me some spoor. If we can run these bastards down and end this quick, so much the better." Somehow, given what Gurke had found, I didn't think Gunny was as concerned about ending Dragon Mask as he was about dealing with our own.

Our own... who were now actively aiding the enemy.

I'd understood Captain Sorenson's logic when he'd attached us to Dragon Mask. I hadn't agreed with it, and had thought he was being dangerously naïve, but I'd understood it. We'd been cut off, far from home and resupply, and so building rapport with the locals had been a viable survival strategy.

He'd taken it to lengths I never would have, not even in Syria, where most of the villagers we'd lived with were as much victims of the jihadis as anyone else. He'd embraced the Dovos nal Uergal as if he were converting to their entire way of life.

Maybe he'd figured things out faster than the rest of us. Most of us had considered the captain a stuffed shirt and kind of a dumbass. He didn't know nearly as much about the job, or much of anything else, as the NCOs and SNCOs in the platoon. Perhaps, though, he'd been far cleverer than we'd given him credit for.

While Gunny had been trying to hold the platoon together, sans the higher chain of command, maybe the captain had already decided his course to survive far from that chain of command.

I'd been thinking that we were going to have to take sides on a metaphysical level in this world. It seemed that the captain already had.

My musings were suddenly interrupted by an unholy yowling and screeching, as the Duergar came swarming out of the rocks all around us, waving short-bladed axes and stone clubs.

We turned, dropped behind cover, and got ready for the fight we'd been anticipating for days already.

CHAPTER 30

WE'D seen these things before. We'd fought them before, and killed them in job lots. Pale, pebbly skin, eyes like obsidian, blank and black and still brimming with hate, jagged teeth sticking up from a prominent underbite beneath a jutting, bulbous nose. They came swarming out of the rocks and the trees, screeching their bloodlust, waving stone axes and spears as they leaped at us far faster than creatures their size should have been able to.

The horses were freaking out, and Baldinus had his hands full trying to keep them from bolting. Applegate and Synar clambered up above them, already taking the Duergar under fire as they tried to get between the evil dwarves and our mounts. If we lost those horses, we'd be in a world of hurt.

Gunfire hammered at the waves of oncoming Duergar, blasting holes through their stony flesh and spattering the snow and rocks with steaming, black ichor. They'd let their own bloodlust get the better of them, and had popped up too far out, so we had the advantage to start with. There would be no VC "hugging" tactics here. As long as we could keep them at a distance, and still had ammo, we could kill the hell out of them.

How long that would last was anyone's guess. There were a *lot* of them.

I was sprinting up toward my team, though the snow and the crumbled, broken earth around the crater slowed me down. I threw myself prone next to Rodeffer, who was leaning around a rock, putting controlled pairs into charging Duergar, as Santos laid down withering machinegun fire, reaping three or four of the little monsters with every burst.

Farrar rose up from behind his rock with our team's 40mm, and dumped a grenade into the charging wave of Duergar swarming over and around the boulders at us like fire ants. The *thunk* was followed a second later by a heavy, echoing *boom* as three of them disappeared in an ugly black cloud.

My first shot caught one of them on the move as it tried to dodge behind a rock to get away from Santos's fire, sending it spinning into the snow and dirt. Another jumped right over the broken corpse and took my next bullet in the throat. Black blood spurted from the wound and its mouth as it kept trying to come after me, stumbling and falling on its face after a couple more strides.

More explosions punctuated the rattle of gunfire, grenades blasting more of the little psychopaths into chunks. They just kept coming, though.

There were enough of them, coming on fast enough, that in the next few minutes, the ones that had survived our gunfire got close enough that it came down to hand-to-hand.

I blew a screeching, pint-sized monstrosity's head apart with what was practically a contact shot, my suppressor almost touching its nose just before I blasted the appendage back through its skull. I got one more before they were too close to shoot without falling back into the crater—which did *not* feel like a good idea; there was something about the darkness down there that felt almost alive, and thoroughly malevolent—then I had to transition.

Slinging the rifle to my back, I drew my sword and lopped off a bulbous, leering head in the same movement. It went flying, trailing a stream of black fluids, and bounced off another Duergar's own head just before Farrar split it with his axe.

"Fall back! Shoulder to shoulder!" Hand-to-hand combat gets messy, and if you get cut off, you're probably doomed. You'll get swarmed and cut to pieces. Room to maneuver is useful in single combat, but so far, we hadn't come up against an adversary in this world with the honor to go for single combat. They'd gang up on a lone combatant in a heartbeat. So, for battle, formation is vital.

We backed up to the edge of the pile of tailings at the rim of the crater, edged weapons in hand, still hacking at the Duergar as they came on, even as we closed ranks into a small but solid formation. Santos and I were at the flanks, with Rodeffer and Farrar between us. I had my blessed blade in hand, Rodeffer had his leaf-bladed Tuacha sword, Farrar his axe, and Santos his own axe, a long-handled job with a bearded head and backspike. He'd been carrying a sword for a while, but had decided to switch to the axe just before we'd left Vahava Paykhah. It fit him a little better, being the barrel-chested freedom fighter that he was. Subtlety wasn't one of Santos's strong points.

With each step back, we killed more of them. The Duergar's numbers were somewhat offset by their small size. Every one of us had a reach advantage, and we used it to the full. Every stroke split a skull, cut a throat, or stabbed through a neck or other vulnerable point. As strangely stone-like as the Duergar were, they were surprisingly fragile, and they seemed to have arteries in all the same places humans did. Which meant that a thrust through the angle between neck and shoulder, or a deep enough cut on the inside of a thigh, would lead to bleed out and death in seconds.

We'd had to learn a whole new way of approaching combat as we'd learned to use edged weapons more. For years—over a decade for some of us—we'd trained to shoot for center mass or the brain box. Hydraulic or circuitry kills. A blade isn't moving as fast or creating as much shock as a bullet, though. If you skewer the heart or the brainstem, it's the same thing, but those are often armored. Easier to go for an extremity that's not as easily protected, where the lifeblood is pumping, and spill that. You've still got to keep the enemy off you while he bleeds out, but often a cut deep enough to sever an artery can send at least a human adversary into shock *fast*.

That didn't apply as much with Duergar. They didn't seem to go into shock. So, we always had to fend them off until they bled out, unless we got a head or managed to stab them deep enough to hit one of their hearts. And we hadn't brought our shields off the horses, most of us.

They were strong little bastards, even as their lifeblood was pulsing out onto the snowy ground. Every blocked blow jarred the hand holding the weapon as it was fended off. I smacked away a stone-tipped spear before the bearer's legs crumpled under it, black blood flowing down its front from a slashed neck. That allowed

the next one behind it, swinging a pair of stone toma-
hawks, to get close enough that I had to beat back the
windmilling axe heads before I could find an opening to
stab the thing.

For a moment, as I panted and frantically blocked
blow after blow, it looked like I wasn't going to get the
chance, even as more of them scrambled over rocks,
hooting and shrieking, trying to get around and flank me.
I heard the meaty *crunch* as Rodeffer split a skull off to
my right, but I couldn't spare the attention. My entire
world had suddenly shrunk to this narrow window as I
tried to kill this one Duergar before it killed me.

Sometimes that delicate balance between overall situational awareness and the immediate fight evaporates,
and you've just got to survive.

I'd fend off one strike, only to have to quickly shift
my blade to block the next. I was barely fast enough to
keep this thing from opening my leg or my crotch, but I
was really wishing I had my shield right then.

Finally, as we were forced back and I had to turn to
put my back to Rodeffer to keep the other Duergar from
getting around behind me, I got desperate.

This time, when the leering little psycho took a swing
at my knee, I didn't block it with the sword, but darted in
with my gloved left hand and made a grab for the tomahawk itself.

I almost lost my fingers at first, but I got hold of the
haft and clamped down, hard, as I hooked my blade on
the inside of the second axe. Then I kicked the Duergar
in the chest.

It felt like kicking a rock, but I still had a lot of mass
and I'd been humping over mountains and hills a lot, so

PETER NEALEN

there was a lot of muscle behind that kick. My sword
scraped on the tomahawk as the Duergar was knocked
sprawling, but with my fingers hooked on the inside of
the head of the second one, I had a better grip than the
Duergar did.

Now I had a sword in one hand, and an axe in the
other.

Flipping the tomahawk around and catching the haft
so I could swing it, I went to town.

Taking a step forward, despite the risk, I hooked the
Duergar's remaining tomahawk with the one I'd taken
and ripped the weapon out of the thing's grip while I
stomped on its chest and stabbed it through the neck. The
sword point grated on its spine just before I ripped it out,
slashing its neck open so far as to halfway decapitate it.

A vicious blow hammered into my side, though
my mail stopped the stone point, and I pivoted, batting
the spear aside with my tactically acquired tomahawk
and plunging my sword point through the collar of the
Duergar's stony armor, driving it down deep into its
chest cavity. The creature stiffened, quivering for a second before it went limp. I dragged the sword free—in addition to never taking a stain, the blade had never gotten
stuck—and brought it down in a short, savage arc that
lopped off a pale, pebbly hand wrapped around another,
bigger stone axe.

The Duergar rarely cried out in pain, but this one
shrieked, looking down at the black blood spewing from
the stump, just before my sword lashed up and lopped
off the top of its skull. It collapsed as I got back into
position next to Rodeffer and fended off another spear

thrust before splitting that Duergar's skull with the stone tomahawk.

Then we held our ground, hacking and slashing at all comers, while the horses kept screaming in terror, almost drowned out by the high-pitched war cries of the Duergar.

I swung sword and tomahawk until my arms and hands ached, my breath stung in my lungs from sucking in the cold, thin air, and I was drenched in black blood to the elbows. The bodies of the Duergar piled up at our feet, but we didn't fall back any farther. Our mail held where they got through, but for the most part, their fury was wasted, as they died in droves for nothing but their own hate.

Finally, as the sun dipped toward the peaks, a brazen, discordant horn call came from higher up the mountains. The remaining Duergar were suddenly scampering away into the rocks, disappearing as quickly as they'd come.

Then movement drew all eyes higher up, to where a figure stood near the shelf where we'd set up overwatch to begin with.

Letting the tomahawk fall to the blackened, blood-soaked ground, I swung my rifle around, my sword dangling from my wrist by its thong loop, and brought my scope to my eye, finding the figure after a moment's searching. It stood brazenly in the open and waved its axes at us defiantly.

It was Duergar. That much was plain from its stature and its shape. But unlike the others, this one was armored, fully decked out in ornate plate, its face hidden by a tall, flat-topped bucket helm. It shook its weapons again, and I saw that these weren't chipped stone like the others, but ancient, verdigris-encrusted bronze, chipped and notched from hard use.

The Duergar bellowed its defiance at us, though the strange, croaking words made no sense to my ears. I probably didn't really need to understand the words. The malice was heavy enough in its tone. I doubted that Duergar were really capable of any other feeling.

"We should leave this place." Mathghaman's own chest was heaving, and he was nearly as blood-spattered as the rest of us, though he was already reaching down to scoop up a handful of snow to wash it off. "They will regroup, and word will travel through these mountains about our presence. They hate each other nearly as much as they hate all who are not Duergar, but they will seek our deaths together, anyway."

"Do we know where we're going?" Gunny asked, breathing hard as he also started to scrub the ichor off his hands. "Those little bastards just wiped out any spoor we might have found."

"I believe so." Mathghaman whistled for his horse, which calmed down quickly and trotted over to him. "Come. We will discuss it on the way."

When I looked up again, before going for Myrsky and Kovaves, the shelf was empty, the strangely armored Duergar gone.

CHAPTER 31

THE snow picked up again as we rode north. It was rough going for a while, and not only because of the weather. The animals were still spooked. It had taken near-superhuman effort on Baldinus's and Conall's part to keep them from stampeding during the fight. They were still flighty and given to bucking and trying to bolt down the mountain—whether they had a rider or not—for miles after we'd left Murtunut Kurnu behind.

Mile after mile, the woods stretched, wild and un-broken, as we clambered over ridges that would have counted as full on mountains themselves if they had not lain in the shadow of the much taller peaks above them. The snow came and went, occasionally turning to rain when we had to ride down into deeper valleys, then back to snow as we ascended again, the horses struggling to regain altitude we'd had no choice but to give up.

So far, the Duergar hadn't attacked again. We saw them from time to time. A squat, menacing figure would appear atop a crag of rock, watching us balefully, then vanish. A deep, croaking bellow echoed down a valley, though no figure could be seen that might have uttered it. They hadn't given up. We hadn't lost them in the snows. They were just biding their time, looking for the right time and place to strike.

It wasn't just the threat they presented by themselves that weighed on us as we worked our way north, through increasingly brutal terrain, often having to climb above the tree line and onto open, snow-covered rocky slopes, painfully aware of how exposed we were to thrown rocks or even natural avalanches from above. The Duergar might be enough of a threat all by themselves, but they could also alert our other enemies to our presence. Those ahead and behind.

About three days after the fight at Murtunut Kurnu, during a break in the weather, I turned in my saddle and looked back, just in time to see the Fohorimans' vanguard crest a ridgeline about five miles behind us. They hadn't stopped, either. The Warlock Kings wouldn't risk Vaelor's freedom—and subsequent revenge—and they still thought that was what we were after.

More worrying still was the question of whether our former comrades ahead of us had heard all the racket the Duergar were making. Given the quiet of the wilderness in those parts, it was entirely possible that our firefight had been heard a *long* way off.

The weather cleared for a couple of days, and we made better time. Yet with every mile we covered, the Duergar got more aggressive.

They'd learned that a frontal assault was only going to get them slaughtered. So, they tried to get sneaky.

As we crossed another valley, great swathes of trees already smashed and uprooted by long ago landslides, a booming, croaking shout went up from above. A moment later, we heard the first *crack*, followed by an earthshaking, thunderous rumble.

Conall looked up, his piercing blue eyes penetrating the drifting shreds of cloud that enveloped the peaks above us, and shouted, "Ride! Ride for your lives!"

We spurred our mounts, tired as they were from almost two weeks of packing and riding through the wilderness, but as the rumble intensified, the horses didn't need much urging. Their sense of self-preservation was as finely honed as any human's, and they'd already sensed what was coming.

Looking up, I saw the leading edge of the avalanche, seemingly coming down from the saddle between two jagged, icy peaks in slow motion, but I knew that that wall of snow, ice, and rocks was already moving at terrific speed, and accelerating with every yard.

Kicking Myrsky in the flanks, I urged him up toward the higher ground ahead. He was already snorting as he pulled hard for the slope, as rocky and thickly forested as it was. Kovaves was a little flightier, and was already pulling on the lead rope, trying to flee down the narrow valley, directly away from the plummeting avalanche. I hauled on the rope with one hand, gripping the reins with the other, so tightly that I was pretty sure my knuckles were white under my gloves.

Any semblance of formation was lost as every man fought to keep his horses from panicking while trying desperately to get to higher ground. For a moment, it was every man for himself. There wasn't much you could do on horseback to help another rider get clear of an avalanche.

Yet even as Myrsky fought his way up onto the ridge opposite, I looked back and saw that Synar was falling behind.

His horse was freaking out, bucking and twisting, fighting the reins as he kicked at its flanks ineffectively. The horse kept trying to turn down the valley and get away from the noise and the onrushing white death. Synar was fighting to turn his her up the hill and away from the danger, but the horse was out of her head with terror. I couldn't see his spare, but right then there wasn't time to worry about it.

Diarmodh was right next to me then, and I tossed Kovaves' lead rope to him. "I'm going back for Synar!"

It took less effort to turn Myrsky down toward the valley than I'd feared. He was a good horse, and somehow he'd sensed that one of our brothers was in trouble, so if I was going to go right into the teeth of death to help, so was he.

Leaning back in the saddle, I plunged back down into the valley. Myrsky was sure-footed and nimble, dodging between trees and boulders faster than I could possibly hope to guide him. I still had to duck to keep from taking a branch the size of a baseball bat to the face at least once.

The avalanche was coming on faster and faster, the rumble shaking the ground underfoot, the thunder filling the air as the billowing cloud of white raced down the slope toward Synar and his now thoroughly panicked horse.

I burst out of the trees just as Synar lost the last shreds of control over his mount. He was looking over his shoulder at the onrushing wall of frozen death instead of paying full attention to his horse, and the horse sensed it. The animal went left, Synar went right, and then he was flat on his back, gasping for breath, having barely missed a jagged boulder that would have broken his back if he'd landed on it, his horse bolting straight down the valley for an illusory safety.

My guts clenched as I urged Myrsky forward. As gutsy as that horse was, he was all too aware of how close this was going to be, and he was starting to shy, to slow ever so slightly, wanting to turn and race back up the slope toward safety. He kept going though, and we thundered down toward Synar, who was starting to sit up, wheezing as he tried to get air back into his lungs.

He still had his weapons, at least, though most of the rest of his gear was gone, bouncing on the backs of his horses as they bolted down the valley. I passed him, brought Myrsky around in a tight circle, and then leaned down, reaching out to him with one hand while I held onto the reins with the other. Even two months before, I never would have dared to try something like that on horseback, and truth be told, I still wasn't actually skilled enough to have pulled it off if it hadn't been for the absolute necessity of it.

Synar reached up and grabbed my wrist. I clamped my hand on his and hauled upward, almost losing my own seat as his weight pulled on me, but he was jumping upward despite having the wind knocked out of him. It was hardly the graceful mount that you'd see in the movies, or that the Tuacha might have managed, but I got him on Myrsky's back, behind my saddle, and kicked Myrsky's flanks, urging him back up the hill.

The ground shuddered as the avalanche got closer. Myrsky was quivering with fright, but he was the greatest horse I've ever known, and he surged up the mountainside as fast as he could, barely slowing even with the extra weight on his back.

The avalanche hit the trees just to our left, and I caught a glimpse of two massive firs getting snapped off like matchsticks, the *bang* of their demise lost in the all-encompassing thunder. Myrsky was panting as he struggled up the slope, still weaving through the rocks and the trees. Synar bounced on his back, barely having managed to get a leg over and grabbing me around the waist, there being no other handhold available. He was holding on for dear life, and it was getting a little hard to breathe.

Myrsky leaped over a fallen tree, and we landed with a jarring impact, just as the wave of plummeting ice, snow, rocks, and broken trees swept by just behind us. We were momentarily enveloped in a haze of flying snow, but after a few more yards we were out of it, and I reined Myrsky in, slowing him as we clambered to the top of the ridge, where the rest of the platoon had slowed and turned to watch the little drama we'd just played out.

I finally brought Myrsky to a halt. He was blowing hard, his flanks wet with sweat despite the chill. I let Synar down first, then quickly dismounted, pulling the saddle and rubbing him down as soon as the saddle hit the ground. That horse had just performed heroically, and I didn't want to kill him through neglect or over burdening him before he'd had a chance to recover.

There wasn't much time, so it wasn't a thorough rubdown. We had to keep moving. I switched my saddle to Kovaves, while Synar accepted Bailey's spare mount. The rest of the platoon was on security, watching the trees and the slope above us, where the ridge climbed toward the forked, jagged peak that blotted out a quarter the sky overhead. We couldn't hear the croaking calls of the Duergar over the still-echoing rumble of the avalanche below us, which was still going strong down the valley, a fine white mist of powdered snow rising above the treetops, but we knew they were still there.

A shot rang out. "Let's go!"

Looking up as I swung into the saddle, Kovaves quivering with nervousness beneath me, I could see more of the Duergar swarming through the patchy snow on the rock-strewn slope above. There were hundreds of them, bellowing and croaking their hate, waving stone weapons. A few had slings this time, and fast-moving stones started to whistle through the trees. Fortunately, they weren't all that accurate, though the *crack*s when the stones hit trees were loud enough to give a pretty good idea how bad it would be to get hit by one.

"Ride!" Mathghaman's voice echoed over the rest of the noise. "Ride now! Slow for none of them!"

"Save your ammo!" Gunny probably wasn't thinking so much of the ammunition supply as he was the risk of spooking already frightened horses with a lot of gunfire. "Use your blades if you have to!"

I cinched down my rifle sling and drew my sword as I kicked Kovaves into a gallop, following Santos as he took lead. Once again, there wasn't much of a formation, at least not by teams. We quickly—almost instinctively—gathered into a wedge as we pounded over the top of the ridge, even as the first of the Duergar got down in front of us.

One went down under the hooves of Conall's horse, pounded to a blackened, slimy pulp. Another took an upward stroke of a long-hafted axe to the skull, splitting it like a melon as Diarmodh hit it like a polo player hitting a ball.

I had deliberately worked my way to the uphill wing of our wedge, my sword in my left hand, and brought it down in a great, circular blow that just about took a Duergar's head off as I batted its spear behind me. Kovaves was scared, his sides quivering as he ran, but he didn't bolt. He held his course as black blood spurted behind us and the Duergar went down.

Then we were over the ridge and heading down into the narrow valley on the other side, forced to slow as the ground got steeper. A raging cataract foamed at the bottom of the V-shaped valley, and soon Conall, at the tip of the wedge, had turned down the valley toward slightly more level ground. I looked over my shoulder, careful to keep my sword from hitting a tree or accidentally stabbing or cutting Kovaves—that would have been disastrous—only to see the Duergar halted at the top of the ridge, only a few of them visible through the trees.

One, in the same ornate plate armor we'd seen before, waved a bronze or copper hammer and croaked at us as it stamped its feet. It reached down, picked up a rock the size of its own head, and lobbed it down the slope after us. It hit a tree with a crash, and then the Duergar were gone, the ridgeline above us empty and still.

We would have kept going, but Conall slowed, reining in as he rode onto a narrow shelf above the raging stream below.

Gurke twisted around in his saddle, looking up behind us. "Why'd they stop?"

"Maybe they've got a new trap in mind." Applegate was scanning the top of the valley, where the stream ran down from the snowcap atop the mountain above.

"No, I do not think so." Bearrac pointed. "I expect they do not want to get too close to that."

Atop the ridge on the other side of the river stood a castle. At least, a sort of castle. Towers, ramparts, high, arched windows, galleries, and steps from one tower to another had been carved into a massive upthrust of rock, crowned with a single, tall tower, topped by a round, peaked roof.

If the vampire Unsterbanak's castle had looked like something out of Bram Stoker's *Dracula*, then whoever had built this place was going to give him a run for his money.

And we had to ride past it to get where we were going.

CHAPTER 32

IT took a couple of hours to work our way down toward the foaming rapids of the river at the base of the steep-sided valley, during which we saw no trace of the Duergar. It appeared that Bearrac's assessment was spot on. Whoever—or whatever—lived in that castle in the rock, the little psychos wanted nothing to do with them.

That might be a good thing. I remembered the way the Dovos had feared the tor where we'd first set up after we'd broken contact with the sea trolls that had been our welcoming committee to this strange world. We'd found out later, from Mathghaman, that the tor had been one of the last redoubts of those men and Tuacha who had stood against the Fohorimans before the fall of Teac Mor Farragah. Maybe this was another one of those places, though Mathghaman hadn't spoken of any such in these mountains.

Given the fact that the old temples and high places we expected Dragon Mask to be making for were all scattered through this country, it seemed unlikely that such a bastion would exist here. We'd seen stranger things, though. We'd found Brother Melchorius walking calmly right through the middle of the twisted, darkened woods of Lost Colcand, as if on a morning stroll, after all.

The Tuacha, however, didn't seem to think we'd found such a place, and I wasn't inclined to be particularly optimistic. I'd learned in Syria that the enemy of your enemy is not necessarily your friend. Just because the Duergar didn't want to go near that place didn't mean that whoever or whatever lurked inside it wasn't a threat to us, too.

Of course, the resident of that forbidding structure, which was curiously black against the white of the snow, making it more visible even as the wind blew flurries between us and the massive block of stone, was the least of our immediate worries. That stream was deep, and *fast*. The horses would make crossing a little easier, but we still needed to find a ford, because trying to swim it was going to be rough, even for the sure-footed Menninkai mountain horses.

No one was prepared to find an actual bridge in that wilderness.

A single stone span arched from one bank to the other, the flagstones dusted with snow, wide enough for two riders to cross abreast. The stonework looked solid, the craftsmanship strange to see in in that savage, haunted land.

Two figures waited at the far end.

Armored from head to toe, each held a long spear in one gauntleted hand, one in its left, the other in its right. Tall, vaguely Corinthian-looking helmets sported tooled metal wings on either side, and the T-shaped vision slits were as dark as night. Scale aventails draped from under the helms across muscled cuirasses, while more scale covered their shoulders clear to splinted vambraces, and scale kilts hung to their knees, with more sculpted greaves beneath. Every bit of armor was enameled in deep purple, shading to black.

At first, I was reminded of nothing so much as the animated—and empty—suits of armor beneath Taramas's citadel, and I felt my blood run cold as I looked at these things. That had been a fight that only the blessed sword I carried at my side had been able to win, and I didn't want to think about how I was going to get inside the reach of those spears.

Yet while the sepulchral knights beneath Taramas's citadel had attacked in eerie silence, one of these things spoke. Maybe both; it was hard to tell since neither one moved, and we couldn't see mouth or eyes in the stygian blackness under those helms.

"Declare yourselves." The voice was hollow and distant, as if coming from within a deep well. The language was strange, neither the guttural tongue of the Dovos or the more musical *Tenga Tuacha*. But there was mind speech at work there, or the sorcerous version of it, because I could still understand the words.

Mathghaman rode forward and halted his horse next to Conall, at the end of the bridge. For a moment, I wondered if he was going to respond or charge. There didn't appear to be another good way across the river, but it looked like these things could cause us some serious trouble on their own. If they had reinforcements…

The question was, what were they? They stood motionless as statues, and if they hadn't spoken, I would have thought they were statues.

Not that that made *that* much difference here, as evidenced by the aforementioned animated suits of armor.

Now, my first instinct would have been to ignore their demand and either push forward—which would probably mean a fight, presumably with something that didn't die honestly when you shot it—or find another way around. Mathghaman wasn't as constitutionally sneaky as a Recon Marine, though.

"I am Mathghaman Mag Cathal, King's Champion of Caedmon Mag Nuada, King of the Isle of Riamog. I am beholden to no dark power, and will be stopped by none." Mathghaman didn't give a damn whether or not the enemy had his sense of honor. He wouldn't be buffaloed by anyone.

This *was* the man who'd jumped over a ruined wall to tangle with Fohorimans hand-to-hand, *outside* the formation and defenses, in Teac Mor Farragah. Mathghaman was gentle-spoken at times, but it would never pay to forget that he was a badass, and could probably kill any one of us as easily as breathing if he took a mind to.

Strangely, the statuesque armored figures didn't move, didn't react to his challenge. Almost as if their own had been little more than a recording. When he started his horse across the bridge, hooves clattering on the stones, they didn't move.

They didn't *seem* to move at all as the rest of us followed him. Only when I came abreast of the two figures did I see that their helms had turned to watch us as we crossed.

The fact that the castle's occupant had placed such guardians here, yet they did nothing but watch, bothered me. I was used to everything in this place trying to kill and eat us. We were a *long* way from Menninkai territory, too, which told me that *everything* was suspect.

Especially the farther north we got, closer to the Teeth of Winter and the deep, dark hole where Vaelor was imprisoned.

Unfortunately, the terrain on the other side of the bridge was not conducive to just going up over the ridge and avoiding that castle altogether. We got a couple yards from the end of the bridge and found ourselves faced with a sheer cliff that drove us uphill, along the riverbed and toward that looming massif of rock which the castle was carved into.

As we turned our horses to follow Mathghaman and Conall, Santos looked back, and his face clouded, that haunted look that wasn't *quite* fear, but definitely wasn't comfort, entering his eyes. He looked at me. "Those weren't there before."

I followed his gaze. Two more armored figures, their armor enameled in the same dark indigo, stood at the far end of the bridge, facing us, rather than the way we'd come. They'd appeared without a sound, without any of us noticing their approach.

And, unlike the first two, which had turned, without apparent movement, to watch us, they were standing in the middle of the bridge, instead of off to either side. That way was blocked, at least for now.

There was definitely something spooky in this valley, and I suspected it had something to do with that castle. And the terrain was still forcing us steadily up toward its gates.

It stayed that way as we climbed the mountainside. There was no path, no road, but the lay of the land and the thickness of the stands of trees wherever the steepness of the slope eased enough that we could ride a little higher, always seemed to force us toward that looming, black shape, only partially obscured by drifting feathers of windblown snow.

It didn't escape my attention that when I looked up at the peaks above, through the gaps in the trees, the clouds were getting thicker and darker, slate gray billows lowering over the mountains.

Halfway up the mountainside, Mathghaman reined in. His face was set and grim. "We're being herded."

I don't think any of us disagreed. Nobody wanted to get too close to that black edifice that loomed ever closer above us, but try as we might, we kept getting pushed toward it.

We'd seen this before. Lost Colcand had done the same thing, forcing us deeper in when we wanted out, driving us toward that eldritch abomination lurking at its heart.

Judging by the looks cast at the woods and mountains around us, nobody in the platoon missed the parallel, either.

"From the looks of things, we're not the first." Gunny was looking down at the ground in front of his horse's hooves. Swinging down, he bent and picked something up, holding it up where it glinted in the quickly dimming light that got past the clouds and the thickening snow.

A 5.56 shell casing.

"So." I looked up at the castle. "They came this way, but it looks like they didn't want to go there any more than we do."

Gunny was squinting at the gateway, which we could see clearly now, looming like the open maw of a blackened skull in the rock. "Question is, did they get out of the trap, or are they still in there?"

All eyes turned toward that forbidding edifice as the clouds descended still lower, then swept the surrounding woods and rocks. I could have sworn, several times, that I'd seen more of the armored, utterly still figures atop boulders or outcrops of rock on the mountainside, though there was never anything there when I looked directly at it.

I wondered if that was what one of our former comrades had taken a shot at. We certainly hadn't come under attack yet. If Dragon Mask had kept summoning his pet horrors, though, I could see even Recon Marines getting strung out and jumpy enough to shoot at shadows.

Especially if one of them was Captain Sorenson.

"I guess that raises the question," Bailey said slowly. "Do we go in there to check? Or do we push on and see if we can cut their trail farther on?"

"If they went in there, they might not have made it out." Gurke was rubbing his bearded chin. "How far are we going to go? I'd hate to spend another week in these mountains, only to have to double back and go in there, anyway."

Gunny sighed heavily, watching the castle. The snow was starting to come down more thickly, fat white flakes plummeting out of the solid gray ceiling overhead, obscuring even the far side of the valley as they settled on shoulders and hoods that had been thrown up against them.

Mathghaman sat his horse quietly, watching Gunny. The decision, ultimately, was on Gunny's shoulders. And it was a hell of a decision.

We were, ultimately, on a mission to rescue our missing Marines. The fact that it *looked* like they'd gone bad complicated things, but the basic mission remained the same. Find them and deal with the problem. If the problem boiled down to freeing them from Dragon Mask, so much the better. If it meant putting them down, that got stickier, but at that point, I doubted anyone in the platoon who had survived the bloodbath that had been our trek halfway across the Land of Ice and Monsters in Dragon Mask's company would hesitate very long to put a bullet in the captain.

The point was, we were there to find them, and that meant if there was a possibility that they were in that castle, we needed to confirm or deny. The tricky part lay in whether or not *we*'d be able to get out once we went in. That place was clearly not just an empty, abandoned ruin. There was *something* in there, and the fact that we were being steered toward it was not a good sign.

"We're going in and clearing that place." Gunny clearly wasn't entirely comfortable with the decision, but as was his way, once the decision had been made, once we'd "slapped the table," it was made, and we were going to roll with it. "Heads on a swivel, and if you see anything spooky, *do not* hesitate to call it out."

"Hell." Santos's mutter was low, but it carried anyway in the sudden silence as the snowfall got even thicker. "I seen this movie, too, and I didn't like the ending much then, either."

CHAPTER 33

VISIBILITY had dropped to less than fifty yards by the time we reached the gate. It seemed that whoever or whatever lurked in that castle was happy enough that we were coming to them not to mess with us further. I might have caught a few more glimpses of those statuesque armored figures out of the corner of my eye as we'd climbed to the top of the ridge, or maybe it had just been my imagination lending their shapes to trees seen half-obscured by the falling snow.

We dismounted and closed in on the gate, Eoghain and Conall staying outside with the horses. That hadn't taken much discussion, though Cairbre had inaudibly expressed his disdain at the idea of Tuacha taking second place to Recon Marines. Mathghaman had ignored him, though. This was *our* mission now.

The gate stood open. A portcullis had been drawn up at the front, and massive, iron-bound doors stood open behind it. Eyes and muzzles were raised toward the machicolations cut into the rock above it, and no one wanted to stand directly under them.

Yes, I'd learned what machicolations were. When you're living and fighting in a world where ancient and medieval weapons and defenses are common, you have to learn how they work. Machicolations are essentially vertical murder holes set up above a potential breach point. They're not that different from the holes knocked in the ceilings of houses in Fallujah, that the AQI guys used to drop frags in on some of my first infantry instructors, back in the day.

With two teams, mine and Mathghaman's, lined up on the gateway, stacked against the rock walls where we could fit, out of the fatal funnel, while the other two teams held exterior security, I looked across at Mathghaman. We traded a nod, and I gave Rodeffer the squeeze.

He moved in, taking the left wall, while Diarmodh took the right.

We flowed through the open gatehouse, cross-covering on the murder holes in the ceiling. Nothing moved except us, though we had to look carefully, since the gatehouse was dark and shadowed, even compared to the dimmed gray light outside, where the snow and the clouds had long since obscured the sun.

Despite all the miles we'd covered, on horseback and on foot, we fell easily back into that fast, smooth glide that you have to develop in CQB. "Only move as fast as you can accurately shoot." That was the maxim that had been drilled into us during shooting package after shooting package. So, you learned to move smoothly and quickly, keeping a steady shooting platform from the waist up.

It had some applications to swordplay, too, we'd found. But right now, we were guns up and looking for targets.

Reaching the open doors at the far end of the gatehouse, we didn't even pause. Rodeffer and Diarmodh went through the doorway simultaneously, Mathghaman on Diarmodh's heels, me on Rodeffer's. We swept the courtyard with our muzzles as we flowed in, clearing every corner we could see.

I call it a "courtyard," but it was almost more of a cave. Remember, this entire thing was cut out of the rock, not unlike the tor where we'd first taken refuge after landing here. Like the great hall in the tor, this was lit by shafts carved in the rock from outside, but unlike there, these shafts were letting in considerably more light, to the point that it almost looked like we were outside, standing in an open space before the second gate, which was carved into the rock above us at the top of a wide flight of steps, flanked by more of the tall, narrow, peaked windows.

The interior, on the other side of that open gate and the looming windows, was black as night. But there was no other way to go. The courtyard was empty and still.

The cave's ceiling rose a good hundred feet above our heads, and the façade ahead of us was carved all the way to the top. The gate was framed by pillars carved into stone trees and vines, with countless little creatures peering out from under the boughs. None of it looked as overtly evil as we'd seen elsewhere, but that didn't count for a lot. Low bar to clear.

Two more of the armored, purple-black figures stood at the top of the steps, flanking the slightly open door, their spears angled outward, toward us, the butt of each haft resting on the stone steps, the point aimed high above, at the ceiling directly above the gatehouse.

For a long moment, we stayed in our crescent against the outer wall, guns pointed up at the gate, the windows and those two armored figures. Neither one of them moved. They may as well have been statues, just like the others down below. Nor did they speak, like the first two had at the bridge. They just stood there, motionless yet watchful.

I can't explain that last part. I could *feel* their eyes on us, even though none were visible. There was an aura of vigilance about them, an oppressive sense that we were being scrutinized closely.

We could stand there and have a staring contest with what may as well be stone statues, or we could advance and continue the clear. One of two things was going to happen. Either they'd come to life and we'd have to figure out how to kill them, or else they'd do the same thing as the others down below, and simply stay in place, watching.

I started forward, since it seemed like nobody else was going to take the first step, my weapon up at the ready, watching the armored figures over the top of my sights. They didn't move, even as I mounted the steps, still staying slightly offset from the doorway, the faint padding of boots behind me an assurance that I hadn't just thrown myself solo into the middle of the killing ground.

A Tuacha rifle muzzle entered my peripheral vision off to my right, and I glanced over in time to see that it was Cairbre. He still didn't say a word, and he didn't look at me, but he'd been the first to step out and join me on the steps. That said something. I couldn't be sure what, but something. Maybe he was getting over his superiority complex. Or maybe he was just pissed that the outsider was the first one to move on the gate.

We came abreast of the two armored figures, which was when I realized that they were bigger than they'd initially appeared. Each one stood probably two feet taller than me, and I'm not a small man.

They didn't move, their helmets still turned toward the gatehouse. We passed them, rotating to clear the dead space in the shadows behind them , and then we were at the doors.

Massive, sheathed in verdigrised bronze, they stood only partway open, the gap just wide enough for one man in full gear to slip through. The hall beyond was dark, and I paused just beforehand, tucking my buttstock up under my arm to keep my muzzle trained on the opening while I dropped my NVGs in front of my eyes with the other hand. Cairbre waited on the other side of the doorway, his impatience palpable. The Tuacha could see in the pitch black without much difficulty, as opposed to us mere mortals who needed NVGs.

So, maybe Cairbre wasn't mellowing, after all.

Able to see the flagstones of the floor on the inside in faintly grainy green, I quickly cleared the space directly in front of the door, then went through, hooking left as Cairbre entered right behind me, moving right to clear that corner and cover my back.

My IR illuminator spilled a circle of bright green on walls and floor in my NVGs as I swept it across the vast hall. More carved pillars ran down the center of the room toward a distant dais, and tables lined the walls between them, seemingly carved out of the same stone as the rest of the place. I supposed if that was the most plentiful building material you had, you took advantage of it.

Fireplaces were set into the walls to either side, all of them dark and cold. More of the spear-wielding suits of armor, all the same, with muscled cuirass, scale kilt and aventail, carved greaves, and the same vaguely Corinthian winged helmets, stood on plinths set on the inside of each pillar, facing the center of the hall.

We moved out to the walls, keeping the pillars between us and the towering, armored figures as we paced up the length of the hall. Weapons stayed up, eyes scanning every angle, every corner.

The resemblance to the great hall in the tor was striking, though that was mainly a matter of layout. The decoration was markedly different. It seemed that every surface was carved with vines, branches, and intertwining beasts. Again, none of it looked nearly as overtly evil as the death and monsters enshrined in the art of the Dovos or anyone else besides the Menninkai that we'd seen here in the north, yet there was something more subtly disturbing about them. Something that reminded me vaguely of Lost Colcand, set in stone instead of living plants.

Light appeared somewhere behind the dais, only a flickering glow in my NVGs at first, but intensifying as whoever or whatever bore it got closer. The light itself was hidden behind the high stone seat that dominated the dais, set behind another big, stone table. The seat back was silhouetted in the glow, revealing two carved, snarling beasts facing each other at the top.

Almost all muzzles turned toward that flickering glow as it grew and brightened. A few were still watching the door we'd come in through, while at least a couple of us were still keeping an eye on the suits of armor along the pillars.

So far, nothing had jumped out at us.

The light came around the back of the chair to reveal a slightly bent old man, his hair and beard both snow-white even in the green of my NVGs, carrying a candle.

He was dressed in a simple tunic and cloak, the latter lined with fur. He squinted at us as he held the candle high, and even as I lifted my NVGs to see better as the light spilled out over the dais, I was struck by the impression that he could see much farther by its glow than I would have expected.

His face was deeply lined, though his eyes were bright, even in the dim, flickering light of the candle.

"Who has come barging into my home at this hour?" It wasn't that late, but the old man didn't seem to notice or care, and given how dark it was inside the hall, he might be confused.

Provided I believed this was actually just a normal old man. Which I didn't. Especially since he wasn't speaking English or *Tenga Tuacha*. He was speaking the same strange, almost Slavic-sounding tongue that the sentinels at the bridge had used, only we could understand him. Which meant he either had the mind speech, or the Fohoriman spell to imitate it, and that kind of precluded his confused oldster act.

Mathghaman lowered his weapon, though he didn't sling it altogether. "We come seeking those men who passed this way before us. They would have had weapons similar to these." He pointed to my M110. "There would have been others, warriors of the Dovos nal Uergal."

"Others?" The old man's voice was vague, though his eyes were still sharp as he studied Mathghaman. "Hmm." He looked up at one of the high, narrow windows, closed off with fogged glass or crystal, that let in a faint, gray glow, too dim to really see by. "The snow must have come again. Well, foolish to try to travel these mountains this time of year. Should have stayed below until the summer." He turned toward the door behind the great seat, and whistled strangely before putting the candle down on the high table. "You are here, though, so I suppose I should be hospitable."

We watched him, eyes narrowed, and I glanced at the motionless suits of armor along the pillars. None of them had moved. Yet.

Light bloomed in the hall as more figures came out of side doors carrying more candles. A lot more candles. Soon the hall was filled with a warm, golden light that made the shadows of the creatures and beasts beneath the carved trees and vines flicker and dance eerily. More of the old man's servants came out with trays of food and big ceramic jugs, like the kind you used to see in cartoons full of whiskey.

Every one of them was a miniature version of the towering, armored sentinels that stood with their spears posted at every pillar in the hall.

Mathghaman's voice was barely over a whisper. "Touch no food or drink."

I wasn't the only one who didn't trust this setup. Good.

The old man had to have heard him, but if so, he didn't appear bothered. He slumped in the high seat and accepted a goblet from one of the faceless, armored servants and took a swig. "I get few visitors here. I have not desired them. What did you say brings you up into these mountains?"

Given the fact that he'd blatantly ignored Mathghaman's first explanation, I doubted he was going to get much out of a repetition. Yet Mathghaman stepped up to the high table and stood over the old man, looking down at him with massive arms crossed over his powerful chest.

The old man didn't seem to notice at first, even as the rest of us moved in around Mathghaman, some facing outboard, watching the servants and the still-motionless sentinels—which had, nevertheless, without anyone noticing their movement, turned their helms to all face us and the high table—the others spreading out to the King's Champion's flanks to cover the old man and the servants that were still bringing trays to the table itself.

The old man looked up at him then, though the befuddled look was mostly gone. Instead, he seemed almost expectant.

"I told your sentinels below who I am." Mathghaman's voice rolled through the hall. "As I am sure that you heard me clearly enough then, I will not repeat myself now. Yet you should know that I also know who *you* are."

"So, you can drop the act." I doubted Gunny knew exactly what Mathghaman was talking about, but the fact that the befuddled old man *was* a façade for something else was painfully obvious.

The creature that looked like a white-haired oldster tilted its head then, its expression clearing, its eyes tightening. Just for a moment, the old man's face *blurred*, and I caught a glimpse of gray skin and glowing red eyes.

Then the great double doors at the entrance to the hall slammed shut.

CHAPTER 34

"BETTER if you had taken the warning the Duergar gave you, even if indirectly." The faint quaver was gone from the old man's voice. He stood, and suddenly he towered over even Mathghaman. He must have stood nearly eight feet tall, almost as tall as his sentinels. He still wore the same tunic, breeches, and fur-lined cloak. His white hair and beard remained, but his face was narrower, harsh and hawkish, his skin a charcoal gray, his eyes gleaming red in deep-set sockets above sharp cheekbones.

"I have had little to do with my kin's squabbling for many years." The Fohoriman's voice was cold, deep, and hollow. "I turned aside from that path long ago, and sought solitude here." He waved a taloned hand to indicate the odd, armored creatures who served him. "I have had naught to do with mortals, preferring to summon lesser spirits to animate my constructs to serve me. So it has been since before your time, Son of Cathal." He almost seemed to sigh, as if he felt some great weariness or sadness. "My kin believe me slain, and damned as I may be, I would have it remain so." He began to turn away. "You may resist for a while, yet soon hunger and thirst will triumph, and you will embrace the oblivion of my hospitality. Perhaps you will seek it out sooner. It would be better so."

"Did the others embrace your 'hospitality?'" Mathghaman had let a little anger slip into his voice, but there was no rage against the trap we'd walked into. Not on Mathghaman's part, anyway. I could tell from the look of pure murder on Bailey's face that we were about half a pound of trigger pressure away from one hell of a fight. "You refused to mention them, yet I know they came here. I saw the traces of violence on those doors behind us."

The red eyes might have flashed angrily. "The shaman among them summoned lesser servants of Vaelor." His mouth worked behind his beard. "They were a match for my servants. *You* will not be." He made to turn aside again.

Mathghaman laughed. "We shall see. I am a servant of Tigharn. Your 'lesser spirits' hold no terror for me." He glanced over his shoulder at us. "Nor do they hold great terror for my friends, who will gladly dismantle the constructs you have built with an eagerness and violence that I think will surprise you." He turned back to the Fohoriman, who stood with his expression frozen, and sobered. "Yet it seems to me that your plan has one flaw. You wish to keep us here because you are in hiding from your fellow Warlock Kings, Fearganagaidh." The Fohoriman's gaze sharpened as Mathghaman named him. I hadn't heard about this one, but apparently Mathghaman had, and maybe he wasn't as good at hiding in the mountains as he'd hoped. "Yet those who came before us have already departed, doubtless with the knowledge of your presence."

Fearganagaidh scoffed. "They seek to free Vaelor. They will not survive the experience."

"Isn't Vaelor's awakening a matter of some concern, even to you?" Gunny had one hand on his hip, the other on his rifle's pistol grip. If he was fazed by the glare of those red eyes as they turned to him, he sure didn't show it.

After all, we'd killed plenty of Fohorimans already. I was starting to suspect that this one was something more, perhaps even a Warlock King himself, but still. He'd probably die if we put enough bullets in him.

I suddenly hoped that nobody was going to get too froggy and crank off a 40mm in that enclosed space. The concussion alone would not be fun.

"I survived his lordship before. I will survive it again." Even as he said it though, I thought I heard a note of dread in Fearghanagaidh's voice.

There was something deeply strange going on here. The very fact that this monster hadn't immediately tried to kill us was weird. And this was the first time I'd ever heard of a Warlock King deliberately trying *not* to dominate everyone around them. A Fohoriman Warlock King who just wanted to be left alone in his survivalist retreat in the mountains? It didn't seem to fit with everything else we knew about those men and women who had turned themselves into twisted, inhuman monstrosities in the pursuit of power.

Mathghaman laughed again, the sound low and faintly bitter. "You hide from death here, thinking that all have forgotten Fearganagaidh the Deceiver. Yet if *my* people have not, what makes you believe that your own brethren have, as obsessed with vengeance as they are? Or that Vaelor will overlook you, should he rise from his prison?"

Fearganagaidh clenched his fists. "I may be damned for the crimes I committed long ago, but I will not go quietly to that damnation. I still live after all these centuries, and live on I shall, if I have to sacrifice every living thing in these mountains to buy one more moment." He glared around at all of us. "You shall not escape this place. No others will go out into the world to bring my reckoning any closer." He turned away, then stopped as Mathghaman drew his sword.

"You sought to stave off your reckoning?" The King's Champion's voice boomed through the hall. "You have brought it to your doorstep. I shall not be detained by a servant of the Summoner, no matter how desperately he would deceive himself that he has broken away."

Every muzzle came up, even as the armored automatons—or whatever they were—stepped down from their platforms and away from the pillars, footsteps booming in the stony hall. It looked like we were going to get that fight that Bailey was spoiling for, after all.

Fearganagaidh straightened, his hands at his sides. "You would challenge *me*? I have wielded the powers of the spirit world for many lives of men." Once again, he swept that taloned hand around the room. He had a stone table between him and Mathghaman, so he was probably feeling confident enough. "My servants are legion, and they have none of man's vulnerabilities!" He scoffed. "You would do better to taste of my liquor. I am not without mercy. The oblivion you would face at the bottom of my cups would be far preferable to what awaits you should you fight me."

Mathghaman laughed again and leaped over the table.

At almost the same moment, Fearganagaidh let out a shout, sweeping his hand in a commanding gesture, and the armored sentinels turned and closed in on us. The smaller servants didn't seem to be interested in joining the fight, but simply stood motionless, waiting.

I spun and snapped my M110 to my shoulder, my finger already tightening on the trigger as I found the red dot, tracking up the huge, sculpted cuirass toward the ominous helm above, even as that big bastard lowered its spear toward my chest.

Santos had already opened fire, laying into the other sentinel that was closest. He walked a line of bullets up the advancing monstrosity's cuirass, punching craters in it but hardly even slowing it down.

I dumped three rounds into that dark eye slit, as fast as I could pull the trigger and recover from the recoil, leaning into the heavy rifle even as I backstepped to stay away from that massive spearpoint. The rest of the platoon had also opened fire, but against a dozen of the gigantic monsters, we couldn't focus all our firepower on one or two, which looked like what it was going to take to drop one of these things.

That, or explosives, which had their own drawbacks in that stone hall.

I could hear the clash of blades as Mathghaman and Fearganagaidh dueled on the dais behind us, even as Gunny bellowed over the crash of gunfire, "Close in! Skirmish line, use the tables for cover!"

The big automatons, or whatever they were, could easily reach over the tables with those long spears, but it would probably still help to put something big and heavy between us and them. I sidestepped as that big spear jabbed for my face, chipping stone from the table behind me, and shot the thing in the face again, but while the helmet rang as the bullet disappeared into that cavernous darkness behind the T-shaped eye slit, there was no sign that I was doing any substantial damage, even with 175-grain 7.62 rounds.

We came together quickly, moving behind the tables along one wall, though the sentinels turned and followed almost as quickly. It was fast becoming apparent that we weren't going to scratch these things just by shooting at them, and they were going to flank us fast.

While it seemed counterintuitive to give up a firearm for a blade, I slung my rifle and drew my sword. My shield was back on my horse, outside, but I'd learned to fight without one, too. I'd much rather *have* a shield than just a blade, particularly against a twelve-foot-long spear, but wish in one hand…

The sentinel coming around the corner of the table was the most immediate threat, and I moved around Gurke and Chambers, putting my hand on Chambers' shoulder to make sure he ceased fire before I stepped in front of his muzzle. He'd figured out that it was pointless at about the same time, and dropped his weapon, drawing his axe. It was questionable how much any of our hand weapons would do, but while mine was clearly special, blessed from its first forging, Brother Saukko had blessed each of the more mundane blades before we'd departed Vahava Paykhah, knowing what we were probably getting into.

That huge spear came flying at my face, and I deflected it as I leaned to one side, ducking beneath it as Chambers hooked it with his axe and slammed the point into the stone table, putting his boot on it even as he grabbed the haft with his free hand. He was almost yanked completely off his feet as the sentinel pulled the spear back, but I'd gotten the opening I needed.

Dodging toward the wall to avoid the questing spear-point that stabbed over the top of the table and rang off Franks' helmet, knocking him sprawling, I pushed off the flagstone floor, the palm of my off hand pressed against the pommel of my sword as I drove the point at the bottom edge of the breastplate, trying to get under it and over the scale kilt.

It was like stabbing a boulder. The sword rang, the impact traveling right up my arms. If I'd tried that with any lesser sword, it would have shattered.

As I pulled back and ducked under the scything sweep of the spear once again, as it chipped stone from the wall behind me, I realized that this wasn't going to be as easy as dropping the animated suits of armor beneath Taramas's citadel. Those things had had joints I could get the point into. These things were solid. Seemingly, solid stone.

If I'd been some movie swordsman, I would have run up the spear to stab the thing in the eye slit. I'm just a mortal man, though, weighed down by my gear, a rifle hanging on my back by its sling, and days and weeks of accumulated fatigue. I wasn't doing any jumping or vaulting anytime soon, never mind some kind of Hollywood elf stuff.

Fortunately, as big as they were, they weren't nearly as big as the giant we'd fought in the pass off to the west, the first time we'd encountered the Duergar. I could still reach that helm, if I could get in there fast enough. As the spear finished its long, sweeping arc, I stepped in and thrust for the eye slit.

The sentinel tried to rear back, the first time any of these things had tried to evade any attack at all. My point skittered off the edge of the helmet, but if there had been a face in there, it would have gotten cut.

A low, distant moan sounded, and the sentinel actually staggered backward, its back foot stopping it with a *boom.* For a brief moment, every one of the sentinels seemed to hesitate.

I followed up, pressing the thing, grabbing the arm that held the spear to use it as a fulcrum as I drove the point at that slit again. I didn't get far before the thing interposed its other arm, driving my blade out and away again, but I'd still hurt it. It staggered even more noticeably.

I'd been too occupied with the immediate fight to pay much attention to the duel between Mathghaman and Fearganagaidh. I'd heard the clash of their arms in between gunshots as our Recon Marines and those of Mathghaman's companions still with us fought to keep Fearganagaidh's sentinels at bay. But the sudden shout, full of hate, fear, and despair, that echoed through the hall suddenly silenced everything.

The sentinels froze. Almost. Every helmeted head turned toward the dais. Our eyes followed as that terrible cry fell silent.

Mathghaman had been knocked sprawling, his sword flying from his hand with enough force that it had left a mark on the nearest pillar and had then skittered into the shadows near the far wall. Now he lay on the stone floor, one hand beneath him, looking up at Fearganagaidh, who stood above him, sword drawn, his eyes wide and wild, his chest heaving.

Mathghaman made no effort to defend himself, but stared the Warlock King in the eye. That seemed to bother the gray-skinned, white-haired figure the most.

"*Get up!*" The words were a strangled scream. The point of Fearganagaidh's sword quivered.

With a grim smile, Mathghaman slowly rose to his feet. He made no move toward his sword.

"What is he doing?" Gurke whispered. Anything louder seemed out of place.

I didn't know. Something was going on beneath the surface, something we couldn't see but that Mathghaman had perceived, and now he was taking advantage of it.

Mathghaman, instead of moving toward his weapon, took a step forward. To my surprise, Fearganagaidh stepped back.

"What do you fear, Faceless Man?" Mathghaman's eyes were hard as he took another step. "Adding one more murder to your tally? What is one more upon the myriads that already stain your hands? What is one dead man, more or less, to one who sold his soul so long ago?"

Fearganagaidh continued to retreat, his red eyes wild. I frowned as I watched him. The sentinels were still frozen, as if just as confused as I was.

"Is my punishment not enough?!" The ancient Warlock King retreated before Mathghaman's inexorable, if empty-handed advance.

"You think to hide from eternal justice in this high place, as if the abominations you summon to serve you and your own indifference to Vaelor's stirrings would be enough to mitigate what you have done." Mathghaman

314

spoke low and evenly, though every word cracked like a whip, and I could have sworn Fearganagaidh flinched with every syllable. "Is murder the line you will no longer cross?" He took another step, nearly bringing Fearganagaidh's point to his throat. "Such small mercy at so late a date will not save you."

I didn't hear what he said as he stepped even closer. His voice dropped low, and he kept talking, each word striking Fearganagaidh like a whip. Soon the Warlock King, now looking more like a shrunken, beaten man, rather than the towering, commanding sorcerer he had been, shrank back against the high table on the dais.

Then, with a scream that drove me almost to my knees as it hit my eardrums like an icepick, Fearganagaidh collapsed.

He wasn't alone. Every one of the armored sentinels and servants in the hall cracked, then began to crumble to rubble and dust. A distant, hollow wail was almost drowned out by the sound of collapsing masonry.

A long, heavy, despairing sigh drifted through the hall, as the candles all went out at once. I reached up, fumbling for my NVGs.

By the time I got them focused, Fearganagaidh was nothing more than a desiccated corpse, leathery flesh shrunk tight to the bones, slumped back against the stone table.

The floor shuddered, and dust sifted down from the ceiling as the entire mountain seemed to quake beneath us.

Mathghaman turned toward the doors. "Come. We have far to go, and this took far longer than it seemed."

CHAPTER 35

"OKAY." Bailey had held his peace until we were back outside, swinging back into the saddle again. The sun was almost down; we wouldn't get far before we had to stop and light fires. We were high enough and far enough north that fire was a necessity for survival again. The snowstorm had stopped, but the air was bitingly cold, the snow ankle deep where it hadn't drifted deeper. "I gotta ask. What the *hell* just happened back there?"

Mathghaman had already started his horse moving toward the north and the next valley on. He turned in his saddle, his face somber.

"There have long been tales of Fearganagaidh and why he disappeared. Once he sought to imprison us rather than kill us, I began to believe that some of the tales were true." He took a deep breath, smoking in the frigid air. "He was long thought dead. A servant of Vaelor before the uprising that imprisoned him beneath the ice, it was said that he balked at taking Vaelor's place. He had accepted the power offered, dragged step by step into the darkness and evil that is all that sorcery leads to, yet some part of him still wished he had not become such a monster. He fought his fellows, though he was outmatched, and even his spirit-driven automatons were forced back steadily, until he disappeared in a great conflagration at the feet of the mountains." He looked up at the black castle, darker than ever against the fading light of the sky. "It seems he has hidden here for centuries, terrified of the thought of death and judgement."

"That's a history, but it still doesn't answer the question." It was hard to say whether Bailey was just pissed about being confused, or if he was pissed that he hadn't managed to actually kill any of the Fohoriman's monstrosities himself. It hadn't been a good feeling, backed up against the wall by those towering automatons, unable to so much as scratch them.

"His entire existence was dominated by his fears, many of them conflicting. He feared discovery, lest the other Warlock Kings learn he still lived. He feared judgement, which was why he was reluctant to kill us, but sought to imprison us instead. He knew that he would face consequences at the end, and his terror of it knew few bounds, which was why he clung so desperately to life as to live in a keep in the mountains, sustained by sorcery. To have killed us out of hand, he feared, would only make things worse at the end, even though he was prepared to cling to life until the end of time to postpone that end." Mathghaman sighed slightly as his gaze became distant. "He was not entirely rational any longer. His own sorcery and his fears had long since caused his sanity to flee. Until the last.

"I simply told him the truth. That even killing us would not make things any worse than his own clinging to power meant for no mortal man, power taken from the denizens of the Outer Dark. That his judgement would be as bad either way. Unless he turned aside from it fully."

There was a stunned moment of silence. "You mean you just killed a Warlock King by *guilt-tripping* him to death?" Bailey sounded simultaneously thunderstruck and slightly angry.

Bearrac laughed. "I suppose that would be one way to put it."

"It was a grave risk," Mathghaman admitted grimly. "He might easily have decided that I was right, and that a few more deaths would count for little. Yet there was a part of him that has regretted his service to Vaelor, and his embrace of the powers from the Outer Dark, all this time. He thought himself damned, but he regretted, nevertheless. In the end, faced with what all he had done, he thought to try to redeem himself. He let go his sorcery, and since that was all that had kept him alive for centuries, he now faces his judgement."

"So, what? He repented and died?" Bailey looked over at me and I shrugged.

"So it would seem." Mathghaman turned back toward the north. "His fate is beyond this mortal realm, now."

It was a quiet column that threaded its way across the snowy crest of the ridge and down into the valley below, as the last light of the sun died in the west.

* * *

We didn't get far before we had to halt and light the night's fires. We still set security and stayed at fifty percent as the temperature plummeted, the clouds having cleared, letting the meager heat of the day escape into the dark.

Bearrac went around to each of the teams after we'd set security and rubbed the horses down. "Keep a sharp watch tonight, but if you hear voices or see lights moving in the trees, pay them no mind. Block them out. Do not watch them."

"More ghosts and spirits?" I asked.

He nodded, looking around at the trees, the lower branches lit by the flickering light of the fires. "It is likely that the spirits which animated Fearganagaidh's servants were banished when he relinquished his hold on them, but it is just as likely that some were far more potent than even he realized. Such creatures are deceptive, and his soul would have been a great prize, as tortured as it was. Some of them might linger, searching for new prey."

That was comforting. I looked around at the dark under the trees. I didn't see any apparitions or will-o-the-wisps floating around. But that didn't necessarily mean we were in the clear, either.

Still, it wasn't my shift on security, so I had to wrap myself more tightly in my cloak and Ranger roll, my head on my saddle and one hand on my rifle, the fire behind me.

Just before exhaustion claimed me, I could have sworn that not all the shadows under the trees were moving with the firelight.

* * *

My dreams were chaotic, disjointed, and disquieting. I wouldn't remember most of them when I woke up, but finally I found myself in one of those vivid, lifelike ones

319

that you're never quite sure if it's a dream or not until you wake up.

I stood on a flat plain, featureless and dark. Smoke or mist drifted above the ground, and while I could see, there was no sun in the sky, nor even any stars. Everything was a sort of slate gray, except for the utter darkness just ahead.

Something about that darkness was more than the absence of light. It was alive, aware, and, worst of all, it was *angry*.

A bitter wind plucked at me, and I stumbled forward, toward that vast blackness. One step, then another, as the inexorable pressure shoved me in a direction I didn't want to go.

A voice was chanting in the distance, but the presence beneath the darkness didn't seem to notice. It was as if all its attention was focused on me, and despite the fact that I could see nothing there, I knew there were eyes, many eyes, fixed on me.

There was a rumble then, like distant thunder, more felt than heard. As if whatever was in there, far in the distance yet entirely too close, had shifted its weight, or turned over in its sleep. It was terrifyingly aware, and I was filled with a terrible dread at even the non-sight of it. Its very presence radiated hatred... and something worse.

This thing wasn't just aware of me. It *knew* who I was. It knew *me*. And it wanted to see me utterly destroyed, in a way that meant I would suffer for an eternity along the way. It hated *me*, with all the intensity that it hated everything else.

I knew then that I was looking at Vaelor, in whatever strange realm he inhabited in his deathly slumber beneath the ice. And I was alone, exposed to his bottomless malice.

No, not alone. A hand closed on my shoulder, and I felt more than saw the glow of the luminous figure I'd first seen in a dream or vision in these northlands, shortly after we'd arrived.

My guardian didn't say anything audibly, but I heard him, nevertheless. *He is not all powerful. Resist him. You are not alone.*

Then Santos nudged me awake, and the vision faded.

* * *

My time on security was undisturbed by strange apparitions floating through the trees, and I was glad of it. That dream, or vision, was still bugging me, and with Santos and Farrar asleep, and Gunny down as well, I couldn't discuss it with anyone. Even Bearrac and Mathghaman were in that distant sort of trance the Tuacha substituted for sleep.

I was shook, and that didn't come easily. I'd seen some pretty horrific stuff in Syria, and even worse since we'd come to this world. I'd fought savages, trolls, Fohorimans, other things I had no names for, and even the walking dead. I'd beheaded an ancient vampire with the sword at my side. Yet none of that came close to the sheer depth of evil I'd seen in that dream.

So, I wasn't in the best frame of mind when the cloaked figure came out of the dark and sat down next to the fire.

It didn't walk past me, or else things might have gotten sporty a lot faster. It came out of the south and sat down across from Bearrac and Mathghaman. I saw the movement out of the corner of my eye and came up fast, my rifle tracking toward it, but Mathghaman's eyes had snapped open, and he held a hand up to forestall me.

I still prodded Farrar awake to take my place and moved in toward the fire, weapon ready if not aimed in.

"You spoiled my sport." The voice that came from beneath the hood was almost a hiss.

"You were not invited to this fire." Mathghaman's reply was as cold as the night's chill. "Depart back to the pit from whence you came."

The thing tilted its cowled head. "You are on *my* turf, Son of Cathal. You have no authority here."

"I am a servant of Tigharn, serpent from the Outer Dark," Mathghaman retorted. "That gives me all the authority I need."

Another faint hiss. "And are your hands completely clean, Son of Cathal?" I'd noticed that it had recoiled, ever so slightly, at the name of Tigharn. "No sins whatever to weigh upon your soul?" A low laugh made my hackles stand up even higher than they already were. "I think not. None but your master are pure, and He has little use for those less *perfect* than Himself. Let yourself slip, even a little, and He will abandon you, and leave you to *me*."

Mathghaman didn't laugh. None of the Tuacha who had gathered around behind him did, either. In fact, they didn't respond to the cloaked thing at all.

It was Mathghaman who moved first. From where he sat by the fire, he rose to a kneeling position, spread his hands, and looked up at the star-strewn sky. One by one, the other Tuacha joined him as he began to chant.

The sound was deep and resonant, the language that ancient tongue that I still hadn't wrapped my head around. The *Tenga Tuacha* was complex enough. The chant rose toward the sky, echoing off the distant mountains with a soaring, piercing beauty that stunned even a jaded Recon Marine.

In response, the cowled figure at the other side of the fire began to snarl, growl, and spit, the noises getting steadily nastier and more horrifying, rising to earsplitting shrieks and dropping to low, menacing promises of death and worse. There were words in that feral, seemingly incoherent noise, and even though I couldn't understand those words, I was a Recon Marine, well-versed enough in profanity that I could recognize curses and obscenities when I heard them.

As loud as that thing got, while it twitched and spasmed with anger, it never quite managed to drown out that chant. It was trying. But while the Tuacha never quite seemed to strain to raise their voices, they were always just slightly louder than the discordant, malignant noise coming from the cloaked hooded figure.

Then, with a final, echoing blast of hate, it was gone.

I blinked. I could have sworn it hadn't just vanished like a soap bubble, but it just wasn't there anymore. If it had gotten up and left, I hadn't seen it happen.

The chant continued for a few minutes, finally fading away as the Tuacha fell silent. The echoes seemed to linger, and in that cold, dark place, it was a small comfort. Especially after what had just been present there at our fire.

"What was that?" When I found my voice, it was hoarse, my throat dry as the desert.

Mathghaman lowered his gaze and looked at me across the fire. "That was the source of Fearganagaidh's power. A creature of the Outer Dark, kin to Vaelor, if considerably lesser than he."

Bearrac snorted, and his sardonic laugh seemed jarring after what had just happened. "The Warlock Kings fancy themselves gods, yet still must borrow their power from the same things they say they rejected and imprisoned."

I unclenched my hand from my sword. I'd barely noticed that I'd been gripping it so tightly that my fingers hurt.

Looking around, I saw that everyone was awake, more than a few weapons clenched in gloved fists. Fortunately, they were all swords or axes. If anyone had been pointing a gun at the fire in the *middle* of the perimeter, we would have had to have a bit of "mentoring" in the trees, involving eight count body builders until the snow melted.

Mathghaman noticed. "There are things in this world, my friends, that cannot be fought with bullets or blades." He looked around at the darkness beyond the firelight. "We will encounter more of them as we near Vaelor's prison. You must prepare yourselves."

As I moved back out to take up security, I nudged Farrar and indicated he should try to get some sleep. The look on his face in the flickering firelight suggested that was going to be far more easily said than done, but he headed back to his saddle anyway.

I settled back into my own position, watching the darkness outside the perimeter. It seemed darker, somehow. Intellectually, I knew that it was probably because my night adaptation had been shot when I'd turned back toward the fire, but I couldn't shake a lingering sense of oppressive dread after that thing's appearance, despite how seemingly easily the Tuacha had banished it.

Thoughts of my earlier musings about taking sides came back as I tucked my cloak around me to keep the chill away. Surviving in this place might just require more than speed, surprise, and violence of action.

That was an odd thought for a Recon Marine. I mean, I think we'd all considered such things at some point or other, but it wasn't something you talked about much. It went counter to the stereotype of the hardened killer that we all strove to cultivate. Toughness, courage, and skill were all that mattered.

Until they weren't.

That line from the Recon Creed popped into my head, then. *Conquering all obstacles, both large and small, I shall never quit. To quit, to surrender, to give up is to fail. To be a Recon Marine is to surpass failure; to overcome, to adapt and to do whatever it takes to complete the mission.*

I guessed that we were going to have to *adapt* in ways we'd never considered before.

CHAPTER 36

NO more demons or monsters came out of the dark that night. We were still dragging when we swung into the saddle the next morning. I doubted any of us had gotten much sleep after that little confrontation.

All eyes kept scanning the woods and the mountainsides as we crossed the much wider valley on the north side of Fearganagaidh's fortress. I saw more than a few nervous looks over shoulders, seeking not only the monsters we could shoot, but also the ones we couldn't.

The valley was empty and still, except for the faint waving of the treetops in the wind sweeping off the peaks, and the swirls of snow flurries that rode that wind. That quiet could still be deceptive. There might be armies of monsters waiting in the shadows beneath the trees, or even in holes in the ground on the open meadows that lay between windblown stands of firs and spruces.

We rode carefully, though cover and concealment take on different meanings when you're potentially fighting things that can hide in the smallest shadow or depression in the ground. Still, we maintained a wide, dispersed formation, riding in traveling overwatch across the open areas, and making sure that we had clear fields of fire and could quickly maneuver when we passed through the woods.

Any spoor left by our quarry had long since been blown away or covered in snow. We couldn't follow them directly, so we were making for what the Book of Audur Cohm had pointed to as their probable next target: a hanging valley in the shadow of the peak named Tumsanag, where the greatest high place for the worship of Vaelor had once been carved out of the living rock.

We still had a long way to go. If the maps in the Book were remotely accurate, that temple was nearly at the base of the Teeth of Winter. If things had changed appreciably since they'd been drawn, it might even be buried under the ice by now.

That could be a win, at least from the perspective of keeping Vaelor buried. It wouldn't solve the problem of finding our missing Marines, though.

There wasn't a lot of unnecessary talking as we rode north, over increasingly rugged, stony mountains. The woods were still there, but the closer we got to the Teeth of Winter, the more wind-wracked and stunted the trees seemed to get.

More than once, we had to change course to get around sheer cliffs or nearly bottomless ravines. The weather got colder and more unpredictable. It was slow going, and while I was sure I wasn't alone in worrying about how far ahead Dragon Mask was, the sorcerer and our former companions weren't our only concern.

* * *

I looked back as we topped one of the last ridgelines before Tumsanag, about a week after the confrontation with Fearganagaidh, and stopped, reining Myrsky in for a moment as I squinted through the haze at the farthest ridge, about ten miles behind us. Lifting my rifle, I peered through the scope, but I couldn't see what had caught my eye again. Still, I'd been sure I'd seen a glint of pale, wan sunlight on metal.

It was almost certain that the Fohorimans hadn't given up their pursuit. And even if that was only their scouts, ten miles was far too close We'd opened the time-distance gap since the last time we'd seen them, but not nearly enough. The Duergar might have done some of our work for us, not that I was going to feel the slightest bit of gratitude to those little bastards. Now, I was starting to think that we needed to find some way to slow them down even further.

Ambushing the Fohoriman react force had been one thing, though. Numbers hadn't been quite as unbalanced. For seventeen of us to ambush an entire army would be suicidal. We'd get a lot of them to start, but the rest would probably steamroll us in pretty short order.

There were ways to get around that. I remembered stories from BRC about Recon teams in Vietnam, five or six dudes in the bush, getting walked on by entire VC or NVA battalions, and proceeding to bleed them white over a couple miles of jungle. Often with air support, but sometimes just with guns and violence of action.

We didn't have the knowledge of the terrain to make sure we weren't going to get cornered in a box canyon or pinned against a cliff, though. And with Dragon Mask and our missing Marines being our primary objective, we simply didn't have the time.

Gunny saw me halted and looking back the way we'd come, and he turned his horse and rode back up to join me. "See something?"

"Maybe." I turned Myrsky back toward the north. "I don't think Uergal and them have given up."

Gunny squinted at the far ridge, even as the clouds began to close in over the peaks above once again. We'd had a relatively clear couple of days, but as we got closer to Tumsanag, it looked like our respite was over.

I wondered, as I headed down the opposite slope, into a shallow hanging valley overshadowed by a razor-sharp ridge so steep that the snow struggled to cling to the rocks, just how natural that incoming weather really was. The Teeth of Winter could now be seen above all but the peak of Tumsanag itself, a jagged, dirty white wall stretching from horizon to horizon. Somewhere up there lay Vaelor's prison, and if we hadn't been fast enough, then Dragon Mask might already be poking the bear, trying to wake him up. There were all sorts of weird influences up here, and nothing could be taken for granted.

Not that we generally did, but we'd been learning for several months now that there's taking nothing for granted the way we'd done it back in The World, and then there was here.

We rode down the slope and toward the shadow of Tumsanag, weapons up and heads on a swivel.

* * *

"Well, that's something." Gurke's voice, as hushed as it was, seemed achingly loud in the rocky defile where we'd halted, looking down at the hollow below.

It was late afternoon, but it was *dark* down there. Clouds lowered over the peaks, and the summit of Tumsanag itself was lost in mist and gloom. Even the clouds, though, didn't seem to be enough to account for how dark it was in that valley. It looked like End of Evening Nautical Twilight, the last dying glow of the evening after sunset.

That wasn't what Gurke was observing, though. The darkness was far from the strangest thing we were looking at.

First was the evidence of another fight that had happened right at our feet. More shell casings glittered dimly in the rocks, and shattered stones, turned black by scorching or something more unnatural, had been blasted across the narrow defile, some embedded in the boulders nearby, hurled there with terrific force.

The remnants of a dozen stygian suits of armor were scattered across the ground, torn and rent in ways that looked like they'd been torn apart by huge claws. Dragon Mask had definitely been here. And he'd kept going, down that defile, into the darkness beneath.

The strangeness under that shadow made the demolished sentinels seem mundane.

A line of massive standing stones marched down from the crack in the rock where we stood, our horses all shifting nervously, joining the five rings of even taller obelisks that encircled the stony floor of the hollow. They would have looked a bit like Stonehenge without the topper stones, except for one, very disturbing, detail.

The nearest stone slab had a human face, contorted in agony, jutting from its side. It *might* have been carved that way, except that it would have meant carving down the rest of the eight-foot-tall stone level with the face's ears.

I really wanted to believe that it was just the result of some *really* intense craftsmanship, but given the fact that *every* stone had one or more of those faces, and sometimes an eerily realistic arm or hand, rising out of the weathered rock, I doubted it. Especially given what else sat down there in the hollow.

The idol had to be fifty feet tall. It sat on a throne, though whether the folded, batlike wings to either side were supposed to be the back of the throne or the idol's wings, I couldn't tell. Four great, clawed hands rested on the arms of the throne, and the creature squatted atop massive talons.

Its head was enormous, thrust forward and bent between its shoulders. Ten horns rose in a crown above it, and seven eyes glared out above a gaping, tusked maw that hung open nearly to the center of its chest.

An altar of skulls stood atop a stepped, stone dais at the idol's feet. Even in the gloom that clung to that place, and from the distance where we stood, we could see a corpse sprawled atop that gruesome pile.

"Leave the horses here for now." Gunny hadn't waited for Mathghaman's suggestion. It was pretty obvious that the animals really did *not* want to go down there.

We might have no choice in the long run. Even as we picketed them, even the most level-headed of the animals was pulling at the lead ropes, trying to shy away from the horror below. I looked up with a frown, and wove through the horses to come up to Gunny's side.

"We might need to grab our rucks from here, Guns." I glanced over as one of Chambers' horses whinnied in terror and reared up, while Chambers tugged on the lead rope and spoke quietly, trying to calm the animal down even as his suppressor tried to knock against his own knees. "If we lose the horses, we lose all our gear, not to mention what little is left of our chow. And I don't think they're going to stay put for long, even if we drive those picket pins down *really* nice and hard."

He glared down at the idol, then up at the horses, as Rodeffer fought to keep his own mount from bolting in response to Chambers' horse's panic. Then he nodded. "Everybody ruck up." It was going to make maneuver difficult, but there wasn't a lot of choice.

We'd moved and fought this way before, sure. It had sure been nice to leave the rucks on the horses for all this way, though.

It took some time to get everyone rucked up, especially since we couldn't drop security. Nothing had popped out to eat anyone's face yet, but that idol, stone though it was, seemed a little too alive for comfort.

The frozen faces in the standing stones just made things worse.

By the time everyone had his ruck on his back, three of the horses had broken loose from their pickets and run back up the defile and out of sight. Baldinus and Synar had started to run after them, but Bailey had called them back with an angry hiss. The other horses milled and shifted nervously, clearly terrified by their surroundings.

After a moment, Gunny caught my eye, looked at the horses, and nodded, a little sadly. I returned the nod, moved to where Myrsky was picketed, and pulled the picket pin, then shucked his saddle and harness off and left them against the rocks. I rubbed his neck as he nosed at me and whickered. "You've been a good boy, Myrsky. Gonna miss you." I kept my voice low. "I hope you make it back in one piece." It was a long shot, but he was a canny animal, and if any of the horses had a hope of making it back to Menninkai lands, he did.

Then I turned and smacked him on the hindquarters before turning to set Kovaves loose. He looked at me for a moment before turning and heading back the way we'd come.

The others, whose mounts hadn't bolted already, were doing the same, switching out with the guys on security. Gunny had already released his horses, and he turned back toward the idol, his jaw tight. We'd all bonded with the animals over the last couple of weeks. It sucked sending them off to fend for themselves in the wilderness.

Finally, the last was cantering off into the defile behind us, and we rucked up and got ready to move.

The rucks were considerably lighter than they had been. *If* we survived to head south again, we were going to have to hunt if we weren't going to starve. It would be doable—we'd seen some game on the way north, though nothing for the last several days—but it would be rough. Especially if we were running for our lives the whole time, which seemed likely.

Finally, we began our descent into the hollow. There was no other way to go. If Dragon Mask had come here—and between the shell casings, the shattered armor, and the corpse on the altar it was pretty obvious that he had—then he wouldn't have been able to go back south without being spotted. We'd crossed a barren slope to get to the defile leading to this high, hanging valley, and we'd had eyes on it for over a day.

That meant the only way to get to them was to go through this nightmarish place.

It was quiet as we paced down that eerie lane toward the idol and the altar. The crunch of our boots on the gravel and scree was painfully loud, yet I could still hear the wind moaning through the standing stones.

At least, I hoped it was the wind. I found my eyes drawn to one of those hollow-eyed, screaming faces as I paced past, pivoting to cover the dead space behind the stone with my muzzle. I tore my gaze away with a shudder. The detail was uncanny, and unlike any other carving I'd seen in the Land of Ice and Monsters, or any-where in this world besides the Isle of Riamog, for that matter. There were sculptures in Aith an Rih that were just as detailed, though every one of those was edify-ing, uplifting, turning the mind to thoughts of beauty and courage. These were the exact opposite.

And I could not shake the feeling that I wasn't look-ing at carvings so much as I was looking at men and women who had somehow been made one with the rock.

As if this place wasn't already going to haunt my dreams for a long time.

We reached the bottom of the hollow without inci-dent, the idol looming above us, still all too visible as a deeper black against the darkness of the sky. Its seven eyes were bent on the altar, but even in the dark, barely relieved by our PVS-15s, it still seemed to be staring at us malevolently. And that gaping mouth seemed far too close as Bailey, Gunny, and I stepped up toward the altar, as if that enormous head was about to dip and bite one of us in half.

The cavernous maw was easily large enough for a man to fit in, even with all his gear on.

The dais the altar sat on was taller than it had appeared from a distance, and the steps were all larger than a normal set of stairs, sized for an average human being. By the time we reached the top terrace, we were about six feet below the bottom, fanged jaw, and a good twenty feet above the floor of the hollow. It was dark enough that I had to turn on my IR illuminator to get a good look at the corpse.

"Holy shit," Bailey blurted out. I couldn't disagree with the sentiment.

Captain Sorenson hadn't been dead for all that long. The blood around the gaping wound in his abdomen was still glistening, the cavity that had been gouged out under his ribs still steaming slightly. He stared up at the starless sky, his eyes still fixed open, his face slack. There wasn't even the look of agony one might have expected on the face of a man who'd had his heart ripped out.

That face, which had been the bane of my existence for months, was leaner than I remembered it. Life with Dragon Mask, on the run through the mountains and wilderness from the Fohorimans, must have been hard. Not that our lives had been easy, except for the spare few weeks that we'd been able to spend on the Isle of Riamog. But Sorenson looked like he'd been starving before he'd been murdered.

"Well, I can't say I'll miss him." Bailey's hostility had never been as well-disguised as mine or Gunny's. I'd had to work hard to restrain him a few times. Fortunately, we had always been close enough that he'd never resented it. Now, I didn't have the energy, though it seemed vaguely obscene to speak ill of the dead, no matter how he'd met his end.

"Why'd they kill *him*, though?" Gunny was genuinely perplexed. "If anybody was going to participate in a little casual human sacrifice, I would have expected it to be the captain." When we all looked over at him, he shrugged. "The man's dead. I don't have to show any deference to his rank anymore."

"He was sacrificed for two reasons." Mathghaman had joined us quietly. He pointed up. "His heart would have been cast into the idol's maw, the crime of his murder feeding Vaelor's hunger for slaughter. It is one more step in freeing the beast. His blood, however, would have been squeezed into that." He pointed at the idol's inner left hand, which, unlike the other three hands, was held palm up. I hadn't noticed that before. I must be tired.

There was a cavity in the center of the palm, that was currently empty. "That would have held the key to the next passage." Mathghaman pointed again, this time I thought to the idol itself, but he began to step down the side of the dais, clearly heading for the back of the enormous statue.

Bailey followed him, and the rest of the platoon moved to join us, guns up and eyes on everything where possible, watching the walls of the hollow, the standing stones, and never straying far from that menacing representation of Vaelor, carved from stone yet frighteningly *aware*. Only Gurke and Gunny lingered on the dais for a few moments.

"Seems wrong to just leave him here." Gurke hadn't been a huge fan of Captain Sorenson either, but he'd never butted heads with him as brutally as Bailey and I had.

"We don't have time to bury him." Gunny turned aside and started after the rest of us. "And don't think about dropping a thermate on him, either. I've seen it done, and it didn't work out that well. If we survive this, maybe we can come back and dispose of the body properly." He looked up at the cloud of vapor that streamed from his mouth and nose, barely visible on NVGs. "He's not going anywhere."

With one more glance at the body, I descended the dais to join my team.

It was even darker behind the idol. The walls of the hollow closed in, and the standing stones seemed closer together, as if they were crowding behind the statue, the frozen, screaming faces trying not to see the carnage on the altar.

The rock walls stood sheer above us, though I could just make out a gap pointing up toward the shoulder of Tumsanag and the Teeth of Winter just beyond. I could feel the frigid wind coming off the glacier.

The base of that gap was blocked by a vast stone door that stood a good twelve feet tall and eight feet wide. It looked like it was all one piece, a giant slab carved off the side of the mountain and dropped straight down into the cleft in the rock. There was no way we were moving that by main force. Mathghaman stood in front of it, his arms folded. This was, presumably, what Dragon Mask had sacrificed Captain Sorenson for. The key had to open this gate, whatever form that key took.

Somehow, I couldn't get the picture of a gigantic, antique key out of my head, though I was sure it had been something far creepier.

Gunny took a look at it and scratched his beard. Then he turned over his shoulder.

"Breachers up!"

CHAPTER 37

"I have control, I have control, I have control." Gunny's voice echoed through the darkened hollow. It had taken a lot longer to set the charges than I think any of us had liked, surrounded by hellish stelae marked by screaming faces and overshadowed by the oppressive shade of Vaelor himself. When you're trying to blast through solid rock, though, it takes a lot more prep than when you're slapping a strip charge to a door, or even a ghostbuster against a cinderblock wall.

Now we had almost all the explosives we'd brought packed into every joint we could reach, tamped with whatever we could pack in behind them. It was, frankly, a crap shoot as to whether we were going to crack that big slab of rock, or just waste the last of our explosives.

What we were going to do then, I had no idea.

With Gunny's call, we all got to some shelter, turning away from the cleft in the rock, or lowering our heads to put our helmets between us and the blast. Gunny started the countdown. "Five, four, three, two, one."

Given that we were trying to breach the gate, the charges had been set up with an electric initiation system, tied into a claymore clacker. As he hit "two," Gunny pumped the clacker three times.

The shockwave in that stony hollow was *brutal.* It felt like getting punched, not in the face or the gut, but all over. And at first, it almost looked like it hadn't worked. As the smoke and dust cleared, the slab of rock filling the cleft was still intact.

Then it cracked. A chunk calved off one side, falling to the bottom of the hollow with a crash that seemed muted after the world-ending thunder of the charges going off. The top six feet of the slab began to tilt with an awful grinding noise, then overbalanced and fell, fortunately on the other side. The stone's impact shuddered through the ground as the *boom* echoed across the mountain.

There was still about six feet of rock solidly blocking the cleft, the sides chipped and blasted by the charges, but that part of the slab hadn't been breached. Still, we could get over a six-foot cliff. Even with rucks, that wasn't a big deal.

Especially since those rucks were even lighter now, lacking the explosives. We might pay for that later, depending on what we encountered farther north, but there was nothing for it.

"Conor, your team's got point." Gunny pointed to the still-smoking gap in the rock.

Rodeffer and I moved quickly to the wall of stone that still stood in the cleft. Santos and Farrar took the other side, where the stone stood a little higher, not quite seven feet. Santos nodded to me and hefted his Mk 48. He'd take security to start.

Farrar dropped his ruck and put his back to the stone, taking a knee and bracing himself, his rifle slung to his back. Santos likewise dropped his ruck and pointed his Mk 48 at the sky, put a boot on Farrar's thigh, as the smaller man winced a little, and then hoisted himself up. He got just high enough to lay his belt fed over the top of the stone, covering the defile beyond as Rodeffer and I dropped rucks and got ready to go over at the lower portion.

I almost went first. Rodeffer was lighter than I was, though, and he'd be quicker to get on his feet and ready to rock. So, I took a knee, cupped my hands, and boosted him up.

With Santos covering him, Rodeffer still paused just long enough to clear his immediate area, then hauled himself up until he got his waist on top of the stone, flipped one leg over, and adjusted his position to where he was lying on the top of the stone. He lowered one hand to me, and I grabbed it, pulling up as he slid down the other side, using his weight to propel myself over the stone, my boots scrabbling for purchase as I got high enough to get a good purchase on the top. I waited up there until Rodeffer was down and out of the way, his rifle up and covering the slot in the mountain ahead, then dropped the rest of the way, hitting harder than I'd meant to. My rifle bounced off the rock with a *clack*, but stealth was a non-starter at that point, anyway. Anyone or anything within ten miles or more would have heard those charges going off.

The defile was narrow and dark, even through NVGs. It curved up and away, toward Tumsanag itself, cutting off visibility after about seventy-five yards.

"Rucks." Santos called the warning just before one of them slid over the top of the stone slab and dropped the six feet to the rocky floor. It took moments to get all four over, then Santos boosted Farrar up to the top, and they clambered over, somewhat faster than Rodeffer and I had, since we were covering security.

We'd left the rucks where they'd dropped and pushed forward to leave room for Santos and Farrar. Right then, Rodeffer and I were alone and unafraid on the far side, and security was our sole priority.

Nothing had stirred in that darkness beyond the cleft the entire time, as Santos and Farrar moved over, collected their rucks, then relieved us so we could get our own. By that time, Mathghaman and Bearrac were already on the top edge of the remains of the slab, climbing over with an ease that I could only envy.

It took the better part of ten minutes to get the whole platoon over. We'd trained for this sort of thing before, and I'd done it for real in Syria. So had Gurke, Chambers, and Applegate. Usually there, though, the guys going over the wall would move to the compound gate and open it for the rest of the strike force. Usually. We'd run into a couple of cases where IEDs had made that a bad idea, and we'd had to bring the whole platoon in over the wall. This wasn't that different.

As soon as my team was rucked up and ready to go, we pushed up to that curve, if only to get out of the way. There wasn't a whole lot of space on that side of the door.

The curve was short, the ravine twisting back toward the shoulder of Tumsanag. The bottom was still dry and empty, though patches of snow had drifted along the wall in places. The wind whispered and moaned through the rocks above.

It was dark as midnight, even though it was barely after sunset. There *should* still have been some faint light remaining in the sky.

We split, Rodeffer and I moving against one wall of the ravine, Santos and Farrar the other. I could just see about fifteen yards ahead as we took a knee and waited for the rest of the platoon to catch up.

As still and quiet as that ravine was, I couldn't help but sense a restlessness, a hostile *presence* somewhere nearby. Every shadow seemed to flicker and shift when I wasn't looking directly at it, usually outside the green circle of my NVGs' field of view. Whenever I turned my head to look, though, I saw only bare rock, snow, and the broken scree underfoot.

Above, the darkness of the sky only deepened.

I couldn't put my slowly growing dread into words. The act of human sacrifice back there was bad enough, but it felt like something else had happened, something worse. From the Book of Audur Cohm, we knew that the high place was where the key to the far north had been kept, even before Vaelor's fall, but there were other gates, other safeguards that the Fohorimans had put in place to bind Vaelor to his throne in the north, under the ice.

Vaelor's fortress, the seat of his power, had already been up there before the Warlock Kings' rebellion, which was why the idol and the high place had been the primary opening that anyone needed to get past. The Fohorimans had imprisoned him in his own palace, as it were. We'd just passed the outermost line of defense.

I wondered if Dragon Mask had already forced one or more of the inner gates, and if he had, just what he'd let loose in the process.

Fortunately, before my imagination could start to run away with me, the rest of the platoon was up, with all our gear, on this side of the door. Rising to our feet, guns at the ready, we started moving, climbing toward the shoulder of Tumsanag and the first gate.

Hopefully, we'd catch up before they got all the way into the ice.

Hopefully.

* * *

That ravine ran higher and higher, widening as it reached the shoulder of the mountain and the base of the ice sheet. By the time we reached the top, almost ten hours after leaving the hollow and the idol behind, we were slogging through snow at least a foot deep, the stark, barren peak looming above us, the trees left far behind.

A pair of stelae faced us, now, black against the lighter ice. They were huge, standing almost as tall as the idol had down below and behind us. Rough, uneven in outline, they loomed threateningly overhead, warning anyone crazy enough to climb this high, this close to the Teeth of Winter, to turn back.

We spread out, security set in three hundred sixty degrees, as Gunny called the team leaders in to join him and Mathghaman in the center of the perimeter.

"We need to halt. We've already gone damn near a day without rest." Gunny nodded toward the hole in the ice between the standing stones. "It looks like they got in.

I don't particularly want to follow them on no sleep." He glanced at Mathghaman. "That drink of yours is good, but I don't know that it's going to be enough in there."

If he was remotely offended by the doubt, Mathghaman didn't show it. "We may not have any choice once we go in there, but I would agree. I only hope we *can* rest here."

No one asked what he meant by that. It wasn't just the wind and the cold, either.

It was hard to tell where the wind stopped, and the angry voices began. It wasn't like night land nav after midnight, either, where you're not sure if it's just your imagination, or if there's someone out there in the dark, talking. No, there were definitely voices out there, and they were *pissed*.

"Fifty percent security." Gunny glanced at the sky. "I don't think we can spare much time, and I also don't think we can expect to see the sun again before this is over. Make sure whoever's up is keeping an eye on their watches. We can spare maybe six hours. No more than that."

That wasn't good news, but there wasn't going to be much good news up there. We were all strung out, far leaner than we had been when we'd stepped off, thanks to the increasingly short rations as we'd climbed higher, the exertion, and the cold. Heading in there on about three hours of sleep was going to suck.

Gunny was right, though. There were dark marks on the ground and crawling up the ice, signs that something bad and weird had happened here. If this was the first gate, then Dragon Mask had already forced it, which meant he was that much closer to his goal. Time was short, and getting shorter.

Rodeffer and Farrar would take the first watch. They'd be fresher when we stepped off again. Santos and I wrapped ourselves in our cloaks and Ranger rolls, leaned back against our rucks, and tried to sleep.

It didn't go well.

CHAPTER 38

IT was every bit as dark as it had been six hours before when we finally got moving. The voices hadn't let up, but nothing had come at us, yet. We rucked up and headed into the gap blasted in the ice between the stones.

The voices intensified as we passed between the stelae. The darkness beneath the ice seemed to get even deeper, and I could have sworn my NVGs were getting dimmer.

Rodeffer got about three yards inside and stopped with a whispered, "What the fuck?"

I stepped up next to him, and stopped as my boot *crunched* in something. Looking down, I saw that there was a skeleton lying on the icy floor.

It was big, easily standing seven feet tall in life. From the looks of what was left, it had been bound in something like either barbed wire or dark, thorn-bearing vines. It lay spread-eagled on the icy floor of the passage, its skull—still wrapped in the black, prickly bindings—lying separate from its spine by several feet.

Dark stains were splashed against icy floor and walls, and when I looked up, there might even have been some spatter on the ceiling. Something bad had happened here, no doubt about it.

"What's up?" Gunny had pushed up to join us when we'd stopped.

"Looks like there was a sentinel here, and Dragon Mask or one of his summonings went right through it." Except for the never-ending, susurrating voices, we appeared to be alone in the passageway, but I still kept my voice low, barely above a whisper. In truth, a whisper often travels farther than a murmur. That was one of those counterintuitive truths you learned in Pre-BRC, but it works.

Gunny looked down at the bound skeleton and the slightly deformed skull, the jaws jutting just a little too far out, the teeth a little too long and a little too pointed. He took it in, along with the stains and the hanging remnants of the bindings, dangling and drifting from the sides of the stones. "When the book said that they'd 'bound' some of their own to hold the points of the prison, I guess I hadn't pictured this."

"It is worse than you think." Mathghaman's voice echoed hollowly through the passage. "This thing was still alive up until the point that our quarry cut him down. He has hung here, suspended between life and death, for all the centuries since Vaelor was bound."

"That sucks." It was a succinct assessment on Rodeffer's part, though it might not have fully encompassed the horror that Mathghaman had just described.

"Prepare yourselves. This sentinel would not have been bound willingly, but he would have fought to defend the way, and the Warlock Kings did not set their weakest sorcerers to watch Vaelor's prison. Whatever our enemy summoned to tear this one down, it was formidable indeed."

"I take it they'll only get more potent, the deeper we go?" I was looking down the passage, into the gloom beneath the ice.

"Undoubtedly." Mathghaman flexed his hands around his rifle. It was the closest to nervous I thought I'd ever seen him. Even when we'd been descending into the dungeon beneath the vampire's castle, he hadn't been visibly perturbed. "We may hope it will slow them down somewhat, but be prepared for a fight unlike any you have faced before."

Given what twisted horrors we'd already seen Dragon Mask summon, that was not a thought calculated to make any sane man want to go deeper.

But we were Recon Marines. We went in anyway.

* * *

The passage didn't go straight into the ice. There were still mountains, if smaller ones than Tumsanag, that had to be gone around. At least, I assumed so. It was possible, I supposed, that the Teeth of Winter might have just ground everything flat as it had advanced south from the pole. Besides, the twists and turns didn't seem like they were formed by terrain. I started to suspect, the deeper we got, that there was some other design involved in the weird, writhing way the passage bored into the ice. I couldn't tell what it was, but it creeped me out.

Just like we'd needed to under Taramas's citadel, we were moving on IR illuminators. There was no other light down there. We stalked through a frigid, dark underworld, sweeping the icy passages with cones of pale green light, visible only through our PVS-15s.

The Tuacha could probably see just as well as if we'd been walking in daylight, but that was one of their gifts.

I'd lost track of how long we'd been down there. We just kept going, eyes stinging with fatigue, putting one boot in front of the other. The icy floor made for treacherous footing, though it was at least crunchy with frost and pulverized snow and ice, rather than a solid sheet.

The voices never went away. In fact, they were getting louder the deeper we got—at least, it seemed that way. All it took to realize that they weren't *really* going up in volume was to pay attention to the rasp of breath, smoking in the freezing air, and the crunch of boots on the frozen floor of the passageway. They were as quiet as ever, but somehow they were more insistent, capturing more of our attention, the deeper we got.

Then the scream came.

It echoed down the passageway, sounding like it came from a long way off, but all the same, it raised gooseflesh on my arms. It was a sound of hate, rage, fear, and despair. It was worse than hearing a mountain lion scream in the dark when you're deep in the woods, fifty miles from the nearest town.

Everyone froze at first. It was that kind of scream. IR illuminators swept the chipped, blasted ice around us, searching for monstrous attackers that weren't there. Even the voices fell silent for a moment.

"Keep moving. That means we can't afford to slow down." Gunny was already pushing forward, and the rest of us had to move just to make sure he didn't jump the stack and leave us all behind.

The passage twisted twice more, never quite the way we thought it was going to, and then we came out into a vast cavern in the ice.

The packed ice and snow underfoot gave way to bare rock, and the walls vanished to either side. The ceiling above was low, only standing about four feet or so above our heads, the ice chipped and faceted, like a flint arrowhead. It was so low that it felt like a threat in and of itself, an ever-present reminder of the millions of tons of ice overhead, waiting to collapse and crush us all.

Light flickered at the far end of the cavern, pale in my NVGs, still too far away to see what exactly was going on. I could guess, though, especially as I heard the high *snap* of suppressed 5.56 fire amid the insane shrieks and growls that reverberated through the cavern. A thunderstorm sort of pressure started to build, along with a crawling sense of *wrongness* that made the lizard part of my brain want to run and hide, gibbering and screaming. There was sorcery going on up there, and it wasn't the Fohorimans' tamer version, that just did things like set fires and blow holes in fortified walls.

It was more like the twisted defiance of natural laws that had turned three of Taramas's hunters—and Sergeant Clarence Nelson-Hyde—to black mist in the snowy hills on the other side of the Land of Ice and Monsters, months before. Like the horror that had reduced the Lasknut outside the walls of Vahavah Paykhah to ravenous, mindless psychos.

I'll confess, I didn't want to go into that. None of us did. I'd seen it before, and it had haunted my nightmares ever since. Still does.

For a long moment, no one moved. Not even the Tuacha.

But Gunny knew what had to be done, and without a word, he started across the rocky floor, his M110 in his hands, his face set and grim, lit dimly by the green glow of his NVGs.

We followed. It was Gunny. We weren't going to let him down. Spreading out into a skirmish line, we followed, stretching our paces out to catch up with him.

The flickers of IR floods and lasers were all we could see, with the occasional muted flash of a suppressed gunshot. I wondered, my mind desperately reaching for anything *normal* that could distract from the abject, twisted *strangeness* of what we were walking into, just how much ammo those of our remaining brothers could have left.

And just where they'd point those weapons when we caught up, given what had already been done to Captain Sorenson.

The rocky floor wasn't completely flat. Boulders were scattered across the long, shallow slope leading toward that heinous light show, probably dragged down from higher elevations by the advancing ice sheet. As we advanced, we started to get down, moving from boulder to boulder, and before long, without a word of coordination, we were leapfrogging across the cavern, covering each other as we went. There were guns in the equation again, and we knew how to deal with gunfire, at least.

I was beginning to pick out detail in the gloom, as the IR lasers danced across the far wall. The ceiling rose higher at that end of the cavern, though still not high enough to clear the two black stelae that stood at the wall, flanking the narrow opening that went deeper into the ice. Their tops disappeared into the frozen ceiling above.

Three figures in furs and bump helmets were crouched behind boulders, shooting at the thing that hung suspended in the dark, thorny web strung between the standing stones. They didn't seem to be doing much more than annoying it.

The other dozen fur-clad figures, crouched behind another boulder, were up to something far more danger- ous. The blackness growing between them as they chant- ed was deeper and darker than even the strange, crack- ling whips of darkness with which the sentinel lashed their cover, its ear-splitting shrieks weapons in and of themselves.

A droning, assonant chant vibrated through the chamber. It wasn't particularly loud, yet somehow it penetrated everything, even the screams, the gunshots, and the weird buzzing that rose and fell with the senti- nel's attacks. Meanwhile, that darkness grew and inten- sified, the shaggy, fur-cloaked forms gathered around it dimming and fading into the blackness.

I dropped behind a rock, laid my M110 over the top of it, and found one of those hunched figures, swaying and twitching as he droned and chanted, his own dark shape slowly disappearing into the shadow that was growing up from the rocky ground in front of him. I was about to shoot him in the back, but sorcery counts as "Hostile Act, Hostile Intent."

Even as my finger tightened on the trigger, an old line flashed into my head. *Suffer not the witch to live.* Having seen what we'd seen in the Land of Ice and Monsters and the haunted territory to the east, that just seemed like common sense anymore.

My red dot was right between his shoulder blades, but he was fading into the growing darkness fast. I almost couldn't see him by the time the shot broke. The rifle surged back into my shoulder with a harsh *crack*, heavier and louder than the 5.56 M4s that Zimmerman, Owens, and Gonzalves were shooting at the sentinel.

My target dropped like a rock. The shadow seemed to shrink, just a little bit, and there was a sudden hitch in the chant.

I could have sworn, just then, that Dragon Mask looked straight at me, across the circle where they were summoning that darkness. It was too dark and too far away to see his face or his eyes, or even to be sure that it was him. But I could *feel* the fury and the hatred in that glance, even if I couldn't be sure that I'd seen it.

I was already shifting my aim when a harsh, barking series of notes rose above the sentinel's unholy screeching, and three oily, black horrors sprang up out of the ground right in front of us.

The first one had five limbs sprouting unevenly from a bulbous center body, most of which was mouth surrounded by purple, glowing eyes. No two of those limbs were the same size or shape, but each one was tipped with talons, claws, or simply a whipping tentacle.

A second sprang forward on one foot, three eyes around a lamprey mouth full of glassy teeth, crab claws snapping from limbs that arched over its head from behind its back.

The third was just a writhing mass of tentacles, slithering over the floor of the cavern far too quickly for what it was.

I lost track of the fight at the end of the cavern as the five-limbed one leaped for me, its jaws chomping at my face.

CHAPTER 39

MY first shot went straight through that slavering cavern of a mouth, spraying black fluid out the back of it. It didn't even slow it down.

I backed up, unwilling to turn my back on it, absolutely sure that it was going to jump on me and tear me to shreds as soon as I did. I kept shooting, blowing holes through the monster and spattering black ichor across the rocks, black ichor that turned into oily smoke as soon as it settled. Nothing I hit it with was even slowing it down.

I could feel the sheer, animal panic scratching at my mind as I backstepped as fast as I could, dumping rounds so fast that I could barely feel the trigger reset, the suppressed reports blending together into a single, thunderous crackle. The bolt locked back on an empty mag, and I almost lost my mind, knowing for sure that it was going to be on me before I could either reload or transition to my sword. Even if I could grab the blade, fighting that thing at close range was certain death.

Then a hand gripped my shoulder, just for a moment, and one of those long, elegant-looking Tuacha rifles came up in my peripheral vision as Bearrac took up the fire, blasting more holes into the five-limbed horror, the big man standing his ground, his feet solidly planted on the rock, leaning into his rifle as he hammered at the unnatural thing of hunger and malice as it kept swarming over the boulders toward us.

"Hold, Conor!" Bearrac's bellow rose even over the hellish noise that echoed from ice and stone. "Listen not to the fear!"

Something in his voice penetrated the gibbering panic clawing at my brain. I started to calm down just a little, my near-hyperventilation slowing as I felt my combat calm start to come over me. Then I noticed that the fire wasn't having no effect. It was slowing these things and driving them back. I just hadn't noticed.

Dropping the empty mag, I smoothly slapped another one in and hit the bolt release, leveling the red dot at the thing's center mass and opening fire again. This time, one of my rounds popped one of those glowing purple eyes, and as Bearrac, Rodeffer, Farrar, and I slammed round after round into it, it actually began to stagger backward. Only a little, but it wasn't advancing any more.

It wasn't giving up, though. It shrieked its fury, lashing at the rocks with all five limbs. One boulder the size of a couch cracked under its onslaught as it redoubled its efforts to get to us, despite the brutal hammering we were giving it.

Then Santos came up on our left, laid the Mk 48 over another boulder, and opened up.

Four ball, one tracer makes for a lot of lead when it's being poured into a point target at less than fifty yards. He chopped into the gibbering horror with a long, thunderous burst, holding the trigger down for half the belt. His suppressor was glowing brightly in my NVGs and smoking by the time he let off.

The creature had been reduced to a writhing pile of offal by that time, two of its five limbs completely blown off, all but one eye gone, many of the teeth it had sprouted from its maw shattered. It wasn't done yet, though. It kept clawing its way toward us, reduced as it was, even as Rodeffer and Farrar kept shooting at it. Bearrac and I were reloading, as the heavy *thud* of an explosion sounded off to the right. The shockwave of the 40mm grenade traveled a lot farther in the enclosed space of the cavern, and only the horror of the sorcery flying around that place meant that my head didn't start to hurt any more as the overpressure washed over us.

"Get back!" Gunny roared. More rounds began to *crack* past our heads, smacking into the horror on the ground and the rocks around it.

That wasn't the time to wonder at the order. Nor was it the time to worry about turning my back on that thing. I turned and ran for the first boulder I saw, making sure I wasn't about to run right into another Marine's line of fire before I moved.

As I ran, I looked up and saw Gunny bringing one of our standalone M203 grenade launchers to his shoulder.

Thunk.

I could see the 40mm ogive as it sailed past my head, though only for a moment. I threw myself flat just before it hit.

Boom. I don't think I'd ever been that close to a grenade explosion, even counting that one ill-advised frag into a mud hut in Syria, when I'd taken a bit of shrapnel through the wall. Dust and smoke boiled over us, and I heard the thousands of bits of serrated wire whispering against the rocks and pattering on the icy ceiling. A chunk of ice fell free and dropped to the ground with a crash, only about a foot from my boot.

The shockwave had stunned me a little, and the cold of the ground was rapidly sucking away the body heat I'd built up. I had to get up. I had to move. I could still hear that thing snarling and gibbering through the ringing in my ears. It wasn't done yet.

Then all of reality *blinked.*

At least, that was what it felt like. It was as if the whole world shuddered, not just the ground, but the very air itself. My ears rang, and for a moment, I couldn't hear anything. I felt like I was falling, even though I was still on the ground.

The scream that tore through the cavern felt like it was never going to end. It pierced through gunfire and explosions alike, drowning out every other sound, until there was nothing but darkness and that scream.

Then it fell silent, dying away with a despairing wail that sounded more like a wordless curse. My stomach twisted, and I felt like throwing up.

As the scream finally ended—it seemed like there was still an echo of that thin, malignant wail ringing in my ears, though that might have just been my imagination combined with the tinnitus I've been walking around with for over a decade—the cavern went momentarily still, as if even the oily black horrors from the Outer Dark were stunned.

I levered myself up off the floor. It wasn't easy; everything hurt, and I felt like I'd just joined "The Five Hundred Club" all over again. Though that night of standing in a mud puddle of my own sweat outside the cadre shack, arms and legs aching from hundreds of eight counts, seemed like paradise compared to that place of darkness, cold, and despair.

A low, evil gurgle came from behind, where the gibbering horror had been smashed back by the 40mm grenade blast. It was still there. I staggered to my feet, turning and practically falling against the nearest boulder. Dragging myself back up, I hauled myself halfway around the rock to bring my rifle to bear against the monster.

What was left of it. One clawed hand dragged the shrunken, blind creature forward, its broken teeth gnashing and snarling. It seemed slow and woozy, twitching strangely, almost like it had been animated in stop motion, as it grabbed another rock and pulled the basketball-sized remnant of its body over the bullet-and-shrapnel-scarred boulder.

I shot it through that chunk of oily gristle, blasting another spatter of black out the other side. It shuddered, but kept coming, though it was still slow and uncoordinated. Santos let rip another burst, spattering the rocks with that fast-dissolving, unnatural slime. More gunfire echoed in the dark, and another 40mm went off with a resounding *boom*.

You might think that, with my panic having been suppressed, and the monster being reduced to one limb and a body smaller than a medicine ball, I wouldn't have been scared of it. That's just because you've never seen one of these things. It could be the size of a housecat and I'd still have to fight the screaming urge to just turn and run, even as I knew that it would probably catch me. Those things were the embodiment of predatory hatred, dragged out of the void where there was nothing good, nothing natural, given form only to wreak destruction on our plane. They weren't just dangerous and scary; they were *wrong* in a way you can't really understand until you've looked one in the teeth.

So, as I stood to get a better shot, I kept the boulder between me and it, leaned into the gun, and dumped the rest of the mag into it. It jerked, shuddered, and shrieked as Rodeffer, Farrar, and Bearrac joined in, spattering more of the inky muck that made up its physical form across the rocks and the ground.

We kept shooting until there wasn't more than a fist-sized chunk left. It had no limbs, and only part of a mouth, but it kept screaming up until Bearrac walked up to it and stomped on it, hard enough to spatter the black fluid all over the surrounding boulders.

Only then did everything go quiet.

Bearrac shook the last, smoking bits of the thing off his boot, which looked whitened and scarred, as if he'd just stepped in some caustic chemical. I was sure that he'd just crushed something far worse than that.

I looked around me, then. By some miracle, we were all still standing. Some looked in better repair than others. Everyone was a little unsteady on their feet, as if we'd all gone through a massive IED blast, and were suffering the aftereffects of TBI. Maybe we were. I was pretty sure that whatever had happened, whatever that "blink" had been, it was probably a lot worse than an IED.

When I looked up at the end of the cavern, I saw that it really was.

All that was left of the sentinel was its deformed skull, hanging from a single strand of that thorned web, its eye sockets darkened. The rest had been smashed to smoking fragments scattered down the passageway behind it.

The stelae looked wrong, somehow. As I stepped closer, I saw that they looked melted, though they were still cold enough that they looked black in my NVGs. If they'd truly been melted by extreme temperatures, they'd be glowing brightly on IR. No, whatever had done this had managed to make them flow like a candy bar in a microwave without raising the temp at all.

I came to the man I'd shot. The corpse was desiccated and fleshless, one clawed, skeletal hand stretched out toward the center of the ritual circle.

It was better than what had happened to Nelson-Hyde when he'd been too close to that kind of sorcery, I guessed.

"One gate remains." Mathghaman's voice was grim. "And now they know for certain they are being pursued."

"We must hurry." Bearrac was already stepping it out toward the stelae and the passageway beyond. Whose mission it was didn't matter anymore.

If Vaelor was freed, none of us were going to get out of those caverns alive.

I just didn't think we'd get the kindness of dying that year, if that happened.

CHAPTER 40

NOW that he knew he was being pursued, Dragon Mask was really in a hurry. We hadn't gone far when the cavern shook and heaved under our feet, and a deep, menacing rumble sounded from somewhere up ahead.

We slowed, weapons coming up and eyes searching the darkness for the next attack. The narrow passage through the glacier stretched almost straight in front of us, our IR lights disappearing into the blackness beyond the reflections glittering off the fractured ice.

Nothing came howling out of the dark at us. The shaking stilled. The rumble faded.

"What the hell just happened?" Baldinus's voice was a rasping whisper.

"Nothing good." Gunny stepped forward, peering into the dark. "Keep moving."

I can't say there wasn't a little extra caution as we kept going. Marines pride ourselves on our aggressiveness, but when you're confined to a narrow corridor, and you've just spent a good chunk of your combat load on gibbering horrors that weren't even the primary target, some caution is called for.

It took another half a mile or so to discover just what had made that noise.

The passageway was caved in, piles and blocks of shattered ice filling the way in front of us. Baldinus halted, playing his IR illuminator over the pile.

"Well, shit." Bailey glared at the obstruction. "And we used all of our explosives on that slab of rock back there."

"Aside from the forty mike-mike, anyway." Applegate tilted his head as he studied the pile of shattered ice and rock.

"Don't even think about it." Gunny stepped past Bailey's team and started to grab chunks of ice with his gloved hands, digging at the pile. "I guarantee that any more shocks will probably bring the rest of this passage down on our heads. Which is probably exactly what they had in mind." He looked over his shoulder at the rest of us. "One team on six o'clock security. Everyone else, start digging."

We couldn't fit the whole of the platoon on digging duty, but we still needed more hands behind the guys digging away at the mound itself to keep the chunks of ice moving backward, clearing the way so that we didn't just move the obstruction back a little farther. Everyone got to work, even as Gurke's team watched back the way we'd come, just in case.

All indicators pointed to the threat being in front of us, but we'd learned the hard way to take nothing in this frozen hell for granted. After all, that idol and whatever weirdness lurked around it was still behind us, too.

A gap began to appear at the top of the pile. It was too small to get one of us through it yet, but it was big enough that Gunny pointed to Synar and told him to climb up there and cover the opening. Again, just in case.

Three-hundred-sixty-degree security is a requirement that any fighting man forgets at his peril.

Even as Synar clambered up and stuck his muzzle through the gap, the ground and the walls shook again, and a piercing scream echoed down the cave.

Gunny didn't stop digging. "Sounds like they just got to the third gate," he grunted, levering a chunk of rock-hard ice twice the size of his head out of the pile and sending it tumbling down toward the rocky floor.

"We are running out of time." Mathghaman clambered up next to Synar and went to town, shoveling ice and rock aside, sending a small avalanche tumbling toward the cavern floor.

The screams continued, joined by ominous rolls of thunder and an electric crackle that wasn't gunfire. All hell was breaking loose down there.

As evil as the Fohorimans were, I could only hope that their bound sentinel held out long enough. The alternative didn't bear thinking about. They were almost to Vaelor's Throne.

Something in that pile of detritus gave way, and Gunny, Mathghaman, and Synar suddenly slid backward in a rattling avalanche, catching themselves with gloved hands thrown deep into the ice and stone before they could be swept away. The gap between the pile and the ceiling was suddenly much larger, the mound of debris having cleared away from the inverted crater in the ceiling from where it had fallen.

"Get moving." The screams intensified for a moment, then, with another nauseating shudder in reality itself, fell silent. For a moment, as the sorcery made reality blink, we all shuddered and stumbled, but as soon as we were able to move again, we were clambering up the unstable slope and toward that still-narrow opening.

Synar and Gunny got there first, checking to make sure nothing that needed to be shot was waiting just on the other side. Then Gunny tapped Synar on the shoulder with a fist and started to crawl through himself.

Everybody started moving faster at that. Gunny didn't usually jump the stack, and I knew he was only doing it now because he was there and time was short, but nobody in the platoon wanted to be back in the rear when Gunny got in a fight. He was supposed to be in the middle, at best. The rest of us were supposed to be out there on the pointy end.

Fortunately, he'd halted just on the other side, down on a knee at the wall of the passageway, rifle pointed into the dark. I got there right behind Bailey, as we'd pushed up faster than most of the rest. We bounded ahead of Gunny, taking over security on the passageway, at least until Baldinus, Synar, and Rodeffer pushed up ahead of us.

The last of the platoon was still crawling through the gap when we got up and got moving. Time was wasting. And from the sounds of things, I don't think any of us believed that the sentinel had succeeded in holding the line.

Dragon Mask was on the way to Vaelor's Throne. And we were too far behind.

* * *

Unfortunately, the cave-in we'd just cleared was not the only obstacle Dragon Mask had thrown up in our way. We came across two more such collapses, each one slowing us down as we had to dig through, holding security in both directions as we went. No more noises reached us. One way or another, the fight at the third gate was over.

Part of me was hoping that we'd find the sentinel still intact, bound in the gateway, Dragon Mask and his minions spattered across the rocks, even if it meant that Owens, Gonsalves, and Zimmerman hadn't made it.

Their continued cooperation still bothered me. There had always been a possibility, however distant, that they'd continued following Dragon Mask purely out of the need for survival. Cut off from everyone else, what other choice might they have had? Yet despite everything else, there was a cold dread building at the back of my mind as I wondered just what we'd find when we finally caught up with them. Would they come back with us, or would they fight us? They hadn't had any reason to think that we had been the ones behind them at first, when we'd broken out into that cavern, but every one of them had to have recognized gunfire and explosions. They *had* to have known that it was us as we'd engaged the otherworldly monsters that Dragon Mask had summoned.

Yet even with that knowledge, they hadn't turned back to join us. They'd gone on with Dragon Mask. That did *not* bode well.

The fact that they hadn't turned on Dragon Mask when he'd sacrificed Captain Sorenson, dick though he had been, wasn't a good sign, either.

Had we come all this way only to put them all down? That wasn't a comforting thought.

I just hoped, if it came to that, that we wouldn't lose any more of our own in the process.

That was when I realized that I was already thinking of the three survivors with Dragon Mask as no longer "our own." They were the enemy now.

They'd picked their side.

It was a grim thought, but as we moved closer to the moment of truth, it looked like we *were* going to take care of our own, one way or another.

* * *

It was rough going the rest of the way. In addition to the cave-ins, we had to get across a six-foot crack in the rock that looked fresh. That turned into a combination of dropping rucks, jumping across, and then tossing the packs after those who had already crossed. Nobody fell in, but the delay was still significant enough that I could feel the knots in my stomach as we got moving again. It would really suck to have gotten this close only to be just a few minutes too late to stop Dragon Mask from waking the Devil up.

Barely twenty yards past the crack, the passage curved and opened up on another cavern. This one was smaller than the last, where we'd fought the horrors that had still successfully kept us from interfering in the breach of the gate. We came out only about twenty-five yards from the massive, blackened stelae that framed the gateway.

If we'd hoped that maybe this sentinel would have held out, we were doomed to disappointment.

This sentinel seemed to have been different from those that had come before. Just as tall, and apparently skeletal underneath its armor, it had not been suspended in a web of thorned cables. From the looks of things, it had stood upon the plinth in the center of the gateway, waiting like a statue until any interlopers approached.

It had worn a full suit of plate armor. The plates looked more like stone than metal. Currently, it lay on the ground, its armor cracked, scorched, and blackened, pocked with bullet impacts, the helm detached and lying some distance away. From the looks of things, n either explosion nor blade had decapitated the sentinel, but something with claws dripping with black slime.

Despite the urgency that drove us forward, no one was in a great hurry to approach that thing, decapitated or not. We'd seen seemingly dead monsters come to life again before, and none of us would have put it past Dragon Mask to have pulled some sort of sorcerous booby trap out of his bag of tricks.

When a cloaked figure coalesced out of the darkness between the stelae, it seemed that he had. Half a dozen rifles came up and barked almost in unison, but the bullets didn't seem to faze the figure at all.

"Hold your fire." Bailey didn't lower his weapon, but he slipped his finger out of the trigger guard. Two more shots rang out, but then the shooting stopped. Wasting ammo on a phantom wouldn't help anyone at that point, though I was still wondering just how we were going to fight this thing. My blessed sword *might* have an effect on it, but I still hadn't fought anything that I could see through, and as dark as this figure was, it was still slightly translucent.

It didn't charge us, though. It didn't show any aggression at all. A skeletal face loomed out of the hood, and a cold, hollow, agonized voice filled the cave.

I couldn't understand the words. There was no mind speech there, and the language was far different from the *Tenga Tuacha*, or any other tongue I'd heard in this strange world.

The feel of the words was another matter, though. They were filled with agony, even as the creature—or spirit—pleaded with us. Mathghaman watched it, listening with narrowed eyes.

To my surprise, the figure faded away as soon as it stopped speaking. Mathghaman and the other Tuacha were even grimmer of face as they began to advance toward the stelae.

"What just happened?" Bailey demanded. "What did it say?"

"It is rare," Mathghaman said over his shoulder, "that a spirit is momentarily removed from its punishment to send a warning to the land of the living. Yet this one, as vile as it was in life, stood here where it fell, and warned us that Vaelor even now strains at his bonds. Only a few more murders will break them, setting him free."

Something about that gave me pause, though I was still following them through the gap between the stelae. "So, what happens if we have to kill them to stop them?"

"I do not know, Conor." Mathghaman sounded like he was just as troubled by the question as I was. "Pray to Tigharn that we do not have to find out."

CHAPTER 41

THAT droning chant echoed from the ice and stone as we trod through the darkness, gloved hands gripping weapons perhaps more tightly than we would have otherwise. We'd fought men and monsters on two worlds—some of us, anyway; not everyone had been a veteran on that float— but this felt bigger, the stakes higher, the threat far worse.

The slope in the tunnel had started down again, as if we'd gone over the top of a ridge and were moving toward lower ground. Maybe we were. It was hard to tell, when all we could see around us was ice to either side and above, rock below.

Suddenly, we were in yet another cavern. This one was different from the stark ice caves we'd already passed through, though. A massive stone wall rose above us, only a few yards from the opening where we stood.

Sheer and towering, it disappeared into the ice to right, left, and high above. Every inch of the gleaming, black stone was carved with leering monsters and images of human beings in torment. It was all done in exquisite and horrifying detail, unlike the crude shapes of the stelae behind us, or even the idol of Vaelor, what felt like miles and miles back. These carvings made even the shapes of men in agony embedded in the standing stones around the idol look like crude chippings. They were lifelike in a way that made it feel as if any one of them might spring into motion at any moment.

A towering gate stood in the center, atop a tall flight of black stone steps, flanked by massive, obsidian gargoyles. The doors were just as intricately carved with scenes of horror and carnage.

They also stood open. Just far enough open to let one man through, but they were still open.

Of course, at that point, I suspected that with the Fohorimans' defenses down, defenses designed as much to keep Vaelor in as to keep anyone else away from him, it would be relatively easy to get in from here. If the ancient demon was stirring, reaching out to his disciples, then he'd be trying to help them along as much as possible.

He'd probably eat them once they succeeded in freeing him, but he'd give them every advantage he could up to that point.

Splitting to cross cover on the opening, Bailey's and my teams started up the steps, while Gurke and the Tuacha held security to the flanks, just in case some new monstrosity loomed out of the dark from an angle we hadn't anticipated.

I found myself at the doorway, having outpaced Rodeffer, who tried to push up to replace me in the stack but stopped as I put my hand out to forestall him. Bailey was right across from me, his own M110 pointed at the narrow opening. The doors opened inward, invitingly, despite the fact that it seemed as if the screaming, wailing faces on the panel of the door might suddenly turn and snap at me.

I wasn't feeling the invitation. Especially since there was light in there, and when I turned my head to look past the ocular lenses of my NVGs, I could see that it was blood red.

The mouth of hell was open, and we had to go in.

Bailey and I crossed paths as we went through the opening. I took what I could see, punching across the doorway and into the opposite corner, while he stepped through a heartbeat later, covering my back as he cleared the other side. The rest flowed in behind us, switching off each side.

We found ourselves in a towering antechamber, the ceiling disappearing into the darkness overhead. Two massive, square columns stood in front of us, sconces at their bases flickering with red and purple flames. The flames lit the grotesque faces leering from the columns, making them seem to move and turn toward us as they bared fangs and stuck out tongues that were entirely too long.

The wall between those columns was carved with glyphs that gleamed strangely in the flickering, unnatural light. It made my head hurt to look at them. I turned toward the massive stone staircase, the steps every bit as tall as the dais that had led up to the altar at the foot of the idol of Vaelor. My weapon trained on the landing above, Rodeffer and Farrar on my heels, I started up.

Screams, shrieks, growls, and that same droning, tooth-grinding chant echoed from the darkness above. Bad stuff was happening up there.

We had more to worry about than just what was going on at the top of the steps. Somewhere behind us, a distant *boom* echoed through the passage behind us, followed by a deep, ominous horn blast. The Fohorimans and their minions hadn't slowed, hadn't given up. It sounded like they were closing in fast.

That meant we were now between the hammer and the anvil. Bad spot to be in. I could feel the fear clawing at the inside of my chest.

There's something to be said about being in such a place, though. It's why you always give your enemy a perceived way out. A man with his back to the wall and nowhere to retreat to will fight all the harder.

I reached the landing. The steps opened up on a vast hall, lit from below by a deep red glow that pulsed from a massive crack in the stone floor.

The hall resembled the inside of a vast ribcage, except every rib was formed of stone figures, bound together in agony and violence. There were unspeakable things being done in those carvings, frozen in black stone.

Easing around the corner, I covered each angle with my muzzle before exposing myself. If our missing Marines had gone over, I didn't want to catch a bullet by being careless.

Bailey was on the other side of the hall, clearing the open area in much the same way. No threats presented themselves up close. Dragon Mask and his followers were up at the far end of the hall, lit from below by the glow coming from that big crack.

Only Gonsalves and Zimmerman were standing off to one side, their M4s held ready. Owens was stretched out at the base of the massive black stone that stood at the head of the hall, screaming and thrashing as five Dovos held him down, Dragon Mask standing over him, chanting, a crooked black knife held high.

The whole hall shuddered as the huge stone seemed to rock, ever so slightly, on its base. Cracks had started to form in the stone, and a vague, lurid glow had begun to leak from several of them, high above the floor.

I put my red dot on Dragon Mask's back, my finger slipping inside the trigger guard. Just as I did, though, Zimmerman must have seen something, because he snapped his M4 to his shoulder and fired, forcing me back as the bullet smacked off the black stone carvings just over my head, leaving a bright scar but otherwise doing no damage to the stone itself.

More rounds struck the stone as Zimmerman and Gonsalves flipped their weapons to "burst" and dumped their magazines at us. I dropped to the floor, taking cover behind the stone before leaning out onto my side and returning fire, forcing them to take cover behind the vast stone that was Vaelor's Throne.

They'd bought Dragon Mask the time he'd needed, though. Owens' screams had been silenced. Dragon Mask held up his dripping heart and began to draw glyphs on the huge stone with Owens' blood.

The stone rocked again. A deep, distant growl vibrated through the hall. The glow in those cracks seemed to be fading...until I saw that it was simply that a deepening darkness was wrapped around that enormous stone.

Vaelor was waking up.

More *boom*s echoed from behind us. The Fohorimans were catching up, doubtless getting desperate as they realized what was happening. We had to finish this fast.

If we could. A shape was beginning to coalesce out of that awful shadow, taking on the rough proportions of the idol at the edge of the Teeth of Winter, miles behind us. It was still vague, and it had none of the presence that lurked in the stone behind it. It was still only an image.

Don't ask how I knew that. I just did. It seemed kind of obvious at the time.

Mk 48 fire rattled behind us, at the base of the stairs. Roars and thunder answered, followed by the distant *thud*s of 40mm grenades detonating. We were out of time and maneuvering room.

More 5.56 rounds ricocheted off the stone floor in front of my face as either Zimmerman or Gonsalves shifted fire, probably trying to buy time for Dragon Mask to finish the ritual. Rodeffer leaned out over me, only to catch a round in the shoulder and get knocked sprawling to the floor with a tooth-gritted moan of pain.

One of our Mk 48s went cyclic behind us, the last of the belt dumped through the doorway. More roars and screams echoed from below. There had to be a *lot* of bad guys pushing through that doorway, clambering over the bodies our guys were stacking in the gap.

Despite years of discipline and training, I stuck my rifle out and fired five shots toward that end of the hall. I wasn't aiming, I was just trying to get their heads down so we could drive forward.

The incoming fire ceased. I clambered to my feet again and started to push forward, as Doc Hartsock pulled Rodeffer back out of the line of fire, only to get shrugged off as Rodeffer shoved himself back to his feet. Blood was soaking his shoulder, but it must have missed the bone, because while he was obviously in pain, he could still work his rifle.

I got around the curved column of tortured figures in time to see Dragon Mask raise his hands to the shadowed stone and let out a reverberating shout, so loud that it sounded like he was using a megaphone. The single word was harsh, discordant, and shouldn't have come from a human throat. A sudden pain lanced through my head behind my left eye, and I staggered for a second.

But whatever he hoped would happen, it didn't seem to have worked.

The stone rocked again, and the rumble that accompanied it might have been a distant voice, but that was all.

The fire ceased, just for a moment, one of those strange lulls in a firefight that just happen sometimes, when not everyone is keeping track of their round count, and too many shooters have to reload at the same time. Over the shrieks, roars, and war cries coming from the entryway behind us, I heard Zimmerman shout, "Fuck this."

Pivoting, he lifted his M4 and dumped the last of the mag into Dragon Mask and the rest of the renegade Dovos nal Uergal. Bullets tore through their flimsy armor, and blood splashed on the stone and the plinth beneath.

Letting his empty rifle hang, Zimmerman stepped up to Dragon Mask, who was down but still breathing. Taking up the crooked knife that the Dovo sorcerer had used to cut Owens' heart out, he grabbed Dragon Mask by the hair, pulled his head back, and ripped his throat open, letting the blood splash on the bottom of the stone.

I ducked behind another rib as Gonsalves shot at me again, and Zimmerman looked up at the stone and shouted. He wasn't speaking English, either.

Having taken cover just in time, I leaned out and shot Gonsalves through the throat, a split second before Bailey double-tapped him through the chest. He crumpled and fell on his face on the rocky floor.

I shifted my aim to Zimmerman, but it was too late.

He was lost in shadow, coils of it writhing up out of the crack in the floor and the stone above. Red points of light, resembling the eyes in the idol of Vaelor where Captain Sorenson had been murdered, began to glitter in the darkness above his head.

Behind me, the rest of the platoon was falling back into the hall, pressed hard by the Fohorimans, who were fighting with the fury of desperation. We were well and truly trapped.

"Zimmerman, you son of a bitch!" Gunny moved up past me, even as I braced my rifle against one of the screaming faces carved out of the shiny black rock next to me and started to dump rounds into the shadows, hoping I could hit him. The shadows just swallowed my bullets as they thickened and darkened, starting to take on that same oily sheen that Vaelor's horrors had displayed every time we'd fought them.

I didn't think this was going to be as easy as fighting those. And that had been no picnic.

A bellow of fear and rage sounded behind me. I didn't turn to look. There was no point. I just kept shooting, as Vaelor continued to manifest in front of us.

Gunny was advancing on the towering thing of shadow as all seven glittering eyes, lit with an infinite malevolence, bent on him. He was moving fast, too, his own rifle up and barking. There was almost no point, but the sheer act of fighting back was about all we had left. We were caught between Vaelor and his former servants, outnumbered and with zero escape route. The only thing we could do was sell ourselves as dearly as possible.

Gunny's bolt locked back on an empty mag, and he dropped it and reached for a reload. I was moving up on his flank, blasting away at where I thought Zimmerman was, in the vain hope that if I hit him, maybe Vaelor wouldn't have a physical body to latch onto. I didn't know what made me think that was a possibility, but it seemed vaguely logical, and what else did I have to go on at that point?

Then, with a voice so terrible that it dropped us all in our tracks, Vaelor spoke.

"Such pathetic vermin. Fools. I could have rewarded you with power beyond your imagining. Now, your torment shall be legendary. You have dared to strike at me, the greatest of elder gods, and before you die and are hurled into the Void to vanish forever, you shall serve as an example to all who would oppose my will." The seven eyes lifted. "Is it not so, Uergal? Slave and betrayer! Your suffering shall be far greater than even these. For I owned you before, and despite your rebellion, I own you still." That massive head, still made of smoke and oily nothingness, turned toward Gunny, who had gotten closest, even as the rest of us had tried to catch up.

"See now the folly of defying an Elder God!" A great limb rose up, sharpening to a massive spike, like the T-1000's arm in *Terminator 2*.

I was suddenly knocked aside as a blur of movement barreled past me. My limbs weren't doing quite what I told them to, and I felt blood trickle out of my nose and into my beard. My head ached abominably from hearing

Vaelor's voice, and I struggled to get my weapon up. I knew it wouldn't scratch that thing, but I was still going to try to kill it, even if it amounted to nothing more than one last act of defiance.

Lifting my head, I saw the shape of a Tuacha warrior throw himself in front of Gunny at the last moment. When he looked up at that descending spike, I saw that it was Cairbre.

That haughty expression on his face never left it as that giant black talon slashed down and skewered him through the collarbone, bursting out through his guts in a shower of gore as it nailed him to the stone.

Vaelor snarled, a growl that shook the ground, and flung Cairbre's corpse away to smash limply against the curved columns of tormented figures in stone before tumbling to the floor in a welter of blood and offal. Then he lifted that talon above Gunny's head again. None of the rest of us had been able to move much.

The talon froze. A new sound had entered the hall.

Mathghaman was chanting.

The power of the chant before wasn't there. Actually, that's not quite right. It was different. This wasn't a call for help, it was a dirge, mourning Cairbre and commending his soul to Tigharn.

Even as I realized that was what the words were saying, it turned out that it was a little more than that.

A light began to glow in the darkness. I couldn't tell for sure where it was coming from, but it grew and intensified until that terrible room was filled with a brilliant glare, so bright I couldn't see anything else. It wasn't the red glow from the crack in the floor, or the red/purple light of the strange flames in the entryway. It was more like the sun itself had descended into that chamber.

As the weakness that had stricken my arms and legs under Vaelor's baleful gaze and at the sound of his terrible voice faded, and I held up my hand to shield my eyes, I was suddenly reminded of the flash that had hit down in the catacombs beneath Taramas's citadel, just for a moment. This was brighter. It lingered much longer. But it was similar.

Then it faded and was gone, though not without leaving the sense of a burden lifted.

I blinked as I looked around. Gunny was still on one knee, shaken but alive. Zimmerman's body lay on the plinth, contorted, ripped open, and clearly dead. There was no sign of the stygian apparition that had been Vaelor.

Cairbre's body was gone.

A shriek of terror rose behind us. I turned in time to see Uergal, towering, apish, his green-tinged black helmet almost too large for his shoulders, scramble to his feet and flee, throwing himself down the steps and out of sight.

One by one, we struggled back to our feet. "Rear security!" Bailey's voice was a harsh rasp, and I didn't doubt that the rest of us might sound much the same. I felt like I'd been hit by a truck.

I didn't need to ask just what had happened, though.

Cairbre hadn't ever liked us, and he hadn't made any secret of it. He'd followed Mathghaman, even as that had meant associating with us barbarians. He hadn't been as much of a dick as he could have, but he'd been cold and distant from the start.

Yet he had willingly sacrificed himself to save Gunny. And that, it seemed, had been the tipping point on the more mystical side of the struggle.

There are a lot of monsters we can shoot or blow up the old-fashioned way, for us anyway. There are other fights in this world that, as Mathghaman had said, we couldn't win with bullets, blades, or explosives.

Cairbre had just won one of those fights for us. Whoever had come in answer to his self-sacrifice, they hadn't only banished Vaelor back into the stone—I could *feel* the malice still radiating from that giant rock—it had put the Fohorimans to flight.

Gunny staggered forward, pulling a thermate grenade from his chest rig. He looked down at what was left of Zimmerman, then popped the grenade and dropped it on Owens' body. He turned away as the flames popped and sizzled. His face was set as he walked away from the plinth.

Nobody asked. We all got it. There was still a chance that Owens hadn't gone over all the way, and that that was why he'd been sacrificed. Zimmerman and Gonsalves had shot at us, fought us so they could summon that ancient demon out of the stone.

They weren't ours anymore.

At the same time, they had been, once. And now we'd cleaned up our mess.

It was time to go. Without more than a cautious backward glance over weapons, just to make sure some new monster wasn't about to come after us, we headed out of that terrible place, leaving it to the ice.

EPILOGUE

IT was a long, hard slog to get out of those mountains and back to Menninkai lands. The horses were long gone, so we were on foot the whole way. Unlike the flight to Teac Mor Farragah, we faced no pursuit, and no real opposition aside from the terrain and the weather, either. A few beasts and monsters stalked us, but the mountains seemed emptied of Fohorimans or their minions. It was as if that light's descent into Vaelor's Throne had terrified all the forces of darkness for miles and miles. Uergal and his army had fled as fast as their feet could carry them.

Still, it was a long way, and we'd been getting short on rations before we'd reached the Teeth of Winter. It was a lean, almost skeletal bunch of mail-clad scarecrows who finally came out of the woods at the northernmost Menninkai outpost of Kaukan Kevi.

About fifty wary Menninkai warriors came out to intercept us as we came down the slope through the trees. They were ready for a fight, spears leveled and arrows nocked, until Mathghaman lifted a hand and greeted them. He spoke the *Tenga Tuacha*, but with the mind speech, the Menninkai heard him as clearly as if he'd spoken their own tongue, even those who didn't know our friends' language.

An especially short, wiry man stepped through the front ranks, pulling his lamellar helmet off to reveal a shaggy head of gray-shot red hair, sticking out like a lion's mane. "Who are you? None but the Lasknut or the servants of Lusken come from the north. Yet you wear none of their foul talismans, and you speak the tongue of the Gifted Ones from across the sea."

"I am Mathghaman Mag Cathal, King's Champion of the Tuacha da Riamog, and brother in arms to Gunny Taylor and his men." He swept a hand to indicate all of us, even though most of us had taken cover, spread out across the hillside, weapons leveled at the Menninkai, just in case. None of us had more than about two mags left, but we could still do a lot of damage.

Well, the Recon Marines were aimed in. The Tuacha were hanging back, watching what was going to happen.

The Menninkai leader frowned, looking around at the strange gear and weapons. "What takes a lord of the Tuacha so far north?"

"We rode to stop a sorcerer who sought to unleash Vaelor, the Shadow of the North."

Even from where I knelt behind a fallen tree, I could see the Menninkai leader go pale. The warriors behind him shifted nervously, many of them making protective signs furtively behind their shields.

"He will not return yet." Mathghaman started forward, apparently confident enough that the Menninkai wouldn't attack him. "How fares Vahava Paykhah?"

"The city stands." The rest of the Menninkai had relaxed somewhat, spears now pointing at the sky and arrows returned to quivers. I've got to hand it to Mathghaman. The man has the presence and the charis-

ma to just walk into an ally's camp who have never seen
him before and convince them in a few words that he's
one of the good guys. All without being the slightest bit
deceitful. "She is wounded, and our tribes have taken
terrible losses, but our lands are now ours again." The little man scratched his head. "The entire Fohoriman army
abandoned the siege and left about two months ago, and
has not been seen since."

"They pursued us." Mathghaman looked back at
Gunny, who raised his eyebrows and shrugged. So, we'd
achieved both objectives.

Not bad for a desperate roll of the dice.

"Now, we are weary and hungry. We would ask your
hospitality for a few nights."

The leader blinked, then seemed to shake himself,
as if remembering something. "Of course. If you are the
Mathghaman Mag Cathal who came to the aid of Vahava
Paykhah, the entire Menninkai nation owes you a debt."

"It owes my companions a debt," Mathghaman said
as we were escorted within the timber palisade around
the stone tor that formed the heart of Kaukan Kevi.
"Most of all, to one who is no longer with us."

* * *

That night, gathered around the fire in the great hall,
which was considerably smaller than King Karhu's in Vahava Paykhah, but still the largest structure in the fortress
town, we sat quietly, sipping the potent yet tasty liquor
made from fermented berries that the Menninkai distilled
in the north. The warmth and the booze were making my
eyelids heavy, yet I found I still fought the drowsiness. We'd

been in a constant state of alert for weeks, and it's not easy to come down from that.

"So, my friends." Bearrac took a deep swallow of the amber liquid, seemingly unfazed by the alcohol. "You have found your missing Marines." He paused somberly as we all thought back to what that had ultimately meant.

There are those back in The World who make idols out of men like us, but the fact is, we're still just men. We train to a higher standard, but we're every bit as human as anyone else, in or out of uniform. Some of us are better men than others, and I'm not talking about skill or fitness level. Others are far worse.

I wondered, looking at the fire as the warmth of the liquor flowed down my throat, if I could have held out if I'd been in those guys' shoes. Trapped behind enemy lines, relying on savages and dark sorcery just to stay alive... how long before I'd have been justifying each little step into the abyss, just like I'm sure Sorenson, Owens, Gonsalves, and even Zimmerman had?

I don't know. Maybe there was something rotten in them to start. I'd seen enough over the years, seen choirboys become bloodthirsty killers and stone-cold, borderline sociopaths turn away and try to become something better, that I doubted it. We all have choices. Sometimes, our circumstances and the people we surround ourselves with make those choices easier or harder.

"What will we do now?" Bailey finished Bearrac's question for him. He glanced at Gunny. "I don't know. Seems like there are still plenty of fights out there."

"There will always be fights. The war never ends, it only changes." Bearrac took another swig, his voice at once sad and grim. "Vaelor is still imprisoned, not destroyed or banished. In time, he will reach out again, through dreams and visions, and bring more men under his sway. And he is not alone."

Mathghaman, who had been speaking softly with the Menninkai leader, Huono, stood up then. "We are brothers, be we Tuacha or Recon Marines. We have no hold upon you, but you shall always have a place with us. You know, however, that such a place means constant warfare, for the dark forces have nearly conquered this world, and seek our destruction always."

Gunny looked around at us, and he got nods all around. "There never was a Recon Marine who wasn't addicted to the fight in some way, shape, or form." He stood and raised his horn cup to meet Mathghaman's. "I'd say that we'd be better off staying with our Tuacha friends. Where else will we always be able find a fight and know it's going to be righteous?"

Mathghaman nodded as we all drank. I felt something different then, apart from the heat of the alcohol burning its way down my throat.

Dragon Mask had promised—I had no doubt he'd lied—to help us get home to The World once he had Vaelor's power. But I wasn't thinking of going back, not anymore.

As my hand strayed to the hilts of my sword, feeling the runes inlaid in the pommel, and as the smoke rose from the fire, which threw flickering golden light against the walls, the beams, and the faces of my brothers, Recon Marines and Tuacha warriors both, I knew I *was* home.

Peter Nealen is a former United States Marine who now writes full time for a living.

https://www.americanpraetorians.com/

Other WarGate Titles Available now:

Forgotten Ruin
Tier 1000

For Updates, New Releases, and Other Titles, visit
www.WarGateBooks.com

Made in the USA
Las Vegas, NV
13 February 2023